EKO

Loren Walker

Octopus & Elephant Books
PROVIDENCE, RHODE ISLAND

Octopus & Elephant Books
www.oandebooks.com

Publisher's Note: This is a work of fiction. Names, characters, places, and incidents are a product of the author's imagination. Any resemblance to actual people, living or dead, or to businesses, companies, events, institutions, or locales is completely coincidental.

Book Layout ©2015 BookDesignTemplates.com.

Cover by Deranged Doctor Designs.

EKO / Loren Walker. -- 1st ed.
ISBN 978-0-9973922-0-3

Contents

For the ones that I love.

PART ONE

Sydel took a deep breath, her first in hours. Her lower back ached, but the cold floor of her room was a relief to her swollen bare feet. Stripping off her blue high-necked tunic and trousers, her apprentice uniform, the stink of antiseptic and layers of sweat was overpowering. But when cool cotton slid down her body, her nightgown's hem grazing the floor, she couldn't ignore the ache in her throat anymore, or the frustration burning in her sternum.

It was immunization day. Sydel was in charge of the operation, her first assignment as Yann's medical assistant. She had taken care to dress neatly, pinned up her hair to look older, straightened the equipment and syringes again and again, prepared friendly suggestions or comforts for patients who were nervous.

None of it mattered. Not one of the fifty residents of Jala Communia would look her in the eye, not one all day. Each man and woman gave mumbled answers to her questions; they offered their arms for injection without comment. She tried smiles, reminders, silences, but no one would lift their head. Failures, one after another. The community still shutting her out.

It should have been better. Yann told her it would be different when she turned eighteen, when she was made his official apprentice. What was she doing wrong?

Deflated, Sydel sat on her bed and pulled the pins from her hair. Six ropey braids fell over her shoulders; she itched at her scalp, sighing with relief. Then she loosened each braid, running her fingers through the strands. Her gaze wandered across her cell, taking stock of her few possessions to distract her from her thoughts. Textbooks on anatomy and physiology, borrowed from the library. Meditation beads hanging from a nail. The armoire in the corner, one door higher than the other, with her clothing and toiletries inside...

Take her with you.

Sydel froze at the sharp command, her hands on her last braid. Confused, she swiveled to the door, mouth open to ask what Yann meant by such a command. But the door was still closed, the lock fastened. There were no shadows in her cell.

I said take her away.

Sydel rolled onto her hands and knees, looking over the windowsill. The courtyard was silent, following the rainstorm. She strained her ears to listen: no creaking doors, no wet sounds of walking, no voices. Even the crickets were quiet, forced underground by the downpour.

Sydel sat back on her heels. She put her fingers on her temples, massaging the skin, debating. Should she open her mind and call back to him? No. Yann hardly used Eko, and in the medical clinic where they worked, he strictly forbade it. What could be happening? Again, Sydel searched the landscape for signs. But all was quiet.

No lights in the sky. Barely a trace of wind. Peaceful, on another night.

Just an accident, she reasoned. Yann had a random thought, accidentally projected it, and since Sydel was the only other Eko, she picked up on it.

Take her with you. Take her away.

Was he being threatened? Impossible. Yann was the leader of Jala Communia. He was brilliant and powerful. Everyone deferred to his judgment. They always had. No one would dare. Would they?

* * *

Sydel tried to keep her breathing even, but her body thudded with adrenaline. Her stomach burned with anxiety. She crossed her arms over her midsection, heading for the latticework gates. They were open, just enough to let someone slide through.

The grasslands stretched before her, dark red and shimmering from the rain. To the left was a round stone building, its whitewash luminous, even with no moons to reflect off it: the medical clinic.

And by its doors: two black silhouettes, struggling.

"Get away from him!" Her voice was shrill in the night.

The shadows stumbled backwards. Then one face came into the light: Yann.

Sydel made the connection via Eko. *Are you all right? Should I call for help?*

No response. The other silhouette, an incredibly tall man, loomed behind Yann like a specter. Sydel gripped the sleeves of her nightgown, torn between running away and doing something, doing anything to defend Yann.

"Do you work here?"

The question came from the stranger. His voice was low and liquid, with a slight drawl to it. A foreign accent.

Sydel opened her mouth, but no sound came out.

The man jerked his chin towards the clinic. "You have a patient."

The moon broke through the clouds. The right side of his shirt caught the light, dark and shiny. Wet with blood, Sydel realized. His? Or someone else's?

"No," Yann interrupted her thoughts. "Take that woman and leave. I refuse treatment."

"You can't," the stranger corrected. Even with the moon's appearance, Sydel still couldn't make out his face. "You're Jala. You people follow your chosen paths for life, working in total devotion, righteousness and perfection. So if you're a healer, you can't refuse a request for help."

"It doesn't matter what you think you know," Yann sputtered. "I refuse to help a criminal."

Sydel gaped at Yann, and then the stranger. Criminal?

The man shrugged. "Fine. Then she dies. I've done my part."

And the tall man began to walk away, Yann scampering after him like a desperate puppy, yelping: "You cannot do this! What if retribution follows?

"It won't, if you keep her here in Midland and hidden for the next week," the man said brusquely. "If she dies, do whatever you want with the body."

Sydel stared at the clinic door. Someone was in there. Someone was dying.

A rumbling sound. Engines and sweet gasoline in the air, a stench Sydel secretly loved, but hardly ever encountered. Yann's silhouette stood at the crest of the low hill, gesturing wildly.

Then a shimmer of lights, as something large and metal rose from the grass: a ground rover, not rusted and rattling like the one in the Communia, but sleek and nearly silent in operation. It skimmed the desert rocks, neatly navigating the rise and fall of the landscape, until it finally disappeared into the night.

Once again, the world was silent. The wind picked up again, like an afterthought, and swirled Sydel's hair around her face. Sydel pushed it back and waited.

Yann's huffs came to her ears, coupled with the sound of his lumbering, angry gait. As he drew closer, her mind rolled with questions. Who was that man? Who was inside the clinic? Why in the dead of night?

"Master - " she began.

"Not now," Yann snapped, sweeping past her. "Inside."

He stomped on each step, bursting through the clinic doors.

After a few seconds, Sydel followed.

The florescent lights burned her retinas. Then the white walls grew clear; with its simple, open concept design; the clinic was only thirty feet in area, but well stocked, and immaculate. The linoleum floor glimmered with red drops of blood, smeared blood brushed by footprints.

Up ahead, a squirming body lay on the gurney.

Yann was pulling on gloves. "You always wanted something exciting, Sydel," he spat at her, in a tone she'd never heard before, his eyes rimmed with pink, his bushy eyebrows raised high. "You were bored with vaccinations and blisters, well, here you go."

Hurt and bewildered, Sydel held her tongue, and snapped her own gloves on. As Yann cut through the patient's shirt, Sydel helped to pull it free. Underneath, there was blood everywhere, dried and brown, all over the left arm and torso.

"Gunshot wound to the left lateral chest," Yann announced.

"Gunshot?"

Yann ignored her shock, probing the patient's ribs.

"But -" Sydel sputtered. She couldn't stop shaking her head. "How could - who would -"

Her voice died as the patient writhed under Yann's hands. It was a woman, Sydel realized, underneath all that jagged blue hair. Then the woman's head jerked back, and Sydel could see her sharp, pinched features: how the patient's eyelids were rimmed with heavy black, her lips the color of a deep bruise.

Before her, Yann's shoulders dropped. "Superficial," he sighed. "See? Looks like it glanced off the rib. We can handle this."

Sydel forced herself to look. He was right. It wouldn't take much repair to stop the blood flow. Oddly, she felt a little disappointed. The word 'gunshot' was not something she ever expected to hear; as scared as she was outside, there were still little visions of possibility playing in the back of her mind: surgeries, complex repair work, bringing hearts back to life.

"Strip her. Check for other signs of trauma," her master instructed. "This shouldn't take long. Then we need to talk about next steps."

As Yann began to work, Sydel went to the foot of the gurney. The woman's black boots were knee-high, worn leather, tied with difficult knots. Finally, she managed to yank one off. As soon as she did, something tumbled out. Sydel caught it before it fell to the floor.

A thin cylinder made of metal, one inch long.

Sydel looked over the planes of the woman's body. Yann was still absorbed in cleaning the wound. The cylinder lay in her palm. There was a tiny engraved sun on one end, a little button at the top. Beautiful.

Sydel slipped it into the neckline of her nightgown. She felt only a pinprick of guilt at the sensation of cold against her collarbone as she pulled off the other boot. Then she cut off the woman's pants, and bundled all the stinking, chemical-laden articles into a bin.

Retrieving the handheld ultrasound, one of the few modern devices that Yann allowed in Jala Communia, Sydel swept it over the woman's legs, then her arms. No breaks, no other signs of immediate injury. There were so many scars, though, lines crisscrossing the woman's arms, some still pink, some long since healed over and white.

Sydel forced herself to concentrate. The patient's heart rate was rapid, but not dangerously so. Blood pressure was acceptable. Then Sydel put a stethoscope to the woman's chest, listening. The lungs were constricted. Strange. Not drowning in fluid. Why was her breath so strangled, then? Sydel glanced at the woman's mouth, but she couldn't see the true color under that artificial dark. She picked up the woman's hand. The fingernails held the faintest shade of blue. She wasn't getting enough oxygen.

"Something else is wrong," Sydel announced.

Yann looked up. Sydel leaned over and fit her stethoscope in Yann's ears so he could hear for himself.

He listened intently, his bloody gloves hovering.

Suddenly, the floor was a sea of glittering tools, the table upturned, wheels spinning. Jumping back, Sydel almost slipped on a pair of scissors. On the gurney, the patient thrashed. Yann grabbed at her wrists, but the woman's naked arms were frighteningly muscular. With a sudden burst, she shoved Yann, and he slammed into the countertop, a loud crack echoing through the clinic. The woman tried to roll off the stretcher, her hair sweaty and sticking to her face, her arm wrapped around her bloodied ribs, her feet searching for the floor.

If she weren't retrained, she would kill herself, or the both of them, Sydel realized. She didn't have the physical strength to hold the woman down.

But she could shut down her body.

Sydel leapt over Yann's groaning form. Darting behind the gurney, she grabbed hold of the woman's head, her fingers pressed into her temples, and concentrated, searching for the part of the brain that controlled sleep.

"Don't!" Yann cried from the ground.

But she couldn't break through.

Stunned, Sydel tried again. No, there was a barrier there, as sturdy as the stone wall of the clinic.

How could that be?

Then the woman's head went heavy in Sydel's hands. Strained, sucking breaths came from that dark mouth.

"Please," Sydel said, working to keep her voice from trembling. "If you can hear me, you need to stop fighting us."

The woman's inhalations grew shuddery and wet, like she was on the verge of tears.

Surprised, Sydel eased her grip. "Trust me," she whispered. "Let me help you."

A tap on her thigh. Yann had silently crawled over, a fresh syringe in hand. Before the blue-haired woman could react, the needle was embedded in her thigh, the contents injected. Within seconds, the stranger's head lolled. She was unconscious.

Only then did Sydel let go. Wobbling, she put a hand to her brow. Strands of hair stuck to her forehead and hung wet behind her ears. A headache encircled her skull, pressing and pounding.

How dare you, Sydel.

She looked up. Her master slumped into a chair. His face was back to a normal color, but his mouth twisted with anger.

Using Eko on someone like that - what did you hope to achieve? What were you trying to do?

Even her thoughts were stuttering. *I don't know - I was just trying to s-s-stop her, protect you.*

If we are discovered, everything will be destroyed. Time and again, I've told you this, and still you defy me.

The rush of angry words in her head made her light-headed. She held onto the edge of the gurney.

"Enough," Yann spoke out loud. "Go to the chamber, restore your focus. Come back in the morning, when you are in control."

Tears pricked at her eyes. She didn't have the strength, or voice, to argue.

Outside, Sydel welcomed the cool wind on her flushed face. No sign of the stranger, in any direction. No stirring of life in the Jala Communia, either: the doors to the men's ward, the women's and the children's, were closed, all the shades drawn. But there was something in the air. Fear rippled across the landscape, like a swarm of bees. People were awake. People were afraid.

If we are discovered, everything will be destroyed.

She had heard those words so many times, growing up in Midland: a thin, ragged state in the center of the continent of Osha. The Midland was sparsely populated, occupied by those who rejected government and modern society. People in Midland established their own schools, communes, monasteries, ways of life and business; separate, but equal; poor and often scrounging from year to year, but free to do as they pleased.

Yann told her, time and again: they were lucky to have found the tiny, devoted Jala community, in desperate need of a healer. It was their saving grace, and they could never do anything to jeopardize it. She and Yann had to remain quiet, obedient, devoted to their independent paths. And no one could know about their secret.

But, he admitted when she began as his apprentice, to keep their secret, she had to learn how to control her Eko.

So, under his watchful eye, and in the privacy of the clinic, she practiced. And every week, her abilities grew. She could hear thoughts; see people's dreams; the energy pulsing through their skin. She could see through Yann's skull, into the hazy gray parts of the brain, the spots that triggered sleep, happiness, sadness, and memory. Sometimes she longed to touch them: with what, she couldn't quite pinpoint, but the longing was there.

Every evolution seemed to add more lines to Yann's face. "Remember," he cautioned her. "We have to stay hidden. We have to be content with a small life. Our chosen destiny. I know it's difficult to understand, but it's the only way."

Now, those words were like knives in her brain.

So Sydel focused on her trek: stepping heel to toe, concentrating on the feel of gritty, cold sand on the soles of her feet. There was a pinch on her shoulder, under her nightgown. The cylinder. She withdrew it and kept walking. Why had she stolen it? She grazed her thumb over the slim metal, coming across a little button. There was a tiny click. But there were no lights, no change in its appearance. Sydel sighed. She'd give it back to the woman as soon as she went back to the clinic. Yann never had to know. More important to do as he asked and make amends for her behavior.

In the corner of the courtyard, behind a privacy wall of rocks, the metal cylinder came into view. Technically, sensory deprivation was open to anyone in Jala Communia, but for a long time now, Sydel was the only user.

Sydel stripped off her sweaty, blood-smeared nightgown. The water was freezing. She didn't care. Every shock, every shudder, it drove her thoughts off-course, suffocated them, forced them into the background.

Finally, with a gulp of air, she submerged her whole body, pulling the hood shut after her. Her head shrieked from the cold, but she gripped the handles on either side, installed just below the surface to keep her from floating up. Slowly, her brain grew numb. Her nerves went still. Her body tightened with resistance, but finally relaxed.

One more minute, she chanted, exhaling a stream of bubbles. *One more chance to prove myself.*

* * *

Yann's voice hovered at the edge of her sleep. She lifted her head a hundred times that night, shoulders stiff with anticipation, certain that she heard a summons from her master. But there was nothing but the four plain walls of her cell, and slow-moving shadows.

Dawn came. The clouds lay heavy in the sky, but the Communia was awake. Feet sloshed through puddles outside her window; rain bounced off the brims of hats. Some would be in the meditation center, she knew, searching for insight; she could imagine the rise and fall of their breathing, the gentle hum in the back of their throats. The smell of wood burning came next: fires in the kitchen. Her stomach growled.

Sydel sat up in bed. No. She had to make things right first. She was such a mess the previous night, she recalled with embarrassment: working in her nightgown, hair wild around her face, acting so rashly. She had to remind Yann of her potential.

So she took her time braiding each section of her waist-length, copper-brown hair, winding it into knots and pinning it, just as she had done every day for the past two years. She chose her most mature outfit: loose trousers and tunic, with embroidery, faded from washing, but a cool, soothing blue. As she scrubbed her face with cold water, worries pressed into the back of her head. Would Yann pretend that nothing ever happened? Would he still be furious?

Finally, Sydel left the women's barracks, making her way through the courtyard under a woven bamboo parasol. Heads swiveled as she passed. Voices quieted. She chose to focus on the gates ahead. The residents had questions: of course they did. They would never ask her directly, though. They hadn't spoken to her in two years.

There were no strange silhouettes on the plains anymore: no smell of gasoline, no sound of engines, just purple sky, red rocks and patches of gray-green vegetation. Sydel licked her lips and made her way up the stairs of the clinic.

Yann rose as she entered, his face drawn with fatigue. The overhead lights were dim, as if the bulbs were just as exhausted. The floor was clean, all the spilled instruments put away. The patient was in the little twin bed in the corner: pale, bandaged, strapped to an intravenous unit, hair combed off her face.

"Good morning," she said, unable to think of anything else.

"She's stable," Yann said curtly. "Wound is repaired. I've given her pain medication."

"And the respiratory distress?"

"Nothing to be concerned with."

Doubt billowed in her chest. Last night, the woman was turning blue, she saw it. He wasn't telling her the truth. But Sydel forced herself to nod.

Yann sighed, his hands pressed to his lower back. "Monitor her blood pressure and heart rate," he instructed. "Keep her comfortable. Meds to a minimum. Change the saline when the bag runs out."

"And if she wakes," he added. "Don't speak to her. Come and get me, immediately."

Sydel gathered up her nerve. "What about the man from the night before?"

"He won't be back."

But what if he did come back? What if the man came through the doors, and there was no time to call for help? If a threat appeared, she should be prepared, shouldn't she?

"They're mercenaries."

The word surprised her, as did his candor. "Mercenaries?" She looked at the woman, lying under the clean white linen. She'd never met a criminal before.

Oddly, Yann wouldn't look her in the eye. "I shouldn't have even let either of them in," he muttered. "I'm sorry, Sydel. But we must resolve this, and get her out of here as quickly as possible."

"Do you know him, master? Or who she is?"

Yann shook his head. "I've known people like them."

How? she longed to press him. *When? Before you took me on as your ward?*

He lifted a finger to emphasize his point. "Remember, if she wakes...." He let his words trail off.

"Yes, sir."

"I will relieve you at sunset."

"Yes, sir."

This is an opportunity, she reasoned, staring at Yann's retreating back, and swallowing her questions. *This is your chance to make him proud.*

Growing up, Yann's attention was all she craved. Though her legal guardian, she was raised in the children's ward with all the other offspring. The supervisors met the children's needs, kept them all clothed and fed, educated and healthy, but with little warmth, or tolerance for idle chatter. Even a few minutes of Yann's undivided attention were precious; he was never affectionate, and there wasn't much conversation, but he looked her in the eyes and he listened when she asked questions.

When she turned ten, he told her the story of their arrival: how he discovered the Communia, deep in Midland; how the community took them in and became their unexpected saviors. He was a medical student from the east; she was an orphaned baby, placed into his care. Excited by his confession, Sydel let out a flurry of questions about her parents, how she came to him, why they had to hide. But the man only flinched, and went silent. Then he sent her away.

When she was twelve, Sydel announced her Jala path: she would become a physician, just like Yann. Small, bony, and shy with other people, she took care of stray animals in the plains: birds with injured wings, rabbits with twigs stuck in their throat. Such a commitment meant moving past her social anxiety, but she was confident in the choice. There was a barrier between Yann and the people he treated, she noticed; there was medicine, and solution; little sentiment, but great respect.

His response: books and assignments, diagrams and diagnostics, lectures late into the night. She was finally of interest to him, and she eschewed the few friends she had to study, to memorize, to fix the walls of her path. And when she turned sixteen, Yann made her his apprentice. Granted permission to move into the women's ward, she finally had her own space, away from all the chatter and gossip. She had a role to fulfill, a destiny to manifest. To her, the clinic was a beacon of light; every time she walked through its doors, she knew she would gain the respect of the Communia, and find peace and fulfilment on her chosen path.

Inside the clinic, the day stretched on. The patient perspired, though she bore no fever. When Sydel sponged down the woman's arms and legs, the woman never woke. And when Sydel wiped the sweat from the woman's eyebrows and upper lip, the dark colors remained. Permanent? It made her look so ghoulish. Why would she choose to look like that? She wasn't much older than Sydel, maybe in her mid-twenties. Could she really be a mercenary? What did that mean?

She thought to the books she'd memorized: tales of pirates and marauders and ancient knights. From what she knew, a mercenary was a violent person, who could be hired to injure or steal or kill; someone void of values, despicable to the core. She thought about the very tall man, and shivered. Were they rival criminals? If so, why would the tall man bring the woman to the Communia?

She had no idea. She didn't really understand how things worked in the world outside of Midland, other than what she'd read in books. Sydel had never left its borders; only Yann made those trips to Daro, the capital city in the North, hundreds of kilometers away, in the old ground rover to make supply runs, or for medical emergencies. His stories were always grim: stabbings, robberies; callous, judgmental, cruel people. It was his responsibility, he told her, to secure what the Communia needed on his own, without putting anyone else in danger. No one seemed to mind his decree.

The woman shifted in her sleep. The corner of the sheet rose, revealing her bandaged rib.

Yann's words pricked at Sydel's ears. *Nothing to worry about.*

Sydel drew her chair closer. Then, slowly, she peeled away the gauze from the woman's wound. Underneath, the sterile strips held the gash together. It was as Yann said, she noted with dismay, just a wound: no signs of infection, or anything to suggest a reason for respiratory distress.

Pretty lucky, she thought, *to glance off the bone like that.* What was it like to be shot?

The woman moved again. A soft moan rose from her throat, and under those dark lips, her teeth grit, so hard that Sydel could hear the squeak of molars.

Sydel quickly replaced the bandage. But the woman continued to writhe, back and forth, her blue eyebrows angled. Her eyes fluttered; Sydel caught sight of the irises underneath, a strange gray-green color. One hand lifted, clawed at her chest, leaving behind pink trails. Sydel put her hand over the patient's, holding it back. The woman's palm was rough, her fingers calloused, and strong.

Her heart thrumming, Sydel checked the saline drip. Still active. Pain medication, then? But Yann told her not to do more than the minimum, and hours remained until the next dosage.

Her mind turned back to the previous day, and those blue fingertips. Something else was wrong, she knew it; something was still in the woman's body, constricting her.

Could she run blood tests? Yann might be angry, but if she could get the results before his return....

Her hands were hot, still gripping the woman's fingers.

They were burning.

The world blurred.

She couldn't take in a full breath, like the lower half of her lungs refused to expand. But an image rose in her mind's eye: black and twisted threads, woven among red spheres, strangling, choking them, splitting them in two. Then a sharp, nauseating smell: chemicals, the strange smell of the woman's clothes from the previous night. And the black threads were moving, rolling away from the red, as if pulled by a violent force. The red spheres doubled in size, swelling with strength. And Sydel was on fire.

Gasping, Sydel jerked her hand away. Her vision cleared. The patient was quiet in her bed. The walls were white and familiar.

Sydel stared at her hand. There were no threads inside. But her palm pulsed, like a heartbeat. Like a snake undulating under her skin.

She ran.

Bracing herself in the doorway of the clinic, Sydel shut her eyes and gulped in breaths.

Be calm, she told herself, rubbing her burning palm against her tunic, wiping away the sensations.

It's nothing. It was a dream. You're exhausted.

When she opened her eyes, a man was staring up at her. The stranger from the night before.

She shrieked.

The man held up his hands, backing away. The light hit him; he was dressed in gray and brown wool layers, his head shorn to the scalp. His brown face was smeared with sweat and sand, but his eyes were bright. "I'm not going to hurt you, I just want to know if she's here," he begged. "Is she alive?"

Her hands clasped over her mouth, Sydel forced herself to calm down and assess the facts. Her eyes swept over the man: he was tall, yes, but he was also wide, and his voice was different, younger, and rougher. It wasn't the same man from the night before.

"Please," the man said. "I'm sorry if I scared you."

He opened his right hand, revealing a handful of coins. Sydel gaped at their bronze etching, their harshly cut ridges. She'd only seen actual rana a few times in her life; Jala Communia functioned on credit, and purchases were made on-site only...

"I know it's not nearly enough," he apologized. "But we'll find a way to pay you back. Just do whatever it takes to keep her alive."

What was wrong with her? Yelling in his face like a child; she had to compose herself. The man shifted from foot to foot. Anxiety billowed around him like a cloud.

"Tell me your surname," she managed.

The man shook his head, his full mouth twisted to the side. He kept looking over his shoulder to the hills beyond. Sydel followed his line of vision. There was nothing on the horizon, though several eyes were fixed on them; the residents of Jala Communia were lingering by the gates, watching their exchange. And if she opened her mind just a little, Sydel could hear their disdainful thoughts: *Look at his clothes. Look at his face. He's from the North.*

She flashed back to the encyclopedia in her room; Daro contained the mining and manufacturing centers of Osha, but also high rates of poverty and criminal activity. And the coastal area was one of the impact sites of the meteor, so many years ago, that shortened the borders and created the skerries...

She shouldn't be speaking to him, the taunts continued. *She should know better.*

That made Sydel bristle. They had no right to judge her. She was only eighteen, but she was still a medical professional. She could speak to whomever she liked, regardless of where they came from. "Well, I'm Sydel, the medical apprentice here at the clinic," she announced, louder than necessary. "And we offer charitable healing to the public. There is no cost. She's inside, stable, and sleeping."

The man slumped with relief.

"And you don't have to tell me your surname," she offered. "But your given name?"

It took several seconds for him to mutter: "Cohen."

"And her?" she tried.

"Phaira. Her name is Phaira."

Sydel straightened her shoulders. This was an opportunity. She could give Yann valuable information, if she did this correctly. "I need to know what happened before the - accident."

The man's brow furrowed. "Accident?"

Sydel searched for the right words. "Did some - action - prompt Phaira to - get shot?" She flushed at her awkwardness. "I'm sorry, I'm not saying this right."

The man ran a hand over his face. "I don't know what happened," he muttered through his palm. "Or where she's been, or what she's been doing. I haven't seen her in months."

He glanced at her, wary. Gray-green eyes, she realized with a start, that same eerie color as the patient's. Were they related?

But the whispers from the tunnel were growing louder. She had let this go for too long. When Yann found out what she was doing…

"You need to come back later," she whispered. "When my master has returned."

"Your master," Cohen repeated, a strange look on his face. Heat rose in her face. Was that the wrong word?

"Later," she instructed. "Sunset."

The look on his face made her heart hurt.

"I'll make sure you can see her," she added. "Okay?"

His face brightened.

She hoped she could keep her word.

II.

Sydel paced the clinic floor and practiced her story. Yann must know by now about the new arrival; word spread so fast in the community. But it wasn't the original tall man, she reasoned. This was something wholly unexpected. She had resumed her duties immediately afterwards. And the patient hadn't woken in her absence. She would remind him of those facts when he came through the door, before the first accusation flew.

The room grew darker. He'd sworn to return and relieve her at sunset. So where was he? Should she seek him out?

Standing in the doorframe of the clinic, Sydel shielded her eyes and searched for any sign of Yann. She couldn't quite see over the walls into the courtyard, but there was still some activity there: residents finishing up their tasks for the day, heading for the kitchens for dinner....

"Sydel!"

To her shock, it was Cohen calling, waving at her as he trotted into view. "Hey, it's me, Cohen! Remember, from earlier? Is Phaira awake? Can we see her?"

We. The word struck her.

Then Cohen's companion appeared. Slighter in build and inches shorter, the new stranger's blond hair was shaved on the sides, the fringe flopping over his forehead. Glasses hid his eyes from view. He wore the same layers of dull wool as Cohen, but his clothes were sizes too big, sleeves hanging over his hands, trousers rippling with every movement of his legs.

Sydel's heart hammered so hard that she put a fist to her chest.

"Stop."

The men froze at the command.

It came from Yann, who finally emerged from the courtyard, his face flushed, his jaw tight. Sydel gripped the doorway, uncertain of whether to step outside or withdraw.

Yann climbed the stairs to the clinic. Sydel watched the strangers. Cohen's eyes were big, his shoulders stiff, like he feared a reprimand. The blond man had no reaction. Though far smaller than Cohen, he had an air of authority. He spoke first, his voice quiet, but sharp. "You in charge here?"

Yann stood in front of Sydel. "I am. And you are?"

"Renzo. We'd like to see our sister now."

Sydel couldn't hide the surprise from her face. Sister?

"Of course," Yann said.

Sydel's mouth dropped open. So did Cohen's. The blond man merely nodded.

Sydel stared at the back of Yann's balding head. He was so masterful at hiding his thoughts from her. She never had a hint of his inner workings. But she didn't mishear; Yann's tone was respectful, and welcoming.

"Gentlemen," he gestured at the door. "Please come in."

Sydel flattened her back against the wall. Cohen bound up the steps and into the clinic, flashing her a quick, bashful smile as he passed. Renzo was slower, visibly limping on his right side. As he rocked his way up the stairs, she saw the lines on his face; still young, but weathered. He smelled like metal and smoke. He didn't look at her, before disappearing inside.

"Sydel."

She turned to her name.

"Supper is ready. Go and eat, and then retire. Thank you for your service."

Yann's clipped tone gave her no room to protest.

But even as shame colored her cheeks, she made a vow as he swept past her.

She's my patient, just as much as yours. I won't just give up.

* * *

From the second floor of the women's barracks, in one of the empty cells, Sydel watched the two men as they walked the perimeter of Jala Communia. Cohen walked slowly to accommodate Renzo's gait. Their mouths moved constantly, their brows furrowed. They were anxious, and frustrated.

When the sky turned dark and the moon slid overhead, she went to the clinic. Inside, Yann was washing his hands, his shoulders stooped with fatigue. Sydel studied the open drawers, the cabinets, even peered in the disposal unit. No sign of empty vials. No chart to review. Why was he being so secretive about the woman's treatment?

"I'm sorry."

Surprised, she glanced at her elder. His pockmarked face twisted. "My behavior has no excuse. Forgive my harshness earlier."

Sydel winced. "I know - I mean to say - you only mean the best for me," she managed.

Yann sucked in a breath, as if in pain. For a moment, he looked like he might cry.

Long seconds passed. Before them, Phaira gave a sigh.

Finally, Yann waved Sydel off. "You've been here all day, you should be resting."

"I'd rather stay." And she meant it. "I can sleep here if I need to. But if the brothers come again," she added. "May I let them in?"

Yann frowned. "Is that wise?"

"They are worried about their sister. I'm not afraid of them."

Yann chuckled. "You are too magnanimous. But don't worry: they won't come back until morning." His smile dropped. "But if you need me, reach out."

"I'll be fine."

The door closed behind him. She was alone again.

To fill the time, Sydel took stock of the clinic supplies. The routine soothed her, forcing her to be present in the moment: making lists, neat piles of supplies, of white linens...

"You again."

With a gasp, Sydel dropped the last towel in her neatly folded pile. When she turned to look, Phaira's head turned on the pillow. Navy and aquamarine strands of greasy hair fell over her cheek. Her gray-green eyes were clear now.

Sydel forced her hands to her sides, digging her fingernails into her palms. The pain was a reminder. Calm. Control.

"You - you're in a medical clinic," she began. "In Midland. Do you remember what happened?"

The woman said nothing, her dark mouth pinched.

Suddenly, Phaira arched her back. Little pops echoed through the space. Then the woman swung her legs over the edge of the bed. As she held the sheet to her chest, she studied the swath of bandages on her ribs, touching the edges.

"You did this?" she asked Sydel, her tone skeptical. "How old are you?"

"Eighteen," Sydel said, stung. "How old are you?"

The woman smirked. One of her bare feet kicked in the air. "Where are my things?"

Sydel flushed. "We had to cut off your clothes. But there are clothing donations on the shelf behind you. I kept your boots, though," she added. "I thought you might want them."

Phaira dropped her head back, searching for the folded pile. As she reached, the sheet fell. Sydel turned away. For many seconds, she only heard the sound of fabric brushing on skin.

"You can turn around," the woman's voice wafted over. "Very considerate."

When Sydel completed her circle, she froze at the sight. Phaira was so tall for a woman, at least eight inches taller than Sydel. Standing upright, she had broad shoulders and a narrow waist, and even the muscles above her clavicles were pronounced.

Mercenaries.

A knock on the door. Phaira paled. Her eyes darted around the clinic, finally resting on the clinic door.

The only exit, Sydel realized.

The door opened. Sydel barely avoided a collision with Cohen as the man barreled inside, and swept Phaira into an embrace, lifting her off the ground.

"Ack!" Phaira cried, smacking her brother. "Put me down, I'm still hurt!"

"Sorry," Cohen apologized as he set her down. "I'm just glad you're all right. That was scary."

The sound of hinges again. Then the threshold grew dark, and stayed dark, and the warm sentiment in the room began to cool.

"Hi Ren," Phaira said pointedly.

Half in shadow, Renzo's face had no expression.

Then the man glanced over at Sydel. "Thank you for your help - Sydel, right? She looks good."

"Are you going to come in or what?" Cohen asked impatiently.

Renzo shook his head. Sydel's curiosity bubbled up inside her, and a strange confidence. Buoyed by the rush, she moved into the line of sight between Renzo, Cohen and Phaira.

"I have a few questions," she announced, in what felt like a brazen voice.

Instantly, all three wore the same wary expression. *They really do look alike,* Sydel thought. She pressed on. "For our records. I need clarification on what happened. It's required," she added. "As part of public healing services. Full disclosure."

The threesome glanced at each other. They were weighing their collective impulse to run, she realized. And, really, what would she do if they ran? Chase them?

"And when there's evidence of narcotics, we have to report it." Yann's voice echoed through the space.

All turned, save for Sydel, who bit her lip and lowered her gaze.

"So the truth, if you please," Yann said, sliding past Renzo into the clinic.

"Narcotics," Cohen said. He sounded ill.

"Mekaline," Yann corrected, as if speaking to a child. "In addition to the gunshot wound, your sister was in withdrawal." Sydel sensed her master standing behind her. "That was the cause of her respiratory distress."

Silence.

Then Renzo exploded. "What have you been doing?"

Phaira lifted her chin, eyes glittering.

It just seemed to make Renzo angrier. "We spend months looking for you and you're -"

"I didn't want you to come after me," Phaira corrected hotly. "You should have let me disappear."

In the bitter hush that followed, Cohen looked between his brother and sister. A ping of sympathy rang in Sydel's chest. But she remained quiet.

Finally Phaira spoke up. "Please leave us to discuss our personal matters. Then we will comply."

"Very well," Yann agreed. "I'll return shortly."

He took Sydel's arm and steered her out of the clinic. Sydel gladly followed.

Outside, the moon had broken through the clouds. Sydel kept pace with her elder as they moved to stand by the latticework gates. Under the soft white light, it was almost peaceful.

But Sydel couldn't hold back her question any longer: "Master, are you certain that a narcotic caused her distress?"

Yann studied the wood of the gates, running a finger along the grooves. "Mekaline abuse is easy to recognize. It's a street hallucinogenic, highly addictive. Very foolish girl to even try it."

"You ran a blood test to confirm it?"

He shot her a look. "I could smell it on her. You wouldn't understand, you haven't been exposed to those kinds of people."

"But it wasn't medically confirmed," Sydel pressed.

"Sydel." The tone of his voice made her stiffen. "Why are you questioning my judgment?"

"I - I just fear to cause a rift between these people if none truly exists."

"And that's all?"

Sydel worked up her nerve. "I want to know what this is all about."

"You already know. They are criminals, all of them, and we are caught in the crossfire."

Sydel bit her lip. "How can you be so certain of that? Other than the gunshot wound -"

Yann shushed her, looking around. It just increased her frustration. "Who was the tall man from that night?" she insisted.

"Keep your voice down."

"No, I won't! Not until you - "

"You are acting like a child," Yann growled. His cold hand was on her arm.

"I'm not," Sydel retorted, jerking away from his grip. "I'm asking for honesty."

"You're not ready to know what's out there."

Sydel recoiled. Did he really say that? Did he really think that about her?

"You have no idea what I'm capable of," she burst out. "What I've been able to do - "

"What did you do?" His eyes pierced into hers, but they weren't angry anymore; they were full of dread.

Sydel swallowed her words, staring at the ground. "Nothing," she said through gritted teeth. "I spoke out of turn."

When she glanced up, the look on his face was the coldest she could recall.

"Go to bed, Sydel."

Tears welled up in her eyes. But before he could see her weakness, Sydel ran, not stopping until her feet hit the steps of the barracks, then the floor of her cell.

III.

When the sunrise eased into Sydel's room, a folded note slid under her door. Sydel sat up in bed and uncoiled her hair from the top of her head. The braids fell over her shoulders; her scalp was numb from sleeping on them. Stumbling to her feet, she picked up the paper. Yann's handwriting, scribbled on the diagonal, as if in a rush: *Phaira has been cleared to leave,* it read. *All three are leaving at dawn. Met us at the main gate.*

She had to make amends. When the strangers left, she would ask for Yann's forgiveness. She would do her best to listen and learn. She would be the heir to the clinic; she would set herself on her chosen path, and embrace Jala Communia and all its blessings from now on.

Outside, the inner compound was deserted. Walking its breadth, Sydel kept looking over her shoulder, searching for signs of life.

Ahead, the latticework gate was open. In the growing light, Sydel caught sight of the vertical line of the planetary ring, arching up and disappearing behind clouds; the one time of the day when it could be seen clearly Normally, she would be spellbound. Now she could only focus on the siblings, who were on the other side of the gate, waiting. Were they waiting for her? She slowed her pace, uncertain of what to say to them.

But none of them would even look at her. Renzo's face was in profile, staring up at the orange sky. Cohen's eyes were at his feet, arms crossed over his broad chest. Phaira had changed clothes; she now wore a black overcoat with heavy collar and cuffs, her throat wrapped with a silver scarf. Her hands were in the back pockets of her grey trousers, her gaze overlooking over the rocky plains.

The sound of footsteps behind her. Sydel stopped walking, and lowered her head. When Yann's shadow passed her, she stayed close, behind her master.

"You are ready?" Yann asked the siblings.

Renzo gave the slightest nod. No one else moved.

Sydel wondered what the medical records said, what secrets were divulged to Yann when he returned to the clinic. Would he ever show her?

"Regarding payment..."

All three strangers looked at Yann with surprise, as did Sydel. What was he talking about?

Something bumped into her feet. A leather satchel.

"... take Sydel with you," Yann completed his sentence.

She must have misheard him.

"Take - what?" Phaira said finally. The brothers wore the same perplexed expression.

"I'm placing her in your care as payment for services rendered," Yann said. "For three months, until we reconsider her for residency. Until then, she is your responsibility."

Was she still asleep? This was wrong, all wrong.

She saw Renzo crane his neck, staring at something behind her. An audience, Sydel realized: several eyes fixed on the back of her head, pinning her in place.

The whole community had gathered to cast her off.

She was being excommunicated.

"Look," Renzo began. "We're not taking anyone - "

"You have no right to refuse," Yann cut him off. "Unless you want the details of this visit released to the public, you'll do as I ask. Take her to a safe location, find her shelter and occupation, and then ensure that she has the means to return in twelve weeks."

Sydel couldn't feel her skin, only her frozen, cracking insides.

"But - but why?" she finally choked out.

"The vote occurred last night," Yann said, his voice strangely flat. "It's out of my hands."

"But why would they - "

"I'm sorry, Sydel." Now there was a strangled edge to his words. "But that you are of age, you must earn the trust of the community. And at this moment," he faltered a little, before resuming. "You're a hazard."

"A hazard?" Sydel heard Renzo exclaim. "Her?"

Yann continued to talk, but Sydel couldn't make out the rest of his words. Her senses had dulled into nothing. She couldn't breathe. She couldn't think. She was breaking apart.

Then someone touched her arm from behind. A rush of warm breath hit the side of her face.

Startled, Sydel's hearing sharpened, just in time to hear Phaira's whisper: "Don't let them see you cry. Control yourself. You have to leave with pride."

Somehow, the words registered in Sydel's brain, and her senses began to thaw, slowly expanding until her body felt functional again.

"She comes with us, then," Phaira announced. "Co?"

As if moving through water, Sydel turned around, finding Cohen in her blurry vision. He was staring at her. Then, jerking to attention, he walked over and offered his arm to Sydel. It was warm, and solid.

The other two siblings loomed over Yann, glaring down at the man. Finally, Phaira muttered something unintelligible and turned her back. Renzo remained standing. "You're disgusting," he spat. Then he lifted his voice, addressing the audience in the distance. "You're all disgusting! She's just a kid!"

"She's older than she looks," Yann replied. For a moment, Sydel thought she saw a flash of regret in his face, before his features settled into cool regard. "I wish you a peaceful three months, Sydel. And wise choices from here on out, to ensure your safe return."

Sydel forced her body to bend over, for her hand to reach for the satchel at her feet. But Phaira beat her to it. As the woman slung it over her shoulder, Sydel caught the tiniest shake of Phaira's head. *Say nothing*, the motion seemed to say. *Show nothing.*

Then Phaira stood next to Sydel, Renzo just behind. The strangers' collective energy was a vibrant orange; it buoyed Sydel with the strength to walk.

As a foursome, they passed through the main gate, and into the plains. They walked in silence, never turning their heads.

But within the mile, hidden in a flushed-out gorge, the vessel appeared: boxy and brown-gray, bulky with mismatched parts, patched with corroded metal. Its wings jutted out like a broken bird's, spray-painted with graffiti in languages she didn't understand.

A Volante. Sydel had only heard of them in books: cheaply manufactured, used for transient living, often by criminals to avoid registration. They really were mercenaries. And Yann placed her in their care? How could he?

The Volante released little hisses as they came closer, as if it lived and breathed. Frightened, Sydel's hand dropped from Cohen's arm. Her nerves itched; her skin itched; her mind screamed at her to run away.

But what else could she do?

As Renzo yanked open the rusty door, every step forward was a reminder.

This is the last time I will see the Communia.

The last time I will smell the rush of rain and the sand.

IV.

At the back of the Volante, there was a storage compartment filled with water tanks, and a small pocket of space in the center. Sydel barricaded herself in. She slept on a coiled-up quilt, soothed by the sound of water rippling all round her. When she woke, she stared at her reflection in the metal walls: the circles under her eyes, her waxy brown skin, her still-round face, her slightly hooked nose rimmed with pink, waiting for the next wave of fatigue to come and take her away.

Thankfully, the siblings let her be, their presence shown by a meal pack left inside the door, or water with M-purification tablets affixed to the bottle. Sometimes Sydel heard them through the ventilation system, whispering.

The Volante seemed to be in constant motion. Sydel's stomach dropped every time the world lifted; her insides shuddered at the backwards push of gravity. She wondered where they were going, how far she was from home. Sydel couldn't tell how many days had passed since her expulsion.

Excommunicated. It didn't seem real. Was it real? Maybe this was a test. In her heart, though, she knew how the Communia was governed. Despite Yann's guardianship, and her lack of exposure to the outside world, all adults had to be formally accepted into the community.

And she had fallen short.

She couldn't bear to think about it.

So instead, she slept.

* * *

"Sydel?"

The door opened, and then closed with a soft click. The sister looked different than before, healthier and far softer with her blue hair tucked behind her ears, wearing gray cotton trousers and a matching shirt that slipped off one shoulder. As she approached, Sydel pushed herself up to a seat, rolling her loose, greasy hair into a knot at the nape of her neck.

Phaira crouched down, peering into Sydel's face. "So we need a plan here," she told her. "You can't keep hiding in our closet."

"Yes," Sydel said. "Where are we - where are you going?" she corrected.

"I'm not sure yet," Phaira said. "We're still trying to figure out where to take you. You've got no rana, no connections, and we don't have any to spare." She sighed. "This is a strange situation you've gotten us into. And lousy timing."

"I have been thinking." Sydel closed her eyes, drawing in her focus. When she opened them again, Phaira hadn't moved from her precarious position, her heels hovering in perfect balance. "While I realize that you are..."

She tried to think of the politest way to say 'criminals.'

"...strangers," she finally inserted. "Given my circumstances, I believe the wisest course of action would be to remain with you, and be of service for the next three months."

Phaira raised an eyebrow. "Doing what, exactly?"

"Healing, of course."

"Sydel," Phaira said. "I respect the situation you're in, how difficult it must be, but your master, or father, or whoever that was, he said that - "

"I noticed the number of scars on your skin," Sydel broke in. "I could ensure that any future wound heals twice as quickly. No matter the circumstances around it. I won't question your activities...."

Maybe this is how I'm to regain my Jala path, she thought as she spoke. *Maybe this is my destiny.*

"...and if you are concerned about another mekaline reaction, like the one you experienced," she added nervously. "Having a healer nearby can only benefit you, correct?"

Phaira didn't say anything. Sydel's heart thudded. She had gone too far.

Then Phaira stood. Sydel caught a flash of tight jaw, a flush on Phaira's cheek, before the woman left the closet.

Some minutes later, whispers moved through the ventilation pipes, into the little storage unit. They were talking about her, Sydel knew it. Making decisions.

She couldn't remain a recluse.

So Sydel braided back her hair. A wrinkled, sleeveless pink dress, unearthed from the depths of her satchel, replaced her dirty chemise and trousers. It was better than before. Then she crept into the narrow corridor.

Lights flickered overhead. The Volante was split down the middle, with rails, grated floors and wires snaking along the edge. One side housed the three cabins, one for each of the strangers; the other side held a small kitchen, a lavatory, and a common room. The three strangers were in there now.

Clasping her elbows, hovering by the entrance, Sydel listened to the hushed argument inside:

"She's ideal. No connections to the outside world. Dependent on us for basic needs."

"Ren, I can't believe you're actually considering this."

"You could have died, Phair. And what about the other times? If another attempt's made while we are out here, we wouldn't have to scour for medical options."

"Wait a minute, we can't involve her! Not without being honest about Phaira's - about our situation."

"Co's right. You realize how sheltered she is? She doesn't know anything outside of that creepy commune."

Sydel winced, stung by the judgment. The strangers continued to argue the same points, their voices growing louder. She had to intervene. She rehearsed her speech, gathering her courage. Then she stepped inside.

The common room was dim and musty. Sydel could make out one chipped table and two makeshift desks made of storage containers. Papers, parts and wires dangled off the edges. A dusty console ringed the room's perimeter, with buttons that hadn't been touched in years, by the look of it. Cohen and Renzo sat in two chairs; the third turned slowly, abandoned. Phaira stood by one of the windows, looking outside.

The two men looked up as Sydel entered. Cohen's face turned a funny shade of pink. Renzo ran a hand through his blond hair. "I guess you overheard some of that," he mumbled.

Sydel wet her lips, clasped her hands in front of her, and announced: "As I told your sister, I can be of service to you."

She quickly checked for Phaira's reaction. The sister didn't turn around.

"I chose the path of medicine when I was twelve. I've been training for six years, and I can manage several illnesses and injuries."

No one spoke. Sydel continued, concentrating hard to not stutter. "Your sister was brought to my clinic because you had no funds. And you still don't, so I've learned. This can be seen as a benefit to your situation."

The brothers had identical expressions of surprise on their faces.

Sydel pressed on. "And I can help in other ways. Whatever is useful. And I can be discreet. Please, let me stay."

Then she bobbed a small curtsy and hurried back to the storage closet.

She didn't want to stay with them, of course. She loathed the idea of living in a machine, choking on recycled air, healing the wounds of terrible people. More than anything, Sydel longed to run back to Yann and beg for forgiveness.

But even as she wished, it was a unanimous vote. If she wanted any chance of returning to the Communia, she had to wait out her banishment.

A knock on her door. Sydel lifted her forehead from the cold metal.

Phaira's blue head poked through the opening. A decision already? Sydel braced herself for the news.

"You said someone brought me to your commune." The woman's voice was low and rushed. "Who was it?"

"You don't know?"

"Clearly, I don't. The last thing I remember - "

Phaira stopped, her dark mouth pressed together.

"Man or woman?" she asked instead.

"Man," Sydel said nervously. "I couldn't see his face – but he was very tall..."

Before Sydel could finish, the woman was gone.

* * *

Another day passed. Sydel didn't leave her little space, moving through sleep and half-hearted meditations. More conversations wafted through the ventilation system.

"It's creepy that someone's living here and we never see her," she overheard Cohen say. "It's like there's a ghost or something."

It hurt to hear Cohen's words. She suspected that he was the one who left the water, food and blankets at her door. She disturbed him? Didn't he understand how heartbroken she was?

"You want to draw her into some deep conversation?" came Phaira's sharp reply.

"She might understand what we are going through."

"Right, because we've seen such a great history of that."

Sydel removed her ear from the metal vent. If Cohen saw her as a ghost, she might as well act like one. It was time to learn the danger she faced.

So when they landed again, and siblings left the old ship, Sydel began to explore the Volante.

On the left side of the corridor, the kitchen was cramped and lined with rust, with little in the cupboards other than cups and utensils. She had already braved the lavatory, and she didn't have the courage to sneak into the cockpit, but she found another storage unit off the common room: the same size as hers but filled with stacks of meal packs. Her heart jumped at the sight of the rifle, tucked behind all the bins. Even Sydel knew that firearms were illegal to the public. They really were criminals.

On the right side were the crew cabins. Sydel stood in the doorways and studied the contents of each. They were all the same, structurally: curved ceilings, lined with ventilation pipes, cracks and rust, but each had a different energy. Renzo's space was full of half-assembled, slowly-turning mechanisms. Cohen's room was surprisingly neat and sparse, save for the enormous bed. Phaira's quarters had the window covered, but Sydel could still see the pile of clothes in the far right corner, and the crooked bed with twisted sheets.

When she wasn't exploring, Sydel remained in solitude; she ate sparingly, she rested and worked to rebuild her focus, one meditation at a time. Her mind began to clear. She asked Phaira where to bathe and put aside her disgust of the lukewarm water supply and its copper stink. She resumed her practice of braiding and pinning her hair up. And she went through the supplies in the leather satchel again and again, cataloguing what she had, and what she needed.

Finally, the siblings asked her to join them in the common room. They had made a decision.

"You can't stay with us. I'm sorry; but that's not going to work," Phaira apologized. As she spoke, Cohen picked at the hem of his black shirt. Renzo looked down, one boot scuffing at the floor.

Suddenly Renzo thumped his forearms onto the table, startling them all. "Are you sure your people won't take you back? I know they said three months until the next review, but what would happen if we just punched in their See-See, and apologized and - "

"The what?" Sydel interrupted. "See-See?"

"Connection Code," Cohen spoke up, furrowing his brow. "Letter and number combo - so you can talk to people or places? CC. You don't know?"

Sydel shook her head, confused. She didn't know what to say.

Renzo sighed. "Well, whatever. What if we just went back there?"

"Nothing," Sydel said.

"So you can go home?"

Sydel winced. "You misunderstand me. Nothing would happen. When a decision is made to excommunicate, there is no argument. For the next three months, I no longer exist." She looked at Renzo pointedly. "So you see, I am quite at your mercy."

"Ugh," Phaira groaned, putting her face in her hands.

"Phair," Cohen warned.

"Okay, okay," Renzo interjected, waving his hands. "You can still find work elsewhere. You're right; you have a valuable trade skill. Every place needs a healer. So we teach you the basics of society, you find some temporary housing, and you can survive on your own. Right?"

Sydel remained silent, though she knew he was right.

Renzo sighed. "I registered for work at a Vendor Mill. This is as good a time as any to start your education."

* * *

From the outside, the Vendor Mill looked like a square, squat box, plopped in the center of the city. Inside, the smell of grease and gasoline was overwhelming. Waves of people knocked into Sydel, first on the left, then on the right, as she followed the strangers down the dank corridor. Ahead, a break of light: the marketplace. Cloth banners of every color draped over makeshift stores, stalls and display tables. Vendors in magenta robes called out their wares, sometimes grabbing at people's sleeves to force them to look. The multi-pitched voices, mixed with the roar of transport ships and ground vehicles, made for a weirdly melodic backdrop to all the commotion. That was what Sydel told herself, anyways, as she cupped her hands over her ears, trying to process all the stimulation.

Leading the group, Renzo suddenly stopped. "My repair job's this way," he gestured to a dark opening to the left. "Shouldn't take long. Meet back in an hour."

He limped off into the masses. Cohen and Phaira kept walking. Phaira hovered behind Cohen's enormous frame, her eyes darting in all directions. *Why is she so afraid?* Sydel wondered. *Should I be afraid too?*

As they reached the center of the Vendor Mill, people moved in a kaleidoscope of color. Sales took place at rapid speed, with lots of fingers pointing. Sydel slipped on a puddle of oil, and she resisted the urge to moan.

Then Phaira was backing away from them, moving into the surging crowds.

"Hey, wait, where are you going?" Cohen yelled after her. "We should stay together."

"I'll be right back!" Phaira said sharply. Then her expression shifted. "I'm not going to a dealer, Cohen," she continued, her tone gentler. "Of any kind. I promise. I just want to buy my things in privacy. Okay? Take Sydel and show her how to barter. I'll be right back."

Before Cohen could say anything more, Phaira disappeared. People rushed into the void left by the woman; when their frantic energy crashed into Sydel, she felt the urge to just let her body be carried away....

Then Cohen's enormous bulk was before her. The crowd curved around them and she could breathe.

"Sorry," he told her. "I can take you around, if you want. Or we can just go back to the Vol, if it's too much. It must look pretty crazy to you."

Sydel lowered her hands from her ears. "It's - you're very considerate," she managed.

Cohen shrugged. "I know it's strange. It's strange for me too sometimes. Don't know what's happening half of the time." He kicked at an oil spot as his voice trailed off.

A tiny flicker of affection grew in Sydel. She expected such a large man to be aggressive. But he was kind. He meant well.

So she forced a smile and touched his arm. "Phaira mentioned bartering? I've never done that. Show me how?"

Cohen grinned. "I can do that." He practically bounced as he made a path for her. Thankful for his great shadow in the crowd, Sydel studied the little swirls in Cohen's hairline, shorn so close to the scalp. He was a good man. Renzo did repair work; there was nothing evil about that. Phaira acted strangely and she still wondered about the circumstances of that gunshot sound, but maybe she was wrong about them.

A ripple went through the air.

She froze in place. A flash of magenta caught her eye in the distance, perhaps a balding head.

Sydel.

"Yann?" she whispered. Had he followed her all this way?

Cohen didn't notice her stopping; he kept walking, weaving around a pillar towards the open market.

Then everything burst into white.

V.

Her ears rang so loudly that it took a moment to register her own whimpers of fear. But Sydel's mind filled with collective terror, voices screaming and crying in a million octaves. She squeezed her head with both hands, trying to manage the overflow. Her right hand grew wet and warm. She was lying on the floor, covered in dust. Cohen was - Cohen? She strained to see through the billowing smoke. A few people lay on the floor, moaning and writhing, but Cohen....

There he was, ten feet in front of her, lying on his side. Sydel crawled to him, coughing. She put her hand on his shoulder. Cohen didn't move.

"Cohen?" she whispered.

He screwed up his face in pain. Sydel quickly assessed his condition. His pulse was slow; his blood pressure was probably dropping. His breathing was ragged, but no sign of a lung collapse. There were spots of blood on his shirt. Tiny pieces of shrapnel had torn through his chest, but Cohen gave no reaction when she swept her trembling hands over his arms and legs checking for broken bones.

And where were the siblings? Were they hurt, too? Should she run? What if he was dying? What if they all were dying and she couldn't do anything?

Panicking, Sydel broke open her mind, her thoughts soaring through the Vendor Mill. *Phaira! Renzo! Please!*

Suddenly, Phaira burst through the smoke and slid next to Cohen's body. "Co!" she panted, her clothes smeared with soot, her hair wild around her face. "Are you okay? Are you awake?"

"Prefer not to be," Cohen mumbled, ending his sentence with a cough and a groan.

Phaira flinched at the sound of sirens in the distance. "Please tell me we can take him back to the Vol," she begged Sydel. "And you can heal him there."

Sydel stared at the woman. "I've never done anything like this alone."

"But you can manage, right?" Phaira's gaze dropped as she spoke under her breath. "We can't go to a hospital, we can't have any records taken. We have to get out of here."

"I - I need an ultrasound to be certain," Sydel said. "In the Communia, we had a device for remote imaging - do you have those out here? Can you buy one? Or - ?"

Before Sydel could finish the sentence, Phaira had disappeared into the smoke.

Cohen tried to sit up, but his face went gray with the movement. Sydel took hold of his big hand. "Be still," she ordered.

"Dizzy," he muttered. His hot fingers gripped hers. "What happened? You alright?"

"I'm fine," Sydel told him. "We're going to take you back to the Vol, just as soon as your sister -"

Phaira emerged again, a white metal box tucked under her arm. "There's an ultrasound in there," she told Sydel, shoving it at her. "Do it quickly."

Sydel popped open the case; a gleaming remote ultrasound lay inside, along with gauze, scissors, sterile cloths, a stethoscope and blood pressure monitor, all neatly arranged. She quickly screwed the device together and activated it; holding the screen to her eye, she scanned down Cohen's body, starting at his head and working down each arm and leg.

Past her point of vision, Phaira's foot tapped over and over. "Is he okay?" she asked twice.

Sydel swallowed as she lowered the ultrasound. "I think I can manage."

"Good. And he can walk, right?"

"I think so. The drop in cardiovascular output - "

Phaira waved her hand impatiently. Then the woman ducked underneath Cohen's arm and gestured for Sydel to do the same. "Come on," she told her brother. "Time to get up."

Sydel replaced everything in the box and gripped it in her left hand. She put her right shoulder under Cohen's arm, and with Phaira, together they rose to their feet, straining under Cohen's weight. The brother groaned, but he was able to support his body enough for them to walk as a trio.

Slowly, they made their way back to the garage, maneuvering past the injured. Paramedics ran past them, carrying the same white metal boxes. Sydel's mouth dropped open.

"Did you steal this kit?" she hissed at the blue-haired woman across Cohen's chest.

Phaira just shot her a look.

Sydel gripped the handle of the white box as they ran. Should she drop it? She didn't dare. It was too valuable.

When they had dragged Cohen into the Volante and onto his bed, they split off: Phaira to start the engines, Sydel to her little storage unit. She didn't have much from the Communia, but Yann had been kind enough to include her personal medical kit, complete with healing balms.

On re-entry to Cohen's room, the smell of burnt flesh and chemicals choked her nostrils. Sydel snapped on a pair of gloves and tore his shirt in spurts until she could pull it off his body. Little chunks of metal were embedded in his chest and right arm. Shallow, though, and small. There were some pink patches on his hands, possibly second-degree burns. But it didn't seem like there was anything more. He was lucky, so lucky. She recalled the pillar in front of her, before everything went white; it probably kept her from serious injury. Just as lucky as Cohen.

The Volante shuddered. Sydel felt her stomach drop as they lurched into flight. A few seconds later, Phaira returned, staring at her brother from the doorway, wringing her hands.

A strange anger rose in Sydel. "Come in here and help me," she ordered Phaira. "Go into my kit and take out the burn ointment. In the green jar."

Phaira rummaged through the bag and withdrew the container. Sydel nodded; she had mixed it only one week ago, so it should be at full potency, ready to trigger the skin to regenerate its lost layers. Sydel kept that detail to herself, though; she didn't know much about medicine in the outside world.

"You can apply it," she told Phaira. "Put gloves on and be gentle. Just where the skin is pink on his hands."

"Me?" Phaira looked ill at the thought.

"Yes, you."

I sound like Yann, Sydel thought suddenly. She didn't quite know how to feel about that.

As Sydel began to extract the metal pieces and staunch the flow of blood, the sister scooped the milky white gel from the jar and applied it to her brother's hands. Cohen's body stiffened, shaking with pain.

At the sight, warmth prickled in Sydel's palm again, but this time, she could breathe. Red circles swam behind her eyes, and instinctually, Sydel mentally chanted: *Be calm. Be still.*

Cohen's hands unclenched and his breathing began to slow. The red receded into nothing.

When his body was clean and bandaged, Cohen struggled to sit up. Both Sydel and Phaira moved to push him back. "You need to rest," Phaira told him.

"Where's Ren?" Cohen mumbled.

"Don't worry about him," Phaira soothed. "We're on our way to pick him up. You need to sleep."

As the women exited, Phaira headed in the direction of the cockpit. Sydel retreated to her little storage unit, slid behind all the water units into her little alcove. Then she allowed herself to crumble into a ball on the floor.

An hour later, a knock on the door. Sydel lifted her head from the quilt she'd bunched into a pillow. She had cleaned up her head wound, and hoped to sleep a little, but it was no use. The scenes of the Mill were on constant rotation in her brain: the sounds of the market, the burst of hot white, the moaning, broken people.

"Sydel? Are you in there?"

Renzo's voice made her instantly nervous. But she brushed away any hint of tears and stood up.

"Yes," she called. "I'm here."

The door creaked open. Over the top of the crates, Renzo looked exhausted, his blond hair sticking up, his tanned face streaked with soot.

After a long, uncomfortable silence, Sydel spoke first. "Your brother will be fine."

Renzo nodded, avoiding her eyes.

The silence continued. Sydel didn't dare to say anything more.

"I'm just -" Renzo said abruptly. He cleared his throat. "I'm very - we're very lucky that you are here."

Before Sydel could respond, he was gone.

She had done the right thing. It felt incredible.

But only for a moment, as the sounds of arguing travelled through the open door.

Leaning over the threshold, Sydel saw Renzo grab Phaira's arm, just outside of the common room. Phaira brushed him off. "I need to get back there before it's wiped clean," she was saying.

"This had nothing to do with you!" Renzo snapped, hobbling after her.

"How do you know that?" Phaira challenged. "I told you, one of them is still out there - "

"That guy is not going to expose himself in public," Renzo shot back. "If he knows you're alive, and if he cares that you are, he'll attempt something a little more direct."

Something clicked in Sydel's brain. "You speak of the one who shot Phaira," she impulsively called out.

The siblings stopped fighting. First they stared at her, and then at each other.

Sydel exhaled with a huff. She was already so tired of their secret looks. "Please just tell me the truth," she insisted. "I have a right to know if I am in any immediate danger."

"She's right," Renzo said.

Phaira whipped around to argue, but he held up his hand. "You know she's right. We can provide some details. Some," he added pointedly. "It's only fair."

Several seconds passed. Sydel did her best to refrain from blinking.

Finally, Phaira stomped past Renzo to enter the common room. Renzo exhaled, rubbing the bridge of his nose under his glasses.

"Let's go," he told Sydel. "You asked for this."

Inside, Phaira slumped in a chair, her head in her hands. Renzo leaned against the chipped table, his long fingers tapping the edge.

"Sit down," he instructed, as Sydel hesitated by the doorframe.

Sydel took the seat closest to the entryway. Her fingers plucked at her dress; she hadn't noticed, but there were speckles of blood in the fine fabric. Hers? Or Cohen's?

"About a year ago, a very - notorious - man died in an accident," Renzo began, glancing at the top of Phaira's head. "Phaira was blamed for his death and driven into hiding. Co and I searched for her for months. Then her solar tracker went off in your commune. You know what that is?"

The little cylinder, with the sun etching. The tiny click. That's how the brothers came to Communia. She had summoned them.

Sydel pressed her mouth together, and shook her head.

Renzo shrugged, continuing. "It wasn't until we came back on the Vol that we found out..."

His voice trailed off.

Then Phaira's blue head lifted. "Four bounty hunters tried to kill me. That's how I got shot. But one got away, and I think he might be behind the bombing."

Her eyes met Sydel's. "And the reason I came into your clinic."

It was a pointed remark. She was talking about the very tall man, but she didn't want Renzo to know about it.

Sydel blinked a few times, processing.

"He got away," she repeated. "There were four hunters."

"Yes. And I had to defend myself."

So the rest were dead? By her hand?

She is a murderer.

I have healed a murderer.

As she stood up, Sydel did her best to speak without trembling. "It would be best if I were to leave now."

"No!"

Sydel shrank back at the man's outburst.

Phaira bolted upright, her boots making a loud thump on the floor. "Ren!"

Ignoring his sister, Renzo lifted his palms to Sydel. "Please don't go yet," he pleaded. "Please."

"Ren!" Phaira warned. "If she wants to leave..."

"No!" Renzo fired back over his shoulder. "I'm thinking of Co now. And you too."

Renzo turned back to Sydel. His hands clasped in front of his sternum. *He is begging me*, Sydel realized with shock.

"Sydel, we'll make a decent room for you," Renzo said. "Whatever you need or want. I'll make sure you transition into a new life, a safe one. But I need to know that if something else happens..."

He wrung his hands as he paused. The man's energy was white and frantic.

"Please. Please stay for a little longer. "

* * *

Thrown by Renzo's plea, and terrified by Phaira's confession, Sydel chose to focus her efforts on Cohen. His burns were beginning to heal, thanks to her ointment. He was bearing the pain well too. Twice now he had refused medication to ease the heat of his injuries. A little of his refusal had to do with ego, Sydel sensed; he wanted to appear strong in front of her. She didn't argue his choice, but tried to be as gentle as she could be when changing the bandages.

As she worked, Sydel could hear the other two siblings, lost in their own worlds: clicking noises from Renzo's quarters; dull thuds and smacks from Phaira's.

"What are they doing in there?" Sydel murmured, wincing at a sudden bang.

Cohen shrugged. "Ren's building something, Phaira's punching a bag. That's what they do when they're upset. You know, they pretend they're so different from each other? But they react the same way."

"But you don't seem to be like them," she countered. "Are you adopted?"

Cohen gave a little bark of laughter. "I wonder sometimes."

"Cohen?" She kept her eyes low as she tore off a strip of tape. "Are you - is your family...?"

As she stumbled, Cohen rose onto his elbows. His jaw was covered with thick stubble; it made him look both older and more intimidating.

"Are we what?" he murmured, his eyes shifting to the wall.

He knows, she thought. *He knows that I'm afraid his brother and sister will hear.*

"Am I in mortal danger?" she whispered back. "Should I run away? Please tell me the truth."

Cohen looked at her for a few seconds. Then he shook his head.

"No," he said quietly. "I mean, if you want to leave, you should leave. But none of us would hurt you. We're not bad people. We've just - "

He ran a thick hand over his face and let out a sigh. "Thing is, I just don't know how much to say, Syd. It's not really about me, so I don't know what's okay to share. You know?"

Syd. The term struck her. She had never been called that before. Always Sydel, Healer Sydel, Apprentice Sydel. Cohen's term had a different sound to it. Warm. Familiar.

She realized that Cohen was grinning at her. "What'd I say?" he teased.

Sydel blushed and got up from his bedside, smoothing down her skirt. "Nothing. I was just thinking - I don't know what I was thinking." She headed for the door, embarrassed.

"So are you going to leave?" he called after her.

On her way out, Sydel rested her hand on the doorframe, her pink face hidden from his view.

"No," she murmured. "No, not just yet."

* * *

The Volante broke through the clouds, revealing parched land below, greens and dead browns. Through the window in the common room, Sydel saw the outline of a city in the distance, the flashing lights, pinpricks of motion. Within minutes, the Volante slowed and began to turn, rattling the whole while. Sydel heard the landing gear unfurl in rusty protest, and then the final clunk of the parking magnet.

Curious, she crept into the hallway, looking for one of the strangers. Cohen slept, she knew. Renzo's door was closed, and there were no sounds within.

But Phaira was in her quarters, the door ajar. She was fastening buckles on some kind of black, rubbery, sleeveless bodysuit. The slick fabric shielded her neck, covered her torso, and then disappeared under a pair of gray trousers. A holster sat on her hip.

"Are you coming with me?"

The question made Sydel jump. Phaira's head turned, that sharp profile over her shoulder.

"Where are you going?" Sydel asked, huddled by the doorframe.

The woman looked like she was about to tell Sydel to go away, but something shifted in her expression.

"I'm going to reconcile this misunderstanding," she said. As she spoke, her hand drifted to her ribs. As if to challenge Sydel.

"You're going to kill him," Sydel said, aghast. "The tall man."

Phaira pressed her dark lips together. Then: "No, not necessarily."

Not necessarily. Sydel swallowed hard. "But he saved you."

Phaira rolled her eyes. "I don't expect you to understand."

Sydel bristled. "I might, if there is any logic behind your action."

Anger burst through the room like a firestorm, and Phaira suddenly loomed over her. "You have spent your life with your head in the sand," the woman spat. "You don't know what we've been through. So don't you dare to judge how I keep my family safe. Understand?"

"But I - I do," Sydel stammered, backed into the wall. "I mean, I'm not judging. I just don't understand why – "

"It's a game," Phaira shot back. "A sadistic game. And I'm not exposing Ren and Co to it."

"But there has to be another way to resolve this," Sydel said passionately. "Something that doesn't require violence and - "

Phaira glared at her. Then, unexpectedly, she shrugged. The tension in the air dissipated.

"Fine," she said coolly. "Come see for yourself. When I go to meet this guy, convince him to walk away and leave me be. I won't touch him."

"You're meeting him?" Sydel asked, still shaken. "Why are you meeting with him if he tried to kill you?"

"Because he asked me to," Phaira said, as if the answer was obvious.

Sydel couldn't think of what to say. Did she not understand something?

As she backtracked through their conversation, Phaira slid her arms into her long black coat, the one with heavy collar and cuffs. There was a pistol in the holster now, glinting at her hip.

Firearms are illegal, Sydel almost said out loud, but thought better of it.

Then Phaira sifted through a pile of clothing on the floor and drew out another jacket, this one navy blue. She held it out to Sydel. "You'll blend in better."

Sydel looked down at her dress. It didn't look so unusual to her, but she took the jacket. When she slid it on, the coat was so long that the hem almost brushed the floor; she had to loop the belt around twice. A pretty design, though, the way the coat fastened together with a series of folds across the chest, like an outstretched wing.

What if this is stolen? she suddenly thought. *If it is, and I wear it in public...*

Sydel looked up at the sound of tiny clicks. Phaira was fitting a metal half-circle around her hairline. As she slid it back, Phaira's blue hair turned mahogany. Sydel gasped with surprise.

"You've never seen a CHROMA?" Phaira asked, surprised. "It's not permanent; I set it for three hours." She offered it to Sydel. Phaira's eyes were even paler with that red hair at its edges; the effect was unnerving. "Do you want to try it?"

Even as she shook her head, Sydel couldn't help but ask: "Does that thing keep your features dark, too?"

"Does it what? Oh. No, that's just how I look." Her hair fell over her face as she secured one of the buckles on her jacket.

Was she embarrassed? Sydel tried to get a better look at Phaira's profile. "Why is that how you look?"

"You don't need to know," Phaira said curtly. "Come on, then."

She strode out of the room. Her heavy boots thudded down the corridor and down the steps towards the exit.

Hovering in the hallway, Sydel desperately looked back to the brothers. Where was Renzo? Should she wake up Cohen?

But there was no one to go to for help.

So Sydel followed the woman to the outside.

VI.

Enthralled, Sydel turned slowly, taking in the panoramic view: the cluster of tiny apartments with curved roofs, the slim towers with a million glittering windows. Pods and private transports zipped down gridlines, as did ground cycles. The air was flavored with spices, overlaid with the sweet smell of gasoline. The heart of Daro, the capital city. She never imagined it would be so spectacular.

Past all the heads of the crowds, she caught a glimmer: the coastline. Her breath caught. The skerries. Were the skeleton buildings there, just like she'd read in books, those ghostly remnants of the old coastline? She hadn't been born when the meteor broke apart in the atmosphere, when three unexpected masses crashed into the sea, and the coastlines of Osha were swallowed up five miles inland: cottages, highways and hotels destroyed, waterlogged, swept away, though thankfully, few lives lost.

It was too expensive to rebuild what was lost – instead, rana would be poured into building a reinforced stormwall, creating a new border between the devastated and the still-standing, separating the wreckage from what remained. What was left behind was nicknamed "the skerries," and it was forbidden to go there: too dangerous, too unstable, too vulnerable to another impact.

But even Sydel had heard the stories: how the abandoned wasteland was the setting for evil deals and secret murderers, where thieves and smugglers did their trades. When she heard the tales, the skerries seemed mythical. Now she wasn't so sure, staring at the shimmering horizon and the hint of dark lines jutting out.

When Sydel came full circle, she saw Phaira approach a beggar, slumped on the side street. A girl with a cloud of curly black hair sat next to him. Phaira crouched down to speak to the man, and then the girl, her trench coat rippling behind her. Sydel took a step forward and then back, uncertain of what to do. Her memory clicked back to Yann's diagnosis of mekaline withdrawal. What if Phaira sought to use Sydel's presence as an excuse to purchase narcotics? What if Phaira involved her in an illegal drug deal?

Nervous, Sydel looked over her shoulder to the looming black parking hanger, stretching thousands of feet high; somewhere in there was the old Volante.

After several seconds, Phaira pressed something into the beggar's hand. Then, rising to her feet, Phaira gestured for Sydel to follow down the bustling main street.

Sydel held onto the cuffs of her borrowed jacket as she darted to the woman's side. "You gave that man money. What did you buy?"

Phaira ignored the question, keeping pace with the crowd.

She could be on narcotics now. She could be leading me into danger.

As they continued to walk, Sydel let her mind open, just a little, reaching over to measure the aura around Phaira.

Still looking ahead, Phaira's mouth drew tight. "I'm not lying to you. Do you want to check my pockets for mekaline?"

Embarrassed, Sydel closed off her senses. Phaira never looked at Sydel, but her voice rippled under the noise of the crowd: "I bought information, if you must know. That girl just told me that our man is here and waiting. So let's get on with it."

She forged ahead of Sydel, effortlessly gliding between the surging bodies. The vibrations of heat, sourness and impatience surrounded Sydel, and she held her breath, scurrying to catch up to the woman. Her thoughts raced. What was she going to say when she saw the tall man? What if she couldn't speak? What if he tried to hurt her?

Phaira finally turned into an alley, lined with trash barrels and street rubble. Together, they climbed up a series of wrought-iron stairs, up and up until they reached the building's red rooftop. Phaira hoisted herself over the edge easily. Sydel strained to roll her body onto the concrete.

Panting from the exertion, Sydel stared at the elevated horizon: the crooked skyline, the incredible, fiery sunset. For a moment, she forgot about her precarious situation.

Then something tiny and cool slipped inside her palm: a smooth, flat black square, one inch in area. Sydel peered at the thing, turning it over and over. What was she supposed to do with it?

"You've never seen a Lissome, either?" Phaira asked, with that same note of surprise. "Okay. Well, here's one thing you can do with it."

Phaira held the Lissome at chest level. With a twist, she separated it into two components. The tiny piece, no bigger than her little fingernail, she affixed behind her ear. The larger part was slipped into the cuff of her jacket.

"Transmitter and receiver, in this form," Phaira explained. "We can hear and talk to each other."

Sydel copied Phaira's movements. Despite her fears, the Lissome broke apart smoothly. But when pressed behind her ear, the small piece moved automatically, and tiny prongs attached to her skin like an insect. Sydel held back her shriek at the quick pinch. When it subsided (was that normal in this world? How could that ever feel normal?) Sydel unclenched her fingers and stared at the remaining square in her palm. There was nothing to it: no buttons, no ridges, just a little slip of plastic. How did it turn on? How did it work?

"Listen, Sydel," Phaira said, her tone serious. "I need to keep watch. You stay here and be quiet."

Panic hit Sydel like a shockwave. "You're leaving me?"

"For the moment. If you sense any kind of danger, if anything strikes you as wrong, just say a word, any word. I'll hear you, and come right back. Don't speak, otherwise. I'm counting on you."

Then she stepped off the roof.

Sydel gasped. But her hands fell away from her mouth when she saw Phaira turn in mid-fall and catch the crest of the shingles. The woman readjusted her grip with her right hand, the left holding steady. Then Phaira let go.

Sydel scrambled to the edge, just in time to see Phaira land on a ledge two floors down. The woman inched over to an open window on the diagonal. With one quick leap, she grabbed the sill, swung her legs up and slipped through the opening.

"Can you hear me?" Sydel jumped at Phaira's voice in her head.

"Yes," Sydel replied loudly as she sat down in a heap, a drop of sweat trickling down her spine.

"You don't need to shout," the voice lectured. "Now stay hidden, and speak if you sense any trouble."

Sydel did as she was told. Her borrowed coat wrapped tightly around her, she waited. Though, as the minutes crept by, she began to wonder why. *I could just leave,* she thought. *I could just disappear in the crowd. Maybe I can sell this Lissome-thing. And this jacket.*

Her mind switched to a new possibility: she could go to a law enforcement agency. She could tell them what she knew about the strangers, and the very tall man. They would protect her, help her find somewhere to stay.

"I wasn't sure you'd come."

There was a man's voice in Sydel's head: low and rolling, with a hint of a smirk.

Her skin broke out in goosebumps. She knew that voice; she had only heard a few in her lifetime.

"I'm here." Phaira's voice was sharp in Sydel's ear. "How high is the bounty on me, anyways? Know upfront that I can't match it. So I guess we're at a standstill."

"I'm not a bounty hunter."

"You might not have pulled the trigger, but don't insult me."

"I'm not. Hence the meeting."

Through the Lissome, Sydel heard a click, and then a small thump.

"What are you doing?" Phaira was yelling. "Pick that back up!"

"I'm trying to make peace," the man said. "I was meeting with a potential partner when the others dragged you in. You defended yourself, one of them took a shot at you - "

"Why did you take me to Midland?" Phaira demanded.

The man said nothing. Sydel concentrated, trying to hear any little whisper as she simultaneously reached out with her mind. She found them two floors below. The man's heart beat fast. Phaira's energy was yellow and intensifying.

"This is a mind game," Phaira finally spoke. "You must have been known Nican well."

Nican. Sydel mouthed the name.

"I'm familiar with your bounty. And I've heard of the Macatia family," the man countered. "Never met the son, though given his reputation, it sounds like he deserved what he got."

Nican Macatia. Sydel committed it to memory.

"I don't believe you," Phaira accused. "Are your friends here, surrounding the building? Sydel, who else is here?"

Startled, Sydel looked wildly for any sign of men approaching.

Then an explosion rocked the building.

Sydel fell to her knees with a shriek. Clouds of black smoke billowed past the rooftop. Then it started again, just like the Mill: one voice after another, building into an assault of screams and death rattles, terror roaring through the streets. The loudest voices were right in front of the building. Sydel peered over the edge of the roof, her eyes tearing from the heat.

There, in the midst of the panicking crowds below, two faces looked skyward, one man, one woman. Both clad in the magenta robes of merchants, both with brown hair and skin, they were serene and smiling in the fog of smoke, and looking straight at Sydel.

At the edge of Sydel's peripheral vision, a splotch of dark red entered the frenzy.

"Phaira!" Sydel screamed, pointing. "Those two! They did it!"

Then she clapped her hands over her mouth. What was she doing?

On ground level, the man and woman were backing away. Phaira vaulted over the wreckage in their direction. All three disappeared into the rush of crowds.

Sydel sat back on the terrace with a thud, her hands still over her mouth. The fire blazed below on street level.

Long minutes passed before she could stop shaking. Then she leaned over the roof's edge, searching. Below, firefighters were spraying some kind of foam on the explosion site fifty feet away. There was no sign of Phaira or the very tall man. Why had she yelled to Phaira about those two on the ground? What did she expect Phaira to do?

I should just take shelter until things quiet. Find some form of law enforcement. Find a kind face and ask for help.

"Sydel." Phaira's voice rumbled in her ear. Behind her voice came a medley of awful sounds.

"Phaira, did you - is that man - ?"

"Time to go," came the reply. "Now."

* * *

The brothers were in the Volante's common room, huddled around a pixelated screen, rife with images from the destroyed marketplace, the voiceover droning: "...already apprehended the persons behind the attack, perpetuated just one hour ago...."

On hearing the reporter's words, Sydel took in a sharp inhale. Phaira shot her a warning look and brushed past her.

Renzo glanced over. "Where have you two been?"

"Supply run," Phaira said. "Never got a chance to stock up, last time we stopped. What are you watching?"

"Did you see this happen?" Cohen was bundled into one of the chairs, wrapped in a blanket, staring at the bulletin. Sydel squinted as the report switched to live video. Her mouth dropped open: it was that man and woman from the street, bound at the wrist, their robes torn, surrounded by law enforcement.

The audio continued: "...both exhibiting questionable mental stability, possibly under the influence of street narcotics...."

Wide-eyed, Sydel opened her mouth to speak, excited to get Phaira's attention. But none of the strangers turned around.

"Just the aftermath," Phaira finally answered Cohen's question. "We weren't in the zone."

How easily she lies to her family, Sydel thought, sickened. Should she say something, anyways?

"Well, I'm glad you're both back," Cohen said, getting to his feet. "I'm going back to bed."

"You shouldn't have gotten out of bed in the first place," Renzo said pointedly.

"Okay, okay." Cohen shuffled out of the room, giving Sydel a grin as he passed, his eyes flicking up and down. She still had Phaira's jacket on, she realized. Sydel shrugged out of it, yanking her hair down from its knot. The strands reeked of sulfur and smoke.

Neither Phaira nor Renzo noticed her shedding. They weren't looking at each other, either, their faces lit by the broadcast as they spoke.

"Two bombs go off in the two locations we dock at."

"Phair, it has nothing to do with you."

"Have you talked to Nox yet?"

"Not yet. I thought you should call him first. This is his parents' old Volante, you know."

"I figured. Saw some of his stuff in the closet."

"He was really worried about you."

"Hm."

Bundling the coat in her arms, Sydel chose that moment to duck out of the room. The bombers' faces drifted into her vision again. Had they set off the bomb in the Vendor Mill too? Why did they smile at her like that?

"Sydel."

Sydel froze. Phaira's soft footsteps drew closer, finally stopping six feet behind.

"I shouldn't have taken you into the capital," she heard the woman murmur. "I don't know what I was thinking. I don't want to be that person, who takes advantage of another's - "

Then she fell silent.

Sydel waited. Weakness? Misfortune? What word was dropped?

"I'm sorry," Phaira said instead. "It won't happen again."

When Sydel turned to protest, Phaira was already gone.

VII.

Secluded in her closet, Sydel puzzled over all her collected facts, replaying Phaira's words and the overheard conversations, rolling the foreign names around, trying to understand. Things were changing so quickly. Phaira's behavior was so confusing. She couldn't rely on Cohen's word that she was safe. She needed answers, real answers. And from sources outside of the siblings' circle.

That now-familiar dip in her stomach told her that the Volante was in flight. When a half-hour crawled past, and Phaira and Cohen were sealed away in their quarters, Sydel made her way to the cockpit. Standing in the doorway, she gawked at the sight of so many screens, switches and lights, the barren landscape a hundred feet below, streaking past.

From the pilot's chair, Renzo turned to look, frowning. "Oh," he started to say. Then he faced forward again. "You need something?" he asked, his hands busy on the ship's console.

"I want to stop," Sydel said, working to keep her voice steady. "And purchase some personal items."

"Didn't you already do that with Phaira?"

"I didn't have the chance, with the explosion." Her heart sank at the deceit, how easily it unfolded from her lips.

"You understand - " Renzo trailed off for a few seconds before continuing: "I'm a little spooked at the idea of stopping anywhere right now."

"You believe your sister's suspicions?"

The question wasn't meant to be a challenge; she genuinely wondered about the older brother's thoughts on all that had transpired. But regardless, it had an impact. Renzo's face darkened. "No, I don't," he declared. "But someone should go with you."

"I want to go on my own," Sydel said firmly. "I promise to return within minutes. I will not speak to anyone. If the goal is for me to eventually become independent - "

"All right, fine," Renzo huffed. "There's a rest station below. We land, you head straight into the center of the market and get what you need."

He popped open a compartment to his left and rummaged through it. Then Renzo spun in his seat to face her. "Come here," he said as he opened his hand to reveal five coins. "For services rendered," he added. "Take it."

When she followed his instruction, Renzo's pale eyes met hers for a moment over his glasses. Then he took hold of the flight controls again, and Sydel made her escape.

Back in her space, Sydel slid on Phaira's navy jacket again, and slipped the bronze coins into the right pocket. Her ears popped as the Volante began to descend. Sydel waited until she heard the click of the magnets, securing the ship in place.

Outside her door, the corridor was deserted. She crept down the hall and the stairs, opened the exit door as quietly as she could. Then she ran to join the flow of the crowd, all heading to the center of the tiny marketplace.

Sydel quickly found the magenta robes of the vendors, and accepted the first price offered for a hairbrush and serum, a scarf and gloves; there was no time to barter. Then she studied the rusty signs hanging from the ceiling and followed the arrows.

The public info-lab was dank and cramped, with a constant buzz that made her feel jittery. A few travelers talked or typed, the light of their screens illuminating their weary faces. There were two open workstations with privacy shades on either side. Yann had a similar station in his quarters; she'd watched him research once or twice. She'd never touched it herself. But she could figure it out. She had to.

Sydel took in a deep breath, checked the time and ducked behind the plastic shields. Two screens flickered and fuzzed, waiting to display information. Above her head was a camera lens, likely for security measures. Sydel shook her hair loose and lowered her head so the long brown waves hid her face. Then she used her two index fingers to type: *Phaira.*

The console whirred. Sydel's nerves sparked with every sound.

Then lines of text scrolled down the screen: thousands of entries, the name Phaira, again and again.

It's a common first name, she realized with embarrassment. *Ridiculously common.*

She needed more.

Then she remembered the names spoken in the capital city.

The first listing was a death notice posted three months prior. Nican Macatia, twenty-two, son of a wealthy manufacturing entrepreneur and beloved social figure, died in a tragic fall in the city of Daro. Ruled an accident by the law enforcement. The Macatia family released a statement, thanking the public for the outpouring of support. Memorials were planned. Pictures accompanied the story: a man with a confident smirk, black hair, pale skin. No mention of the siblings in the article. But Phaira was involved in the accidental death of someone powerful; Renzo had said so. It must be this man, Nican. But why?

She couldn't stay out any longer, not without arousing suspicion. Sydel gathered her items and ran straight through the marketplace, back to the landing platform. Her mind swirled with questions, the closer she came to the old Volante.

The door swung open when she tried it. No one was waiting on the other side.

But Sydel had barely set down her items in her little closet when she heard Phaira calling her name.

The siblings were back in the common room, seated around the table, with one of those little black squares placed in its center. Sydel cleared her throat nervously. "I'm here."

Phaira spoke first. "Where were you?"

"She went out," Renzo said. "Why are you calling her in here?"

Phaira's gaze remained on Sydel, unwavering.

"I'm making an introduction," she finally said, tapping on the black square. "Officer Aeden Nox. Say hello, Nox."

"To who?" echoed a man's deep, scratchy voice. Sydel jumped back a foot, from both the voice and the revelation. They had a friend in law patrol?

"Our stowaway," Phaira said wryly. "Never mind. Just tell them what you just told me."

"Those two brought in for the capital city bombing are dead."

"Dead?" Sydel exclaimed without thinking. Cohen and Renzo turned to stare at her. She flushed and shrank back.

"That's your stowaway, I gather," the voice rumbled. "Yes, dead. Heart failure. Thirty minutes ago."

Silence. Sydel stared at Phaira's profile, but the woman's gaze remained on the black square. "Tell them the other thing, Nox."

"In the past month, four other similar explosions were set off throughout Daro. No civilian deaths or serious injuries, but - "

Sydel started as the black square clicked. Two translucent screens unzipped above it, and two portraits flashed: an older male, a young man. "The only two suspects ever arrested and brought in for questioning? Died from heart failure in the station. Autopsy linked it to a stimulant mix on the market, called Zephyr. It's most likely the same for these two new ones."

Phaira studied each picture intently, her face a few inches from the projection. "Heart failure," she murmured.

"That's my line," Nox quipped.

Phaira threw a grin at the device. The sudden change in her face was unnerving.

"The bombs were the same in all those cases?" Renzo asked, disturbed, but clearly curious.

"All improvised explosive devices: alkali-based, water, aluminum, sodium hydroxide. Basic and effective, though small scale. More of a noisemaker than anything serious."

"Yeah, injured party right here, Nox," Cohen broke in.

"I'm talking in comparison to others I've seen."

Renzo's face grew pink. "I appreciate the information, Nox, but what does this have to do with Phaira? Or us?"

"Your sister seems to think that these recent incidents were meant to draw her out of hiding."

"Maybe not," Phaira broke in, casting a dark look at the device. "I just think it's strange that the last two have been so close to us. Do you have a list of the injured? The witnesses?"

"Not all in one place, but statements were taken. It wouldn't be difficult to compile a list." Nox paused, his voice growing low. "Are you going to tell me where you've been all this time?"

Sydel saw a blush in Phaira's throat. "Later."

A huff of air rippled through the soundsystem; Nox didn't like that answer. There were a series of beeps and static pulses, then the screens disappeared from view, sucked back into the Lissome.

"Why are you getting involved in this?" Cohen asked Phaira.

"Because these people hurt you. And hurt a lot of people," Phaira said, like she couldn't believe the question. "There's more to it than just random - "

"Didn't you hear what Nox said?" Renzo interjected. "It's been happening for the past month. Part of a series of planned attacks, separate from you, or us, or anything. So let the patrol deal with it."

"Well, I'm not convinced yet. There's something more to this."

Renzo threw up his hands. Sydel saw fiery white anger around Phaira, coiling like a snake, ready to strike.

In his own way, Cohen seemed to recognize the danger, stepping between his brother and sister. "You're going to get killed if you keep poking around," he told Phaira.

"Co," Phaira said, her tone gentler. "I've been running for so long now, I'm not going to sit in this ship and wait to be hunted down - "

Renzo snorted.

Phaira's voice lost its softness. "Say it, Ren."

"You might convince him, but not me," Renzo said. "You haven't changed at all. You're still being foolish, and reckless, as - "

Phaira leaned around Cohen to scowl at Renzo. "How many times can I tell you that I'm sorry, Ren? You keep lecturing me on - "

"No, I'm just stating the truth," Renzo shot back. "Co won't say it because you're his big sister and he hates it when people are mad at him."

"Hey!" Cohen objected.

"At least he pretends that he still likes me," Phaira accused. "If you hate me so much, you should have let me remain a ghost."

The tension in the room rippled like an earthquake. Finally, Renzo pushed off his chair and limped away. Stopping at the door, he spoke without turning around: "You're not the only one who has nothing, Phaira."

"I know," Phaira murmured, surprising Sydel. "And you know I'm sorry for it."

Renzo ducked out of sight. Cohen covered his face with his hand. Phaira sighed and nudged his leg with her foot. "It's okay, Co. Really."

"You know it's not," Cohen muttered through his palm as he left the common room. Sydel heard his footsteps in the hallway, slow and dragging. She wondered if she should follow him. Did anyone ever follow him?

"I need to speak with you."

Phaira's tone made Sydel shudder. She let her hand rest against the wall, bracing her will.

"You have questions."

"Do I?"

"Don't play coy," Phaira warned. "I know what you've been up to."

Sydel lifted her chin. "I'm not up to anything."

"When you search for sensitive information in public, you put all of us in jeopardy." Phaira's tone was cold, every word exacting. "You cannot do that and expect to remain here with us."

"How could you know that?" Sydel retorted. "Were you spying on me?"

"If you want to snoop around, we'll get you a Lissome of your own," Phaira said, ignoring Sydel's outburst. "There's a million vending machines, and after we encrypt it, you can pull up any kind of information: photos, video, whatever you want to know about us, or Nican Macatia."

Sydel recoiled. Then Phaira's voice grew quieter. "Ren may not want to listen, Sydel, but there are people out to hurt me. I'm not looking for you to get caught in the crossfire too. Understand?"

Phaira is concerned for my safety? The notion stunned Sydel. But she had to ask, regardless of the consequence. "You were involved in Nican Macatia's death?"

Phaira flinched. Her grey-green eyes zeroed in on Sydel's, but they weren't fearful. They were full of hatred.

Murderer. Serial killer.

Her hand was on fire.

Gasping, Sydel jerked her fingers away from the wall. She stared at the center of her palm; the flesh was bright red and stinging. Waves of heat reverberated off the wall. What just happened? Had Phaira noticed? No, Phaira was looking at Sydel, not her hands, with a strange expression on her face. Almost like hurt?

As Sydel cradled her hand, a memory floated up to the surface, something Cohen had said days earlier in response to Phaira's skepticism: "She might understand what we are going through."

There was a beeping sound. Phaira turned back to the table, waving her fingers over the black square. The Lissome clicked open and projected a new screen, smaller this time and full of names. Phaira's hand waved slowly up and down, the blue light scrolling over her face.

Her eyebrows lifted. Then she rose to her feet and swept past Sydel.

Sydel slumped against the wall, lifting her raw, pulsing hands to her eyes. Blisters were already rising. Her blood quivered through her veins. She flexed her fingers, trying to block out the pain, trying to keep breathing.

VIII.

Cohen wasn't in his massive bed, but slumped in a chair wedged beside it. Standing in the doorframe, Sydel hesitated, a fresh pack of gauze in her bound hand.

Then his eyes opened. "Hi."

"Is it okay to come in?"

Cohen nodded, shifting his position. He looked wan and exhausted as he shrugged out of his shirt. Sydel sat on the edge of his bed as she ripped open the bandages.

"What happened to your hand?" Cohen asked suddenly, his brow furrowed. "Did you cut yourself?"

"I'm fine," Sydel deferred. "It's nothing."

But Cohen's forehead remained in a bunch. His concern made her feel lighter, somehow, as she peeled the gauze from his chest.

"How?" came Renzo's voice, startling them both.

He limped into the room, staring at Cohen's chest.

Then he turned to Sydel. "How did you do that?"

"Ren!" Cohen protested, one hand lifting as if to push his brother back. "What are you doing?"

But Renzo shook his head, pointing to Cohen's chest: tiny, pale pink notches dotted his chest, hardly any trace of evidence that shrapnel was once removed.

"That is impossible in a week's time," he announced. "That's impossible."

He was right. Sydel stared at the scars, their smoothness, their light color. Not even the balm could heal that quickly. How could this be?

Sydel balled her right hand into a fist, pressing the nails into her palm. Her left hand drifted towards Cohen. "Let me try to explain," she began weakly.

"No," Renzo shot back. "Don't touch him."

"Ren!" Cohen exclaimed. "Stop it!"

"No, this is wrong - this is freakish - "

As the brothers argued, Sydel sank into the mattress. Did she do this, somehow? When she saw red, when her hands burned - was she capable of healing? Was this a part of Eko that Yann never told her about?

A ripple struck her, like a sudden gust of wind.

Sydel frowned, looking past the brothers. There was something strange in the air, some kind of anticipation.

"Where is your sister?" Sydel interrupted the argument.

"She's flying the ship," Renzo said shortly. "Why?"

Then they all heard the screech of the landing gear.

"We're stopping again?" Cohen asked.

Renzo limped over to the window. Sydel peered over his shoulder to see.

They were descending into an industrial area: great swatches of flat concrete, with hundreds of metal warehouses lined up like pins. Dread formed in her stomach at the sight. But why? She let her mind wander, searching for the source.

There was nothing.

* * *

Sydel longed to retreat into her little storage unit. Instead, she watched as Phaira and Cohen clomped down the rusty stairs, leaning against the exit doorframe. Her uneasy feeling wouldn't go away. Something was going to happen, she could sense it, and the siblings had no idea.

Before landing, when confronted by her brothers, Phaira would only say that she was meeting someone named Meroy.

"Come with me, Co?" she'd asked. "To be safe," she added, glancing at Renzo.

"Do whatever you want," Renzo muttered. He slumped into the pilot's seat, flicking switches, shooting derisive looks at his sister, and at Sydel, who hovered at the edge of their conversation.

"Who is this guy? Dangerous?" Cohen asked Phaira.

"No," she said. "Just someone I used to know."

Sydel strained to see in the twilight. A light from a lone transport swept past. In the brief seconds of illumination, Sydel saw the man, Meroy: bone-thin with grizzled features, pale, with sunken cheeks and grey hair pulled off his face. A man that could squeeze and sneak his way into any crevice, by the look of him. *How does Phaira know him?* Sydel wondered, repulsed.

She felt Renzo shuffle next to her. He said nothing; he just stood and glowered over the tarmac. The silence stretched on and on.

"What are they saying?"

At his voice, she glanced at him. His eyes glowed in the dark behind his glasses.

"I don't know," she finally said.

"So find out."

Sydel balked. "I'm not going to go out there."

"You know what I'm talking about."

Her body went stiff. What did he know? What did he suspect?

"Let's be straight with each other," Renzo continued, his gaze still fixed on his siblings. "Your commune saw you as a hazard because you can do some weird things. Accelerated healing for one thing. And some kind of telepathy."

"You're mistaken," Sydel said faintly.

"Then explain what happened with Cohen's injuries. And with Phaira in the clinic," he added pointedly. "She told me what happened. You might as well confirm it."

Exhaustion surged over her like a wave. What was the point of lying about it? She was so tired of lying.

"Are you going to kill me?" she muttered, her shoulders drooping.

"What?" For the first time emotion registered on his face: surprise. "Why would you say something like that?"

"Because – " Yann's warnings of destruction wove through her mind.

"Phaira wouldn't want me to read her mind," she finally muttered.

"Then go through Cohen."

Appalled, Sydel opened her mouth to argue, but thought again. Why not? She wouldn't go into Cohen's mind, though; even excommunicated, she still held true to Yann's rules.

So Sydel let her mind stretch across the tarmac, finding the blood that rushed through Cohen's ears. Then she closed her eyes to listen.

".... the last person I expected to call and want to meet," Meroy was saying. His voice was as slick as his appearance.

"I just need some information," Phaira said. "Your name came up during a search of mine. Bombing two weeks ago?"

"As you can see, I'm fine. More of a nuisance than anything. Why?"

"I just want to know what you saw that day. Anyone acting strangely, maybe someone with long black hair, very tall?"

The tall man? Phaira suspected him of the bombings?

Even from a distance, Sydel could see that wolfish look in Meroy's eyes. "You look good, you know," the man remarked. "It hasn't been that long, we can get you back into the circuit, set something up."

"I'm retired, Meroy," Phaira said, shifting in place.

Then something changed in the air.

Alerted, Sydel turned her head to the right. Storage crates stretched in every direction. Crickets chirped in the far distance. The Volante's engines pinged as they cooled.

But her senses continued to fire, striking her like tiny fists. Anticipation in the air.

"Someone is here," Sydel whispered.

Renzo's eyes bugged behind his glasses. He opened his mouth to yell out a warning, but Sydel held up her hand. "No, don't."

"Then use your - whatever it's called." Renzo whispered, panic in his voice.

"No, send them a message with your Lissome-thing," she whispered back.

As Renzo fumbled, Sydel's heart thudded. She could hear the shadows holding their breath.

Another explosion, she realized. *It's about to go off.*

Across the blacktop, she saw Cohen look down at his belt; it was flashing red.

Read it, Sydel begged internally. *Back away. Come back to the Vol.*

Then an alarm went off, shrieking through the metal warehouses. Meroy cowered like a scared rat; Phaira gestured at him angrily as she and Cohen broke into a run. Disoriented, Meroy turned in place, and finally started to move when the storage crate behind him exploded. The man caught the edge of the blast; his body slammed into a warehouse wall and crumbled to the ground, out of sight.

Cohen reached the vessel first, pounding up the stairs. "Get inside!" he yelled to Sydel. "Go!"

"Wait! Phaira!" Sydel cried, pointing past Cohen.

But she was already gone.

"Phaira!" Cohen yelled into the crackling night. Sydel stared at the wall of fire, spreading fast across wires and walkways. The searing heat crashed into her again and again, followed by the stench of chemicals.

A gunshot rang out.

Cohen froze next to Sydel.

Then a shriek of pain echoed over the tarmac.

Cohen prepared to jump down the stairs again when Phaira emerged from the smoke. Someone was being dragged behind her: a woman with long blonde hair wound through Phaira's fist. Phaira never slowed her stride, her features highlighted by the flames. In her free hand, she held a firearm, rimmed with fading orange.

Cohen and Sydel backed over the threshold as Phaira shoved the blonde woman up the stairs. The woman's sobs punctuated each step and stumble, her hand to her bleeding thigh.

Sydel pressed her back to the corridor wall as Phaira and the blonde woman passed. The woman's cries echoed down the hallway. Then came the dull, scraping sound of the door, pulled inward and sealed.

"Syd? Are you okay?"

She didn't want to look at him. But Cohen was touching her shoulder, trying to see her face through her tangled hair.

She opened her eyes, just a little. Through the strands, she could see his face lined with soot. "It's okay, Syd, we're safe now," he soothed.

Tears welled up. She swiped the back of her hand over her eyes. Then she turned away from him, and pressed her forehead into the metal wall.

"Okay, okay. I get it."

His heavy footsteps clomped down the hallway. Following Phaira, no doubt. And that hysterical blonde woman.

The wall vibrated under Sydel's fingertips as the ship's engines roared to life. Her stomach dropped, lifted, and finally settled.

She pushed off of the wall. Her trembling hands moved over her face and smoothed back her hair. Then Sydel began to make her way to the cockpit. Every step was a mistake, she knew it. She should lock herself away until she could escape. She should threaten to expose the family if they didn't drop her at the nearest safe location. Renzo wanted to throw her overboard; Phaira had already threatened the same. They would leave her behind, happily.

But her desire to comprehend this world, this odd family; it overwhelmed any logic she could muster. Every turn, every fright seemed to trigger the same reaction: she had to know what would happen next.

Inside the cockpit, the strangers huddled together: Renzo by the flight controls, Phaira and Cohen on either side. There was no sign of the blonde woman.

"There," Sydel heard Renzo murmur.

Confused, she went to respond, but realized he was speaking to the console. On one of the archaic screens, two shadowy figures ran into what looked like a freighter transport, a greyish-white box, like a million others that Sydel had seen in the cities. The camera zoomed into the ship's rear paneling; a series of numbers flashed before the video cut out.

Renzo punched in some numbers and clutched the flight controls. Phaira and Cohen remained close, talking under their breath.

How odd, Sydel thought. *They are so hostile with each other, yet now they come together.*

"Hey, Syd."

Sydel snapped out of her thoughts. The three strangers were looking at her.

"Thanks," Cohen smiled. "Thanks for warning us."

"Yes," Renzo added gruffly. "Thank you, Sydel. That was close."

Phaira regarded Sydel for several long moments. Finally, the sister gave the slightest nod.

Relief flooded through Sydel, along with shame.

Was she that desperate for Phaira's acceptance?

"Found it," Renzo transcribed. "Registered six months ago to a cargo company, now defunct. My guess: stolen from a junkyard and rebuilt."

"What do we do now?" Cohen asked Phaira. "Should we get the law involved? I can call Nox."

The sound of a moan startled Sydel. Craning her neck around the siblings, she gasped.

The blonde woman was squeezed underneath the flight console, bound to an exhaust pipe. Her pink-tinged skin was covered in sweat; her thigh was bandaged, but blood seeped through the gauze.

"Not again," Phaira muttered as she gave the woman's backside a push with her boot.

"What's wrong with her?" Cohen scoffed.

A wisp of sound moved through Sydel's mind. Was she hearing things? No, there it was again: a whispering, wavering voice calling for help.

Phaira's cold hand clamped down on her arm. "What is it?"

Sydel wondered if she should remain silent. But by the look on Phaira's face, the sister already suspected the truth, so Sydel confessed: "She's trying to contact someone for help."

"What?" Cohen exclaimed, but Phaira interrupted him. "How?"

"She's an - she's an Eko, I think," Sydel pushed out the words. "Skilled in telepathy, memory retrieval and manipulation, and other mental aptitudes."

She glanced at each of the siblings, long and hard, before screwing up her courage to confess: "Like Yann in the Communia. And like me."

The cockpit was silent. Her words hung in the air.

The blonde woman moaned again. Desperate for distraction, Sydel knelt down to examine her: the damp smell of her skin, the red veins in her hazel eyes, the over-excited beating of her heart.

A fragmented, dusty memory came to the surface; something Yann had mentioned while discussing the

history of the commune. Sydel frowned, trying to remember his words. But again, a cry for help mewed
through her mind, distracting her.

Sydel lifted one finger. *STOP*, she commanded via Eko.

The woman was instantly still. Then she opened her
sunken eyes. Their glassy texture shifted to an adoring
gaze.

Sydel took the woman's wrist and pushed up her
sleeve. There, in the crook of the woman's elbow: an injection site. And the veins were blue and bruised; this
wasn't the first time.

What is it?" Phaira asked, crouching next to her.

Sydel shook her head. "She's a drug addict."

"Is that unusual in your kind?"

"I don't know about my kind," Sydel said awkwardly.
Her memories grew clearer as she recounted. "But Yann
warned me once against using any kind of stimulant
to artificially heighten my abilities. He knew someone,
once, who did that. Someone outside of Jala Communia."

She looked back at the brothers. "With increased
neural activity and increased heartrate, psychic ability
is naturally increased," she explained. "An accelerated
evolution, instead of learning over years and training the
brain to accommodate." Her voice trailing off, she studied the blonde woman. How did this person know about
that method? Why would they subject themselves?

"So those bombings are, what? A group of Zephyr
addicts going crazy?" Renzo asked, looking over his

shoulder. "Doing this for fun? Why draw attention to themselves?"

The cockpit was quiet, everyone considering. Leaning on the back of Renzo's chair, Phaira stared at the canopy of clouds through the windshield.

"I should storm their ship," she murmured.

"Don't be ridiculous," Renzo shot over his shoulder. "Co, get Nox on the line."

"That piece of junk is just an old carrier freight," Phaira continued, seeming not to hear Renzo's protest. "No weapons, no shielding. They're either bounty hunters with a really sick hobby or some small-scale group of troublemakers. Either way, I get in and get some answers."

"I'll go with you," Cohen broke in. "Just tell me what to do. I won't - "

"Phaira," Sydel found the courage to interrupt. "Twice now, I have had to block this girl from sending a distress call. If her partners are gifted, and using those artificial means to evolve, they could be even more powerful."

"So we take them down quickly," Phaira replied. "Element of surprise. Very simple." Her eyes were hazy with planning.

"And I'm coming with you," Cohen added. He crossed his arms over his chest and stared at Renzo, as if daring his brother to protest.

Aghast, Sydel looked to Renzo. The brother kept his back to the conversation, his hands on the flight controls.

But Sydel could see black waves rippling off of him: a brooding, building desire for retribution.

IX.

The blonde woman had long since passed out. Though the bleeding had stopped, Sydel still fought her instinct to heal the woman in some way. But she knew better, and kept her hands at her sides.

Even with her tolerance, the strangers still ignored Sydel as they made preparations. Clad in that black rubber bodysuit again, Phaira sheathed twin blades into her two hidden pockets. This time, Sydel got a clear glimpse at one of Phaira's illegal firearms before it was holstered.

Sydel watched Cohen tape his hands. He wore heavy, laced boots, some kind of armor strapped around his torso, and Phaira's other handgun holstered at his waist. Though his physical appearance was formidable, to Sydel, he looked nauseous.

Phaira shouldn't make him do this, she grieved, her chest tight with dread. *They don't even know what they will encounter. If these people are careless enough to inject narcotics in search of power, what else are they capable of? How advanced might they be?*

Too soon, Sydel heard the landing gear unfurl, and the heavy settling of the ship into its shocks. She should warn them again.

"Ready, Co?" Red crackling energy surrounded the sister. In contrast, Cohen was framed in sickly yellow.

"Sure," Cohen replied curtly, his face unreadable.

Phaira put her hand to her ear. "Ren?"

"Half a mile up," Sydel could hear Renzo's tinny voice through the soundsystem. "No sign that they see us. Powered down, and locked into landing."

Phaira walked out, Cohen followed, and Sydel tailed them both as Renzo's voice travelled through the air: "There's an access panel between the four ion engines; if there's any shield built into the ship, it can't overlap them. That's the best point of entry."

"Just make sure that woman stays unconscious, Renzo," Phaira said. "Sedate her if you have to. When we leave, knock out the mainframe, just in case."

"If it looks bad, you tell me," Renzo told them. "And it's just restrain and question. Right? Don't fire unless you absolutely have to. I'll have Nox's cc on standby."

Sydel remained in the corridor. Neither Phaira nor Cohen looked back. The sounds of their steps echoed away.

The exit door closed with a thunk. They were gone.

Suddenly, the lights went out, and the ship plunged into darkness. Walking blind, Sydel felt her way into the common space. Her fingers groped and finally found the edge of the console, then a chair. When she sat down in a heap, it struck her how many times she had longed for silence over the past few days. Now it was the most unnerving state she could imagine.

Time passed. She waited. The ship was eerily silent, save for a faint pinging noise every seven seconds. Almost peaceful. No emotions slamming up against her. No anger or pain or fear. Nothing.

Nothing?

Sydel opened her mind and searched for Cohen.

Nothing. She couldn't sense him at all.

But that was impossible. Even with some distance between them, she should still be able to pick up his presence.

Phaira? She reached out again.

Nothing. There was a wall, forcing her back. Something intentional, and powerful.

When Sydel fumbled her way to the cockpit and slid open the door, Renzo was yelling into his console: "Phaira? Cohen? What's going on? Are you all right??"

Then a smoky voice echoed through the cockpit. "Renzo Byrne."

Renzo went pale. His hand moved over the console.

"I could refrain from doing that.

Renzo stopped. Icy-cold fear rushed down Sydel's spine. Then Renzo shot to his feet, popping open a hidden compartment filled with artillery.

"Renzo."

She can see us. Our every move. How?

Renzo slowed his movements as the voice spoke again. "I will wait on final judgment of your brother and sister if you comply."

Renzo muttered something under his breath and shoved a pistol into his waistband.

"Renzo?" Sydel began, trying not to panic.

"No weapons, please," came the voice again, eerily calm. "No communication with your patrol friends. Bring

my student outside to the plains and let her lie. Then
walk to our vessel and wait. Trade off in thirty minutes."

Then the smoky voice dissipated. The screens went
dead: no flashing numbers, no alarms. Silent, and
horrifying.

Renzo's shoulders slumped. As his body curved into
itself, he gripped the edge of the console with white
knuckles.

Bewildered, Sydel opened her mind again, trying to
gain a sense what was out there. The moment she reached
out, something took hold of her: a soft, enfolding murmur that threatened to squeeze out her last breath.

Sydel.

* * *

Gripping shoulders and ankles, Sydel and Renzo were
able to drag the blonde woman through the Volante and
down the stairs. They stumbled several times in the process; neither was used to the physical exertion, it seemed,
but the woman never woke. Finally, they swung her onto
the ground, panting as they let go. The wind cut into
Sydel's skin, even with the mountains surrounding them.
She was afraid to shield herself, though. If they were still
being watched, it might be seen as weakness.

Instead, Sydel slowed her pace so she remained beside Renzo, who limped heavily as they made their way
through the brush. He still intimidated her, but Sydel

was so numb with fear that she felt desperate for any kind of companionship.

Inside Renzo's coat pocket was the firearm; he insisted on it, despite her protests that it would only cause trouble. Sydel carried no weapons; what could she possibly bear? But the more they walked, the woozier she felt.

Then the pain hit her. White-hot pain, jumbling snapshots of a life, racing together, overlaid with a scream that seemed to reverberate off the mountains. Sydel stumbled and grabbed Renzo's arm.

"What's wrong?" Renzo said sharply, his hand moving to his inner coat pocket.

Her mind consumed with blood, anguish, and exhilaration, Sydel could barely speak: "They are torturing -"

Renzo broke into an unbalanced run. Sydel could barely see his retreating body, so overwhelmed by waves of agony. She shook her head once, twice, then in rapid succession.

Stop, she screamed inside her head. *STOP.*

And it did. Her head cleared instantly. Her skin grew cold with its fresh sheen of sweat.

Frightened, she rushed to catch up to Renzo, pushing through the spindly trees and long grass.

When she broke through, the freighter from the video loomed before her.

A groan of metal on metal. Above, a door broke open. Stairs began to unfold. Renzo brought his firearm to his eyeline.

A woman emerged from the carrier ship. Her gaze was that of a sovereign surveying her lands: regal posture, short silver hair, golden skin, white cape swept over her chest and rippling with the wind. She noted the line of fire of Renzo's pistol. Then she shifted her gaze to Sydel. Her eyes softened, and she spread her hands apart, smiling.

"Sydel," the woman called with a thrilled, triumphant voice. "I can't believe you're here. It's an honor, truly."

She knows my name. And she's happy to see me.

"I'm called Huma," the woman continued, her name pronounced with a soft, bird-like hoo. "Please, come inside. We have so much to talk about."

Sydel looked to Renzo. He didn't move.

"And Renzo Byrne, once again, I have requested no violence," Huma said. "My final warning."

"Warning?" Renzo exploded. His finger tightened on the trigger.

From within the folds of her winter's cloak, the woman's hand emerged, pale and elegant. Her index finger flicked. Renzo's pistol was wrenched from his grip, skittering across the dirt path.

Gasping, Sydel forged a barrier around her mind, her terror mixed with genuine wonder: was telekinesis a part of Eko development, too?

"Sydel," came the woman's voice again, softer this time. "Please, come and speak with us."

Despite her gentle words, this woman had Phaira and Cohen somewhere inside that old freighter, Sydel knew.

And Huma was likely the one who tortured Phaira only a few minutes prior. But what choice was there? She put her hand on Renzo's arm. "We need to go."

"No," Renzo shot back. "If we go inside, we might not come out."

He raised his voice, addressing Huma. "I just want my brother and my sister. Then we will leave and never speak a word of this. You have my word."

Long seconds passed. The wind intensified, yanking threads of Sydel's hair from her braids.

Then another figure emerged from above, stumbling down the staircase, arms bound behind her back. Phaira had been stripped of her armor and weapons, and wore only a shapeless grey dress. They had even taken her boots. Her bare toes gripped the stairs. When she reached the ground, Phaira lost her balance and fell to her knees. The wind whipped at her hair and exposed her face for a few seconds: pale and sweaty, her eyes rimmed in pink.

A second silhouette emerged: Cohen! Sydel's heart leapt into her throat. But something was wrong. His head was slumped forward, his feet barely supporting his weight. Something was propelling him down the stairs. When Cohen reached the earth; he promptly fell into a heap in the ground. Renzo darted to his brother's side. No response, though Cohen still breathed.

Huma made her way down the stairs. She had a cold, classic beauty to her face: fine eyebrows, high cheekbones, and elegant wisps of lines around her eyes and mouth. Those eyes, an intense green, remained on Sydel. A gangly teenager with shorn strips of black hair followed Huma, carrying a metal case. As Huma moved next to Phaira, the youth withdrew a thin syringe from the case. Taking it, Huma bowed her head in gratitude, and the boy flushed with pleasure.

Huma studied the needle tip for a few moments. It glinted wickedly in her hands, a pinprick of light travelling along its length.

"Renzo," Huma finally said. "Please understand that I have been forced to take drastic steps to secure our safety."

The youth clapped his hands onto Phaira's shoulders, shoving his knee into her back. Phaira thrashed, but with her hands tethered, she could barely move. With a viciousness that surprised Sydel, the young man yanked Phaira's hair to expose the right side of her throat.

"Get off her!" Renzo yelled, fumbling to his feet.

But it was too late. With one smooth motion, Huma injected the contents of the needle into Phaira's neck.

The man let go of Phaira and stepped back. No one moved.

A rumble of thunder sounded overhead. Huma looked up at the clouds. She was waiting for something.

A shuddering inhale made them all look to Phaira. The woman's face was ashen. Sydel could hear her heartbeat, skittering and uneven. She wavered on her knees, as if caught in a whirlpool.

"She may not last long," Huma mused. "It's very hard to say who can tolerate the Zephyr mixture and who cannot. You're now the second-in-command, aren't you, Renzo? The decision is now yours. The counteragent in exchange for Sydel."

"Sydel?" Renzo gasped. "No!"

"Then your sister might die," Huma said. "I regret this route, but you and your siblings set the tone for violence - "

"You've been setting off bombs, you crazy - !"

"And Sydel," Huma continued. "You've known her for, what, a week? What loss is it to you? She frightens you; I can see it. She should be with those who understand her."

Huma's green eyes travelled back to Sydel's. "Truly extraordinary," she murmured. "You cannot even comprehend, Renzo. To discover someone like her in a common Vendor Mill - "

The whisper I heard, Sydel realized. *That was someone from this group. And when the bomb went off, when I panicked and called out to Phaira and Renzo, I confirmed my Eko to them. That's what they do. They use explosions and fear to root out other Ekos. And they have been pursuing me ever since. Testing me. Studying my reactions. All those poor victims. Meroy. Cohen.*

Sickened, Sydel looked to Phaira. The woman keeled over in the grass, gasping for air.

Then Sydel glanced up at the carrier ship. Faces pressed against the rusted windows: hopeful, curious, enthralled. A ripple of voices descended to ground level, soft and excited: *Sydel. Sydel. Sydel.*

"I have a few conditions," she finally said.

"Yes, I know," Huma said kindly.

"Sydel, no," Renzo pleaded, limping to her side. "This is not an option; we'll figure something out." His eyes kept darting back to Phaira. She was deteriorating with every ragged breath, Sydel could see it. Cohen had not awakened either.

Poor Cohen, Sydel thought. *He will be upset that I'm gone. But so it is.*

"I will go with you," Sydel said to Huma. "But there will be no more explosions. Nor will anyone use that narcotic; it's dangerous and an affront to the gifts we carry."

Huma shrugged one shoulder. "Merely two methods to experiment with. With you here, they are not needed."

Sydel nodded. "Give Phaira the counteragent."

"Sydel, no," Renzo said weakly.

But the youth was already grasping Phaira's arm. Another syringe emptied into the crook of her elbow.

Within seconds, Phaira's breathing began to slow. Soft moans emerged as she buried her face in the dirt.

As Sydel moved to Huma's side, the woman drew her hands back under her cape. "I have your quarters prepared, Sydel," she said pleasantly. "We are so honored to work with you."

Sydel looked over at the siblings, one last time.

"Goodbye," she murmured.

Then she followed Huma up the stairs.

PART TWO

I.

This was what Phaira could remember.

Under cover of woods, she and Cohen came upon the enemy freighter: no sign of activity, no sounds, cold and looming. She found the access panel between the ion engines. They forced it open and slipped inside.

Her XK-Calis firearm primed, Phaira did a basic sweep of the engine room. Deserted. Cohen mimicked her every move, wielding her other Calis. They crept into the adjoining compartment. Trash in piles everywhere. A corpse lay half-buried in the corner, surrounded by more junk and abandoned technology. Cohen covered his nose with the crook of his elbow. Phaira breathed through her mouth and kept moving.

Voices rippled from the next section. Phaira slid her back against the wall as she glided to the entryway. The sliding door was open just a crack, light and activity on the other side. Phaira nudged it with her foot. It would move easily when pushed.

She caught Cohen's eye, and with her free hand she counted down from three. Then she kicked the door open.

Seven men and women knelt on the floor amidst debris and wreckage. They didn't move at the loud bang.

Cohen ducked in behind Phaira, his Calis at eye level. Phaira's laser target swept the room, searching. It found its mark in the older woman, who slowly stood up. The leader: mid-sixties, five-foot-six, olive skin, short silver hair, hands concealed under a white wool cape, swept over her right shoulder.

"Stay where you are," Phaira ordered. "Hands up."

The woman didn't move. She didn't blink either, observing Phaira and Cohen without expression. Phaira opened her mouth to issue another warning.

Then her vision blurred. She blinked to clear it, but her eyes refused to focus. And her heart was beating hard and fast.

Still aiming the Calis, Phaira groped with her free hand, trying to find the doorframe, something to hold onto for support. Inside her head, blurry images and distorted sounds flashed, whispers and accusations layering upon themselves.

The grey-haired woman raised her hand. The voices grew louder. Next to Phaira, Cohen dropped to his knees, clutching at his chest. All Phaira could see were red spots, bleeding together.

She put all her focus into squeezing the trigger of her Calis. Then everything went dark.

Did she dream? She wasn't sure.

But suddenly, the blackness lifted. A single light bulb flickered, wedged into the corner of the ceiling. Stale, claustrophobic air. The sound of her brother breathing, his body at her feet. Her head pounding in pain.

Phaira ran her hands over her body, taking stock. Nanotube armor removed. Calis pistols gone. Lissome removed, and no boots either. She flexed her cold, bare feet. No major injuries, other than being naked under some ugly dress. Stripped while unconscious. Fantastic.

Phaira sat up and scanned the room. Six feet, squared. No visible exit. She let her fingers roam over the walls: there had to be some kind of panel, or vent...

Cohen groaned. Phaira laid a hand on her brother's shoulder. His immediate wince told Phaira that he shared the same headache. "What happened?"

"I think they drugged us," Phaira coughed, her throat dry. "Through the ventilation system. And then that leader did something to knock us out."

"I heard things," Cohen rasped. "In my head. When she looked at us."

"I know," Phaira confirmed, resisting the urge to shudder. "Me too."

Cohen lifted his head, his eyes bulging. "Wait. Maybe we shouldn't talk. Or think."

"I don't think it matters at this point, Co." She resumed her search for an exit.

"Then why try to break out?" he bemoaned. "What's the point?"

"Just because they can read our minds doesn't mean we just sit around and wait to - "

Phaira closed her mouth on the last word. She didn't want to say it out loud. But she knew how much trouble they were in. Unarmed, no obvious means of exit, held captive by a powerful gang with untold abilities...

Suddenly, a crack broke through the wall. The room flooded with light. Three silhouettes stood in the threshold of the secret door. Cohen scrambled to his feet but they were fast; two of the men pushed him back into the cell. The other grabbed a hold of Phaira's arm and yanked her out. The door slammed shut, reverberating from Cohen kicking at the door.

Phaira turned on her heel, grabbed hold of the guard's arm and flipped him over her shoulder. Then her head exploded with pain. Her hands flew up by reflex, just long enough for the two remaining guards to restrain her.

Writhing, Phaira used everything from her teeth to her fingernails on them. The guards slammed her face-first against the wall, knocking the breath out of her, and bound her wrists beyond her back, followed by her ankles. Then one hoisted Phaira over his shoulder and carried her into a windowless cell that smelled of lilacs and sour body odor. Waves of fabric were tacked to three of the walls; bright sheaths of color drooped in places, exposing the dull, rusty decay underneath. Books were piled in every corner, along with crumpled papers, and pictures in organized stacks. The fourth wall held no decorations: just five metal strips, spaced two feet apart, running from floor to ceiling.

The guard set Phaira in front of one strip, while the other flicked a switch by the door. Phaira's wrists jerked back, magnetized to the wall. Then her ankles followed.

Surprised, Phaira leaned her body forward and wiggled. No give.

This was an old freighter, she remembered. Magnets were used to keep crates from sliding around.

I'm like a prow of a damn ship, Phaira thought suddenly, fighting the urge to laugh. Instead she just grinned, aware that her dark mouth, pale eyes and wild hair made her look like a maniac.

"Please leave, gentlemen."

That gray-haired woman again. The guards bowed their heads at the command. The woman took a moment to touch each of them on the forehead before the two men shuffled out of sight.

All pretense, Phaira thought. *Oh so magical and spiritual? You're a stereotype, lady.*

"I hear that, Phaira Byrne," the leader said. "And rather than 'lady,' you may call me Huma." There was a light gash across the woman's cheekbone; Phaira's Calis had made contact after all. She enjoyed a small twinge of satisfaction in that.

"So what now?" Phaira asked loudly. "You going to kill me, or take me back to the Macatias? I don't think they care what condition I arrive in."

Huma's thin eyebrows knitted together.

"Well?" Phaira pressed.

Huma smirked. "We don't want you at all. How arrogant you are."

The truth struck Phaira like a slap across the face.

They were after Sydel.

She cursed herself for being so blind. Dammit. And she'd brought the girl right to the slaughter...

"No slaughtering, Phaira," Huma corrected. "Nothing so barbaric."

"You're one to talk about barbarism, with all those people you blew up," Phaira shot back.

"If you read the facts, Phaira, you would have seen that no one lost their lives," Huma pointed out. "And true: not the noblest methods to use. But in the short-term, wonderfully effective in uncovering others like us. Like Sydel."

She smiled then, flashing even white teeth. "Such an unexpected gift. I didn't believe it when my students returned with the discovery. But tests proved they were correct, and all the pieces fit together."

As she spoke, Huma's jugular vein pulsed through her skin. Phaira fixated on that throbbing artery. It was taunting her: so exposed, so close. She moved her wrists, back and forth.

"Well, she's a pacifist," Phaira said, keeping her tone bored. "So good luck with convincing her to blow people up. I don't envy you."

"It's so much more than that, Phaira," Huma sighed in a way that made it clear she believed Phaira to be an idiot. "You have no idea what she is capable of, do you? For someone so young, she is - "

"She's not as young as she looks," Phaira interrupted, echoing Yann's words back at the Communia.

It did its trick; a tiny pin of uncertainty showed in Huma's face.

"You don't know what you speak of," Huma said finally.

"Says you." This was fun, finding ways to irritate this woman.

Huma studied Phaira for several moments. "You're an Eko," she determined, surprise in her voice. "Not much of one, but you can receive, at least. How curious. But given that, I will be generous. I will let you go, and your brother too, for a simple exchange. Your brother and your life, for Sydel."

Phaira shifted her position. "She doesn't belong to me."

"Sydel is used to following orders," Huma said. "If you tell her to, she will. And she will be the key to stopping a great tragedy, I promise you that."

Phaira stopped fidgeting. "What tragedy?"

Huma ignored the question. "That is my offer."

"The answer is no." Phaira shifted her body again, trying to slip one hand under the other. It was so close; the bone of her right wrist ground against the restraint, the only barrier left....

Huma's left palm pressed into the top of Phaira's chest, hot and dry.

Startled, Phaira tried to jerk away, but Huma held firm. Then the edge of the woman's right thumbnail streaked down Phaira's forehead, as if to peel her open.

The world went cold. Phaira's brain ran over with faces, emotions, sped-up memories. An icy hand dragged its talons over the surface, over and over again, digging into the crevices of her mind. Phaira tried to twist her body away, but her brain wasn't listening to her pleas, releasing all her thoughts into Huma's waiting hand. Over the din of her exploding consciousness, she heard Huma's murmur: "Oh, Phaira. What a catalogue of experiences."

A memory swam to the surface: nineteen-year-old Phaira, her first overseas mission, firing a Vacarro sniper rifle; dragging an injured comrade into shelter. Fixed defenses. Slopes and sand dunes. Platoon scattered. Heroics are the best way to get killed. Just like that, a man is dead: his intestines blown, his eyes bulging and sinking. The assault seems like hours, but it's only twenty seconds.

A more recent memory: Phaira huddled under a bridge, counting the rana coins left in her pocket. The smell of garbage and filth. Her skin crusted with dirt. No one would hire. No one would help. Was her only option to offer her body? The humiliation, the burning temptation to press her knife into her wrist, to press down and stop pretending.

Then: bright lights and roaring crowds. Her hair in braids to keep it from being pulled; too-tight, borrowed gloves; the taste of bitter plastic in her mouth. Keep to the center of the ring, get out of the fence. Wait for an opening, then cut an elbow across the face. Double leg pick-up and drop: an explosion of punches. The pulse, the sweat and breath. Blood on the mat, blood on her hands, speckled over her face. The satisfaction when the muscle tore from the bone, when the ligament finally snapped, her arm raised in victory. Backstage, in celebration, one of the other fighters gave her a roll of mekaline, so readily available in the roster: then that first hit of blissful, blood-pumping, ecstatic shame...

"Stop," Phaira gasped.

"Do you concede?"

Phaira wrenched away from Huma's hand, desperate to escape, to release a limb, to hit this woman as hard as she could.

"No. Not yet," Huma concluded. "Let's go deeper, then."

The icy claw plunged through Phaira's brain. The pressure made her body spasm as a deeper memory was hauled out.

Renzo. Ren. Barely breathing. Hooked up to machines, doctors scurrying around him. His leg destroyed, his skull caved in on one side. Her brilliant brother, older by just one year; her stubborn, bossy, prickly brother who barely saw the sunlight with all the work he did: the victim of a brutal assault for no good reason. Wrong place, wrong time. His genius gone, his life ruined forever.

Another silhouette came into her mind's eye. Phaira shook her head, trying to push him back down, but that icy hand drew his face into the light. Black hair cut short. Perfect, pale skin. Brown eyes that barely blinked.

Handsome, sneering, arrogant. Young, untouchable heir to a fortune.

And she was back on the bridge. Midnight. His hands around her throat. Blood oozing through his perfect smile. The satisfying crack of his head snapping back. A stumble and trip. His hands gripped the edge, and then were gone before she could take a breath. His mouth a perfect black circle as he fell. The sickening smack echoed through the concrete ravine. Her hand still outstretched to catch him. The surge of relief. The sickening drop of her stomach.

Then it was over. The walls and the smell of the freighter returned. Phaira could breathe again, could hear Huma's smug, breathless voice: "So she defends you, even though you are a killer. How curious."

Phaira lunged at Huma with teeth bared. Huma shrieked, jumping out of reach. Glaring, unseeing, Phaira tried to form a strategy on how she would make this woman suffer. But she couldn't stop shaking.

Her hand to her throat, Huma settled her features again. "They are outside now," she said finally. "Come. Let us negotiate."

She swept out of the room. The magnets released suddenly. Phaira dropped to the floor; her muscles had given up. The guards returned and loosened her ankle bonds. Her legs were trembling, but the guards grasped her on either side and marched on.

Filtered light through trees, and sharp wind. The rusty metal platform dug into Phaira's bare feet. Sydel and Renzo stood in the grass below, aiming one of her old Compact pistols at Huma, who waited on the ground with one of her followers. Standing next to her brother, Sydel's brown skin was ashen, her long reddish-brown braids lifted by the gale. No sign of Cohen.

When prodded, Phaira made her way down the stairs, willing her body to remain upright. Despite her determination, her muscles gave out when she reached the ground. Her knees sank into the cold, wet mud.

Then one of the boy followers was behind her, his knee in her spine, yanking on her hair to expose her neck. She thrashed, trying to get away. But her throat caught on fire, and everything turned red and breathless. Voices wove in and out, warped and garbled.

And when she woke up, she was in the old Volante, bed sheets twisted around her legs, like it was all a dream.

* * *

Renzo was sullen when questioned. Again and again, he explained the decision made to give Sydel over to Huma. No, not even give; Sydel had volunteered. A sour taste grew in Phaira's mouth as he talked and talked.

The real shock was Cohen's reaction, when he too woke from unconsciousness. The shouting match went on for several minutes, Cohen's voice booming through the old ship as he berated Renzo for sacrificing Sydel. From the other side of the room, Phaira rubbed the injection site on the side of her throat. Sometimes she felt for her heartbeat.

They did everything they could think to find Sydel. But every search came up empty. The records on the carrier freight had been erased from the public network. No one from the Jala Communia would reply to their messages. Phaira even tried to mentally call out to Sydel, foolish as she felt in trying. No response, of course.

So, finally, they called Nox. First, he berated them on not calling him sooner. Then he did a search in the global patrol database. But no one named Huma existed in public record: no birth record, no fingerprints, no genetic record. They gave Nox a rundown of Sydel's features: eighteen years old, just over five feet tall, bronze skin, dark eyes, copper hair. But there was nothing else to offer. They didn't even know if she had a surname.

Frustrated, Cohen argued with Nox, demanding that the law intervene for what had been done to him and Phaira. Nox's reprimand was sharp: they had been the aggressors, they had entered without consent, and therefore Huma and her followers had the right to defend themselves.

He was right; Phaira knew it before he said it. The guilt overwhelmed her, and she had to leave the common space.

An hour later, Phaira looked up from her perch at the sound of knocking. She'd taken a shower, put on warm clothes and bundled herself into the corner of her bed, but she was still freezing.

Cohen sat on the edge of the mattress. He looked as exhausted as she felt.

"Phair, we gotta find her."

Phaira shook her head. When she ran a hand through her damp hair, she felt her fingertips tremble against her scalp. "There's nothing we can do."

"How can you say that?" Cohen exclaimed. "They're terrorists! We have to get her out of there."

"Even if we found them, those people, that woman, they have abilities that I can't even explain," Phaira said. "We're lucky to be alive."

"It doesn't matter. We have to get her," Cohen said firmly. "She doesn't belong with those people."

"Where does she belong, then, Co? With us?"

"Why not?"

Phaira shook her head again. "I can't. I can't do it."

"Phaira, please - "

Turning her head, so her chin brushed her shoulder, Phaira stared out of the window at her bedside as the night sky streaked past. Soon, she heard his angry footsteps, stomping down the hallway and into the next room.

I'm sorry, Sydel, she thought. *I doubt you can hear me, but I am. I was reckless, and arrogant, and blind. But I don't know, maybe it will all be okay. You'll find a place where you belong, somewhere better than that creepy commune. You'll change those people for the better....*

The self-talk wasn't helping. Guilt pulsed under Phaira's skin, tiny stabs of shame. The girl would have seen past the speech, anyways, looked at her in that steady, discomforting way that made it clear she saw Phaira for who she really was.

Phaira got up and went to her door, locking it. Then she resumed her position on the bed, this time with the lights off. In the darkness she could focus on what was going on inside of her body: how the core of her being, that thin central cord, wouldn't stop shivering. Her nerves were hypersensitive to every sensation. She couldn't sleep, and when she did, her dreams were filled with dark water, of sinking into an endless pool, scrambling, panicking, her lungs on fire, coming so close to breaking the surface, but her vision turning black a few inches from life. That brief moment with Huma, nothing ever registered so strongly: no combat mission, no scenes of death and destruction. Even Nican's plunge was now twisted around the memory of Huma.

And not only her mind, either. That woman had stripped Phaira of her most precious possessions: remnants of her brief other life.

The black nanotube bodysuit had been specially designed for Phaira's body measurements when she turned eighteen, now eligible for special operations. It withstood most heavy firepower, applied automatic pressure to any wounds or bone breaks, adjusted for heat and cold. The circuitry within the suit pumped enzymes and nutrients into the body to combat fatigue, constricted around wounds to stop blood blow, and regulated temperature. The very latest in warfare.

And her two 765-Calis pistols: the first models after the experimental prototype, powerful, but heavy recoil. No one in her division would touch them. It had taken her days to master them. When Phaira was dishonorably discharged, she only managed to keep them both through Nox's help. He still had influence, despite his early retirement. In her weeks of exile she had kept them close, as a reminder of when she was considered to be extraordinary.

So little of her was special anymore. Nican's family had seen to that.

II.

Renzo finally docked in a tiny seaside town, Inna, a place renowned for its white beaches. With constant rainstorms over the past month, however, contamination had broken out in the beaches, so tourists were sparse. It was a good place to regroup, and figure out what to do next.

Phaira made her way through the wet streets, a thermal belt looped around her waist, the collar of her raincoat high. Now and again a Subito speeder flew by, spraying water onto her back. She didn't care. The shoreline was rough and desolate, but she walked up and down the empty coastline for hours where the waves beat against the sand.

Cohen wouldn't come with her. He'd barely spoken to her since the incident, and he was the first to leave when they landed. Phaira suspected he walked the town too, burning off his frustration.

Renzo's mood alternated between angry outbursts and intense, impenetrable thought. All the same, he stayed busy, seeking local repair work, ordering supplies, working on the ship's bad wiring and corroded power system, disappearing for hours on end.

On the rare occasions when she was alone in the Volante, Phaira paced its narrow corridors. It felt smaller every day. It suffocated more every day. She could barely look at the door to the little storage unit, where Sydel's satchel still lay. When it got too overwhelming, she trained for hours in her locked quarters, using her body as resistance, trying to focus on her strength, stamina, and flexibility, trying to regain that cool blue focus.

One day, as she wandered into the common room, lost in thought, a call came on the public line. The console blinked at Phaira. It wasn't Nox's cc, or any other cc she recognized. She hesitated. Then she clicked the audio connect.

"Are you there?"

Him again. Unbelievable. She had changed the cc to the Volante twice now. How did he keep finding her?

"If you're going to go out in public, Phaira, you should probably try and blend in a little more."

Phaira let out a huff. "Who asked you, Theron? Stop calling me."

"There is always someone watching," the man continued, very serious. "No matter how abandoned a town is, or how solitary a beach seems - "

"Are you listening to yourself? You are equally as creepy as that statement," Phaira interrupted. "Stop tracking what I'm doing! Are you looking for me to come back and shoot you?"

Theron chuckled. The sound made her uneasy. "I had a question for you. About your stowaway."

Phaira's heart skittered. "Is she researching us in public again?" That was the subject of his second call to her, the first being the invitation to meet and 'sort the truth out.'

"She left on her own?"

Phaira took a moment to compose the tone of her voice. "It doesn't matter. She's gone."

"Back to Jala Communia?"

She said nothing. But in her mind, she was back in the arena, waiting for her combat time slot. Guaranteed a percentage of the night's take, she would finally have enough rana saved to run again. Three promoters stood in the locker room, but they didn't have the right look about them: their bodies on edge, a little too slow to approach. She was high on mekaline, though; it didn't take much for them to overpower her and smash her in the head.

When she came to, she saw the peeling walls of an old hotel room. She was bound to a wooden chair. She could hear the movements of the three bounty hunters behind her. And there were two new men standing before her, staring down at her. One was young, but incredibly tall, with a warm, sandy complexion that spoke of good food and lifestyle, and long black hair tied back with red cord; the other with deep wrinkles, a stooped back and grey hair, far less healthy.

As she blinked, trying to focus, the man with the black hair kept looking between his associate and Phaira. His eyes were the color of amber.

Then time became a blur of light and blood; they hadn't secured her wrists tightly enough. She went for the bounty hunters' throats: crushing one's larynx; snapping one's neck; slashing one's jugular vein and sending a spray of red in an arch across the wall.

A blast of white and the stench of gunpowder. Burning pain exploded through Phaira's body and everything went sideways. She tried to keep her eyes open, to clear her vision, but all she could make out was darkness, pierced by red lights, then white. And pain in her head, endless pain, her dreams filled with red and black threads, bundling together.

Then: Sydel, folding towels at her bedside, in that country clinic. And everything after.

Until he called and asked her to come to the capital. She assumed it to be some sick endgame, but in that windowless room, Theron laid down his Aegis firearm, and his explanations rang with truth. She didn't know what to make of him, or any part of the past few weeks. Why did he keep getting involved? Wouldn't it be easier to just forget that they ever crossed paths? Did he expect her to repay him, somehow? Did she owe him that?

"Phaira?"

He was still on the line. Phaira studied the blinking light.

Then she disconnected.

Just as the connection broke, an auto-news alert sounded: a developing story of a vessel on fire in town, torched in a waste disposal, unknown if people were inside. Fire officials on the scene, warning locals to remain inside until the smoke's toxicity was determined.

Then the reporter broke in: "...the freighter formerly registered to a courier service, abandoned six months ago...."

When the brothers returned, Phaira was still in front of the broadcast. Renzo and Cohen clustered around her to read the bulletin.

"Oh no," Renzo said, growing pale. Cohen looked like he might vomit. Phaira put a hand on his arm as she watched the flames on screen.

"Wait," Cohen said suddenly. "Wait. Look. No one inside. No victims."

Phaira let go of her breath. Renzo removed his glasses and pressed his fingers to the bridge of his nose. Cohen just watched the ongoing broadcast, looking sadder than Phaira could recall in a long, long time.

When hours had passed and the fire officially extinguished, Renzo was the first to leave, a scarf wrapped around his face. Cohen followed, a hat pulled low over his brow.

Shrouded in the cockpit, a musty blanket around her shoulders, Phaira watched the projection from Renzo's Lissome, propped up the flight console. The space echoed with her brothers' breathing and the sound of mud squelching under their feet.

Then the scorched skeleton of Huma's carrier ship loomed into view. Phaira's chest grew tight at the image.

"Do you see it?" came Renzo's voice.

"I see it," Phaira said grimly.

The video zoomed closer to focus on the charred windows, the exit door hanging by a hinge. Phaira could almost smell the gasoline and burnt rubber.

As he stepped inside, Renzo turned his Lissome screen outward so Phaira could see. The space was a jumble of burnt wires, scorched storage containers, piles of ashes. The cockpit was trashed, the console ripped apart. Blobs of melted glass had cooled on the windshield from the fire's intense heat. In the corner of the screen, Phaira could see Cohen stepping through the wreckage, searching. Then he noticed he was on Renzo's video feed, and stepped out of frame.

"There's nothing here, Phair," Renzo reported. "They cleaned it out completely. They're gone."

Gone, Phaira mused as her fingers drifted to the side of her throat. *Not just gone, but warning that we should not pursue. Why else would they torch the ship in the beach town? Huma knew we would see the report and make the connection.*

But they were missing something; Phaira's senses were pricking, telling her so.

When Renzo stepped back outside, his Lissome swept past the half-dangling door.

Something was burning.

"Ren!" Phaira cried.

The video jumped. Renzo's face suddenly filled the screen. "What?"

"Show me the door. Just make a sweep. Anything there?"

The video rotated to focus on the door again: blackened along the edges, composed of a hard greenish metal.

Something sparked in the center of the door. Phaira's face was inches from the image, squinting. What was that?

Then a faint yellow line unspooled on the door's surface. Phaira's mouth dropped open as words formed in cursive. "Do you see that, Ren?"

"See what?"

"What's going on?" Cohen asked, off-camera.

Phaira stared at the message. Was this some kind of trick?

"Nothing," she finally spoke. "Sorry. I thought I saw something. Come on back."

The link to the Lissome went to static. Phaira sat back in the pilot chair. The blanket dropped from her shoulders, but she barely noticed.

They can't see it, Phaira thought. *But I can.*

A trap? No, Huma had one purpose in mind when she torched the ship, and it wasn't to string them along.

Could it be from Sydel? But why could Phaira see it and not her brothers?

Her mind turned back to the incident, when Huma called her an Eko, a 'receiver,' whatever that meant. Sydel had used the term Eko, too, talking about that blonde bomber.

Expanding the digital screen above her Lissome, Phaira did a general search of the term. Information was scarce, but there were a few stories posted. Just as Sydel had mentioned, an Eko was the term for a particular psychic being whose abilities fell into the 'mental' field: telepathy, clairvoyance, that sort of thing. Reflect, project and receive, read one description. Still, no proof of such a condition existed, only the notes of theorists.

I'm psychic?

True, Phaira could sense when Sydel was being nosy. And she heard Sydel yelling her name when the bombs went off, even though Phaira was on the other side of the Vendor Mill....

The whole idea made her head hurt, so she went back to the message.

Find the missing Hitodama.

What was a Hitodama? Why would Sydel leave that kind of message for her? If only for her eyes, which she suspected it was, she couldn't bring it up to her brothers. Not yet, anyways.

Information first. Then she could move.

* * *

The pub was half-sunken into the street, with a splintered doorframe that patrons had to duck under to enter. Inside, rows of dusty bottles lined the wall, reflecting the dull red lights. The circular booths were patched over, but their design curved into themselves so the table within was hidden: ideal for private conversations. There were no monitoring devices in this privately owned business, a favorite meeting place for local hit men. Plus, the place played great music, old songs with a rhythm and ache to every lyric.

Phaira took a sip of the SunFlare she'd prepared: burnt orange with yellow wisps, cayenne pepper around the rim. Pungent and familiar. She peered into her Lissome screen, waiting.

"Sticking with the blue, I see," a voice floated through. Aeden Nox appeared in the live video feed, his spiky red hair showing at the edge of his hood. By the look of his pale, shiny and annoyed face, he had been soaked by cold rain on his way. "I thought it was just some CHROMA fun."

"Says you," Phaira retorted as she stroked her chin, mocking his neat beard. "Is that thing supposed to make you look older?"

Nox slid into the booth and adjusted the screen with a twist of his hand. Then they both leaned back: Nox into the torn cushions, Phaira against the metal wall of her bedroom.

Phaira gestured. "I ordered you a SunFlare."

The glass sat to Nox's right hand. Nox didn't smile or touch it. "I have twenty minutes left on my break."

"All I need. I just had some questions."

"You haven't even told me where you've been all this time."

Phaira looked away. She ran her finger over the glass's rim to collect some of the red spice. "East," she offered. "And North."

Nox sighed. "What do you need?"

"Have there been any more of those public bombings?"

"No," Nox said, swirling the ice in his drink. "Not since we last spoke. Has your brother calmed down yet?"

Phaira's temper flared. "Don't joke about Cohen, you have no idea."

"I would if you told me," Nox said pointedly. "I lend out my parents' old Volante, which you're still running around in, by the way, and I barely get a thank you."

"Sorry," Phaira admitted. "You're right. Thanks for helping them out."

Nox shrugged. "The most interesting thing I've done in months."

Phaira felt a sting of pity. Then again, if she had remained in the military and retired from active duty at the age of thirty, as she would have been entitled to, Phaira would have ended up where Nox did: working with database management or some other entry-level deskwork. There were no special favors, even with their history; if anything, the government wanted to enforce the idea that one civilian was never above another.

Still, Phaira knew Nox. She could see how he vibrated with stagnant energy. It wasn't a shame, exactly, that he was out of harm's way. But it seemed so in that moment.

Nox took a sip of his drink and winced a little. "Wow, that's strong."

"Lightweight."

"Shut it. What do you want? I'm down to fifteen before I'm due back."

"Ever heard of the term 'Hitodama'"?

"Sure, it's a hacktivist group," Nox nodded, taking another sip. "They wear a lot of black and that scares people. You'd fit in well."

"Ha ha," Phaira mocked. "Anything else?"

"Funny you mention them," Nox mused. "A couple of Hitodama were killed last night in the Mac. Another one has been reported missing. My desk mate thinks the lack of response is due to prejudice: he's been ranting about it all day. I just figure they made the wrong person angry."

Phaira thought about it. Macnus, or "The Mac" as it was better known as, was one of two major cities on the East Coast. When she'd toured it with the fighting circuit, so many weeks ago, she'd stayed clear of the shadows.

"Gang retaliation?" she asked. "Do hackers have gangs? Or gang wars?"

Nox shrugged. "Maybe." He took another long swallow of his drink. "Surprised you haven't seen all their campaigning. There's Hitodama protests all over the Mac; they even started info-bombing all the stations, demanding action." His green eyes flicked to hers. "Why are you asking? Have they come after you?"

"No," Phaira said. "That's one group that hasn't tried. Not yet, anyways."

"You know, you shouldn't be doing this." Nox glanced around the booth. "I'm glad you called, but I don't want to be the reason that you're tracked down."

Phaira studied her friend through the screen. Almost ten years of each other's company in service: raiding

144 | LOREN WALKER

together, travelling together, and on a couple of occasions, sleeping together.

She flashed back to the first day they met. Eighteen
and just off the bus, Phaira made her way to her registered hanger, snapping her helmet into place. An auto-
mated voice counted down the time, alarms going off in
every corner of the hanger. The freighter opened at the
rear, with rows of men and women inside, strapped into
their seats, on their way to the frontlines.

Phaira joined the military when she was fourteen,
the minimum age for recruitment. From the start, she
graded high, and advanced quickly. She'd done tests
with various weapons, including new prototypes such as
the Avenger and the Calis pistol, gone through extensive physical training, and tested well in combat, range
weaponry, infiltration and language.

Flight, and her fear of heights, were concerns she
hadn't quite conquered.

"Nervous?"

Phaira's face flushed. "No," she snapped at the young
man beside her. She clicked her seatbelt into place,
checking twice.

"Well, I am," the man said. His eyes darted nervously
around the interior of the freighter.

"Haven't you flown before?" Phaira hollered over the
sound of engines, holding onto her chest strap, trying to
will her heart not to explode.

"Bit different than the commercial flight over here!" he called back. She could see his pale face, how it made the freckles on his face stand out. It was almost cute.

"I'm Byrne!" she yelled. Instinctively, she pushed her shoulder against his. "It'll be fine!"

"I'm Nox!" As the freighter lifted off the ground, he hollered back: "And I don't believe you!"

Phaira snapped back to the present and her cold Volante cabin. There was a sharp ache in her chest. It didn't much matter anymore, what they had been through.

Stop being nostalgic, she told herself. The military life was far different from the civilian world. And it was even more divergent when he was a patrol officer and she was a disgraced soldier with a contract on her head.

"Go back to work," Phaira said. "Sorry if I got you into trouble."

"Phair, come on - "

She didn't let him finish. With a flick of her finger, the screen blinked and disappeared.

Phaira downed the rest of the SunFlare, coughing from the rush of cayenne.

Then she threw the tumbler across the room.

III.

That night, Phaira read everything she could find about the Hitodama. The organized group of hacktivists, with bases in both the North and the East, advocated the procurement of information at any cost. In their few years of existence, the group had exposed government documents, war reports, a few pictures from the very secretive West War, ten years ago. And yes, from the few pictures of those prosecuted, the members did look dark and sinister, sometimes comically so.

But the murders were real enough. Just as Nox had said, two members of the Hitodama were found in the Mac, with the same crushed larynxes and same close-range wound to the thigh. The entry angle had severed the artery and they had bled out.

Oddly precise, was her first thought.

And, as Nox said, one member missing in action: a hacker known only as Emiyo. Hitodama were furious about it, overwhelming law patrol and broadcast stations with alerts, demands and threats. But by all accounts, the public merely shrugged in response.

Why would Sydel lead us in this direction? Phaira puzzled. *It's probably a gang war. I would probably think the same as the law in this case: no good can come of getting involved.*

But the message was clear on the door: *Find the missing Hitodama.*

So Phaira put a message into the public network, written carefully, the cc encrypted as best she knew how. "Locate and recover missing HD. Inquire."

She knew it was an enormous risk. Putting any part of herself into the outside meant that a bounty hunter could track her down. But her guilt over Sydel wouldn't subside. And that message was the only thing to hold onto: not only for her, but for Cohen, too.

Within minutes, a call came in. Phaira listened for any indication that her brothers stirred from sleep. Then she made the connection, both audio and visual, through her Lissome, and moved out of range so her face would remain hidden; the viewer would only see a faint glimmer of metal wall. The caller had the same idea; when the translucent screen unzipped, there was no visual. But the crackle of static told her that the connection was active. She waited.

"Identity yourself," came a male voice.

"You called me," Phaira retorted.

Another crackle of static, and a flurry of tapping noises. Lines of code scrolled down the screen: firewall protection, encrypting at a level she'd never seen before. Then a face slid into view: ghostly white skin, black hair, black clothing, large nose and pinched blue eyes. "This channel is secure now," the man declared. "All can be revealed."

Phaira held back a snort of laughter. When composed, she moved into frame, but at an angle so her profile was half in shadow. Nox said that she looked like one of these

Hitodama; the man seemed to agree, giving her a nod of approval.

"I go by Lander," the man said. "And you?"

Phaira's mind swam. Couldn't use her last name. Should she come up with some nickname? Her middle name was Lora, and she'd used it on the circuit. Better than nothing, and he was waiting.

"Lora. That is - Phaira Lora - Phaira Lore."

As soon as she made the switch, she longed to correct it. It was so pretentious, but she couldn't backtrack now. "I hear your group's had some trouble," she said brusquely, trying to cover her flub.

"We are being persecuted because of our beliefs."

"Do you have any idea who might have wanted them dead?"

"No."

"But you want me to find the one who is missing."

"Isn't that what you do?" His tone was suspicious. "You're not registered anywhere as a LRP."

Locate - Retrieve - Protect, Phaira remembered. No, she wasn't registered as a specialist. She thought fast. "Because I only work with select individuals," she countered. "Who prefer privacy above all else."

That seemed to satisfy him. "This is a time-sensitive situation. Emiyo has a medical condition - "

"Here's what I don't understand," Phaira interrupted. "Most hackers are very good at keeping their position secret. So how were your members tracked down in the first place?"

Lander huffed, looking over his nose at Phaira. "Come to the next gathering in the skerries. If you figure out who's doing this, you'll be compensated."

The mention of the skerries made Phaira pause. "In the Mac?"

"Is that a problem?"

"You're talking about me mingling with your crowd?" she asked, keeping her voice even.

"You're insinuating that the killer is one of our own. Come and see for yourself."

Phaira grinned. "Caught that, did you?"

Then her smile dropped. "If you turn me the wrong way, Lander, you won't be an underground group anymore."

"You have my word."

Hacker's word, Phaira thought with contempt as she broke the connection. The screen zipped into nothing.

The sun broke over the horizon. Her brothers would be up soon. And she had to tell them something.

* * *

"Why are we heading east?" Renzo asked, peering out of the common room's window.

"I've been offered a job. To retrieve a kidnapped victim," Phaira added before Renzo could interrupt. "I can make some money. Which we need. Can't keep relying on your repair work to support three people and a rickety Volante."

"We're fine," Renzo said pointedly. "Why not call Nox, let him handle this?"

"Because the buyers want to maintain their privacy. It's an extraction job. Nothing more. And no different from any other recon mission I've done. "

Then an idea occurred to her. "And it might lead to some protection, you know. The employers are expert hackers. If I'm successful, I can ask them to disable my bounty listing as payment."

Both of her brothers were silent, considering. It wasn't a lie, really. These Hitodama could help her disappear, not just from the registry, but from Osha in general. She wasn't going to say that part to them, though.

"I can help," Cohen finally said. He stood on the opposite side of the room, silent and stony until that point. It was hard for him to offer; Phaira could see the struggle in his expression. She loved him for it.

Still, Phaira shook her head. "Just me," she said gently. "When we land, keep to the city limits. If there's any trouble, leave me behind and go."

Cohen went to protest, but Renzo held up his hand. "Fine," he said. "But don't give us a reason to run."

"Not in my plan," Phaira agreed.

She hoped it might be true this time.

* * *

The instructions came in: midnight, at the intersection of two streets, on the legal side of the stormwall.

Phaira kept to the alleyways until she reached the border. She could smell the sea, and something rotten.

A flicker of movement up ahead. A rope ladder was thrown over the stormwall, slapping against the ground. Lander was already climbing, gesturing for Phaira to follow.

On the other side of the wall, a girl in black helped Lander to the ground. Phaira ignored her outstretched hand, jumping to the ground, immediately rattled by the soft, wet ground under her boots. She stared at the coastline, the old world before the Impact. On this side of the wall, the only light came from the two tiny moons above, highlighting the wreckage: the looming shadows of foundations and poles, disintegrating rovers, and the boggy stink of swamp overpowering. The Mac was one of the worst Impact sites, Phaira remembered.

She held her breath and followed Lander through the muddy path, through a rusty doorway of a crumbling apartment building, and up three rotting flights of stairs.

On the third floor, twenty-odd men and women wandered the halls. Some lay on the floor talking, the light from candles on the floor outlining their bodies. Some hooked up makeshift workstations as they argued. Lander was drawn into a discussion about linguistics when Phaira gestured with a jerk of her head for him to step away.

As they moved to a quieter spot, he studied her face. She did the same, cataloguing all his identifying characteristics: faint scar through eyebrow, pierced ear, triangle freckle pattern on his cheek.

"I ran general searches on our members," Lander whispered. "Everyone has some kind of record, but not for violent crimes."

"That's a start." Phaira said quietly. "I'll leave when I'm ready."

As she walked the floor, her dress felt incredibly tight and revealing, or as revealing as it could be with its high-neck, long sleeves and skirt with blood-red lining at the hem. It was one of the random items that Cohen packed when her brothers came looking for her. Since they re-united, Phaira often wondered if her little brother was drunk when he went into her closet, so random were the gatherings. She hadn't worn this particular dress in years. But she did fit in, visually, at least. And for once, her dark-lined eyes and mouth were almost boring, compared to the visual drama all around. She focused on taking in the hushed whispers, the high-pitched giggles, waiting for a way in....

".... shouldn't gather like this anymore." To her right, a black man with a shaved head hissed at a white man with stringy hair. Phaira leaned against the peeling wallpaper, listening. ".... just setting us up to be killed - what are they thinking?"

"You came out," the stringy-haired man pointed out.

"Because I'm afraid," the shaved man said. "Better to be together than alone. Some operative is just waiting to hunt us down. It's a government crackdown, I tell you."

"Come on," the other man scoffed. "You're making us out to be too important here."

"Oh really? Did you know I got a message asking about a job, but I couldn't trace the cc? You know how weird that is? Not a trace - just one name."

"What's the name?" Phaira broke in.

Both the men jumped

Phaira thought quickly. "I got a request too," she added. "About work. Just before coming here."

"Really?" the shaved man asked eagerly. "Did you recognize the handle? I'd never heard the name before."

"Oh, I know everyone in the system," the stringy-haired man boasted, his eyes darting over to Phaira. "You're just paranoid because of what happened to those other two."

"And you're not?" the shaved man snapped. "I got the request the same day they were killed! So who is to say that it's not a trap? Some plan to lure me in to be murdered like them? Or kidnapped like Emiyo!"

"I wonder if we got a message from the same handle," Phaira interrupted. "What was yours under?"

The shaved man glowered. "Saka. Yours?"

"Saka," the stringy-haired man repeated. "I don't know anyone by - "

"Big surprise," the shaved man said. "You - "

A shaft of light streaked down the hall. The two men shielded her eyes. Phaira didn't need to see what it was; she pulled the hood over her head instead.

"Clear it out of here!" someone bellowed. "You're under arrest for trespassing and public disturbance!"

The Hitodama protested in union, swarming into the light. As they swept past her, Phaira searched for an alternate exit. In a shadowy corner, behind a disintegrating chair, three Hitodama girls waved at her to join them. One by one, they slipped into a hole hidden under a flap of torn wallpaper.

Phaira glanced back; the outcry grew louder. A fight was about to break out. Phaira darted over and slipped through the opening, pulling the greasy wallpaper behind her.

The tinny sound of their bodies on metal made it hard to hear anything. The three Hitodama crawled down the airshaft; Phaira followed. Together they moved along the corroded vent, turning down one corner, and then another, finally coming to a metal grate. The leader, the one with short black hair, fiddled with the screws.

Finally the grate came off with a loud bang. The Hitodama crawled through, stepping down into what used to be a storeroom. Through the walls, Phaira could hear the officers yelling, the sound of glass breaking. Reluctantly, she joined the others crouched in a cleared space, shielded by rusty metal crates and old lighting strips.

Together they waited. Phaira's skin prickled with fatigue and heat. She kept her eyes low and her face hidden.

"Tell your fortune?" said someone to her right.

At Phaira's sour look, the girl smiled. Waves of incense came off her, mixed with the musty smell from the vent. Phaira leaned away, irritated.

Suddenly the girl grabbed Phaira's hand, turning her palm upwards and pressing her nose to her palm. Phaira battled her instinct to punch her.

"I see," the girl began, her voice an octave lower. "You are searching for something."

Phaira's throat closed up.

Grinning, the girl released Phaira's hand. "I'm just teasing. You're Lander's hire, right? I thought we should meet."

Phaira glared at the girl. The other two Hitodama exchanged glances.

The girl raised her hands in defense. "I'm Anandi." One of her thick black eyebrows rose. "Know the name?"

"Should I?" Phaira said cautiously, taking another look at the girl. She was maybe twenty, petite and boyish, with short black hair, golden brown skin and mismatched features: round nose, thin lips, weak chin. But she radiated energy. Or perhaps it was just the glow of her deep orange embroidered dress, peeking through her black cloak.

"Well, at the very least, you know my father." Anandi said. "Emiyo?"

Her father? Phaira turned to face the girl and chose her next words carefully. "Do you know what happened? Do you know someone named Saka? Is that a Hitodama?"

"I read the reports," Anandi said. "And no, I don't know the name. But it's more complicated than that. My father isn't really a true member."

At Phaira's puzzled face, Anandi sighed, her exhale a musical hum. She looked at the two Hitodama watching. "Sorry," she told them. "I'm not a fan. Neither is my father. We're just pretending."

"I wondered," Phaira said dryly. "I can see some color on you."

"Oh that," Anandi said, picking at the colorful cloth of her dress. "I'm not much into black. But I do like secrets, and the Hitodama has some good ones."

This girl was unreal. Phaira couldn't help but ask questions. "So you're just around them for fun? This group doesn't seem very entertaining." She ignored the scowls of the two Hitodama.

"We were getting ready to take our leave," Anandi said. "Then my father disappeared. So my plans changed. Did Lander mention his medical condition?"

"No specifics. Just that it was time-sensitive."

"It is." But the girl offered nothing more.

They listened to the activity outside. Shouts descended into tired conversation. Tables were being moved back into place. It would be clear soon.

Something slipped into Phaira's hand: paper, with a series of numbers and letters scribbled on it. Her cc, Phaira realized.

"Call me if I can help," Anandi said quietly. "My father's real name is Emir Ajyo, and he's worth saving, I promise." The girl touched the ends of Phaira's hair. "I like the blue. Suits you."

Then she darted around the boxes, unlocked the door and ran. The two Hitodama followed.

But Phaira didn't move from her hidden position, studying the paper for a long while.

When she finally got back to the parking hanger, inside the Volante, and secure in her cabin, Phaira peeled off her damp, stinking dress and kicked it into the corner. She slipped into a loose white shirt and shorts, then rubbed her hair with a towel to get the salt out. Sitting on the bed with a thunk, Phaira opened up an audio-only channel on her Lissome, and punched in the cc for Lander. "You get out okay?" she asked when the connection formed.

"Barely," Lander's voice was exhausted and sour. "We lost four members to the patrol."

"Well, there's one bit of good news. I have a name. So hack into the victims' workstations and see if you can find anything from someone called Saka."

A snort of derision rippled through the Lissome. "I will not. Hitodama never invade a colleague's realm."

"Their privacy is no longer relevant," Phaira said pointedly. "If it was, you wouldn't have hired me."

"These two were brilliant at their work," Lander argued. "To try and recover any information - you can't even imagine - "

"Then figure out something. I do nothing until you do."

Phaira disconnected. Then she padded out of the room in search of her brothers.

She found Renzo in the cockpit, half-hidden under the console as he wrestled with wiring.

"What's wrong?" he mumbled from underneath.

"Nothing," Phaira said, leaning against the doorframe. "I just hope I'm asking the right questions to find this Emir Ajyo person. When I was in service, I got the information upfront in a neat package."

"If you're so uncertain, why did you solicit the work?"

Phaira ignored him. "I see two solid options here," she thought out loud. "One, the killer's a former member of the group who's holding a grudge. Second, the Hitodama got into some highly classified material and this is a cover-up. Still seems strange, though."

"Who's to say, Phaira? They probably have a million enemies. These people are criminals: they deface property, manipulate communication servers." Renzo's hand waved, listing each offense.

"Oh, you get that with any kind of youth group," Phaira scoffed. "That's nothing. I used to deface property when I was a kid."

"Yeah, and look how you turned out."

"A joke!" Phaira exclaimed. "A real joke! I can't believe it!"

A red light flashed on the console. Renzo's hand slid out from underneath and tapped the surface. "All yours."

He was right; it was Lander. "I did it," he burst out, when the connection was made. "I found the mail, buried in a hard drive, received thirty-four minutes before the killing. It's this Saka person, isn't it?"

"Possibly. If you knew where he was, I could ask him. Or her."

"I do," Lander said with a smug tone. "I tracked her to the south side of the Mac. You could recover Emiyo tonight."

Before Phaira, the console flickered to life: the symmetrical grid of the city, the outskirts of the Mac, with a single red dot, blinking like a warning.

"Any indication that Emiyo is actually there, too?" Phaira asked, studying the map.

"No. But this is enough information, right? You'll avenge their deaths?"

Phaira felt Renzo's eyes on her. "Find and retrieve is all we agreed to," she told Lander.

"But they - "

"I'll be in contact."

Phaira broke the connection. The word floated through her mind. *Avenge.*

"Avenge?" Renzo rolled out from underneath the console.

"You know that's not what I agreed to," Phaira said. "You heard me. Find and retrieve. That's it."

But Renzo's eyes remained wary.

Phaira raised her shoulders. "That's it, Ren," she repeated.

Renzo hoisted himself up, hopping onto his good leg as he steadied his balance. Then he turned away from her and limped over to the other side of the cockpit.

* * *

When the night sky changed from orange to purple, she moved. She wore a simple black shirt, flexible leggings and her last pair of boots, a black scarf wrapped around her face, her hair covered by another black wrap. A few small knives were hidden on her body, but nothing else.

The coordinates led her to a short, squat, and ugly building. At the rear of the building, one of the basement shutters was loose. She unscrewed it, set it aside and checked for any signs of life. Nothing: silent and black inside. The opening was only two feet wide, but she managed to shimmy through.

Once inside, she moved on the balls of her feet, up the basement stairs, past doorways and windows. There, around the corner: the sound of heavy breathing. A cough rippled down the hallway, followed by a wet sniff. Male, and sick. If weakened by illness, he was heavily armed to compensate. She needed the element of surprise; if this man were as big as he sounded, one direct hit would knock her down and out. A light knock against the wall to draw his attention. A shot to the throat, a kick to the knee, followed by a quick reversal of his firearm so the butt struck under the chin with a crack. He stumbled, and her steel-tipped boot swung into his temple. As he fell, Phaira darted forward and grasped the guard under the arms, following him down as he slid to the floor. Then she removed the charge from the Kivara firearm, leaving it heavy and dead against the wall, and continued to move.

Inside the room he guarded, a silhouette sat in front of glowing blue screens. Alone. Female. Blonde and black-streaked hair, puffed into a halo. Phaira assessed the space: a jumble of mechanics, supply units, half-eaten food. And sitting in the middle of a wire pile, a high-powered magrifle; very likely the weapon that blew through those two Hitodama.

Phaira waited in the shadows, listening to the tail end of the conversation:

"...you don't need her, Keller. Or anyone, for that matter. I can do everything that's needed. You're bringing in too many outsiders. It'll start to draw attention." Her voice was raspy, rougher than Phaira expected.

"You're good, but not that good," came a gruff man's voice through the sound system. "I know what I'm doing. Just hold your position. I'll let you know what's next."

Phaira waited for the click of disconnection. Then she was across the room, her arm looped around the woman's throat. When Phaira jerked backwards, the woman came with her, the chair tipping over on its side with a crash. The woman clawed at Phaira's arm, but her long fingernails couldn't penetrate the material.

Phaira put her face to the woman's ear. "I know you're called Saka," she stated, her voice muffled through her scarf. "I also know that you contacted a Hitodama minutes before she and her friend were hunted down. And a magrifle sounds about right for a murder weapon."

Phaira released Saka. Her halo of hair half-collapsed, the woman grasped her throat, wobbling to her feet.

"You have one option," Phaira told her. "Tell me where Emir Ajyo is and I'll take you to local patrol."

Saka stared at Phaira, her make-up smeared black under her eyes. "Are you Hitodama?"

Phaira said nothing. Stumbling, Saka backed off, reaching behind for her workstation table. A Compact-model pistol lay under papers; she grabbed it and swung the weapon forward.

"Now you have one option," Saka sneered. "Five seconds to leave before I blow a hole in you."

Phaira didn't move.

The pistol in Saka's hand wavered. "Whoever you are, this doesn't concern you."

"If you shoot, I'll be within my rights," Phaira warned.

The woman's finger tightened around the trigger.

"Hand over Emir," Phaira ordered. "And - "

A hole exploded in the opposite wall. Phaira was already knocking the pistol from Saka's fingers, shoving the woman against her desk. Hardware clattered to the floor as Saka ricocheted. Then the woman sprang forward, rolling behind Phaira and snatching up the fallen pistol. As she swung it around to fire, Phaira grabbed Saka's wrist and twisted. The bones ground together. Saka dropped the gun with a cry. Then, panicked, Saka snatched at Phaira's hair, her cold fingers buried in her scalp.

At the touch, something exploded inside of Phaira. She couldn't see, couldn't hear, her heart exploding, synapses frenzied and screaming: *the cold the cold get away get off get off.* Somewhere, Saka was screaming, under the rush of blood in Phaira's ears.

When Phaira snapped back to the present, nearly hyperventilating, she saw Saka holding her broken fingers, sprinting for the door. The Compact lay on the floor. Phaira scooped it up and fired.

The blast caught the edge of Saka's arm. Saka crashed to the ground, but Phaira was there to meet her, grasping the woman by the throat, hauling her up, slamming her back against the wall and pushing her forearm against Saka's wound. Phaira's black sleeve was instantly soaked in hot blood.

As Saka shrieked with pain, Phaira brought her masked face closer. "Where is he?"

Then Phaira's ears pricked. There was a pinging sound over the hum of Saka's broken workstation, something tapping on metal.

Phaira dug her thumb next to Saka's gunshot wound, making the woman howl in pain. As she yanked Saka off the wall, the sound started again in the corner, low to the floor, coming from behind the wall.

Phaira jerked her head towards the sound. "Open it."

With a burst of strength, Saka wrenched her arm away from Phaira, and flopped backwards onto the bundle of wires in the corner, where the magrifle lay. Saka snatched it up, her hands fumbling for the trigger.

It happened so fast. But Phaira's hand was suddenly outstretched, her concealed knife gone and buried in Saka's chest.

The magrifle clattered to the floor. Saka's eyes and mouth were perfect circles of surprise, falling away.

Familiar. Nican made that face. They all made the same face.

Focus, Phaira ordered herself. *Focus and get out of here.*

As Saka writhed, Phaira crouched down, tracing the edges of the wall. There, the hinge: she hooked her fingers around the hidden strip and yanked.

Inside, the man with white hair and ashy brown skin blinked in the sudden light. Phaira offered her hand. It shook just a little as she helped Emir to his feet.

"Stupid - " Saka's voice rasped, followed by the slow, sucking sound of an open wound.

Instantly, Phaira knew what was to come, but Emir was stumbling half-blind and she couldn't get him out of the way.

A swish of air, and a sickening thunk. Emir roared with pain as he clutched his arm, a bloody knife sticking out of his tricep muscle.

Phaira snatched at another concealed knife and flipped it into a reverse position.

But her hand lowered when she saw Saka gulp for air, shudder and finally go still on the floor.

Sheathing the blade, Phaira snatched Emir by his uninjured wrist and led him out of the glowing room. When

Emir started to moan with pain, she gave his arm a jerk, silencing him.

An alarm went off. Panic swarmed through her. She suddenly flashed back to memories of Nox and the others on her team: the voices in her ear, her back up, and her defense. What was she thinking? She was a fool to do this alone.

But she had to finish this first. Left, then left again, down the stairs. Ahead of them, barely visible in the pitch-dark, she saw the open window. Emir might fit through the opening, but barely. Phaira held her breath as she boosted Emir up. He moaned, cradling his arm with the small knife in it. Shifting back and forth on his back, he managed to squeeze through the window and roll onto street level. Phaira kept glancing back at the stairs, listening for footsteps. There were none.

Go, her mind commanded. *Get outside. Then don't stop moving. Stay in the shadows. Take as many twists and turns needed to disappear. Keep Emir behind so he can't identify your features.*

It took nearly an hour to reach the designated safe spot at the city's edge. The scarf around Phaira's face was wet from her breath. Deep inside the alley, and hidden from overhead view, she finally let go of Emir's wrist.

Emir sank to his knees, sucking in the night air. His face was heavily lined, with dirt smeared into the crevices. It made him look ghoulish.

But he does look like his daughter, she thought. *Funny.*

Emir jerked his head up to stare at her. "Who are you?" he said fearfully. "Did my daughter hire you?"

When she nodded, Emir deflated with relief. She took the opportunity to kneel down next to him, examining his arm. The blade was only three inches long, but a good two were solidly lodged into the tricep muscle. This would hurt.

She began to straighten out the arm. Emir let out a shout of pain before muffling it in his throat. Phaira placed his hand firmly against her shoulder for support. A pile of gauze in one hand, she curled the fingers of her other hand around the blade's handle. Phaira swallowed, counted to three, and swiftly yanked out the knife, pressing the gauze down in its place. Emir yelped, and then shuddered. He looked like he might faint.

Phaira shifted Emir so he could lean against the brick wall of the alleyway. Then she took Emir's hand and placed it over the gauze, silently encouraging him to hold it.

Eventually he did. After several minutes, Phaira checked the flood of blood. Slower, at least. She was no Sydel, and with some stitches he would have a nasty scar, but for now it would do.

"Thank you," Emir said, his voice scratchy.

"What's your medical condition?" Phaira asked. "Do you need to be taken somewhere?"

"Just call my daughter. Please."

Uncomfortable at the emotion in his voice, Phaira strode down the narrow alleyway to its end. Digging under a pile of discarded tools and rotten vegetables, Phaira unearthed a Lissome, carefully wrapped in clean cloth, along with that folded piece of paper. As Emir leaned against the wall, Phaira punched in the cc.

"Phaira?"

"South side of the Mac, and bring a suture kit," Phaira said. "Target acquired."

V.

P haira unwrapped the black scarf from her head, wiping condensation from her upper lip and shaking out her sweat-matted hair. Then Anandi threw her arms around Phaira's neck. Phaira stiffened, but let the girl squeeze her tightly. Phaira's brain, however, was focused on berating her own stupidity, her arrogance.

Then she heard Anandi's voice in her ear: "Come with us?"

"What?" Phaira said, backing away from her embrace.

"You're amazing," Anandi sighed, like a teenager with a crush. "We could do so much together. You can stay with us, we'll make you a good meal, and then we can get into some trouble together...."

Phaira looked at Anandi askance. What was the matter with this girl? Why would she offer something like that? She didn't know anything about Phaira...

"I have a place to go," Phaira began.

Then she realized with a heavy stomach that she couldn't be certain of that fact.

"And you should clear out of here anyways," she added gruffly. "Get him whatever medicine he needs."

"Awww - "

"Don't push," Emir told his daughter, his voice still scratchy. "She's right. It's been almost a week since - "

171

"Okay, okay," Anandi huffed, interrupting her father. She clearly didn't want Phaira to know any more about it.

Phaira glanced at Emir. "You know why Saka grabbed you and killed the others?"

"She never spoke to me," Emir said, coughing. "Not once."

Disappointed, Phaira hovered by the alley's mouth, wondering if she should just turn and leave. But Anandi was talking to her again, her smile faded and her eyes now serious. "Will you keep the details of this private?"

Phaira cocked her head. "I'm not sure I understand."

"What's happened tonight, from start to finish," Anandi explained. "I'm asking you to stay silent. If you're willing to do so, I promise: if you need anything, if you are ever in trouble, you have my protection."

Phaira didn't need to think about it. "Consider it classified."

Soon after, Anandi and Emir disappeared into the night, and Phaira headed north, keeping to the shadows. Anandi's words rolled around in Phaira's head; they were significant, somehow, but she was too drained to figure out the meaning.

Within the hour, she wrenched open the door to the old Volante. Her mind swirled with what to tell her brothers about Anandi, about Saka, or any of it. It seemed clear, however, that it was time to make plans to disappear again. It wasn't fair to involve them in her mess. When Renzo and Cohen were far from this area of the country and any potential harm, she could go with confidence. Deal with the aftermath. Maybe seek out Anandi and her father, see what could come of that connection.

"What happened?" came Renzo's voice, startling Phaira from her thoughts. He stood at the top of the stairs.

So much for keeping them away from this, Phaira thought. Still, she chose her words carefully. "I found Emir Ajyo. He's safe. But there might be retaliation. We need to leave."

"Did you hurt someone?"

Pausing at the top of the steps, Phaira lifted her gaze. "Would you believe me if I said that it was in self-defense?"

Then a massive blur shot past Renzo, and two arms slapped around Phaira.

"Cohen!" she shrieked, as he lifted her up in an embrace.

"Glad you're okay," came his muffled voice.

Phaira patted his shoulder, even as her heart raced from shock. "Tough guy."

"Yeah, yeah," Cohen mumbled. As he put her down, a smile grew on his face. "So what happened? Did you get him? I know you did, I bet you can't wait to tell those Hitodama people - "

"I'm not sure we want - " Phaira began, but Renzo caught her eye and shook his head.

"You deal with that group," Renzo said, drawing both Cohen and Phaira's attention. "I'll get us in the air." He limped towards the cockpit.

Cohen looked at Phaira plaintively. She pretended to roll her eyes. "Give me a minute and I'll tell you about it," she told him, relieved that he was speaking to her again.

As the Volante lifted into the sky, Phaira ducked into her quarters to towel off the sweat and grime. *Close enough to normal,* she thought, and opened her Lissome.

"Phaira Lore." The ghoulish face appeared again. "What news?"

Watching from the doorway, Cohen mouthed with a smirk: *Phaira Lore?*

"Target retrieved," Phaira said, ignoring her brother. She needed to end this relationship.

"Where is he?" Lander said eagerly. His face drew nearer to the screen. "Was I right? Was it Saka?"

"Emiyo is safe," Phaira told him. "That's all the information I can share."

A long pause. "What do you mean, that's all?"

"Just as I said. The job is complete."

"But - but he wasn't the only one targeted," Lander sputtered. "Other members are hiding in fear. We are under attack, and you're just going to - ?"

"Your group's security is not my problem," Phaira said firmly.

In the pixelated screen, Lander's face grew spiteful. "I hired you. You do as I say, and you give me the information that I pay for. You don't withhold from the Hitodama."

"Oh really?" Phaira challenged. "You paid for the safe return of a man, which has been accomplished. Not happy with it? Keep your rana."

When she broke the connection, the static backlash made her heart leap. Everything made her react, it seemed.

"That was weird," Cohen remarked, walking into the cabin. "Are you in trouble?"

Phaira ran a hand through her frizzy hair; the smell of dried blood on her sleeve hit her. She brought her arm down quickly. "It didn't go as smoothly as I'd hoped, but still - "

Suddenly the Volante tipped up. Phaira and Cohen slid across the room, hitting the walls with a bang. The wind knocked out of her, Phaira could hear her older brother swearing. Holding onto the walls, she slipped and strained to stay upright.

"Co!" she yelled. "Are you okay?"

The ship shuddered again. The engines grew louder, screaming. Cohen gripped the doorframe, his feet planted wide. "Are you?" he hollered back, gesturing to his forehead.

A hot trickle on her temple. Phaira swiped with her forearm and ran into the corridor. As she did, the vessel seemed to hover in mid-air, as if taking a breath.

Then came the sickening drop in her stomach as the vessel began to plummet.

In the cockpit, Renzo gripped the flight controls with one hand as the other typed in a flurry. The Volante listed onto its side, its speed increasing. Clutching the pilot seat for balance, Phaira stared as the ship broke through the clouds, grasslands stretched below them.

"I can't," Renzo gasped, wrenching at the controls. The screens flashed ERROR. Another alarm began to shriek, a second layer of panicked noise. "I can't control it! I can't access it!"

Phaira's blood went cold. *Lander.* She dug in her pockets. Where was that piece of paper? Had she left it in that alleyway?

The ship tipped to the side again. Renzo fought to keep the nose up, but the system wasn't responding.

Phaira's fingers shook as she punched in the letters and numbers. "Come on, come on," she murmured as it rang once, then twice. "Come on!"

Then the connection clicked. "That was quick. Missed me?"

"Your friends have hacked into our ship!" Phaira shouted, grabbing hold of the console as the Volante shuddered again. "Get him out before we crash!"

"Hey!" Anandi shot back. "They aren't my friends, and I don't - "

"Lady, we have about thirty seconds before we hit the water!" Renzo broke in. "If you can do something, do it now!"

"Stop yelling at me or I won't do a thing!"

"You owe me, Anandi!" Phaira yelled. Her breath caught at the expanse of brown filling the windshield. The engines screamed. The Volante's outer paneling started to peel off, bouncing off the glass. Her mind was a frantic loop. *I've killed them. I've killed them.*

Suddenly the alarms stopped. Renzo grabbed the flight controls and wrenched them to the left and up. The Volante turned sharply, screeching with the effort. Phaira slid across the floor, slamming against the opposite wall.

There was no crash, no fireball. They were alive.

Still, Phaira didn't move for several seconds, even though she was upside down and covered with papers.

"Are you all right?" Renzo wheezed. "You're bleeding." He still gripped the flight controls, his knuckles white.

Phaira pushed the debris off her. "It's fine. Co?" she called out, working to keep her voice even.

"I'm here!" Cohen confirmed, ducking inside the cockpit. "What happened?"

"Hacked," Phaira said, trying not to pant. "I think."

"More than that," came Anandi's low voice through the soundsystem. Cohen jerked a thumb in the voice's direction, mouthing *who's that?*

"Completely disabled your central processor," Anandi continued. "Crude, but effective. But you're fine now. You're welcome."

"Until Lander decides to track us down and attack again," Phaira called out.

A scoffing sound. "Lander can barely find his own face. He won't try it again."

"He tracked down Saka's location, didn't he?"

"No, I found that woman and sent him the information," Anandi corrected, her voice haughty. "I knew he would forward it to you, claiming it as his own discovery. And I was right."

Phaira was speechless. Renzo and Cohen wore the same confused look on their faces.

Anandi continued to talk, her voice growing quieter. "I'm no good against a physical threat. I couldn't have gotten my father out of there. I knew you could, but I had to be cautious. And protect me and my father as best as I could."

No one spoke. The crackle of static filled the cockpit.

"You're quite the professional," Renzo said suddenly. "Maybe we could meet up sometime and you can show me some tricks. I'm looking to learn."

"What?" Cohen yelped.

"Maybe. What's your name?" Anandi asked, some of the old lightness back in her voice.

Renzo cleared his throat. "Renzo Byrne."

Is he nervous? Phaira thought, incredulous.

A high-pitched titter echoed through the cockpit. "You don't remember me, do you?"

"What?" Renzo asked, confused.

"Heh. I'll call you sometime."

Then the line disconnected.

Renzo held up his hands to his siblings. "I don't know her, I swear."

"Sure, sure," Cohen mocked. He punched Phaira lightly on the arm. "Come on, Phair. You've got blood all over your face. I'll clean you up."

It took all of Phaira's willpower to hold her expression in place. But her mind reeled.

Find the missing Hitodama, Sydel wrote on the door of that freighter.

By finding Emir, Phaira gained the protection of Anandi, a powerful hacker. And now Anandi had just saved all their lives.

Sydel knew this was going to happen. She knew we needed someone like Anandi in our lives, to save us.

To find Sydel?

When Cohen looked to her to follow, Phaira forced a smile on her face. Still, as her body moved through the mass of debris, strewn throughout the ship, the same thoughts repeated themselves.

You can't stay here. You can't be around them. You can't be around anyone.

VI.

They flew for hours, heading west, following the coastline and its increasingly rocky edge, before Renzo finally chose to land in Karum, a farm town by the sea, sparsely populated, but quiet and calm. The opposite of how they all felt.

Phaira paced as the Volante settled into its landing gear. With every step, she willed her nerves to stop trembling. They wouldn't.

Her head itched. At Cohen's insistence, her forehead was covered with a thick bandage; she didn't have the heart to shrug off his concern. He stood several feet away now, on top of a hill, surveying the coastal landscape. Renzo jumped down from the ship and arched his back, wincing. His face was still pale, new lines grooved into his forehead.

Finally, they sat in a triangle, like children playing a game. Cohen hunched over, picking at the sea grass. Phaira sat with her knees to her chest. The salty wind was cold. She barely felt it. Renzo was the last to ease down to the ground, shifting to the side and unclicking his prosthetic. He sighed with relief as he set it aside. Phaira watched as he rubbed the edge of his thigh, the empty folds of his trouser leg.

We should have asked Sydel to help Ren, she mused. *He still has phantom pains. Why didn't I think of it?*

When the silence grew too awkward, Phaira spoke: "What are we going to do?"

"I thought you already decided what you wanted to do," Renzo said.

Phaira shot him a look, expecting to see anger or sarcasm, but his expression was neutral.

"I'm not sure," Phaira said slowly. "But whatever I end up doing, protection services, reconnaissance, I do know that I was trained to work in a team, not solo. So before I do anything else, I have to consider how - "

"I can do that." Cohen interjected.

"Do what?"

"Work with you."

Phaira and Renzo both shook their heads, but Cohen kept on: "You've already taught me, Phair. You showed me everything you learned in the military. I can do it."

"No way," Renzo shot back. "Are you forgetting what happened with Huma?"

"No, but I can make my own decisions," Cohen said sharply.

"It's not just that, Co." When his face fell, Phaira smiled to disarm him. "You're a half foot taller than me, and twice my weight. We move differently, we think differently. What you've learned from me isn't going to work in the real world, I realize that now."

"Then I'll do something else," Cohen said firmly. "I want to be a part of what you do."

"What about school?" Renzo interrupted. "I thought you liked the idea."

"School?" Phaira asked, confused. "What were you doing when I was gone?"

Cohen and Renzo glanced at each other. "There's a position I was looking at," Renzo confessed. "At one of the smaller universities in Daro. Lab technician. It's basic and boring, but it's steady. Plus, I could probably get Cohen accepted into some classes."

"Well, maybe," Cohen corrected. "Only if they were willing to overlook my record, which they wouldn't, so it doesn't matter anyways, because I'd rather to do this. Hey, what about Nox? He's a big guy. He can teach me." He pointed a finger at Renzo. "And don't get angry at me, because you were sure interested in that hacker girl. How are you going to use hacking in some lab?"

Renzo harrumphed and leaned back on his hands. "It's a good skill to have out here. I just thought I'd try something different."

"Something illegal," Phaira pointed out, hardly able to believe her words.

Renzo shrugged. "What does it matter? Besides, maybe if I learn the trade, I can get rid of that bounty contract myself."

Phaira flushed. She didn't know what to say to that.

"Not only that," Cohen added, his voice growing more excited. "But Ren and that girl can work together and find Sydel. And Huma. We can't forget about them. There's something more to all of this, you know there is - "

"I should have fought more," Renzo murmured, staring at the ground. "She was a nice girl. Co's right. We were supposed to take care of her. So we should make sure she's safe."

As Phaira listened with horror, her core continued to vibrate, like a string pulled taut and plucked. Nothing would stop: not the tremor in her hands, or the sparks in her brain alerting her to every little sound. Now her mind raced now with images of the future. Cohen would get killed. Renzo would be arrested and jailed for illegal activities. Phaira had already faced death ten times since the bounty went active; it wouldn't be long before someone was successful. It wasn't possible for them to become some kind of team. She wouldn't let it happen.

But Cohen has a resolute expression on his face, his thick arms crossed in front of his chest. And Renzo was looking to Phaira, waiting for her response.

They were serious about this. She had to play along.

So arrangements were made within the hour. If they were to work together, they had to learn how to protect themselves: as individuals, and as a unit.

Nox agreed to house Cohen and take a leave of absence from his position. He promised to train Cohen in conditioning, offense, defense and infiltration. A southbound shuttle would leave in an hour, scheduled to reach Daro in six hours.

Begrudgingly, and only after hearing about their experience with Huma and Sydel, Anandi agreed to teach Renzo the latest in hacking, cracking and information extraction. She was still coy about knowing him, only stating that she would tell him everything when he got back to the Mac, where she was currently stationed.

When he asked if she could teach him how to deactivate bounty listings, a few seconds of silence followed. Then a final, decisive click came through the speaker.

"Already done," came her smooth, high voice.

"What? You mean - just now, you - ?" Renzo exclaimed.

"I'll show you lots of tricks, once you get here."

An overnight ride was arranged, heading east, with Renzo as passenger. Phaira would leave the next day, taking a train southwest. As a girl, she won a poor-kid scholarship for a month of free martial arts training at a school near the Midland border. The master of the temple remembered her, and agreed to let her return, no doubt ready to point out all the flaws in her long-lapsed technique. Probably had some floors for her to scrub as well. But it was the only place they could think for her to stay.

Until the morning, she would remain in the old Volante. Then she would lock it and leave it behind for Nox to pick up; it was already marked as hostile, and the Hitodama could try and hack it again.

Decisions made, they returned to the ship and split off into their cabins. Phaira sat on the edge of her bed, looking at the bounty network on her Lissome, searching for her listing. No sign of it anywhere. The Macatias' contract was gone, just as Anandi said. It was over, just like that? Was it freedom? Or something worse?

Cohen was the first to leave. He shuffled from foot to foot as the shuttle pulled up. Phaira took his arm and squeezed it. "I'll be fine," she told him. "And you know Nox. He'll take care of you. And we'll talk all the time, I promise."

Renzo slapped Cohen on the back. "Behave yourself," he said gruffly. "Don't get into too much trouble."

"I'll see you guys soon, right?"

"Of course," Phaira and Renzo said simultaneously.

Phaira watched as her little brother visibly screwed up his courage and stepped onto the shuttle platform. And then he was gone.

"Weird," Phaira murmured to Renzo. She knew he felt the same undertow of worry when it came to their brother. With their father consumed by mental illness and their mother long dead of bone cancer, Cohen was their equal responsibility for years. It had been a long time since she and Renzo worked together for a common goal. That thread was still there, she could feel it: tenuous, but connected. It felt good.

"I know," Renzo said. "He'll be all right."

"Convincing me or you?"

Renzo just let out a long exhalation. "We're really doing this."

"I know it's not what you dreamed of, Ren."

Renzo shrugged. "What's left to dream? Lives change. We adapt."

"You might have fun with Anandi," Phaira said, noticing that the driver had pulled up.

"I might. Either way, it'd be good to learn something new. Get my brain forming neural pathways," Renzo said. His glasses glinted in the sunset. "You're going to the temple, right?"

"Yes, tomorrow, like I said," Phaira replied with a hint of annoyance.

"I'm just asking." Renzo glanced at the waiting transport, then back at Phaira. "Be careful."

She held back the shiver that threatened to escape across her skin. "You too."

And then she was alone, waiting for the night to come.

* * *

Hours later, Phaira was lying in bed, awake and replaying memories, when she heard a beep from the Lissome at her bedside.

She rolled over, and with a flick of her finger, projected the properties screen, looking at the cc readout. No one she recognized. Maybe something happened to one of her brothers. She had to check, so she flicked the option for audio.

Then she waited. The connection light blinked. The faint crackling sound began, and went on and on. There was definitely someone on the other end.

Then it occurred to her: who else would be on the other end of the line?

"Theron?"

"Nice guess."

188 | LOREN WALKER

"I guess there's not much point in telling you, once again, to stop calling me," Phaira said, pushing up to a seat.

"I thought you might be awake. And since you're in town, I thought you'd consider coming over."

"What?" Her gaze flew to the window, half-afraid of what she might see. "What are you talking about?"

"I live by the cliffs. You flew past my window."

"You do not live here," she accused.

His snicker rippled through the static. "I've been meaning to ask you something, anyways, so if you're not busy - "

Phaira stared at the Lissome as cold rushed over her body. The bounty was deactivated. Why was he still after her? Was this some kind of sick set-up to satisfy his ego, even if he wasn't getting paid for it? Some kind of male pride?

Then her thoughts shifted: how long was she going to run from every thug looking for a payout? Enough tip-toeing around. She couldn't go on with Theron's considerable shadow over her. Especially if her brothers were getting involved in her mess.

"Which house on the cliff?" she asked.

A pause. "You're coming now?"

"Why not?"

Another long pause. Then: "If you walk through the center of town, towards the water, it's the house with all the windows. On the cliff's edge." Then the connection broke.

Phaira surveyed her quarters: still a mess, no bags prepared for her journey tomorrow. She swung her legs over the edge of the bed. Should she be ready for a fight? She studied the pile of clothing in the corner. Subtle protection over her chest and neck, her regular street clothes and boots, and a single blade, concealed. That would be enough. She hoped it would be enough.

Outside the stars were shockingly clear. Phaira couldn't help but stare as she walked. Where she grew up, in the heart of industrial Daro, the swathes of florescent lighting made the sky purple and starless. But here, Phaira could make out the hazy aura of each constellation, even the three specks of other planets in the system, blue, red, green. She'd never seen them so clearly before.

When the town came into view, she kept to the outskirts. The ground turned to sand and rock, the crash of water drowning out any sound. She kept moving.

As she drew nearer, Phaira could make out the glint of windows, framed by rock; the house was built into the bluff, she realized.

Still, as she stared, her curiosity grew, tempted by the unspoken dare that bubbled under all those calls from Theron: *I can find you. Can you find me?*

Phaira caught sight of a terrace, jutting out over the cliff. Then a silhouette appeared, leaning over the railing, framed by an orange glow. "Come on up!" Theron called down to her.

Wary, she eyed the terrace, the boulders below it, the frames of the windows beside it. She could climb, hop from angle to angle, and make her way without much difficulty.

And he could kill her on the way up.

Let him try, she thought.

She leapt. Her hands slid down the glass panels, a split second of freefall until her fingertips caught the frames. Then, with a second coil of energy, Phaira sprang to the next foothold, and the next, moving by instinct, back and forth, up and up, using her upper body strength to swing and grab. Only when she neared the base of the veranda did she slow her movements, dangle for a second over the water crashing below, waiting of some kind of attack.

But there was none. So Phaira pumped her legs, and swung her body over the railing.

In the center of the veranda, a fire burned in an artisan stone pit. The smoke clouded over the stars, turning the edges of the sky violet.

He stood on the other end of the terrace, his broad back to her. Phaira waited, her hands ready.

Finally, Theron turned around. She couldn't see his face, only his outline of his frame. Then something flashed at his hip, highlighted by the fire: a glass, half-full and held by the fingertips.

"You have all this aggression and anger spilling out of you," Theron mumbled, so low that Phaira had to strain to hear. "You're like a walking bomb. And it's even worse now."

He rose his glass in her direction. "Look at you, you're practically jumping out of your skin!" he chortled. "It's amazing that no one has managed to kill you yet. Can't be that hard, even with your background."

He set his drink down on the floor. The fire shifted, and Phaira could make out his features now. Six and a half feet tall; slim but slightly hunched; straight, thick black hair, tied back. By the light of the fire, his square jaw and sharp cheekbones were even more pronounced, and even at this hour, he was meticulously dressed in sleek shirt and trousers.

"I have a proposition for you," he announced.

Theron crouched by a wooden crate in the corner. When he rose again, two dark items flew in Phaira's direction.

She caught them. Sparring gloves, she realized: thinly padded on the knuckles and back of the hand. Theron was already strapping on his two. Phaira stared at the gloves, then the man. He was insane.

"Okay," Phaira called out. "You're a mess! And drunk! You don't know what you're saying - "

"I really do," he interrupted. "Let's go."

"I'm not fighting you!"

"It's not a fight," Theron said, scratching under his chin. "If it were a fight, I wouldn't give you gloves, right? This is an experiment."

He held up his sheathed hands. "I created these. Impact-absorbing gear. So if you're about to land a hit, a reactionary pulse stops your fist from making contact with my face. Means we can spar at full force. I want a test run before the formal manufacturing. Come on."

Confused, Phaira glanced at the gloves again. They looked like any pair found in a training center.

But no, he was serious.

And she couldn't help it: she was intrigued.

"You still might get punched in the face," she finally said, slipping on the gloves.

"We'll see, won't we?" Theron's limbs seemed to undulate, that giant body settling into a stance, his hands up and open, level with his shoulders. Watching, Phaira kept her feet flat and her fists by her face. Theron had eight inches and at least a hundred pounds on her, plus a far superior reach. The odds were against her. She had to be aggressive: fast strikes, vulnerable points. Finish it as quickly as possible.

Theron darted forward. Phaira lashed out with a backhand. Theron pushed her arm aside and sent her reeling, off-balance. Phaira caught herself, pivoted, and went to clip him on the jaw.

But the impact gear did its job; her fist suddenly ricocheted back an inch from his mouth.

Theron took advantage of her surprise and grabbed her from behind, snaking an arm around her throat. She felt for his hair and jutted out her shoulder bone; with one swift jerk, she yanked his forehead into the point of the bone. At his bark of surprise, she managed to slip away. Theron rubbed at the red blotch on his forehead. Despite her better judgment, Phaira grinned at him, mentally daring him to try again.

Theron was the aggressor again, throwing out quick jabs. For such a tall man, he was incredibly agile. Blocking, she saw the opening: with the next punch, she shot out her arms, pinning his on either side, and then slid her hand down to grab his wrist. When she sharply torqued the joint, Theron ducked under, again and again, trying to loosen the grip, using his height and weight to bear down on her. Phaira managed to keep the hold, changing her balance, pivoting, throwing kicks into the backs of his knees.

Then, suddenly, his body slumped forward, like he lost consciousness. With a squawk, Phaira released his wrist and stumbled backwards, falling hard on her tailbone. Theron landed on his knees next to her. His head bowed, and his shoulders started to shake.

Hotly embarrassed, Phaira wiggled away as Theron continued to laugh. She burned with anger, but she was also humiliated. What he did was stupid and childish, but it worked.

In one fluid motion, Theron rocked backwards into a squat, his long arms over his knees. "Truce," he announced. "Okay?"

"Who taught you that toddler defense?" she asked him haughtily.

"What did you do, sharpen your shoulder bone?" he retorted, pointing to his forehead.

Phaira held her breath for several seconds to calm her breathing. Then she asked: "What's the proposition?"

Theron smiled. "Where are you headed tomorrow?"

Phaira thought about lying, but shrugged as she ripped off the gloves. "A temple where I took some lessons as a kid. And no, I'm not telling you where."

"And what are you going to do there, babysit?"

"I appreciate the concern," Phaira said sourly. "But I don't have other options."

"That's not an option at all," Theron pointed out. "If you have a history with the place, with any place, you can be tracked down."

He wasn't wrong. She knew that when Renzo suggested the temple, but she planned to take a detour on the way....

"I think you should stay here instead."

Phaira couldn't do anything but blink for several seconds. "What?" she finally managed.

"This town has less than five hundred residents," Theron said. "No one knows you're here. You can hide out and rest. You look terrible, you know."

"Gee, thanks," Phaira shot back. "And where would I say I'm staying? There are a few people who will ask."

"I thought of that. There's a Jala monastery ten kilometers from here. Gated community. I'll introduce you if you want. A place to go to if you feel the need."

Phaira avoided his eyes as she rolled to her feet. "The answer is no."

"Why not?" He sounded hurt.

"Because you're crazy!" Phaira exclaimed. "I don't know why you keep contacting me, or why you even asked me here. You said you're 'into clarity,' so stop being so vague and be straight about what you want." As she said the last part, her nerves rippled. She had no idea what to expect.

"Okay," Theron said. He tipped backwards so he sat cross-legged on the tile, folding his large hands in his lap. "I'm interested in funding your start-up expenses. To become an independent contractor, so to speak."

For a moment, the ocean winds died down. Phaira realized that her mouth was open in shock. She quickly closed it. "I thought you were a bounty hunter."

"I've mentioned a few times now that I'm not."

"Then who are you?" Phaira shot back. "Who are you, really?"

His amber eyes shifted; he was weighing what to say. It made her all the more suspicious. "Is that why you took me to Midland? Is that why you wanted to spar? To test me, guilt me into becoming your hired thug? No thanks."

"It's just an option, Phaira," Theron said. "The same goes for the offer to stay. I wouldn't invest in you now, anyways. You're a mess."

Phaira's temper rose with every comment. It bruised her ego to admit it, but he was right. She was running aimless. Just like Cohen and Renzo, she too needed to be trained on how to survive. What she knew wasn't enough anymore. Doubly true when it came to Huma or the Hitodama or other sects.

"If all of this is an elaborate plan to shoot me, just tell me now."

The fire behind Theron swelled, casting him into a silhouette again. "I'm not a fan of firearms in general."

"That includes knives too," she quipped.

"I have no violent intentions, Phaira. Truly."

"Why do this, then? Why do any of this?"

Theron shrugged. "I think you have the potential to make a difference. Be a significant player in the world."

It was probably the highest compliment she had ever received.

But she couldn't possibly trust him or anything he said.

Then Phaira's mind clicked on another path: why should that matter? She didn't trust anyone, anyways. But he was a skilled fighter; he had skills in information gathering, some connection to the underworld, by the sound of it. Anything that could give an advantage might be worth a day or two. And if there were any hints of betrayal, she wouldn't hesitate to take him down. She was free of mekaline – no one would get the advantage over her again.

"Do I get my own room?" she asked.

He smiled. "Whatever you want."

VII.

When dawn broke over the shoreline, Phaira sent encrypted messages to her brothers and to the temple compound, explaining that she'd chosen a new location to rest. She didn't specify that it was the farm town, but she promised to be careful and to remain concealed. Then she locked the old Volante behind her, slung her bag over her shoulder and began the long walk back to the glass house.

Theron waited for her by the wall of windows, holding the door open.

Phaira followed him through the house, up one flight of stairs, then another. Neither spoke. Their footsteps echoed through the open space.

Finally, he stopped at an ornate wooden door: unusually tall, like all the other doors they passed. *Custom-made for him*, she thought. *This really is his place. He must be from a rich family, to have a house like this at his age; he can't be more than thirty.*

"Here," he said abruptly, gesturing at the handle. Then he walked away, turning the corner, out of sight.

Okay, then. Phaira thought, unnerved. She pushed on the handle and peeked inside.

It was a small but luxurious bedroom, with plush curtains, soft white carpets, and one enormous bed shrouded with a sheer canopy, so lavish that Phaira felt dirty in

198 | LOREN WALKER

comparison. So she dropped her satchel just inside the door, and left to explore the rest of the house.

Every room was expensively furnished in delicate whites and grays, gleaming metals, granite floors. Art and foreign artifacts were strategically placed. There was a glittering kitchen that didn't look to possess a single fingerprint. The whole place smelled of cotton and ocean air, pleasant enough. Aesthetically, every inch was beautiful, but it didn't seem like much of a home. And the silence of the place was jarring: not a sound, not a stirring in any corner.

Wait, she realized. *Where did he go?*

She turned in place, listening hard. Nothing.

He's gone.

I'm alone in this place.

Her mind reeled. She needed air.

Padding onto the veranda, the sound of the ocean was a relief. Enough light had risen for her to make out the shadows of fish in the water, the orange rust and spidery grass growing in the crevices of the rock. Phaira squinted, searching the landscape. There was no sign of Theron in any direction.

Phaira was used to cities and smoky air. Out here, when she took in a deep breath, her lungs seized, and she coughed and coughed. But she stayed outside, watching the waves roll in for a long time. Then she made her way back inside.

When Phaira locked the bedroom door, she also pushed a dresser in front. Still, she kept her knife at her thigh as she kicked off her boots and crawled onto the canopy bed. She would just close her eyes for a little while. But sinking into the soft warmth, within seconds everything went dark.

When she blinked and saw nothing but white, she panicked. Then she remembered where she was. She lifted her head to study the door. The dresser hadn't moved. And the light was dimmer now in the room: late afternoon, perhaps. Was she still alone?

"Hello?" she called out into the hall. Smoothing down her mussed hair, she rubbed her face to jolt awake her senses. *Wake up. It's bad enough you fell asleep so quickly in a crazy man's house.*

"You're awake."

Theron's voice came out of nowhere. Phaira jumped, her hands flying into fists.

"I was coming up to invite you to train," the voice continued, his tone nonchalant. "If you have the strength."

He was just around the corner, by the sound of it. Phaira stayed in the doorframe. "Train? Where?" she called, feeling ridiculous. "Outside?"

"Come on." She heard his footsteps, growing more and more distant.

Phaira paused, wondering if she should just go back inside. But her gnawing curiosity won out again. She followed the sound until she finally caught sight of his tall frame.

In silence, they went down one flight of stairs, then another, and still another. The final flight opened up

into a dim, expansive basement, gray-walled and sparsely outfitted. The blue floor was thinly padded, pliant under Phaira's bare feet, but sturdy. *I could take a fall on this,
and the impact would be absorbed,* she mused.

But are there exits in this place? her instincts warned. *This
could be the basement of a serial killer: soundproofed, bodies hidden
in the cellar.*

"I thought I could show you my martial arts technique," Theron's voice broke into her thoughts. He
sounded almost shy, standing in the center of the basement, wearing black cotton pants and shirt, and looking
sober this time. "It's based on redirecting energy to both
attack and subdue. You've probably learned about it."

Phaira's eyebrows drew together. This was one of the
strangest experiences of her lifetime.

"Okay," she said cautiously, easing down to the floor.
"Why not? Show me."

Theron's demonstration was impressive: as he moved
through an independent string of movements, each posture rolled into each other, elegant and fully expressed.
It looked easy enough. But Phaira remembered how nim-
bly he unbalanced her on the veranda. So her mind took
photograph after photograph, cataloguing every position of every muscle. Then she stood and joined him on
the floor. Theron restarted his sequence. Phaira stood
behind him and mimicked his movements. Dipping, flex-
ing, flowing and receding, Phaira felt a bit silly. Quickly,
though, she began to realize how powerful this kind of

offensive could be, to use the opponent's energy against them instead of relying on pure aggression.

"Who was your teacher?" Phaira asked when they finally took a rest.

Theron paused before replying. "My grandfather. Now we spar. Shall I get the rebound gloves?"

"No," Phaira said quickly. "They're too weird for me. No offense," she added.

"Noted. No gloves then."

After that, there was little conversation between the two of them, save for quiet comments or brief questions. Yet as the hours went on, a sort of bliss washed over Phaira, a satisfaction that she hadn't felt in a long time. She always loved the artistry of hand-to-hand combat. And she had to admit that Theron was an excellent teacher, patient and concise with his explanations.

They chose to stop when the space grew stagnant with humidity, and they were both drenched in sweat. Phaira was exhausted, but ecstatic. As she pressed her face into a towel, wondering what would happen next, she heard the creak of weight on wood, then the sound of a door opening. He was going onto the veranda.

Well, she wouldn't stay in that basement alone. And the thought of cool night air was too tempting to avoid.

The sky was clear, a thousand pinpricks of light strewn across the pitch-black; Phaira could even see the dusty, brilliant sweep of galaxies. The ocean had calmed, too, its waves a steady brush against the rocks.

Theron lit a fire in the pit. He remained in a crouch, gazing into the flames. Phaira moved to the farthest corner, leaning over the railing, taking in the smoking wood and salty air.

Neither spoke. The crackle of the fire merged with the rush of the water below, a soothing white noise. It was peaceful, in a strange way. And for once, Phaira chose not to question the moment.

* * *

Within the hour, Theron disappeared again. This time, Phaira took advantage of his absence, wandering the cavernous house. She found prepared meals in the kitchen, stored in cold: real, fresh meals, not the cheap meal packs she had eaten for months. The taste was euphoric. Then Phaira found a washroom with a large white bath, and with a chair lodged under the doorknob, she happily sank into hot water. It felt wonderful to soak and scrub clean. After, she made her way back to her room, fell onto the bed and immediately fell into a deep, dreamless sleep.

Once again, she woke at sunset. This time, Phaira focused on her own training routine, lapsed over the past few days: she ran up and down flights of stairs, and used her body weight for resistance. Then she taped her hands, tied up her hair and headed to the basement.

He was already there, his back to the stairway. Though eager for the night to begin, Phaira lowered her voice to a bored tone. "Don't you ever sleep?"

"Maybe four hours a night." Theron didn't turn around as he continued: "I thought you should show me how to work with your Calis firearms."

Shock rushed through Phaira, followed by a sting of embarrassment. "I can't. Someone stole them."

"Who?" Theron asked, looking over his shoulder.

The memory of ice-cold fingers in her brain made her stiffen. "It doesn't matter," she said shortly. "I don't have them anymore."

"Too bad," Theron said. "I've never worked with them. I hear they're incredibly difficult, but powerful."

Think. Get him off this track.

"What if I show you submissions?" she finally blurted out. "I used to specialize in them: joint locks, pins, throws. Not that you get much use out of it in the military, of course, but..." Phaira trailed off, nervous again. "I can show you."

"Okay," he agreed. "Lead the way."

So Phaira began to explain the muscles and bones of the body, how they connected, and what torques would cause excruciating pain, loss of sensation or blackouts. She made Theron stand up, and demonstrated as she talked. Then he mimicked her movements. Again and again, they grasped each other's wrists, shoulders, hands and knees, working the joints and tendons until the movements were smooth. His limbs were remarkably flexible for a man, though not enough to avoid a grimace of pain as she expertly twisted his wrist to the breaking point. Holding the lock, the shades of pink inside his hand caught her attention. Heavy scar tissue lay in the center of his palm, pink cross-lines, old scars, but deep ones. A hell of an accident, or deliberate.

There was a huge element of trust in working so closely together, and Phaira could sense a softening between the two of them, even as they worked to hurt each other. He complimented her on her in-depth knowledge and she smiled at him, surprised at herself. On a break, Theron asked her about the instructors in the armed forces, and the levels of training she had undertaken. She shared a little about her years in the military, and her initiation into active duty on her eighteenth birthday: how scores of men and women had dropped out, and by the end of several weeks, Phaira was one of four soldiers remaining, ready to be sent overseas.

The morning came, gray and hazy. Phaira's bones ached, but it felt good. This time, Theron didn't bother with the veranda. Instead, as soon as she walked upstairs, he offered her a glass of something clear. She took it after a moment's hesitation. Theron had one in his hand already. Then he turned and walked outside.

Through the windows, Phaira saw him emerge onto the beach, walking along the shore, away from the town center, to the edge of the rocky peninsula at the end of the beach. Phaira watched him as he made his way down the length, stepped with the knowledge of one who had made the trek many times before: beautifully nimble, without a trace of hesitation. Then Phaira flushed at her thoughts, sniffed the liquid in the tumbler, determined that its contents would get her good and inebriated, and followed him.

By the time she made her way to the peninsula, Theron was already at the farthest point, placing his glass on an adjacent rock, perched on top of a massive boulder. He didn't look back at her as she approached, slipping in her bare feet, trying not to spill her drink. She couldn't hear anything but the ocean on all sides. Finally, she stumbled to the boulder and hoisted herself onto it, and next to him.

Their legs dangled over the edge, a foot of space between them. The wind was stronger here; there was no option for conversation. All the better.

Staring at the sea, Phaira had a sudden impulse: how easy to just reach out and shove Theron with her foot. Did he know how to swim? If he fell the right way, he might be knocked unconscious and drown. Did he fight the same urge? Was this all a set-up for a surprise death?

Then fatigue overwhelmed her. If he planned to kill her that night, she didn't care.

Phaira leaned back on her hands and let her head drop back to look at the sky. The moons were out tonight, pale pink around the edges. Pretty.

She had another vision, then. If Theron's shadow were to cover her, if he were to kiss her, she would let him. Wind her hands through his hair, yank it out of that red cord that held it back. It had been a long time since she had been touched. The desire for it was sudden and overpowering.

Phaira didn't move, though, and kept her eyes closed.

In the days that followed, Phaira sat on that boulder often, watching the water. And sometimes instead of training, she went back to her quarters, locked the door and slept for hours. Her physical body was exhausted, far more than she had realized. But, strangely, she felt a sense of sanctuary in this place, a peace she had been unable to find in the old Volante, even with the support of her brothers. Her body began to settle, her mind slowed to a cool, dreamy pace. Thoughts drifted in and out: about Sydel, Renzo, Cohen, Nican. How this new life would work, and where they were going to go from here. What Theron's mouth tasted like; her embarrassment at those fantasies; her musing on whether he had the same thoughts. And she worked over the whole situation with the Hitodama, from the first contact to the final attack. There was something unresolved about it all, but she couldn't figure it out.

"You're not concentrating," Theron said flatly one night, landing an easy strike against her jaw.

Phaira crossed her arms, fingers tapping on her bare biceps. "I have something on my mind."

"What is it?"

Phaira considered. She hadn't planned on bringing it up with anyone, but why not? "So, hypothetically - "

"Hypothetically?" Theron countered.

"Yes, hypothetically," she shot back. Then she chewed her lip for a moment before continuing. "Why would someone kidnap an old man and hide him away, with no attempt at abuse, no ransom request, or contact with anyone at all?"

Theron took the question seriously. Several moments passed before he answered: "Do the two know each other?"

"Not as far as I know. And there was no conversation between them, so says the captive."

"Blackmail, then."

"I told you, there were no demands for his release."

"There's more than one way to blackmail," Theron pointed out. "Silence can make a person to do anything for an answer."

Anandi, Phaira thought suddenly. The whole thing had nothing to do with the Hitodama; those murdered members just got in the way. Saka kidnapped Emir to get to Anandi. To force her into servitude? She remembered, then, what Anandi said at the Hitodama gathering, when they were hiding from law enforcement: "Know the name? You've never heard of me?"

And the conversation Saka was having: "You don't need her, Keller."

"You get the answer you needed?" Theron's voice brought her back to the present.

"Yes." She winced as she turned her head from side to side. That strike from Theron had landed in just the spot to strain her neck tendon. *It's always the little stupid moments that screw up your body,* she thought: *a trip over a step, a grain of sand in your eye -*

"Stop. Let me."

Before she knew it, Theron had taken three long strides and his hand hovered over her neck. She flinched and backed away.

Theron sighed. "I'm not going to kill you. Can I please work out your strain?"

She believed him, oddly enough. But she still walked away, to the other end of the room.

"I thought we were past this?" he called out with frustration.

What did he mean by that? She kept her eyes on the wall, her palm cupping the side of her throat.

He didn't understand. He didn't have the same instant panic as she did when it came to the neck. People never considered the throat in battle, but for Phaira, it was a prime example of the vulnerable human body: the airway, the jugular vein, the cervical spine, all contained in one square foot. After the incident with the angry mob, the shots fired, the wooden splinters lodged in her throat and the scars left behind, she always kept it covered.

But she didn't want to fall back into the abyss again. She didn't want to ruin what was happening here, whatever this was with Theron. It had been so long since she felt any connection with someone.

So Phaira unzipped the collar of her sleeveless shirt. Then she pulled away the material to expose the left side of her throat and waited. Her eyes remained on the opposite wall, her teeth clenched to keep from chattering.

When his warm hands landed on her shoulder, a small spasm of panic ran through her. His thumbs found either side of the strained tendon and pressed along the length of the sinew. At the touch, Phaira battled a sudden, maddening urge to cry. But as her neck began to loosen, something began to build in her stomach, relief or fear or desire, she wasn't sure. It would be easy to open her eyes and reach for him, though. Forget about everything outside of this house, fall into the easy routine of nothingness. She never wanted to leave this bubble.

"Better?" came Theron's voice.

Phaira nodded with a tight smile. His shadow moved away.

Phaira rubbed the unknotted tendon. Then she touched the skin at the base of her throat. It was as sensitive as a sunburn.

Quickly, she zipped up her collar again. Then Phaira settled onto her back leg, raising her hands again in a defensive stance. "Come on," she instructed. "Back to it."

VIII.

Phaira woke to the smell of smoke. As her eyes adjusted to the light, she sank down into the warm bed. Her ankles cracked as she stretched. The dawn air was cool, running down her throat, coupled with the faint scent of smoke. Theron had lit another fire.

No, wait: it was afternoon, she could tell by the position of the sun. And the smoke burned her nostrils. Chemical.

Phaira slid out of bed, pulling a tunic over her head. Unlocking the door to her suite, she peered around the frame. No sounds, no movement, just the shine of spotless floors.

Her legs and feet bare, Phaira padded down into the luxurious room with the wall of windows. The glass was cold under her hand as she searched the horizon.

The Volante was burning.

Past the fish houses and fields, Phaira could see the speck of Nox's old transport, consumed with violent orange flames, black smoke rolling into the blue sky.

Something is fueling that fire. It's moving too fast. But there's no accelerant on board that would ignite like that by accident.

Phaira stepped away from the windows. First thing was to get out of there and find somewhere to hide. The Macatias must have issued a new contract on her, one that Anandi hadn't seen. If the hunters had already searched the vessel and chosen to torch it, they were already too close. Theron would have to understand; in fact, it didn't matter if he understood or not. She had to leave. Maybe use one of the artifacts in this room to get some rana...

A knock reverberated through the house. The cool marble floor quivered under her feet.

Phaira swore under her breath. She slid her back along the wall until she reached a weaponry wall display. A longblade was featured among others: intricate carvings along its hilt, ancient and expensive, no doubt. She ripped it off the wall and checked the blade. Viciously sharp.

A knock came again: harder this time, followed by the sound of a drill. They were breaking in.

Phaira gave the longblade a few test swings: light and pliable, perfectly balanced. If she could incapacitate the hunters long enough, she could make an escape without having to kill anyone.

"Phaira." The sound of her name travelled through the room, hushed but insistent. It was Theron, holding open a closet door on the far side of the room. He pressed an index finger to his lips and gestured for her to come.

Bearing the longblade with two hands, Phaira shook her head at him. What was he thinking? To hide in a closet, it was suicide. "I can manage," she whispered. "The Macatias never send - "

"Not them," he said through his teeth.

He mouthed the next word slowly: *Hitodama.*

The sound of glass breaking echoed up the stairwell.

Please, he mouthed, his eyes wide and flashing.

There wasn't time to argue. Phaira sprinted to Theron, ducking under his arm. He shut the door, sealing away the light.

Blackness, and the sound of their breath. Theron stood behind her, his fingertips on her elbow, barely touching, but still sending a message: *Be still.*

Outside, Phaira could hear crashing sounds, footsteps and unintelligible voices. Inside, the pitch darkness threw off Phaira's senses; it felt like everything was getting smaller. By the feel and smell, the space was filled with old, dusty boxes, and with barely four feet of space to move in. Stupid, stupid. Easy targets in here. Theron was a fool. If she could see his face, she would be glaring at it. Or giving it a smack. Phaira's anxiety grew, like an animal desperate for air. Adrenaline burned in her muscles and lungs. *You don't know!* Phaira wanted to yell at Theron. *You don't know what you've done. We're dead. And Ren and Co, I never got to tell them...*

Then Theron's fingers slid over her wrist. Startled, Phaira went to yank her arm away, but he held fast, pressing his thumb inside her palm. He directed her open hand over to something rough and flat with a fastener: some kind of storage container. To the muffled backdrop of shattering glass and pounding hammers, Theron pushed her hand under the lid. Her fingers brushed cool metal, ridged edges, a distinctive trigger. It wasn't the only one either; there were at least six others in that container, neatly stored and waiting. She lifted one pistol an inch off its resting place: lighter than she expected, but modern in its design and brand-new by its smell. She felt for the gun clip. Loaded.

The sounds of chaos continued. The room grew warm and stagnant. She focused on the cool firearm in her hand, the sheathed longblade in the other, and Theron's solid frame behind her. Waiting for that burst of sudden light.

But the door never opened.

And suddenly, she realized that the house was silent.

Theron opened the closet door, letting in a crack of vertical light. Blinking, Phaira glanced around at the stockpile of weapons behind her. There were several more containers in there; filled with what else, she couldn't even imagine.

But outside, the room was destroyed. The great wall of windows contained a hundred spider webs, the cracks stretching from panel to panel. The rugs were trampled with dirt and oil. All of the artifacts were smashed, stomped on, tossed into the corners. Curtains lay in piles, shredded on the floor. There were even holes in the walls, the drywall yanked away.

Phaira surveyed the damage, aching with guilt. The house was strange, and cold, but it was still someone's home. The Hitodama put out a hit on because of what she'd done to them. There would always be someone in the crossfire.

Theron remained by the closet, hunched into himself. Phaira laid down the pistol and the longblade on the floor. Then she spoke carefully: "I'm sorry. Your house."

He said nothing.

Phaira looked down at her bare feet. "I should go," she muttered. "They might come back again."

"Don't." Theron's voice was strained.

His back heaved. Then he crumbled.

Phaira swore, diving to grab him as he fell. Twisting in the effort to keep his head from hitting the floor, she landed hard on her hip, gasping as pain shot up her spine.

Theron continued to twitch in her grasp. His body weight pinned her to the ground. Phaira slid one hand around his jerking forehead, the other around his chest, and held tight.

Please stop, she begged internally as his tremors went on and on. *Please stop. Please. I don't know what to do.*

Then, just as quickly as it started, Theron stopped shaking. His head turned, his eyes drifting over her face, unfocused. He blinked slowly, then rapidly, and scrambled off Phaira. His long black hair hung stringy around his face, and his hands trembled. He clenched them into fists and slid to the wall, leaning his temple to the metal, facing away from her.

Phaira stared at his back, bewildered. Did he just have a seizure? Or some kind of panic attack?

She didn't know what to say. So she held onto her elbows, gazing at the open closet behind him.

"They should have found us in there. Easily," she murmured. "How could they miss it?"

"There's a reason - why I wanted you to get inside," came Theron's ragged voice. "It's designed to protect - it alters brainwaves - makes it invisible to the outside eye - and protects against psychic attack, when needed - "

"You mean Ekos?" Phaira blurted out.

Theron's head lifted from the wall. He twisted at the waist, so his amber eyes met hers. "You know about them?"

Phaira faltered. Should she tell him? She still battled the impulse to run away. But she had never told anyone what happened.

"A week ago, we encountered a group of people - followers." The words were so awkward, rolling off her tongue. "They were - they had abilities that I've never seen before. They knocked us out. Then their leader broke into my mind and pulled out my worst - the most terrible - "

Phaira wet her lips with her tongue, willing her voice to be steady.

Then Theron drew his right thumb down his forehead, and his hand turned into a claw, dragging across the top of his skull.

"The cold, right?"

Phaira's eyes prickled with tears. Horrified, she blinked to push them away.

Theron nodded, sliding closer to her. "Who was it?"

"An older woman. Short white hair," Phaira said haltingly. "Huma. They took the girl from that commune, Sydel. I don't know where. We can't find her. They've disappeared."

Shame flooded through her, too much to bear any longer.

Phaira rolled to her feet and strode out of the destroyed room, intent on packing her few belongings and getting as far away as possible.

But Theron followed, his long gait quickly catching up to hers. "You didn't have any way to defend against that kind of assault. There's no disgrace in what happened, Phaira."

There is if I continue to do nothing about it.

Phaira stopped short at the thought. Theron nearly ran into her back, he was following so closely. He looked even more confused when she stuck out her hand.

"Thank you for everything," she said sincerely. "But I have to go."

He stared at her outstretched hand. Then his face twisted into a scowl. "Really? You're leaving, just like that? Did you forget our agreement?"

"We had no agreement," Phaira said, insulted. "I don't work for you, and I don't need your dirty money."

Those words stung him. Theron took a step back. "You have a strange sense of loyalty," he said flatly. "You barely knew that girl."

Phaira opened her mouth to argue, but his words were true.

"No one else is going to get her," she said finally. "But she said her elder was an Eko, too, back in Jala Communia. If I can convince Yann to show me - "

"You're going back there?" Theron asked, incredulous. "When you know what that man is capable of? He's dangerous."

"No more dangerous than anyone else," Phaira countered.

Theron's amber eyes went cold. His jawline became a hard right angle.

A shame, Phaira thought. *We're the same in a lot of ways.*

"Look," she said, keeping her tone as neutral as possible. "Yann knows Sydel, and he knows how an Eko works. I don't. It's a start. Even if I wanted to work for you, I'd be a useless investment if my mind can be easily destroyed."

She paused, considering. "You could come with me, you know. Learn how to protect yourself so it never happens -"

"No," Theron said. "Those people can't be trusted."

"Fine," Phaira replied, exasperated. She twisted her hair behind her head as she padded back to her bedroom, avoiding the shards of glass and plotting her strategy. What was the best route to get back to the Communia? And how would she convince Yann to talk to her?

Her quarters were similarly torn apart: the mattress upturned, pictures smashed, grease stains across the walls. Fortunate that she had so few possessions.

As Phaira laced up her boots and bundled her remaining items into a satchel, she rehearsed her goodbye to Theron. She wondered if she should try to say thank you again, or if it would be better to just nod and turn away.

But the house was silent again. And on her threshold lay the sheathed longblade, and something small and square wrapped in velvet.

Inside was a fresh Lissome, one ticket for passage on a charter flight to the Midland border, and an identification packet with her picture and the name Ikani Mala.

How romantic, she thought. *The means to disappear completely.*

* * *

Your flight today is on the latest in travel transports, with modern enhancements for speed and fluidity through experimental photon rockets... So read the information card in the seat. Still, just like Theron's house in the cliffs, the commercial vessel was glittering, but cold and overlaid with the smell of sterilization. Phaira kept her head low. Her foot slid over to touch the longblade stored at her feet.

Outside, the landscape grew flatter and full of red, green and browns. She had changed worlds in less than an hour. Now she stood on solid ground, waiting for the shuttle that would take her across the Midland border.

To hike out to the Communia, she reminded herself. *To ask for the mercy of Yann. This is not going to be fun.*

Using the new Lissome, Phaira sent a message to her brothers, explaining her choice to seek training by

Sydel's elder. She promised to check in again shortly with her status, as well as ascertain theirs.

Then she added to her message to Renzo: "Stay close to Anandi. Stay out of sight. Find whatever information you can find on Huma, Ekos, any of them. Whatever it takes.

"We're going after Sydel."

PART THREE

I.

When he tried to open his eyes, the brilliant light burned his retinas. Then his senses began to awaken. Rough sheets under his body, over his body. His tongue was fuzzy, and when he tried to make a sound, the back of his throat was bone-dry.

"Ren?"

A voice to his right. Wait, where was he? Why was he in bed?

"Can you hear me?"

That voice again. Renzo turned his head to the right. It felt like pushing through sand. He tried again to make a sound, any sound.

"Drink this." Something brushed his lips, cool and plastic: a straw. Cold water flooded into his mouth.

If he opened his eyes little by little, the light didn't hurt as badly. The white room grew clearer. Hospital room. Machines, monitors, tubes. His senses grew sharper by the second: the smell of antiseptic, his unwashed skin and his scalp. A headache pulsed through his skull. His jaw itched. Renzo touched his chin against the skin of his collarbone to feel. Decent growth, at least a week's worth. The backs of his hands felt heavy and irritated; a series of tubes snaked across the bed and ended in the back of his right hand. He didn't need to look at the other hand to know that it matched. One of the monitors began to beep nervously.

"Ren, it's okay," he heard Cohen's voice. "You're in the hospital. Phair's coming."

Phaira? His sister had been in the South for the last three months. Why was she coming? It must be serious. His head itched. Why? He could barely keep his eyes open.

"Ren?"

The light in the room had faded. Night? His mouth was dry again. The headache had subsided, replaced with a swimming, dizzy sensation. Some kind of pain medication, no doubt.

Phaira leaned over him. Her deep blue hair swung over her face, a clean-cut line from jaw to nape. She wore her military uniform, dark grey and yellow trim. She'd been in the sun; her skin was darker, her eyes even paler. There were fresh scars across her knuckles, a healing cut on her forehead.

Moistening his lips with his tongue, Renzo rasped: "Bad?"

Phaira's fingers gripped the heavy material of her uniform sleeve. "We should wait for the doctor."

"No," Renzo coughed. "What."

"Do you remember anything?"

Renzo shook his head.

"You were attacked," Phaira said. "You've been in a coma for over a week."

"Who."

"They don't know yet."

"Bad?"

"They hit you in the head. Then they kept - " Phaira faltered. "There was swelling, and internal bleeding."

Motor skills then. Renzo went to move his right fingers. They lifted, followed by the left hand. Relief washed over him.

Then he thought about moving his toes. The left: he could feel them rubbing against the sheet fabric. The right - the right. He didn't feel the sheet. It felt like they were moving, but -

"Ren."

But he wouldn't look. He couldn't look.

* * *

When Renzo could stay awake for longer periods of time, the assigned physician gave him a rundown of all his injuries, surgical interventions, recovery and rehabilitation needs. As the doctor spoke, Renzo flexed the muscles around his right knee. The knee was there. But when he instinctually tried to harden his calf muscle, he reprimanded himself: *Nothing is there, stupid.*

Between Phaira and the physician, Renzo put together the events. He had been hit repeatedly with a blunt object, cracking the skull and impacting the frontal, parietal and temporal lobes. More damage was done to his right leg with the same blunt object. Then his calf and foot were crushed under a ground transport. A pedestrian found Renzo unconscious and barely breathing. Cohen received the first call from the medical center. Then a telegram was sent to Phaira in her post in the South.

Renzo could barely comprehend any of it. It sounded like a story, like something that had happened to someone else. Why him? Why would be targeted? He lived in one of the poorest neighborhoods in Daro. Even with his position at the university, he had no rana on him. He went to work and came back to the apartment that he shared with Cohen. Once a week, he spoke via satellite to Phaira if she were available. He made simple dinners when his brother got home from his job at the quarry. They lived small, but secure lives, more secure than they could have ever hoped for.

But Renzo could only remember the hours before the assault. That night, he was hunched over his apprentice desk for hours, working numbers, analyzing patterns and trying to crack open their meaning. As the sun began to set outside, he reached for his REM injector and pressed the tip into the hollow in his wrist. It would give the benefit of a few hours of sleep in ten minutes. When the chemicals wove through his blood, he allowed himself to dream, just for this moment, of something other than numbers.

Hours later, he was walking to the public shuttle, wondering whether Cohen was home from the quarry, what was in the apartment for food...

And then, nothing.

Memory loss was normal. Due to the location of the injury, he could expect to experience notable changes in his attention and concentration, his ability to calculate and recognize patterns. The physicians were hopeful that his short–term memory would recover. Over and over, the doctors cited how lucky he was. Renzo listened, he took it in, he played polite and thanked them for their help. He also deferred their offers to set up rehabilitation therapy appointments, or begin the process to fit him for a prosthetic.

Phaira or Cohen stayed in the room with him, sleeping on the cramped chair by the bedside, telling him nostalgic stories from their childhood to try and get him to smile. He knew they were relieved that he was alive and mostly intact. But Renzo was gone.

At least, the person he used to be was gone. He was a poor boy who happened to be brilliant at cracking codes, under the tutelage of some of the top mathematical minds in the country. He was the one who got out, who rose above the pollution and poverty of the neighborhood. His future planned before he left his teenage years.

And now: nothing.

Everything that made him special was gone.

Some of his colleagues showed up at the hospital: bearing flowers, slapping him on the shoulder, with big smiles glazed with anxiety.

Yes, Renzo thought. *Your worst fear in front of you. Thankful that it's my brain that's gone, not yours.*

It didn't surprise him when those visits grew less and less frequent. Curiously, it didn't upset him much either.

After a few days, the nurses ignored Renzo's protests and began to wrap his right thigh in tight bandages, shaping the stump so it would fit into a prosthetic. They sent in a physical therapist to exercise his body, forced him to switch positions to prevent bedsores.

The law patrol came in with questions and an account of the basic procedure followed: looking over surveillance, searching for eyewitnesses, no weapon found, not yet. They asked him the same questions again and again, clearly impatient with his memory loss.

During the interview, Renzo's eyes flitted over to Phaira, who watched from the corner. He couldn't interpret the look on her face, if it was despondent or destructive. But she never blinked.

* * *

Sweating and cursing, Renzo managed to swing his legs over the edge of his bed. His left foot touched the ground. It was unnerving to not feel the cold ripple up his right leg, too. But he was sick of the scratchy sheets and the constant smell of bleach.

As Renzo eased his body into the adjacent wheelchair, Cohen gripped the handles, holding it steady. Phaira waited by the door, out of uniform and in street wear, a hood pulled over her head, looking like her old, sullen self.

The day was overcast: a good thing, as direct sun would have been too intense for his first venture outside. Not that there was much to see. Though the medical center was new and gleaming, the neighborhood was still a wreck. Abandoned warehouses spread in all directions, with sporadic stores and stalls crumbling in-between. Rusty trolleys and Subito landbikes rumbled by. Renzo hated this part of town, but he understood that Cohen and Phaira wanted him to experience some normality. At some point, he had to return to the real world and figure out the rest of his life.

As they walked, there was some kind of activity at the end of the street. Renzo craned his neck to see, trying to ignore the warning throb in his temples. A crowd gathered around the doors of a local diner.

Suddenly, the masses erupted with shrill screams, mostly girls. Looking, Cohen tilted the chair to the side. Renzo grabbed the armrests. "Hey!"

"Sorry," Cohen said sheepishly. "Wonder what's going on over there."

Phaira kicked her foot against the concrete. "Does it matter?"

"Let's go see!" Cohen said brightly, throwing Phaira a sharp look.

Anything other than hospital talk, Renzo thought as they approached the chaos.

There was a break in the crowd. Renzo caught a glimpse of a man's profile: young, handsome, short black hair, bright white teeth. Familiar.

Familiar?

"Oh, it's just that Macatia kid," Cohen noted, disappointed. "Forget it." He nudged Phaira in the side. "You're a girl, why don't you go faint over him with the rest?"

"No thanks," Phaira said sourly. "I don't see the appeal."

"You know why," Cohen scoffed. "Money, money. Everyone loves you when - "

"Closer," Renzo interrupted. "Take me closer." He stared hard at the crowd, searching for that profile again. That face. That sneer in-between the smiles.

Nican Macatia. Everyone knew him. From one of the wealthiest families in the North, Nican was the only son and heir apparent to the M-water purification tablet company. Handsome, infamous, sought after, swooned over. A local prince.

A sleek ground rover hovered outside the diner, waiting for its master. Nican took his time through the crowd of admirers, accompanied by two beautiful girls and flanked by three bodyguards. Renzo barely noticed the entourage as Cohen pushed the wheelchair to the edge of the crowd.

"That's close enough," Phaira said, looking uneasy.

"No," Renzo shot back. "Closer."

They all drew nearer, trying to avoid the wailing girls and their calamity.

Then Nican Macatia emerged before them, flashing a smile at someone over his shoulder.

Renzo pushed off with his good foot and threw all his body weight at Nican.

A cacophony of screams. Nican's fist slammed into the side of Renzo's head, but he wouldn't let go, and he didn't feel any pain, only Nican's rippling throat between his thumbs.

An arm looped around Renzo's neck and pulled, cutting off his air. Nican slipped from his grip, disappearing into the crowd. Renzo clawed at the burly limb, trying to get any bit of air into his lungs.

Then the pressure slid away, and Renzo fell backwards. Cohen's thick arms caught him and swiftly pulled him from the crowd. Blinking through the black spots, Renzo saw his sister in a whirlwind, slamming the heel of her palm into Nican's bodyguard's nose and breaking it with an audible crack, ducking under a wild swing from the bleeding man and driving the heel of her boot into his knee. The bodyguard crumbled, going for his concealed weapon. Phaira already had her Calis out, primed and aimed, first at the bodyguard's face, then at the crowd of shrieking onlookers. Nican was stumbling into his transport, the escorts left on the street as it sped away.

Then the three of them were running down an alleyway, Renzo doing his best to keep his balance while holding onto Cohen and Phaira's shoulders.

Finally, after several twists and turns, they stopped to rest. Renzo panted, hot with humiliation: for his useless stump, for the brief moment he'd locked onto Nican and lost him. He pushed off Cohen's arm and grabbed a lamppost for balance. His joints screamed at the sudden movement, but his brain was busy gathering the new memory fragments.

That smirk, that smile. The way Nican's hands gripped a pipe, the laughter, the hands pulling at his papers, at his glasses, crushing them under an expensive heel.

"What was that, Ren?" Phaira demanded.

"That was him," Renzo said under his breath, more to himself than to his siblings. "He's the one."

"You're kidding," Cohen exclaimed, his eyes wide. "Macatia?"

Was it him?

"Take me back to the hospital," Renzo muttered. "Please take me back."

Holding onto the lamppost, he urged the same images to repeat, to affix them in his broken brain: Nican's laughing face, the crunch of metal on bone, the taste of pavement and coppery blood.

II.

No officers waited at the hospital to arrest Phaira. Instead, Renzo was the one who called the local patrol to make a statement. He told the two officers every detail that he could recall, answering yes every time as they repeated the question: "Nican Macatia? You know who he is, right?"

His mind cleared, with thoughts of justice being done. The daily rehabilitation became a routine. His arms and shoulders grew stronger. The ringing in his head lessened. He still suffered some phantom pain in his missing limb, but with his right thigh and knee now shaped, a doctor came to measure and fit him for a prosthetic.

"You'll be back on your feet in no time at all," the doctor smiled.

Feet. Plural.

There were no visitors. Phaira was in the midst of her service check-in, and working on a request for more leave time. Cohen went back to work at the quarry. He offered to quit and care for Renzo. But jobs were scarce for someone with Cohen's education level, so Renzo insisted that his little brother go back.

Finally, Renzo was cleared for discharge. He was eligible for home visits from a nurse of his choosing. Renzo declined.

Then the university called him, congratulating him on his release and offering him a position as mathematics department assistant, supporting the instructors and students. Easy work. Decent pay.

He said no.

As Renzo counted down the days to his discharge, he spent hours lost in thought, clicking and unclicking his new prosthesis: a rudimentary, low-cost model. It sent blazes of pain around his thigh when he tried to put weight on it. Normal, they said. It's an adjustment. Keep practicing. But now it felt strange to be upright. His right leg was now lighter than his left, and his body felt unbalanced, like he might cartwheel and sprawl across the floor.

The morning of his release, a knock sounded at the door. Lying on his bed, Renzo didn't even look up. "Co, you don't have to knock."

"I'm always gonna knock," Cohen grumbled as he came inside. "It's called manners."

"Aren't you supposed to be at work?"

"I wanted to tell you," Cohen started, and then stopped.

"What's wrong?" Renzo asked, sitting up.

"Your case is closed," Cohen confessed. "No charges. No more hours put into the investigation."

Renzo must have misheard him. "But I told them who did this to me."

Cohen shrugged. "I don't know, Ren. When I checked in, that's what they told me."

Renzo stared at the floor. Of course. What did he expect? Macatia came from money, and everyone had a price. Take this envelope, sweep it away, and it never happened.

Still, it felt like that same old story should be different for Renzo. It was his word, his life. It used to mean something.

"Let's just go home," he heard Cohen say, over the roar of his mind. "Let's just go home."

* * *

A loud bang woke Renzo from sleep. He looked around wildly in the dark. A burglar? He fumbled for his cane and gripped it tightly with both hands as the doorknob to his tiny room turned.

A white face loomed from the shadows. He saw the palm of her hand, her fingers outstretched, groping the air.

Renzo put down the cane and shimmied to the end of his bed. Then he leaned over to take Phaira's wrist and guided her to sit down.

The smell of cold sweat made him recoil. Her shirt was torn, she was bleeding from her mouth, and her knuckles were split open. "What happened to you?" he demanded.

Phaira's eyes gleamed in the dark. "I told Macatia to meet me on the overpass. I told him that I knew what he'd done, and until he settled with me, he'd never be safe. And he came - "

"Why did you do that? What did you do to him?"

"He was high," Phaira continued. "Alone, acting insane. He came at me." She swiped at her mouth; a streak of dull red remained from her knuckles. "Smashed me in the head. We fought, and then he slipped and hit the edge of the bridge. I tried to grab him, but he fell. He's dead."

Renzo's head spun, his stomach both nauseous and euphoric. She had to hide. She had to get out of Daro. No, they should call Phaira's friend from the military, Aeden Nox....

"I know," Phaira said listlessly. "I already called Nox. He's bringing the patrol. They should be there by now." She started to rise from the bed, as if in a trance.

"No, wait," Renzo protested. He forced a deep breath. "It was an accident. Right?"

"Of course it was."

"Was it really?"

For the first time, Phaira's eyes focused on his face. "You think I threw him over on purpose to avenge you?"

"Why else would you do something like this?" Renzo shot back. "Calling him in the middle of the night, making threats?"

He stared up at his sister's silhouette. But even as he tried to ignore it, bitterness began to rise in his throat. And fear, mixed with disgust.

* * *

Law enforcement took Phaira in for questioning. Forensic evidence was collected. And, unbelievably, Phaira's story was confirmed. Nican's blood was full of chemicals, both legally prescribed and banned, including an amplified version of mekaline, a street hallucinogenic. The combination, the coroner ruled, would have made Nican violent and psychotic. Nican's fingerprints were found on the rail, Phaira's blood on the bridge. Her call to Nican was confirmed, but she had far more defensive wounds than Nican's corpse. It should have been dismissed.

But the day after the official ruling, the military took her into custody. No one would say anything to either brother. Cohen begged Nox to find out where she was. But Nox couldn't get any information out of anyone. Instead he came to their little apartment to wait and pace.

Three days passed with no word. On the fourth day, people began to gather outside Renzo's apartment building. At first, only a few, but the numbers continued to swell. When it reached fifty, Renzo, Cohen and Nox kept watch at the window. The people glared up at them, silent, waiting.

Then an official police transport turned down the street. The crowd began to hiss.

Renzo grabbed Nox's arm. "Get down there."

Nox bolted out of the apartment. Cohen went to follow, but Renzo stopped him. "He's an officer," he reminded his brother. "They won't attack him."

Cohen nodded. His eyes flicked back to Renzo again and again. A familiar reaction, that instinctual deferral to his older siblings. Renzo gripped the windowsill so tightly the wood cut into his hands. He had to keep it together for his brother.

And for his sister, now being pulled from the transport by Nox. The crowds swarmed over them, grabbing at her clothes and hair, yelling obscenities. Phaira cowed over, hiding her face. Nox was yelling at everyone to get back, calling for the police escort to help. But the driver stood by his open door, watching the chaos, stone-faced.

Then a shot rang out. The crowd split off in every direction. Renzo leaned out as far as he could, frantically searching for Phaira and Nox, his heart ramming in his chest.

"Can you see them?" Cohen shouted.

The door burst open to the apartment, and two bodies fell through. Fumbling back to his feet, Nox shut the door and leaned against it, panting for air. Phaira remained on her knees. She looked like a ghost: unseeing, barely there. And there were blood on the side of her neck.

"You're hurt!" Cohen gasped, pulling her up to stand.

"The shot grazed the wooden frame of the entryway," Nox explained, mopping the sweat from his face. "It's okay, I think."

Renzo dug out the first-aid kit from the kitchen. When he hobbled back into the room, Nox was surveying the street below, one hand on the hilt of his Compact firearm. Cohen was next to Phaira on their lumpy sofa. Phaira just stared at her feet.

Renzo sat on Phaira's other side. Then, bracing his nerves, he used tweezers to remove the pieces of splintered wood lodged in the side of her throat. *So close to her jugular,* Renzo thought, queasy as blood trickled from the wounds. *Bigger pieces would have killed her.*

They all jumped at the sudden roar of the crowd, screaming Phaira's name. Nox turned from the window and swallowed, his skin pale under his freckles.

That night, someone tried to break into the apartment. Renzo was awake, staring at the clock when he heard glass shatter. As he emerged from his room, bearing his cane as a weapon, he saw a flash of metal and light, followed by a howl of pain.

In the living room, the windowpane had a hole punched through it. Cohen stood next to it, bearing a kitchen knife with blood on the edge, breathing heavily.

Nox was the one to find the online bounty system, and the series of photos framed by different colors to categorize: red for wanted, white for captured, black for kill on sight. And right at the top: multiple photos of Phaira, framed in black, with listings of her physical characteristics, known locations, even her genetic identification code. The reward: 250,000 rana.

It took several calls and a few threats, but Renzo was finally given access to the Macatia compound. Waiting to be seen, he surveyed the grand room before him: the sumptuous furnishings, antique furniture polished to a perfect gleam, the indoor waterfall. It all made him twitchy.

As he tapped his cane on the marble floor, his mind wandered in waiting. He had a sudden memory of his sister from some years back.

Pulled out of a critical theory workshop, Renzo came to the university callbox full of dread. Something was wrong. Child protective services had taken Cohen, who was still underage at the time. Renzo had forgotten to pay some bill. There was always something going wrong.

This call was different, though. Renzo remembered it because his defiant, snarky sister was trying very hard not to cry over the line.

Their father had shown up at their apartment, freshly released from the hospital, and Phaira was caught in his outburst. He'd hit her. Renzo could hear the tightness in her voice, how she tried not to sniff too loudly. He was stunned that she called him in this state, so vulnerable. He remembered how he cradled the Lissome, as if to hug her through the connection, telling her again and again: "Don't let him get to you. Don't let him affect you like this. It's not worth it, Phair."

The memory of fleeting closeness dissipated. Renzo stared at his cane in front of him and swallowed hard. Things had to change. He had to make it happen, for all their sakes.

Finally, an elaborate door swung open and a servant gestured to him. Renzo made his way into the next room, where Nican's parents waited, perched on an uncomfortable-looking but expensive lounger. The father had the same black hair as his son, that same sneering expression. The wife was wispy and graying, shriveled into herself.

Renzo chose to stand as he spoke, despite the pain of his prosthetic. "You know why I'm here."

The father snorted. The mother twisted one of her rings around her finger.

A hot lick of anger flared in Renzo. "You know what your son did to me. You know he should have been punished for it."

"My son," the father spat, "did nothing to you."

"Don't insult me," Renzo growled, striking his cane on the floor for emphasis. "He should be in jail, but you made sure that he never answered for his actions, didn't you?"

The mother crossed her arms tightly. The father said nothing.

"Take the bounty off of my sister," Renzo repeated, with as much authority as he could put into his voice. "It was ruled an accident. Your son took away my livelihood. Phaira has lost hers as well. Leave us be. Let us rebuild what's left."

The father remained silent. Was he considering what Renzo said?

But it was the mother who raised her eyes, her voice limpid, but ice-cold. "There is no comparison.Leave our property."

This won't stop, Renzo realized with horror. *They have the money and the resources to hunt her down, for as long as it takes. She's dead.*

The same thought must have occurred to Phaira. When Renzo returned to his tiny apartment, she was gone.

* * *

"Just take it."

"I'll pay rent for it, Nox, I have the money."

"It's fine! It's been in storage since my parents retired," Nox countered, holding out the ring of keys. "Might need some new wiring, but otherwise it runs. And there's fuel onboard to last a while, some food rations too. Take it."

Looking out the window, Renzo studied the rusty old Volante, parked by the street curb. "I've never flown something like that. Maybe you should come with us."

"I can't," Nox said. "Besides, someone should stay behind. Keep watch for any activity on the bounty. Try to get my colleagues to disable it."

He doesn't sound very confident, Renzo noted. *For good reason. Why would they start to care now?*

"Ready, Co?" he called out.

Cohen appeared from the hallway, lugging two large boxes with a bag looped around his chest.

"You're not keeping the apartment?" Nox asked.

"Nah," Cohen grunted on his way out. "Nothing much to leave behind, anyways."

There really isn't, Renzo thought. He was glad to leave. It felt good, like shedding an uncomfortable skin. He jerked his head towards the door. "Let's go, then."

"What's your first destination?" Nox said as they reached the stairs.

In his peripheral vision, Renzo could see the officer offer him a hand. He ignored Nox and clutched the handrail. "I have a couple of ideas."

He really didn't, though. Phaira had left no trace of where she might have gone. But they had the Volante, fuel, supplies and a few people to visit.

And he had the money: zero after zero, no source, no record of deposit, just there, discovered when he went to close his accounts. A parting gift from the Macatias. Apologizing through rana. Sick people.

But he'd already cashed it out and hidden it in a packet under his shirt. Blood funds, but it was still rana, and more than he could have ever hoped to earn in a lifetime. So they had time on their side, too.

After a quick tour of the transport, Nox apologizing for its decrepit appearance the whole while, the brothers were finally alone. Cohen remained in the back, unpacking, as Renzo slid behind the flight controls.

For several moments, he studied the console. He hadn't flown anything in years. There was never time to indulge in that kind of frivolity.

But when the engines rattled, and finally fired, and the Volante lifted off its gear with a creak, Renzo felt something lift under his ribs: the rush of excitement.

III.

The nickname for the prototype was '*Arazura:*' a take-off on the exterior paneling, which gave off shades of silver-blue. 'Air Azure,' like some commercial flight company. Silly. But it stuck in Renzo's head, and he'd come to like it. During a break, when the others had gone in search of food and cigarettes, Renzo sat on top of the vessel, twenty feet off the ground, surveying his property.

His. His heart beat faster with pride.

When Renzo left for the Mac, he had no idea what the weeks ahead might hold. But when he finally arrived at the meeting point, and the girl stepped out of shadow, the shock burst out of him.

"Ani?" he gasped.

She'd laughed. And it was like they were teenagers again, ten years ago.

When civil war broke out in the West, the government had called in all experts in all fields to strategize. Renzo was nineteen, but already a name in the code breaking field, so he was recruited with several others to analyze communications, satellites and stolen technology.

Anandi, or Ani as he knew her then, was the youngest in his group at fourteen years old. She was also the loudest, the most brightly dressed, and possessed one of the most brilliant minds he'd ever encountered.

Working side by side, she'd made him smile, even laugh a few times. The project had only lasted ten days, until the first armistice came through. Then Renzo was sent home with all the others.

That same girl now showed him all she had learned since their last encounter: how to infiltrate firewalls, break through passwords, and sift through layers of information for that precious morsel. Staring at her profile as she explained, a forgotten memory came to light: even back then, under the watchful eye of the government, Anandi was particularly interested in digging up secrets: family histories, private conversations, stealing away forgotten drafts of memos. She kept everything in a Lissome she kept hidden by her ankle, under the folds of her bright trousers; she showed him a few times, grinning as if he were part of the plot.

A funny fixation, he remembered thinking at the time. He never thought to report her to the authorities; in fact, he was secretly jealous of her brazen attitude.

Still, just like ten years ago, within the first day of their reunion, Anandi managed to irritate Renzo with her chipper outlook, and used her charm to extract far too much personal information from him. He told her about Huma and Sydel, how helpless he had been to make any kind of decision about the girl's ownership. And when Anandi recounted the articles she'd read on it, Renzo told her more about his assault by Nican Macatia, how he and his siblings were still reeling from the aftermath.

"Let me ask you this," Anandi said, sitting back in her chair. "You have time and distance now from all of that. A few weeks on your own. What do you want to do?"

"I'm supposed to be learning from you," Renzo said. "You're not willing?"

"Well, yes, but you have an opportunity, Ren, to do something just for you." As Anandi spoke, she waved her hand and her sleeve slipped down. Renzo caught a glimpse of something taped inside her elbow before she dropped her arm to her side, out of sight.

"For once, you're not responsible for anyone or anything," she continued. "What have you always wished you could do?"

Renzo knew the answer immediately. Anandi caught the change in his expression, and slapped her hand on his knee. "What is it? Come on."

"It's silly," Renzo huffed, uncomfortable with her physicality. "And there's no time to - "

"Just say it. Stop acting like a grumpy old man."

"Well," he mumbled as a flush crept up his neck. "I've always liked to build. And fly. I guess I've always wanted to build my own flight vessel. But - "

Anandi grinned, her eyes crinkling at the edges. "You can build? I didn't know that."

"Well, sometimes. I mean, little things on my own. Sometimes I rebuilt racers or speeders, when I could find scrap material..."

As he spoke, a grin spread across Anandi's face. At the sight, Renzo grimaced. "What?"

"Nothing," Anandi said nonchalantly. "If you want to learn, pay attention." Then her fingers became a blur from typing.

At the end of the day, stiff and sore from sitting for so long, they went for a walk through the Mac. Or as much of a walk that Renzo could manage. He hated walking outside; it felt like everyone stared at him, painfully hobbling on his prosthesis.

But Anandi insisted. "I have something to show you," she told him.

It was an old manufacturing plant. Renzo studied the brick exterior, cracked windows and chains woven over the doors.

"This is why you dragged me out?" he asked flatly. "I grew up in Daro. I've seen this before"

"Right, I got you outside to look at a pile of bricks," Anandi retorted. "It's the inside that counts, Ren."

"Well, it's chained up, Ani."

One of the windows suddenly opened, and Anandi's father, Emir, popped his head out. "Clear," he called. "Come on in."

"What are you two up to?" Renzo groaned, checking over his shoulder for any sign of patrol.

"Come on, grandpa," Anandi called back, dashing towards the building. "Guess what this place used to make."

Minutes later, Renzo stood in the center of a vast hanger, complete with mounting machines, abandoned supplies and welding equipment.

And a rusty old freighter, sitting in the middle of it all.

"They used to build ambassador transports in here," Emir said, stroking his white beard as he studied one of the construction consoles. "Then there was an issue of safety code, and they went bankrupt. They sold some of the equipment, but not all of it."

"Do these still work?" Renzo asked, peering at the joints of one mechanical arm, noting the rust in the screws.

"They should. With some electricity, of course."

"I don't know what she's thinking," Renzo muttered. He ran his hand over the controls, and then glanced at the freighter again. "Whose ship is that?"

"Yours, Ren," Anandi's voice echoed through the hanger.

Where was she?

Then the lights flickered overhead. Some shorted out as soon as they were lit, releasing a brief shower of orange sparks.

"Hey Ren!" Anandi sang out. "I put out the call for help. Guess what you're doing over the next few weeks."

* * *

True to Anandi's word, within the hour the building filled with people. Standing on a platform, overlooking the hanger, Renzo stared at the swarm of faces: young and old, punk and professor, talking excitedly amongst themselves.

Anandi nudged him forward. "Go on. You know you want to."

"I don't even - how did you do this, Ani?" he murmured, paralyzed with surprise. "They're here to build? Really? For me?"

"You don't get it, do you?" Anandi said with a half-smile. "These are people who were fired for not following industry protocol. Scientists who lost funding. Engineers looking for work. They need something to do. So they came running."

"I don't even know where to start."

"At the beginning," said Emir. "One step at a time. You have a captive audience. And a substantial bank account, so the rumor goes."

Renzo looked at Emir sharply, but the older man was gazing across the hanger.

So Renzo turned his glare to Anandi. She shrugged her shoulders. "He's old, I don't know."

Then she jerked her chin towards the buzzing crowd. "Go play. We'll be back to check on you."

"You're leaving?" Renzo asked, panicked.

"Just for an hour," Emir said. "Don't worry, son, you know what you're doing."

Anandi took her father's arm, and the two walked into the corridor, heading for the back of the factory.

Watching them leave, the word *son* hovered in Renzo's mind.

He set it aside, and surveyed the mass of people before him. Faces turned in his direction, some smiling, some wary.

Renzo pushed his glasses up the bridge of his nose and cleared his throat. "Okay, everyone," he called. His voice rang through the hanger. "Let's get started."

I V.

The first day, the crowd divided into groups: design-
ers, engineers, experts in small-scale mechanics
and engine construction. They all contributed to the
planning phase, a huge roundtable of ideas and argu-
ments, raucous at times, with only Renzo's authority to
calm the voices.

Finally, the group was ready to start renovating and
updating the old freighter. The group divided into work
shifts, with a collaborative ease that shocked Renzo.

Soon, days bled into nights. Overseeing all depart-
ments, Renzo saw people find their niches and burrow
themselves into the work. A constant cloud of energy
buzzed in the hanger. Renzo wandered from group to
group, learning, teaching, and focused on nothing else
for the first time in his life. It was heaven.

For all the parts that couldn't be borrowed, found or
stolen, Renzo used the blood money from the Macatias.
At first he struggled with the guilt of using the money
at all, something he had battled time and again on the
crumbling Volante: using that old lie of contract repair
work, withdrawing what he needed and moving the re-
mainder to yet another secure location. At least eight
times, Renzo moved that incredible amount of rana with
an anxious grip. Who could say if the Macatias might
swoop in and take it all back?

But creating the *Arazura* was a blessing, he soon realized. The project consumed vast numbers of rana, disposing of it in a tangible, beneficial way. Something positive out of something horrifying. It seemed right.

One night, Renzo and Anandi retreated from the sounds of construction to the other side of the factory, holing up in one of the old accounting offices. They sat in dusty executive chairs, their feet on the desk, their hands around hot cups of tea.

Anandi nudged Renzo with her foot. "Be honest." Her hair was in several short braids that night, a pink scarf wrapped around them.

"About?" Renzo asked, pushing his glasses onto the top of his head and blowing into the steaming cup.

"I think you're faking." Anandi tilted her head. "I don't think you're as damaged as you want people to think. And I'm not talking about your leg."

Renzo paused in mid-blow.

"I don't know why you don't go back to the university. Or any mathematical department." Anandi's tone was serious, for once in their friendship. "Lots of respect, acclaim, fancy awards, government salaries. Doesn't sound too bad."

Renzo shrugged to delay his response. He wondered if anyone else had noticed. A week before his hospital discharge, he woke in his bed, and suddenly his mind felt clearer. He could recognize the code patterns in his medical chart. He was able to break into his bedside medicine cart in ten seconds.

His brain had healed. But he didn't want it.

The excuse of his brain injury was so easy to maintain. To turn his back on mathematical code breaking, what he was best at, it sounded selfish and arrogant. And maybe he was those things, but he wasn't about to admit to it.

"I like where I am now," he came up with, finally.

Anandi nodded, taking a sip. It occurred to Renzo that she knew what he was thinking. It was no different for her: she could easily take her brilliant skills to some high-paying position in the government. Instead, she chose to live on scraps, sleep in a different place every night, infiltrate top-secret networks and exist only in the underground.

"Now that we're alone," she said suddenly, "I've been meaning to tell you. I got a hit on Huma."

Hot tea spilled down Renzo's chest. He swore, swiping at the burn with his free hand. "Why didn't you say so earlier? What did you find out? Was there any sign of Sydel?

"No," Anandi said thoughtfully. "But the hit I found was in error; someone made a mistake and let the name slip out, just once. It's already gone, no trace left behind. Any information on Huma, for whatever reason, is buried under walls and walls of firewall. It's professional, no doubt. Possibly government level."

So Huma had a connection to some higher authority. Or someone with enough money to buy that authority. Evil woman. Though he would never tell a soul about it, Renzo hadn't forgotten the look on Phaira's face, wrenched with pain from that shot of Zephyr.

And what did Huma want with Sydel? That girl was some kind of dangerous, powerful creature, that was clear from the way she fixed Cohen's burns. But on the other end, she had healed both his brother and sister when he was helpless to do anything. For that, regardless of his trepidation, he owed her a debt.

"Do you think you can get past all the securities?" he asked Anandi.

"I don't know!" Anandi said, laughing. "And that's funny for me to say. But this is pretty extreme. It's going to take a lot of work, especially since I have to cover my path as I break in."

"I don't want to put you in danger," Renzo said. "You've already been targeted. And you've done so much, put all this time and effort into making the *Arazura* happen."

"Hey, listen," Anandi interrupted, her tone serious again. "It's a belated thank-you. You were nice to me in the West. I was a scared kid when they brought me into that wartime work."

"Are you kidding? You, scared?"

"Besides, don't worry so much, Renzo," she ignored his outburst, the teasing note back in her voice. "This kind of challenge is delicious."

* * *

As Renzo worked on the *Arazura* flight console, his Lissome buzzed in his pocket. That familiar wave of panic came over him. Something terrible had happened.

Just as quickly, he chastised himself for jumping to conclusions. Instead, he forced his brain to slow down and take step after step: turn the blowtorch off, lift his goggles, stretch out the ache in his neck and, finally, read the message.

It was from Phaira: a few lines on how she had been accepted as a guest at the Jala Communia, and she'd managed to convince Yann to teach her about Ekos. She didn't know how long she would stay.

She's not happy, Renzo mused, snorting to himself. *I bet they aren't too happy, either.*

Then his smile dropped. He hadn't thought much about the actual confrontation to come with Huma, so absorbed in the *Arazura's* construction. Was that really going to happen? Could he really get involved in something like that? Come to think of it, he hadn't seen Anandi much either; she was working in a secret location, trying to uncover more information about Sydel's location.

"Something wrong?" The question came from one of the volunteers, crouched at the other end of the console, bundling red and blue wires together.

"No," Renzo said, thinking quickly. "Just getting a headache."

The man nodded. "Yeah, I know about that. People don't understand how debilitating it is, head trauma."

"What do you know about it?" Renzo said shortly, fitting his goggles back over his eyes.

The man tapped his forehead. "Frontal lobe. Headaches and seizures. Plus, sometimes I get these blinding flashes of light in my eyes, usually when I'm working. You?"

Renzo paused, suspicious of the sudden admission. But he had never met another person with the same issues.

"Fractured skull. Parietal lobe damage, mostly," he finally admitted. "Some frontal lobe. Long-term memory loss. And yeah. Headaches. A lot of headaches."

The man nodded as he twisted wires into a compact rope, checking for any signs of rupture along the way. "You seem pretty functional for that much damage."

"Lucky me," Renzo muttered, working on lighting his blowtorch again.

"That accident take your leg, too?"

Renzo's irritation prickled again. "Why are you so curious?" he asked, pushing up the goggles again. "What, you want to see the stump? Who are you, anyways?"

The man didn't look up from his work. "I ask because I think I can help you." He gestured at Renzo's right foot. "At least, get you out of that awful thing and into something decent. I'm surprised you haven't built something better."

Renzo blinked, taken aback by the judgment. It was a good question, though. Why hadn't he built his own prosthetic?

Then his Lissome beeped again. "Ren?" came a voice from his pocket.

"Busy, Ani," Renzo hissed.

"You're not that busy. I found her."

Renzo froze. Glancing to the right, he caught the volunteer's eyes: they were golden, like a cat's.

Clearing his throat, he turned away and stumbled to his feet. The prosthesis bit into his right knee joint, as it always did, permanent grooves etched into his skin. He did his best to restrain a wince of pain.

"I'm Theron, by the way. Let's talk later," the man said, his attention back on the wiring.

Renzo limped off the ship, heading for the back of the factory. Inside the old accounting office, Anandi was a tiny silhouette in a glowing blue field.

"What did you - ?" Renzo began. Then his eyes adjusted, and he saw Emir sitting next to his daughter, their exposed arms, and the blood transfusion tube that linked them together.

Catching sight of Renzo, Emir leaned forward and stopped the flow.

"It hasn't been long enough," Anandi protested, glancing at Renzo. "It's okay. I trust him."

"It's fine for now," Emir said, unhooking the transfusion tube with expert hands. Wrapping it in a cloth, he stowed it away in a satchel, along with other steel tools. "You have work to do."

As Emir exited the room, Anandi rubbed the skin around the port, avoiding Renzo's stare as she turned back to her screens. Her fingers became a flurry of activity: camera angles adjusted, images magnified. Her screens showed multiple perspectives of a vendor mill choked with travelers, bright hair colors, dull clothing, faces in profile and out of sight.

Renzo peered over her shoulder. Occasionally, he caught himself staring at her arm. There was a spot of blood on her sleeve.

"Blood disorder," Anandi muttered, her eyes never leaving her work. "He needs transfusions. That's why we stay close."

Renzo tried to think of what to say in response.

Then Anandi nodded. "Wait. There. That's her, right?"

On the video, Sydel stood against a gray wall, separate from the sea of movement. Wrapped in a navy blue cloak, her skin was sallow, her back stooped. As the projection played, her eyes lifted to look into the camera; straight into Renzo's eyes, it seemed. One of her hands emerged, and she rapped the wall twice with her knuckles. Then she shuffled out of camera range.

Anandi replayed the five seconds of video. No question, Sydel intentionally looked into the camera.

"This was timestamped two days ago, from a vendor mill in the south. No sign of anyone matching Huma's stats, though," Anandi said. "And Sydel doesn't show up again."

Renzo stared at Sydel's frozen image. His gaze moved to the girl's hand. "Why the knock on the wall?" he wondered out loud. "What's that wall? Why draw attention to it?"

With a flick of her fingers, Anandi magnified the image by ten, then ten again. Renzo and Anandi leaned in to study the area around Sydel's hand. Nothing. Just a grey slab, like a million others in the world.

Still, she was alive.

"Can you send that image to Cohen and Phaira?" Renzo asked. "They could probably use the good news."

"Already done," Anandi mumbled. By the lines of code, she was already busy creating an algorithm to access local surveillance cameras and identify Sydel if she turned up. Renzo flopped down in one of the executive chairs. His right thigh ached. He rubbed it, mulling over what he'd seen, both onscreen and in the room.

A beep: an incoming call.

"That was quick," Anandi said. She waved her hand to generate another screen to her right. Renzo reached over and pulled it in front of him, waiting for the connection to establish.

Finally, a translucent Phaira shimmered into view. Her hair was pulled back, and shadows cut into the angles of her face. "There's a message, Ren."

"From who?"

"I didn't tell you at the time. I wasn't sure if I should tell you or Co," Phaira explained in a rush. "Remember when you were searching Huma's old ship? And I had you focus on the door with the burn marks? There was a message there: a psychic etching, I guess it's called. It said: Find the missing Hitodama."

"You can see psychic etchings?" Anandi interrupted, leaning in front of Renzo. "That's so interesting! I can't see anything, I don't have a spiritual bone in my body, I wish I did...."

"Come on," Renzo grumbled, pushing at Anandi to move aside. She stuck out her tongue and shifted back into her seat.

"Anyways," Phaira said with a tiny smile. "I think, somehow, Sydel knew that by finding Emir, we'd be able to meet Anandi and work with her. And she'd save our lives," she added awkwardly.

"That's true!" Anandi exclaimed. "So this girl can see into the future, too? That's - "

"Phair," Renzo interrupted. "You said there's a message on the wall. What does it say?"

Phaira's amusement faded. "Feel the fear."

All three were silent, processing those words. Anandi was the first to speak. "What kind of message is that?"

"I don't know," Phaira said. "But she left it for a reason." She glanced off-screen. "I have to go. Stay low, stay safe. I'll call soon."

The connection broke, the screen collapsing into itself and disappearing.

"She thinks we're in trouble?" Anandi asked quietly.

Renzo rubbed the knuckles of his left hand with his right. "I really don't know."

"Well, I'll tell you, Ren: the network is getting hot," Anandi said. "There's a rise in encrypted transmissions. Something is going to happen, and soon. And it's probably not for the greater good."

V.

Cohen made his way through the city of Daro: into industrial parks, past abandoned mills and down unfamiliar paths, the few he could find. He didn't note any street signs on purpose. He wanted to be lost to everyone, and alone.

His stomach ached. He had sharp pains in his chest, too, where the scars lay. Phantom pain was common after trauma, he read that somewhere. Sometimes, he even thought he smelled burning skin.

Finally, Cohen ducked into a back alley, behind copper pipes running vertically up the apartment building. Then he took out his Lissome and brought up the still image. Light and noise streaked over him as transports rumbled overhead. He didn't notice.

It didn't even look like Sydel. His nausea grew at the weird, haunted look in her eyes, at the sickly tinge to her skin.

The first time he saw her, he was running through the desert, his heart in his throat, following the signal of Phaira's solar tracker, the first indication of her whereabouts in weeks. But when they found the Communia, he couldn't help but stare at the girl with the braided hair and big brown eyes. Funny: she was barely five feet tall, but everyone in that place was hyper-aware of her presence. Especially that man, Yann.

Then, when the Vendor Mill bomb went off, she stayed with Cohen, even when he pretended like he wasn't in pain, terrified and reliving the explosion in his dreams. She smelled like soap and vanilla. When they talked, she listened without getting distracted or impatient. It felt like Sydel saw him, really saw him, not just as a little brother, or someone slow and stupid.

And he saw her, too. She was just young and confused, like him. Always a step behind everyone else, unsure of the right thing to say or do. From the first time they spoke, his instinct was to protect that girl from the world.

Nox noted that instinct on his first day of training.

"A team needs multiple components to thrive," Nox told him. "Defense is just as important as offensive. That's your place in all of this."

"What - what were you?" Cohen said, stuttering a little. They were the same size, physically, but the man had extensive military experience, been a part of overseas missions that Cohen couldn't even comprehend. "I mean, on the team? When you were working with Phaira."

Nox half-smiled. "Direct action operations and artillery. Sometimes counter-terrorism. Your sister was all about unconventional warfare and direct reconnaissance. The star of the show."

Cohen thought he heard resentment in the man's voice. Then Nox grinned, and Cohen dismissed it.

The former soldier took Cohen's training seriously. Nox had a connection at the Daro infantry training ground and he worked with Cohen for hours, showing him how to use howitzers and heavy mortars. Cohen learned how to fire a number of weapons, how to adjust for recoil, how to reload in seconds. When he peered through the scope of a Vacarro sniper rifle, it felt natural. Then he blasted three targets, one after another, over two hundred feet away. A rush of pride coursed through him, and Nox seemed to agree. "So that's where your talent lies," the man mused. "Very interesting."

Cohen might have been a natural sniper, but Nox still insisted on physical combat. Nox encouraged Cohen to do as he did: focus on overpowering and overwhelming the target. Both men were over six feet and thickly built, so they naturally unnerved the opponent on first look. Cohen already had high muscle endurance to bodyweight ratio from years of physical labor work; vital, Nox pointed out, for balance and maneuvering. The key was to surprise the opponent with their agility: quick strikes on vulnerable points, or throwing them to the ground with a shoulder toss.

The biggest lesson for Cohen, though, was learning to trust his instincts.

"You're a follower," Nox said bluntly. They were back in his apartment after a long day, and Cohen longed for sleep. But Nox confronted him in the spare bedroom. "There's nothing wrong with that. Not everyone can be a leader. But when you're in a dangerous situation and alone, you have to be able to act independently. And you need the mental toughness to stick it out."

"I'm not stupid," Cohen snapped. "I can think for myself."

"Can you?" Nox straddled a chair and stared at Cohen. "What would you have done about Huma?"

Cohen balked. "I did do something. We tried to stop them -"

"And it blew up in your face," Nox finished. "You're not listening. Was it the right thing to do?"

"It's what Phaira decided," Cohen said. "She knows more than I do about it."

"She's not perfect. She doesn't know everything," Nox shot back. At Cohen's recoil, Nox seemed to check his temper. "Think about it," he continued in a calmer tone. "Was she right?"

This is a mistake. He thought it when Phaira brought up the idea to storm Huma's carrier ship, though he tried to mask it with bravado. But she was so certain, so experienced, and he'd always wanted to do what she did.

"I don't know," Cohen finally said.

"You know."

"Well, I don't know what we should have done."

"Here's your next assignment," Nox said, rising to his feet. "Think about what went wrong. Then figure out what you should have done instead. With or without Phaira."

When Nox left the room, Cohen boiled with anger. What did he know about any of it? Who was he to pass judgment on his sister, on his family?

His anger didn't dissipate. So that night, as Nox snored in the next room, Cohen left the apartment. He didn't know where to go, but he didn't care.

Within minutes, though, the cold began to seep through his jacket; it was colder outside than he realized. But he didn't want to go back yet.

Shivering, Cohen searched the trash-filled streets for somewhere to warm up. As he walked, he rubbed the thick scar on the back of his left hand, soft and sensitive to the dampness. Stupid dare for the fat kid: take a rana coin and scrape it against the back of your hand, back and forth, until you admit pain. Backed into a corner by three bullies, he decided to beat them all. By the time he was done, a bloody groove lay between his bones. He'd won, but no girl wanted to hold that worm-scarred hand. He wondered if Sydel had noticed it.

There was a sudden muffled sound, which quickly faded away. Cohen turned in place, confused. It came again. The ground rumbled under his feet.

Cohen tracked the sound to a rusted-over metal door, tucked in an abandoned warehouse. Curious, he yanked on the door handle. Despite the rust, the door opened silently. A pinprick of light shone at the bottom of a flight of stairs. As he descended, Cohen tensed for any kind of trouble.

The basement teemed with cheering bodies. Two men fought in a makeshift ring in the center of the space. One of the fighters spat up a mouthful of blood. Everyone seemed to scream in unison, as bookies yelled and waved fistfuls of money. Cohen kept to the shadows and near the exit, intending to stay for only a moment. But he was gradually sucked into the bouts, one after another, men and women of all ages in combat.

It was fascinating to watch the outcomes: who prevailed, and who crumbled within minutes. It had nothing to do with size; no, the ones who were successful had the stamina and temperament to outlast their opponent, or else they lashed out with well-placed brutal strikes that ended the match in seconds. And with both, so much of it was influenced by attitude. Just like Nox said: overwhelm and intimidate.

Phaira just had to look at someone, and they shriveled into themselves. She was probably a big hit on the circuit. Maybe she had even fought in this basement. Cohen took in the exposed pipes overhead, the stagnant heat, the smell of sweat and blood. Did she rank near the top of the roster? Was she ever high on mekaline when she fought? How bad did it get in those months after she vanished from their apartment? She wouldn't talk about her time away. There was just a void between the day he found her, and the night she ran.

On that night, Cohen woke to the sound of his siblings' whisper-yelling. He crept down the hallway, trying to make as little noise as possible.

In the shadows of their tiny living room, Phaira hissed unintelligibly at Renzo. He whispered back, waving his hands and clenching them in front of her face. Phaira smacked them away. The sweet smell of mekaline drifted down the hallway; Cohen recognized it immediately.

Then Renzo grabbed Phaira by the upper arms. A loud bang reverberated through the apartment. Renzo had shoved Phaira into the windowsill. As she straightened, Cohen saw the angry glint in her eyes. He knew a fight when it was brewing.

But when he ran to break it up, Renzo had already left the apartment, slamming the door behind him. The sound of his heavy limp and cane echoed down the stairwell. Phaira remained in the darkness. When Cohen touched her shoulder, she'd recoiled from the touch. Her eyes were shiny with despair, her throat still bandaged from the crowd assault. Cohen froze at the sight, grappling with what to say.

But before he could speak, she had retreated to her bedroom.

And the next day, she was gone.

Cohen still hadn't forgiven his sister, deep down, for leaving him behind like that.

Nox is right, Cohen mused as he watched the last match of the night. *I have to make my own decisions. They are my family, but Phaira is a mess. Ren is completely lost. The only thing I know is that I owe it to Sydel to find her.*

VI.

"After you left, I ran into a friend last night."
Cohen tried very hard to muster a look of interest as Nox shuffled around the apartment, talking. "I told him I was training you. And he was really impressed, asked a bunch of questions about you. You won't meet him, of course, but word is getting out - "

Nox kept going, but Cohen tuned him out. Instead he counted the number of days passed since he had arrived. Three weeks? What was taking so long?

Though the training started with an exhilarating rush, Nox's methods were growing erratic, equal parts informative and confusing. Instead of the drills from the first week, Nox's focus changed to recounting all of his missions within special forces. Sometimes he even reenacted certain events, with Cohen as the stand-in.

And at night, another version of Nox came out. Those grand tales continued at the bar, where Nox's group of friends, law patrol, some firefighters and military personnel, swilled liquor and traded stories. The same stories, Cohen soon realized, every night.

Pressured to join their company, Cohen drank, he laughed, he got tangled in shadowy corners with girls with no name. If he acted any other way, Nox and his friends would tease him mercilessly, so he went through the motions. He wouldn't smoke the mekaline when it was brought out, though, or try any of the other drugs, so Nox and his friends still had the opportunity to poke fun at him. But Cohen just watched them smoke and snort, and waited for an opportunity to leave.

One night, when Nox passed out, Cohen crept out of his bedroom window. The moon was out, blazing white, illuminating the rotting city. It was second nature now, for him to navigate one road and then another, winding his way to that rusted door and the roar of the crowd.

But as Cohen watched the last two combatants of the night prepare for battle, a hand clapped down on his shoulder.

"So this is where you've been sneaking off to!" Nox laughed, his breath reeking of alcohol. "So secretive! What, you thought I didn't know about this place? I come all the time! Hey, are they still taking bets?"

Cohen kept his eyes forward. *Decorated, accomplished, and you act like a damn fool,* he thought.

"Hey Cohen, remember that guy I told you about?" Nox sang. "This is him! Keller and Keller's friend, this is Co, the kid I'm working with...."

Cohen glanced to his right. Keller had short black hair, sandy skin and a sharp profile. Nothing remarkable. Keller pushed through the crowds in the direction of the ring, and Nox followed, waving a fistful of rana.

Someone stepped up to take Keller's place. Cohen looked over again, and then up. A rarity: this man was even taller than Cohen, with long, straight black hair tied back.

"Cohen, right?" the man said. "I'm Theron."

He extended his hand. Halfheartedly, Cohen shook it. "Friend of Nox's, huh?" he asked. "Are you an officer, too?"

Theron ignored the question. "Nox is your teacher?" His tone was skeptical. "You don't look like you need his help."

"He's not - " Cohen scoffed, and then stopped. Nox was still Phaira's friend. "He's a good guy," he said instead. "I'm learning a lot. I am."

In the ring, the combatants finished taping their hands, and acknowledged each other with a nod.

"So were you the friend Nox was talking about?" Cohen finally spoke up, shrugging at the same time. He didn't care, but it felt like something should be said. "Talking about my training?"

"He's an idiot," Theron said. "Don't listen to anything he says."

Cohen recoiled with surprise. Theron noticed, and his tone of voice changed. "No, it's not me he's referring to. But how does your friend know Keller?"

Cohen shrugged again. "I don't really care. I've heard enough war stories to last me forever. It's not going to help me - "

He didn't finish the sentence. Frustration bubbled up in his stomach. What was he still doing in Daro? How much longer was he going to wait around for direction?

"So what do you need, then?"

Cohen glanced over at Theron, but the man was watching the fight.

The answer popped into Cohen's head immediately. *To be taken seriously.*

Instead, Cohen gave the second answer he could think of. "The truth, for once."

Theron nodded. "I understand that."

A sudden roar turned their heads. One of the combatants was unconscious on the mat, the other walking away. Nox suddenly appeared, followed by Keller. Cohen tried to sound bored as he asked: "Bet on the wrong one?"

"One kick! That's the whole fight? Come on," Nox groaned.

"You should leave," Theron muttered to Cohen, buttoning the panels of his overcoat. "Don't speak to Keller, he has nothing good for you."

But Cohen barely heard him. In the sea of faces around the ring, one stood out: a long, rat-like face with pale pink burns on one side, yelling at the fallen opponent. Familiar. Where did he know that guy?

Then it clicked: Meroy. The warehouse, the bombing. Cohen assumed that the man was killed. Apparently not.

"You know that guy?" Nox asked. Keller glanced at the two of them, one eyebrow raised.

"Yeah," Cohen said. "Hold on."

He wove through the departing crowds. He didn't know what he was going to do. But it felt like a signal for action, Meroy alive and in front of him.

Meroy picked up on his approach; the man's back curved and his eyes went narrow. Then something clicked in Meroy's face. "Wait, I know you," he said, straightening and looking Cohen up and down. "How do I know you? Are you here to collect? Who do you work for?"

Cohen drew himself up to his fullest height.

"For me," came a voice from behind.

Cohen deflated, confused. Then he realized that Theron stood at his side, glaring down at Meroy.

The weasel man went pale, his mouth dropping open. Cohen was dumbstruck. Why? What was going on?

Meroy raised both hands, palms out. "I'm not making any trouble with your man, sir," he deferred. "I don't even know him."

Sir?

But Cohen couldn't let this opportunity pass. "You know me. From the warehouse bombing."

A flash of recognition lit up Meroy's eyes. "I didn't have anything to do with that. Clearly! You're Phaira's brother, right? Well, your sister contacted me! I hadn't heard from her for weeks, she never showed for her last bout, I assumed she overdosed in some alley..."

"You don't monitor your fighters?" Theron asked sharply. "Or their drug problems?"

Cohen winced, even as anger bubbled in his blood. Meroy was the dealer. He'd gotten her on mekaline, he knew it.

"Not mine, sir," Meroy protested. "Booking and promotions only, I don't represent them. I would have considered it, though; she was a great prospect. You know, I lost a lot of money when she didn't show up for that last fight - she owes me for breaking her contract."

Meroy turned to Cohen. "You can work it off if you're interested, kid, and more. Big guy like you - or maybe I should just take her in for the bounty reward? Heard it's up to 300,000 rana now - "

A streak of red flashed past Cohen, grabbed the yelping Meroy and wrestled him to the ground.

"Get off!" Meroy roared. "What are you doing?"

But Nox was in a frenzy, grabbing at Meroy's hair, his right fist driving down again and again.

Flushing with humiliation, Cohen hauled Nox off of Meroy. The other man cowered on the floor, his mouth bloodied, but Nox kept swinging. Cohen caught sight of Theron, looming above them all, his face twisted into disgust. "Walk away, kid," the man said. "Don't look back."

Then he was gone, and the click of safeties reverberated through the basement. Meroy's associates had emerged, a semi-circle of firearms now aimed at Cohen and Nox's heads.

Cohen pushed Nox towards the stairs. "We're going," he announced to the gun barrels. "Don't shoot. We're going."

The cold air assaulted Cohen's lungs as he trudged in the direction of Nox's apartment. Six feet behind, Nox stumbled, rambling under his breath. A wave of repulsion hit Cohen at the sounds, the smell of it.

Then Cohen heard his sister's name. He spun around. Nox almost ran into him, skidding in the light layer of snow. "What about Phair?" Cohen demanded. "What are you saying now?"

Nox pushed him away with a snort. "Personal relations. You don't want to know."

Nox? And Phaira?

"Long time ago, buddy," Nox added with a snort. "Just a couple of times. Then she wasn't interested anymore."

"You're right; I don't want to hear about it," Cohen snapped. He stomped down the street, willing for Nox's apartment to appear.

But Nox continued to talk. "She's a cold one, you know," he called from behind, his words slurred. "When she needs a warm body, it's good. Then the next day, nothing. What's that about? I stick up for her, I defend her, and for what? You know, I should come with you guys on this Huma mission, I'm rusty, but I'm still ready to - "

Cohen reached the apartment first. He walked straight into his room, shut the door and locked it. Then he flopped onto the bed, his feet dangling over the edge, and put his pillow over his head.

Eventually, Nox stopped banging on his door. The weight of Cohen's pillow grew heavier with each breath in and out. He was so tired of stupid people, of stupid comments...

A sharp knock on the door startled Cohen awake. He had barely moved during the night, the mattress cutting into his ankles. When he lifted his head, it felt like an anvil was dragging his skull down.

The knocking started again.

"Get out of here, Nox!" Cohen groaned.

"Co," came Nox's voice, low and serious. "I'm leaving."

Grumbling, Cohen wrenched his body up from the bed, yanked off the soggy boot on one foot and padded across the room.

Nox waited outside. He had changed clothes, and shaved. A satchel was slung over his shoulder. His eyes gleamed with excitement. Cohen heard movements in the living room; he craned his neck to see two shadows on the wall. "What's going on?"

"I've got a job," Nox said under his breath. "Contract work. I don't know how long I'll be gone."

"Oh," Cohen said, taken aback. "With who?"

"Remember Keller from last night? Well, he came to recruit me. Personally." The word was framed with pride.

Cohen's head swam. Should he go to Ren, or find Phaira? The thought of that creepy Jala Communia made him shudder. Maybe Ren would be better, him and all the technology people. "What kind of work?"

"I can't tell you," Nox murmured. "Sensitive mission. High risk. But don't worry, I've worked with them before," he added with a wink. "I'll catch up with you in a few days."

And with a crisp turn on his heel, Nox walked back into the living space.

Cohen sighed. He should see him off; it was the polite thing to do. Then he would pack up and figure out where to go.

That man from last night, Keller, paced the circumference of the living room. Another man was with him; dressed in a slim-cut grey suit, he had a full head of white hair on a young tanned face. They both looked up at Nox's entrance. Uncomfortable, Cohen nodded at the two men in greeting. Neither of them reacted. Instead, they studied Cohen, their gaze running up and down.

The back of his neck prickled. Cohen did his best to ignore them, and called out to Nox: "I'll just head out tomorrow, all right? Don't worry about me."

"Thanks, kid," Nox grinned as he stepped through the threshold of the front door.

Then he waited. But the two men didn't move.

"Are we going?" Nox called over to them.

"In a moment," Keller said. Under the fluorescent light, Cohen could see thin spidery scars crawling up one eye. His pale blue eyes never blinked. "Cohen Byrne."

"Yeah," Cohen said, wary. "What?"

"You speak to him with respect," the white-haired man snapped.

"Hey!" Nox exclaimed, striding back into the living space. "Easy, Xanto, he's just a kid."

Keller ignored Nox. "How would you like to earn some rana, Cohen?"

Nox dropped his satchel. In three steps, he was across the room and in front of Cohen. "No," he said firmly.

"You hired me. I'm ready to go, so let's go." His voice dropped in volume, a warning in every word. "He's a kid. He's off-limits."

Keller smiled thinly. "You said you wanted me to meet him, Nox. I have, and I'm impressed. Isn't that what you wanted?"

Was Cohen crazy or did Nox's face turn red? "I wasn't thinking straight. Just - let's go. I'm ready to go."

What was going on? Who were these men?

Tension billowed, hot and smoky in the small apartment. No one moved.

Finally, Nox turned his head to the side. There was panic in his command to Cohen: "Get out of here."

Cohen jumped back and sprinted for his room. The sounds of fighting followed him down the hallway. Cohen was halfway out the window when he heard Nox scream. A bellow of pain followed, and a dull thud. Cohen craned his neck to see into the living room. The lower half of Nox's body was visible on the floor, convulsing.

Cohen's feet hit the carpet and he ran.

Xanto was closest. Cohen grabbed him by the collar, spun and threw Xanto headfirst into the wall.

Keller stood over Nox's body. He held a shock-round in one hand, still crackling. At the sound of his partner's crash, Keller turned, his bloodied face exposed.

A flash of blue. Cohen dodged the electric blast and tackled Keller. The current surged past him and struck the wall. The shock-round flew across the room. Springing back onto his feet, Cohen pivoted and struck

Keller's sternum with the heel of his boot. Just as the man coiled into himself, Cohen snatched him by the lapels, his free hand balling into a fist.

Then everything went white. Searing pain tore through his body. Cohen felt his body drop, and his head hit the carpet.

Then something jammed into his spine and everything went black.

PART FOUR

Are you awake?

She opened her eyes. The rumbling had ceased. They had landed again.

Yes, Sydel, we have arrived. Would you join me, please?

The words echoed around her head; her mind had grown lax with sleep. Sydel quickly rebuilt the walls of her psyche. Her stomach moaned with hunger, but she pushed it out of her thoughts and slowly rolled to her feet. She wrapped the navy wool cloak around her body and peered out of the window.

Red desert and gray sky, no sign of any civilization.

She could just stay inside the storage unit. But she had to say it again to prove a point, even if the answer was the same.

Sydel opened the door and raised her eyes to Huma's waiting face. "I wish to leave."

"Oh, Sydel," the older woman murmured. "I understand. But there is no civilization for miles. For your own safety, I cannot allow you to leave."

Sydel kept the barriers tight around her mind. She would give nothing to these people.

Huma sighed, the sound now familiar to Sydel. "I have an announcement for the group. Please join us."

Never, Sydel thought. But uncertainty followed that thought, and not for the first time.

Several weeks had passed since she boarded Huma's transport. On entry, she refused the offered room. Instead, she did the same as she had in the siblings' old Volante; she found a storage unit and barricaded herself within.

Huma's followers were persistent: first the men, then the women, coming to the door with gentle pleas, passionate promises, heartfelt offers to enfold her into their family. It had no impact. She refused to move, or speak.

Frustration was palpable in the old freighter. She didn't care. They were monsters. But she had made a deal to stay, so she did.

From the dusty windows, Sydel had seen endless gray roads, acres of forests, a million bodies and faces of unknown destinations. She has seen wild animals in the South, industrial skylines, lumbering ships that darkened the sun, and the Impact skerries in the North and East. The novelty of the new wore off quickly, as did the cruel, monotonous, depressed thoughts of the public.

But the flashes scared her. Twice now, images had overpowered her brain. First, the old Volante screaming over water, overlaid by a vision of a daughter, wailing for her father, and a strange word repeated again and again: Hitodama. And then a second premonition: Phaira's blue head crushed by icy hands, sinking, screaming, twisting into dust, her white-hot energy sparking and dying.

The visions might have been trickery, or insanity, but Sydel would never find peace if she didn't warn the family. So she stole moments to try. When Huma and her followers abandoned the freighter and set it ablaze, Sydel left a hasty etching on one of the doors. When the group travelled on public transit underground, on route to securing a new vessel, Sydel found a surveillance camera and a wall to write on. Phaira should be able to see the etchings; the blue-haired woman was an Eko, after all. If the family was even looking for her. Those days seemed like a dream to her now.

Sydel shuffled into the cargo bay, which served as gathering space. Inside, the six members of Huma's group sat cross-legged, awaiting their master's arrival. All had the slightly feverish look of the devoted, even days into this journey, when food was scarce. Their faces were lit in sickly yellow-green from the overhead lights. They didn't look up at Sydel's entry. They knew better by now.

From a distance, always from a distance, Sydel had watched as Huma taught these men and women how to invade each other's minds, cripple motor skills or render someone unconscious with a single focused glance.

And Huma's telekinesis wasn't a part of Eko, after all, but something else entirely. Nadi, the woman explained to her students: self-generated energy, or energy manipulation, which could be used to manifest objects and even control them in mid-air. A wholly new skill, another paranormal oddity. The heat Sydel generated in her hands. That's what it was. She was both Eko and Nadi. What would happen when Huma found out?

A few of the followers were also Nadis. They seemed to spend most of their time in meditation, firearms and crossbows lying in their laps. But as Sydel watched through the window, when those weapons were fired outside, the blasts removed trees from their roots; arrows were able to pierce through steel. They had infused their energy into these weapons on purpose to heighten their power. And Huma encouraged it. It made Sydel sick. That was why she refused to speak to any of them. This morning was no different. She made her way over to the corner to stand apart from the rest.

Finally Huma swept into the cargo area. Gliding into the center of the circle, she sank onto her knees, her hands folded on her thighs. The followers bowed their heads, and she returned the gesture. "I am so proud of every one of you." Sydel was struck by the tenderness in her voice.

"You have proven yourselves to be extraordinary," Huma continued. "And truly evolved into higher forms of being. Today, we come to the end of our journey."

End of their journey? Sydel wondered, uncomfortable with the accolades. Was Huma asking everyone to leave?

One of the converts had the same idea, it seemed, blurting out: "Huma, are you leaving us?"

"No. We are all leaving." Huma's expression became serious. "Just a short distance from here, our destiny awaits. Everything I have trained you for, you must be ready to utilize to fight the great enemy - "

"How dare you."

Heads turned as Sydel's voice echoed through the hanger. The navy cloak slipped from her shoulders, but she didn't care. Her skin was on fire.

"I understand your frustration, Sydel," the older woman soothed. "And I am sorry to have been so secretive. But now that we are here, I can tell you the whole truth. I have said that a tragedy is underway, but not who - "

"It doesn't matter who," Sydel shot back. "To use our abilities to hurt others - to show these men and women how to cause suffering on purpose - "

"It does matter," Huma corrected. "Because the hunt is against our kind. Others like you, like me and all of us. Gifted, and misunderstood. They are being tracked down as we speak."

"What others?" Sydel said sharply. "By who? Why?"

"Please," Huma purred. "Be calm, and let me explain."

Sydel's nails dug into her palms. The skin pulsed underneath. She realized she wasn't breathing. "Explain," she wheezed

"Twenty-five years ago, there was a gathering, much like this one," Huma began, "of masters of mind and body, who came together to evolve. But there was a terrible accident, where civilians were killed, and the masters disappeared into the public sphere. Now they are under threat of extinction and we are here to ensure they survive."

Is that true? Sydel wondered. *Is that why Huma sought to recruit me? To save lives?*

"But you said slaughter," she said outloud.

"Everything I have done has been in preparation to protect our kin," Huma said smoothly. "Show them mercy and forgiveness. Establish a new order and learn from them. Though it has required deceit, and some minor violence, I believe it is worth it."

The followers nodded in unison. Sydel's resolve started to crumble. Was she wrong? Was she being too prejudiced? Look at how these men and women were so ready to serve and to protect. And why else did Sydel have these abilities, if not to prevent horrors?

"If your intention is peace, why work so hard on offensive tactics?" Sydel countered weakly.

Huma nodded. "A fair question. If we are to protect the masters from harm, we must be able to defend ourselves. Wouldn't you agree?"

Those intense green eyes held Sydel's for a long moment.

And Sydel couldn't think of what else to say.

* * *

Pain shot through Cohen's body, jolting him awake. When he gasped for air, it hurt even more. Then memory flooded into his brain. Keller. Xanto. Blue electricity. Nox.

Cohen opened his eyes. The world was dim, the air a strange mix of dust and humidity. Where were they? Cohen tried to lift his head. His spine rippled with agony.

"I know," he heard Nox's voice. "They used a lot of voltage. Plus some kind of sedative to keep us down. Take your time."

Cohen forced his body upright, his legs swinging over the edge of a rickety cot. His eyes adjusted. Nox sat on the floor by Cohen's feet. They were in a windowless room. Partitions were set up, creating private spaces for cots. There were other people throughout the space, sitting or sleeping. The air was heavy, recycled. Were they trapped underground?

"Nox," Cohen whispered. "We have to get out of here."

"Co," Nox said moodily. "We've been recruited."

"Those guys were military?"

"No. But trust me, we should just go along with what they say." He turned to look over his shoulder at Cohen, his voice growing even quieter. "I'll do my best to keep you out of it, Cohen. You just have to keep your head down."

"What is this?" Cohen asked, aghast. "What have you gotten me involved in?"

"Quiet," Nox snapped. "It's just some freelance work: protection, enforcement. I do it for some extra rana and to keep myself in top condition." There was a muted excitement in Nox's voice. It made Cohen want to punch him.

"They assaulted you," Cohen reminded him. "And me. Electrocuted us, drugged us, dragged us here, wherever we are. And you're fine with that?"

"It's one day, two, at most," Nox countered. "Then we go home and it never happened. Like I said, maybe I can keep them from - "

Nox's voice trailed off, and he scrambled to stand up. Cohen craned his neck to see.

A man's silhouette was framed in the only exit to the room. His pale blue eyes seemed to glow. Eyeing the crowd before him, Keller jerked his head to the right. Everyone in the room rose, filtered into single file and followed him through the exit. Cohen stared at the men and women as they passed by, maybe twenty in total; a few were young, thin and sickly, but the rest rippled with power, sharp weapons at their hips. Strangely, his mind turned to Renzo and Phaira; were they here, too?

A push on his shoulder. "Come on," Nox murmured, joining the line. "And don't argue."

In the next room, the white-haired man, Xanto, stood on a raised platform, surveying all those who entered. His suit was fresh and crisp, but his face was bruised. Cohen enjoyed a small rush of pleasure at the sight, as he squeezed along the back wall with Nox, behind the gathering crowd.

As the space filled, Keller stepped up to join his companion. Then he turned and extended his hand to someone in the crowd.

A woman's hand glided into his, followed by a blur of white.

At the sight, Cohen's throat constricted. No mistaking that short silver hair and those hard green eyes; those features were burned into his brain. It was the last thing he saw before he went unconscious, and his first memory when he awoke in the old Volante, his sister haunted and mute, his brother justifying his choice to sacrifice.

Cohen looked around the room wildly, his heart pounding so hard that his vision went blurry. Was Sydel here? The room was so dim that he couldn't make out people's faces, they were packed together so tightly....

Nox glanced at him, mouthing: "What?" Cohen ignored him. His eyes slid back to Huma. She hadn't seen him yet. It was hard to not think Sydel's name over and over again. But he had to control his thoughts and remain still.

The overhead lights dimmed, and video screens unzipped above. Everyone's heads tilted up, their features lit by the projected colors. Cohen scanned the room.

No Sydel. No Phaira or Ren, either. His lungs felt like they were sinking into his gut. He was alone.

The images above changed. Cohen's eyes drifted up with the others. The screens displayed grainy surveillance footage: young men and women huddled into groups, deep in discussion, their faces obscured from the overhead view.

"Twenty-five years ago," Xanto began, his voice booming over their heads. "A group of citizens participated in something referred to as the 'NINE.' Privately funded, organized under top-secret conditions, these people were kept underground for two months to undergo experiments, designed to enhance their paranormal abilities -"

"Paranormal?" Cohen heard a woman exclaim.

"- and when they emerged, they killed three innocent civilians, and damaged the minds of four children with them -"

"The minds?" someone hollered out.

"By the time patrol responded, the participants had disappeared," Xanto continued, ignoring the outbursts. "When the law learned who the victims were, the incident was immediately classified, its few survivors relocated, the information destroyed. Privately, the law saw no value in pursuing the case, not with the victims holding such vast criminal records. There was no public sympathy or outcry, so it was easy to sweep aside."

Then Xanto's face darkened. "But we never forgot. And you all are here to help us hold the NINE accountable."

The room went silent for many seconds. Then murmurs carried through the crowd: "Them?" "Who else?" "Did they say four?"

"You were the children?" a woman questioned.

"Me and my cousins," Xanto said.

Every eye in the space drifted over to Keller. The man never blinked.

"Why wait so long for revenge?" someone shouted.

"It's only recently that we remembered what happened," Xanto said. "Our memories were altered. Even now, it's bits and pieces."

He swept his hand across the room. "It took years of searching, but our efforts finally led us here. You currently stand in the birthplace of the NINE: untouched in a quarter-century."

Cohen stared at the walls all around. His skin broke out in goosebumps. Sounds of surprise echoed all around him.

"And with its discovery, the project's abandoned journals, lessons, and, in limited cases, surveillance footage," Xanto added smugly. "Like the video above you."

Eyes shifted up again, as Xanto continued to speak. "Through these records, we've started to uncover what the NINE acronym stands for, and what we are up against. One N is for Nadi: energetic manifestation and manipulation."

A ripple of disbelief coursed through the crowd. But Xanto pressed on: "The I for Insynn: some form of precognition. And E for Eko: telepathy, memory manipulation. We don't know about the second N yet. But we will, when we get our hands on them."

No one seemed to know what to say. Next to Cohen, Nox's red eyebrows were bunched together. Cohen gulped; if Nox was disturbed, then it was even worse than he thought.

Cohen's mind turned back to Sydel: how she healed his burns, the conversation in the cockpit when they captured that blonde terrorist. She said she was an Eko. So was she one of these NINE? No, Xanto said twenty-five years ago, it wasn't possible. Huma, then? But she wouldn't be standing on that platform if that were true, would she?

"How many are left?" someone yelled from the other side of the room.

"We don't know," Keller said in his low, muttering voice, surprising everyone. "But we believe that capturing one will create the path to the others. The first of you to find a NINE receives 500,000 rana."

Sounds of approval moved through the crowd. Huma surveyed the group with a smug expression, that stupid white cape swept over one shoulder like a queen.

Cohen couldn't help it; his temper exploded.

"Where is Sydel?" he roared.

Heads swiveled, including Keller, Xanto and Huma.

Go ahead, Cohen thought, staring into Huma's eyes and ignoring the rest. *Read my mind. I know who you really are.*

Huma cleared her throat. "Cohen Byrne," she called out. "We will be working together to right a wrong - "

"Like hell we are," Cohen shot back.

Gasps rippled through the space.

"One more word out of you - " Xanto spat, his face growing red. Keller had no expression, though his pale blue eyes were locked on Cohen.

A hand clamped down on Cohen's arm, Nox hissing in his ear: "Stop talking, Co. Stop!"

Then Nox stepped in front and waved weakly at Xanto. "He's young," he called. "I'll teach him!"

As Nox made excuses, Cohen battled with the desire to yank his arm free, bolt for the platform, and snap

Huma's neck with his hands. Huma still watched him, and from the stricken look on her face, she could see all that he imagined. With effort, he pushed aside the looping, violent sequence in his brain.

For Sydel, he thought, glaring at her. *For now, you live.*

"This was the not the introduction I planned, but so be it," Xanto huffed. "To my right is Huma. She has recruited and trained seven Ekos and Nadis to shield us."

Disbelief rippled through the crowd. Xanto raised his hand. "To defeat the enemy, we need to counter their offense, whatever it might be. These individuals are currently shielding this base from human detection, and they will also infuse our weapons, rendering them twice as powerful."

The tone of the crowd shifted from confused to interested.

"I thought you might like that," Xanto smirked. "I know I do. Now, back to the barracks. We will have food brought in. If you want to get paid, keep quiet and be ready to move."

The volume in the room raised several levels. Nox pulled on Cohen's arm again. "You can't say things like that with these people," he berated. "You have no idea - "

"Cohen Byrne." Keller's voice made them both jump.

The pale-eyed man stood next to them, as if he teleported from the platform. The crowd gave a wide breadth around the three.

"Follow me, please." Keller's voice was void of any emotion.

"Keller," Nox begged. "I promise, no more issues, he's good - "

"He comes now, or this ends," Keller replied.

Nox opened his mouth to argue, but Cohen held him back. "It's fine," he told Nox. "I'm fine." He jerked his head at Keller. "Let's go."

Everyone stared, or pretended not to stare, as the two wove through the partitions. The thick metal door was locked by keycode; when Keller punched in a series of numbers, Cohen followed the man into a stairwell of red rock, the dust so thick that Cohen had to control his breath to stop from sneezing. Keller didn't seem to notice as he walked down a long flight of stairs, heading for the lowest floor. Cohen's skin prickled in the silence. He assumed that Huma was behind the summons, but Keller could be separating him to kill him.

The man paused on the last step. Cohen stiffened as Keller's head turned to the side.

"You know, I don't just choose anyone to work for me," came that weird, whispery voice again.

Cohen's hands bunched into fists.

"You hate Huma." There was a hard, gleeful clip at the end of Keller's words. "We're like brothers, you and me. We've faced the same kind of evil."

Cohen clamped down on the shudder that threatened to run through his body.

Finally, Keller hit the bottom platform. Six feet ahead, a metal door stood, marked with a 3, fingers of rust around its edges. He waited until Cohen's boots clomped down. Then the pale-eyed man stepped aside. "Go in. First door to the left"

Cohen stared at the door handle. Should he run? Should he try to incapacitate Keller?

"Cohen, my friend. Please."

Was that a hint of a smile on the man's lips?

Cohen steeled his nerves. Then with one hard jerk, he yanked open the door, swooped in and to the left.

The bright light was blinding. He could only make out a silhouette of someone in the room.

Huma, he thought immediately, adrenaline blasting through his body, his hands balled into fists.

Then his vision began to clear. But the eyes before him weren't cold and green. They were deep brown, wide and shocked. He heard an intake of breath. It was his.

"I can be kind, Cohen. To those I consider an ally," Keller's voice carried into the space. "I hear you two know each other."

Then the door closed with a click.

She was hunched over, like something precious had been taken from her. Her skin was ashy, instead of that warm copper he remembered. But Sydel's face was full of relief as she stared at him.

Cohen's mind raced with a thousand things to say. But each sentence died as soon as he tried to speak.

"Co." Her voice was just as he remembered, soft and melodic.

"Hi," Cohen said. Then he internally cursed at his stupid response. "Are you okay?" he added.

Sydel nodded.

He did his best not to fidget. "Nothing bad is going to happen," Cohen declared. "I promise. I won't let it."

One side of Sydel's mouth turned up, even as her eyes stayed sad. "Oh, I'm not worried for my safety."

Cohen didn't know what to say to that, but he took a chance. In his arms, she felt like a trembling bird: bony and frail, so easy to snap in two. But she was unnervingly hot, almost burning to the touch. Cohen ignored the discomfort, and held her with as much steadiness as he could give. Maybe she felt some kind of security, Cohen didn't know. But Keller's words festered inside him, rising up his throat and threatening to strangle him.

They were trapped.

11.

The sun rose, but the shadows in the cell remained cold and blue. Phaira shivered, tucking her body into a ball. She longed to drift off to sleep again, but her body was coming to life, blood pumping, livening her muscles, energizing her, like it or not. This was not a vacation. She had to finish this. Get back to her brothers. Find Sydel. Resolve everything.

"When you grow angry, your defenses drop. It's no wonder that woman was able to invade your mind. She could have done it even without touch."

Phaira's anger flared at the snide comment, but she kept silent, and concentrated. Yann sat in the center of the Jala Communia, ten feet away from her. The ice swept over her brain again, despite her efforts, and Yann plucked out a surface memory with ease: she and her brothers sitting in the grass after the Hitodama hack, deciding what to do and where to go.

"I will say this again," Yann said. "You must learn to control your emotions. Blind emotion, the body's basic chemical reactions, they are of no use to you."

Easier said than done. She always had a quick temper: like touching a hot piece of coal, one girlfriend called it. The structure and physicality of military life had quelled it somewhat. But since her discharge and everything after, her anger had resurfaced, violent and unexpected.

When she trekked across the grasslands, and first caught sight of the Communia's border, and Yann waiting by the gates, she had to take several minutes to calm her rage before walking to meet him.

"Leave, Phaira. Your first and only warning." His hands buried in his tunic sleeves, the elder's face was void of any expression.

Phaira dropped her satchel into the grass. "Sydel's in danger," she declared. "I can't save her without your help."

Yann's expression didn't change.

"Does that make no impression on you?"

"She is not a part of my community," Yann said evenly. "And as I recall, it was your responsibility to ensure her safety until her return."

It was agonizing, but Phaira forced the words out: "I am humbly asking for your expertise, Yann. I need to learn how to protect my mind from an Eko assault."

He stiffened, glaring at her with his watery eyes. "Sydel," he said under his breath, like a warning.

"Yes, she told me," Phaira said pointedly. "And unless you want your secret to go public, let me in."

Yann was silent for a long time.

"I can't save her without your help, Yann. A fraction of your time. Please."

"You want to learn. So focus."

That was Yann's sole retort when she was led into the inner compound, into his barracks and presented with a series of strange tests.

Look at these cards and project the image. That was a complete failure.

Sit quietly, concentrate and receive information delivered telepathically. Phaira managed to relay random words, blurry images and some colors.

Then tests to her natural defenses. *Think about your family. Remember something sad. Recall what last made you angry.*

The results were mixed, but interesting. Yann decided that Phaira had a natural sensitivity to Eko phenomena; she was a borderline receiver and perceiver, but had no ability to project. And when calm, it seemed that her mind automatically generated a thin defensive barrier.

"But," Yann added. "When you cross over to feelings and fear, everything breaks down and you have nothing. You understand?"

It sounded logical; her temper was the catalyst for so many sins.

So Phaira complied. She was shown to Sydel's old cell. She stayed silent at mealtimes, eating sparingly of what was offered, cringing at the under-salted food, but making no complaints. None of the other residents would acknowledge her, or even look her in the eye. Only Yann would speak to her, and then only for one hour a day: sixty minutes alone in the meditation garden, him invading her mind, Phaira flailing to keep him out. After each session, Yann refused to answer any questions. At night, Phaira trained under the stars, scaling the walls and roofs within the compound, working her body to release her burning frustration.

The routine continued for one week, with no change.

At the end of another fruitless day, Phaira drudged back to her cell. It was the same as Sydel had left it: a hard bed, a single light, and a badly-built armoire, a few books stacked under the bed in a language that Phaira couldn't read. Phaira's satchel lay in the corner, still unpacked, odd-looking in the austere space.

But something new lay on the bed: something small and wrapped in brown paper.

Staring at it from the doorway, Phaira's senses pinged, warning her of all the potential danger within. But who knew she was there? Just her brothers.

And that other guy who kept showing up.

A little thrill went through her. Phaira locked the door behind her. Then she went to the window and searched the courtyard. Whoever left it was long gone.

The package had no weight to it, but there was definitely something inside. She unfolded the paper as quietly as she could.

Inside lay a silver half-circle of wire, approximately a foot in length, barely a centimeter in width. A tiny metal chip was fused into the exact middle. Phaira turned the wire over in her hands, puzzled.

She heard a soft pinging sound, coming from her satchel. The Lissome within carried a message: "It's called a HALO. Secure it around the base of the skull, under your hair. Then press the chip in the middle."

Her curiosity won out over any hesitation. The HALO affixed to the hair just behind her ears, looping around the back of her head. But what did it do? She felt along the length until her fingers found the rough chip in the middle. Half-expecting an electrical shock, she tapped it.

Nothing. Phaira looked around her cell, checking for any difference in her hearing, her sight or her thought patterns. Nothing seemed different.

Her Lissome beeped again. Connection request. She turned to sit on the bed, linking only the audio.

"So what do you think?"

"I don't know what to think." Phaira admitted. "What does it do?"

Theron's voice had a satisfied ring to it. "Your mind is now protected from any Eko invasion. In fact, from anyone trying to overhear this conversation."

"It's - what?" Phaira said, one hand drifting to the cold wire.

"You can leave now." His voice was strangely urgent. "This device not only blocks any kind of psychic assault, but projects stock images and thoughts in its place. When you have it on, no one can touch you. So you don't need these people."

Shadows fell across the length of the cell as Phaira tried to think of a response.

"You don't believe me?"

"I believe you," Phaira said. She bit her lip, running her fingers over the delicate wire. No, she knew what had to be done. "But I still have questions. I need answers before I can leave."

"You didn't go for answers; you went to learn how to stop an Eko. Now I've given you the means to do so." He sounded insulted.

Even though he couldn't see her face, Phaira rolled her eyes. *Why am I arguing with him?* she wondered. "And what if it malfunctions?" she said out loud. "Or gets pulled off? Then I'm vulnerable all over again."

Silence.

"I can't rely on anyone or any kind of device to protect me," Phaira continued. "I have to know that it will never happen again, no matter who - "

"Do you dream about it?"

The question made her pause. Through the Lissome's tinny sound system, Theron's words rippled out like waves. "I manage to block out the memory most of the time. But lately it's been resurfacing in my dreams. I barely sleep as it is. Now it's almost impossible."

She understood. The smug look on Huma's face; icy fingers dragging over her brain; Phaira helpless and screaming, grasping at memories as they slipped out, one by one, dying in the exposed light. Then she would wake from the nightmare, covered in sweat and barely able to breathe. Almost every night.

Then Phaira realized that Theron had gone silent. "Are you there?" she asked.

No answer, but the crackle of static told her that the line was still connected.

She wondered if she should ask him to explain what happened to him, if that seizure she witnessed was related to it.

But the silence unseated her courage.

"Huma has followers," Phaira finally spoke. "I have to be able to deflect any Eko attack, even just for a few seconds. Just long enough to get my hands on her."

"You know you can't trust Yann. Or anyone in that commune. They aren't stupid. They all know what's going on, both inside that place, and in the outside world."

Funny he said that. She'd suspected the same for a few days now. Yann was certainly an Eko, but the rest of the Communia, she wondered about them, too. There were too many knowing looks, too many averted eyes. There were missing pieces to this situation: the reason why Yann allowed her to stay, whether his training advice was beneficial or harmful. How could she know for certain, though?

"I don't trust them," Phaira finally said. "Believe me. I never will."

When the call ended, Phaira went to unclip the HALO. There was a sound outside her door; probably just someone taking a walk, but she stiffened just the same. She left the HALO on. Her brothers were expecting her to call that night, and something sensitive might come up.

Phaira punched in the cc for Nox's apartment. As she waited, she rolled her neck from side to side. She wished that she didn't have to talk any more that night. Yes, she

missed Cohen and Renzo, but the conversations were always long and intense, and the aftermath made her think
too much. Theron had already put enough thoughts in
her head.

The Lissome tried to connect for a full minute. Then
an error message beeped. She checked the series of numbers and letters again. It was the right order. She tried
again. Error.

Phaira's heart began to thump. She quickly typed in
the cc for Anandi and Renzo. Scenarios flickered through
her mind. Kidnapped. Dead. Gone.

"Phaira?" Renzo squinted through the screen.
"What's wrong?"

"Have you talked to Co lately?"

"A few days ago. Why?"

"No one is picking up at Nox's apartment."

"So they're out right now."

Phaira was already stuffing her few belongings into
her satchel, strapping the borrowed longblade across her
back, plotting the quickest route to Daro.

"Whoa, Phaira, wait!" Renzo ordered. "Wait until
morning. Let me see if I can reach him. Maybe Nox got
called into work."

"Maybe," Phaira said. "But Cohen would have called
to tell us. I know something's wrong. I know it."

"You're letting those people mess with your mind. I'll
get Anandi on it, okay? Call you back."

Phaira dropped the satchel on the bed. Every muscle
in her body was rigid. The touch of cold metal on the

back of her neck made her jump. Theron's HALO was still attached; she had forgotten about it. She unclipped it and held it in both hands. Simple, but incredibly powerful. Deceptive. A bit of a cheat, too.

Then again, Yann was too. She could tell from the first moment she saw him in that medical center: how he loomed over her with that smug expression; how he lorded his authority over Sydel, a girl who burned with insecurity, aching to please him. How coldly he rejected Sydel, saddling her with three strangers.

Phaira had been going about this the wrong way. Honor and rules had no place in this new world. Yann would never tell her anything.

If she wanted his honesty, she had to make him afraid.

* * *

The next day, Phaira was already waiting in the garden when Yann appeared for their session. Fifteen feet away, the older man settled into a seat on the grass, as per usual, and folded his hands over his knees. Her satchel sat by her feet, along with Theron's longblade. She wore her black street clothes, her hood pulled over her hair to conceal the HALO underneath: inactive but there, just in case.

"Are you leaving?" Yann finally asked. He sounded bored at the thought.

"I have questions first," Phaira replied. She placed her hands behind her back. "And I'm asking one last time for answers."

"I have nothing to share with the likes of you."

"So be it." Phaira took a step forward. Her eyes never left his.

"What are you doing?"

Phaira said nothing and took another step, and then another.

She was five feet away when Yann raised his hand.

There it was: icy tethers, seeping into the back of her head. Panic rose in her throat. But instead of pushing down her emotions, as Yann had taught her, she did the opposite: she let her fear take over.

A flash of cold blasted through her blood, followed by adrenaline, her nerves sparking white-hot. In those rampant seconds, the rush was terrifying and ecstatic. And Yann let out a strangled cry as Phaira looped her arm under his chin, his hand still outstretched as his body jerked for air.

"Questions, Yann," Phaira stated. "Ready now?"

"Yes.... yes..."

Phaira released him. As Yann took in a gulp of air, Phaira reached back to turn on the HALO. Her teeth chattered, her muscles spasmed, and her eyes were wet with tears. But her instinct was correct. Emotion was the key to her defenses.

Feel the fear. Just like Sydel said.

And Yann had been manipulating her this whole time, using her naivety to pick through her memories. She glared down at Yann's bald head, disgusted at believing a single word from his lips.

Then, in every direction, Phaira could feel eyes on her. There was a heaviness growing in the air, like a fog rolling in. The others in Jala Communia. She had to be quick.

"How - your skill-set has developed so quickly - how - " Yann was gasping.

"Questions, Yann." Phaira cut him off. She pushed her knees into his shoulders, and gripped his chin and his forehead. "Say the wrong thing and I break your neck. You'll be gone before anyone can reach you. Understand?" She torqued his neck, putting more pressure on the cervical spine. "Why did you throw Sydel out?"

"There is history here that you cannot begin to understand," he sputtered.

"Try me," Phaira said, twisting more. "Now."

The lines on Yann's face caught the sun. Then he slumped over. "I ran out of chances," he wheezed.

"What does that mean?" Then Phaira asked the question she had held onto for weeks: "And what did you mean when you said that Sydel is older than she looks?"

Yann's body jerked. "When did I say that?"

"When you excommunicated her. What does that mean? She looks barely eighteen."

"She is not." The answer was a whisper.

"I've guessed that," Phaira said, impatient. "How old is she, really?"

Yann deflated again. "I tried to mold her," he murmured, not seeming to hear Phaira's question. "I started her fresh and ignorant again, so many times. She never seemed to age, so it was easy. But always the same result: too powerful, too dangerous, on the brink of exposure."

His eyes rose up to Phaira's. "I never took part in hurting those children," he whispered. "I ran for my life when the chaos began. I've kept myself hidden for twenty-five years, out of respect for those who died. But I always knew they would come after us."

Phaira released Yann's head and stepped back. Her mind swam with all the strange details, but one picture formed clearly: one of Sydel guided, prodded, lectured, chastised for her abilities, and then her mind erased to start the training anew. A fresh start. A blank canvas. Another chance to gain control.

"How many times did you wipe Sydel's memory?" she asked, barely able to comprehend the words.

"Too many," Yann murmured, rubbing the back of his neck. "When you and your brothers arrived, I was on the last restart. My brothers and sisters were tired of pretending that she was normal. They were no longer willing to take the risk of housing her. It was a unanimous vote."

Phaira wanted to place her boot into his back and shove him through the dirt. Instead, she crouched down to ensure that Yann heard her. "Why let me in here and pretend to train me?"

"Sydel, of course," Yann muttered, not turning around. "I wanted to know what you knew. How she lived in your care, if she continued to grow in power. I know I was the force behind her departure, but I couldn't help but worry about her. I never had a child of my own."

"You still don't have a child," Phaira corrected. "Rot here with your minions. You're never going to see that girl again."

Then she swept up the fallen satchel and longblade, walked through the tunnel, and onto the dying grass of the Midland plains.

III.

Anandi's shoulders drooped from exhaustion, but she kept working into the night, trying to uncover information about the so-called psychic attackers, as Phaira had relayed.

I shouldn't bring Anandi into this, Renzo thought more than once. But Cohen was missing. And he didn't know what else to do.

Within the hanger, the *Arazura* stood in silence, complete and operational. After a hearty congratulatory party and some raucous test flights, the other scientists, rebels and squatters had drifted back into the shadows. Standing before the *Arazura*, reliving those moments, calmness settled over Renzo. These past few weeks would remain close to him. Though his brain was still unpredictable, it was one of the first memories since the assault that Renzo felt determined to keep.

As the sun rose, Renzo fired the engines. They barely made a sound. He only had to touch the throttle for the ship to respond. And as the *Arazura* lifted into the air, exhilaration rushed through him, quickly followed by guilt. But in a strange way, he could hear his sister's voice, joking: "It's a good thing, Ren. Don't punch yourself in the face about it. We'll find Co, and he can be proud too."

The *Arazura* travelled out of the Mac and across a stretch of parched grassland. Within the six hours of

319

flight, the landscape dotted with houses, thicker and thicker. Then the *Arazura* descended into the east end of Daro. Building exteriors grew more rundown, mottled with rust. Renzo reduced his speed as the black parking hanger loomed into clarity. On the third floor, he caught sight of a human silhouette, sitting on the edge. That telltale blue hair came into focus.

The *Arazura* seemed to change everything; on entry, the parking attendant offered him access to the higher floors, where the more expensive transports were housed. Renzo smiled and paid the attendant a few rana to ensure the ship wasn't stolen. When the *Arazura* clicked into a landing crate, the magnetic bolts fastening with a groan, Renzo fought the urge to check the exterior for scratches. Instead, he hurried down to street level, where Phaira waited.

"Did you find Co?" she asked him on sight.

The memory of Nican Macatia swept into Renzo's mind. Her anger once led to Nican falling off a bridge. And Cohen was still missing. How would she react when he told her?

But then Renzo noticed her eyes. They were fixed on his feet.

He'd forgotten. They hadn't seen each other for weeks. And he wasn't limping anymore.

And right before him, that dark woman became his little sister again, her face contorted into that baffled expression he'd seen a thousand times before.

Renzo grinned. "I know." He leaned over and lifted his trouser hem. "I made it. Well, Anandi's friend helped."

He took a moment to admire the work. The silver prosthetic had the flexibility and working musculature of a human limb; perfectly balanced, he felt no pain. He could walk, he could even run and jump, though he hadn't worked up the nerve to try the latter yet.

His sister continued to stare. Renzo cleared his throat. "You know, I never... I never apologized to you," he said gruffly. "For that last night in the apartment. I'm sorry. I'm really sorry."

Phaira flinched. "Don't, Ren," she muttered. "It was my fault. All of it. I make some really terrible decisions."

"They aren't all catastrophes," Renzo corrected. It was the most he dared to say, and luckily, it was enough; he caught her faint smile in response. Relieved, he gestured to the curve in the road. "Down this way?"

Within minutes, they were outside Nox's apartment complex. The door was locked, but Phaira twisted the mechanics and popped it open with little effort.

Inside, the place was a disaster. Smashed glass. A smear of blood across one wall, a scorch pattern burned into another. Chairs upturned. Dried blood spattered on the carpet, though not enough to make Renzo panic. Not yet.

Renzo searched the other rooms. Dust was already starting to settle on the few belongings.

Then his Lissome beeped.

"Phair," Renzo said, breaking the silence in that dead apartment. "Phaira."

Phaira's head turned towards him. He could see the sharp angle of her nose, her dark mouth set in a line, but nothing else.

Renzo held up the Lissome. "What did you find, Ani?"

Anandi's voice was tinny and nervous. "I cracked some encrypted surveillance, and I saw them. Cohen and your friend Nox, taken by two men, loaded into a ground transport. Too far away to identify anyone or any registration number. But - "

Anandi hesitated. She was nervous, Renzo realized. Why?

"Did you know that Nox has been working for the Sava syndicate?" she finally asked.

"The what?" Phaira and Renzo asked simultaneously.

"The Sava Family. Crime syndicate in the south cities, though they've started to creep up the coast. They have a lot of eyes and resources. It's why it's taken me so long to uncover even a bit of information, I had to switch routes three times to avoid being tracked. By the look of it, the heir apparent to the syndicate was one of the kidnappers, Keller Sava."

Phaira cradled the base of her skull, her jutting elbows hiding her face. Briefly, Renzo entertained the fantasy of swinging a crowbar at Nox's head. Then he forced himself to focus. "Why would they take Co?" he wondered out loud. "Would Nox have brought Cohen into - ?"

"No," Phaira said shortly, surprising Renzo. "Nox is bored with civilian work and looking for a thrill. I know him, Ren. I have to believe that he wouldn't intentionally involve Cohen."

"There's more," Anandi spoke up. "There are rumors on the network that some kind of big event is about to take place. There are new entries about Ekos, too: more theories than before, more stories of encounters. And other people are missing too. Remember Lander from the Hitodama? He's listed as missing. There's a rumor that he was blackmailed into service, though where - "

Phaira took the Lissome from Renzo's hand. "Like you were?"

A long pause. "What do you mean?"

"Did that woman Saka try to blackmail you to work for her, in exchange for your father's safe return?"

Renzo looked from the back of Phaira's head to the Lissome.

"I wasn't sure at the time," Anandi finally confessed. "A large deposit was made into one of my dummy accounts and a pick-up time and address forwarded. No signature. I ignored it; I get requests like that all the time. Then those Hitodama were killed and my father taken. Five minutes after I got the news, another message with a pick-up time came through, and I realized they were connected. I was so scared, but then I met you, Phaira, and I knew you could get him away and keep us safe..."

Anandi's voice trailed off. "I'm sorry. I was trying to protect my father and me from exposure. I should have told you everything. Both of you."

"Yes, you should have," Phaira retorted. Then she disconnected the line. The Lissome hung at her side. Renzo couldn't tell what his sister was thinking. He wasn't sure what to think of that exchange, either.

"How did you get here, Ren?" Phaira asked suddenly, blinking like she'd just woken up. "Did you take public transit?"

"I flew," Renzo said. "On a private ship. My ship," he corrected, nervous for some reason he couldn't identify. "I've been - well, not just me, but - I restored a live-in transport. With Anandi and some other people."

Phaira exhaled, her breath a sigh. "I don't know what to do, Ren. This is so far beyond anything I know."

As she trailed off, Phaira's hand slipped into her jacket's inside pocket, rubbing her thumb over something. Renzo frowned. "What's that?"

Phaira retrieved the object: a silver half-circle that Renzo recognized immediately. "Where did you get that?" he exclaimed.

"This?" Phaira asked, still half in thought. "It was sent to me. What, you know what it is?"

"Seen it?" Renzo scoffed. "I created it! Well, with another guy in the group. He perfected it, but we drafted up the plans together. I have more in the ship for us, but Theron kept the HALO prototype. Why would he send it to you?"

"Theron?" Phaira exclaimed, her blue eyebrows shot high. Then her body slumped. "Unbelievable," she muttered.

"What are you talking about?" Renzo asked impatiently, but Phaira was already heading in the direction of the broken front door.

Renzo threw up his hands, mouthing curses at the ceiling. All this secretiveness drove him mad. But there was nothing left to do but follow his sister back to the *Arazura* and hope for inspiration.

* * *

Over the next few days, Cohen took stock of his situation.

There were three floors to the underground base. The top floor held the hacker experts, or at least, that was what Cohen overheard. He'd never been upstairs.

Fifteen mercenaries were housed on the middle floor: some heavy and muscular, others slim and silent, but they all crackled with pent-up energy, pacing, sharpening, waiting for further instruction.

On the third floor, at the bottom of the stairwell, were the six Huma followers, plus Sydel and Huma herself. They were shielding the base from surveillance and infusing the weapons supply with energy. Sydel refused to participate, despite bribes and threats from Keller, and was only protected through Huma's intervention. During their daily visits, listening to her recount, Cohen burned with fear for the girl. He already felt nauseous most of the time, worse if he thought about their situation too much.

And Keller didn't help with Cohen's anxiety. The strange man came to see Cohen often, drawing him into private conversations, reminding Cohen that he must be ready to prove his worth at any moment. In the same breath, Keller would remark on how satisfying it would be to get his well-deserved revenge on Huma. Cohen only nodded in response as his insides twisted.

On the fourth day, Keller's shadow entered the second floor. Cohen desperately looked to Nox for rescue. But the man was in the middle of a raucous conversation with the other mercenaries. Nox didn't seem to see how twisted this all was; there was a thrill in his voice, no matter the topic of conversation. Well, Cohen didn't care how much money they were offering or how much potential Keller saw in him. He would never forget the feel of electricity ripping through his spine.

With no available distraction, on command Cohen followed Keller into that now-familiar stairwell and down to the third floor platform. Cohen remained on the bottom step, as Keller wandered over to the door marked 3. The man leaned his forehead against the door: at first gently, and then harder, so the exposed parts of his brow grew white.

"If you had Huma to yourself," Cohen heard the man murmur. "What would you do to her? Would you want her to suffer, or to die outright?"

"I don't know," Cohen responded, his throat tight.

Keller turned his face towards him. So Cohen faked a laugh. "I'd make it quick. But brutal." The consonants echoed up to the rocky ceiling.

Keller pressed his back against the metal. "It's so hard to stay on this side of the door when all you want to do is tear them apart."

Cohen flinched involuntarily. Keller caught it. "Not your girl, of course," the man added. "Though you understand why I am wary around her."

"Of course," Cohen agreed in a hurry. "After what happened to you and your cousins, of course."

A long stretch of silence. Then Keller spoke again. "I hear you refuse to touch the infused weapons. Why?"

For once, Cohen felt like he could be honest. "Whatever it is, energy, essence, whatever, it's creepy. I don't want any part of it."

Keller grinned. He pushed up off the door, clapping a cold hand on Cohen's shoulder. "It was all Xanto, you know, getting Huma involved. I never wanted a part of them. I suppose they serve a purpose, for now, but you're right, we shouldn't rely on their tricks."

If I keep agreeing with him, Cohen thought the whole while, *if I keep on his good side, he'll let me go. If he likes me enough, he'll let Sydel come too.*

It was something to cling to, as Cohen moved through the day, watching the slow build of anticipation, praying for some kind of clue on how to get out.

* * *

Phaira watched the pink petals break from the dying trees and float down. The tiny memorial park had been long neglected, vines and bushes grown over, creating little pockets of privacy, even in the center of Daro. Her long white trench coat belted tightly, the heavy collar was turned up against the damp, cold air, with Theron's longblade strapped across her back on the diagonal.

A rustle of movement behind her. The sound of his steps was to the left, only a few feet away.

She debated whether to punch him in the face.

Her index fingers tapped the bench twice in thought. No. He needed to be able to speak.

But she had to make him drop all pretenses, just to get a sense of the truth.

One method came to mind.

As she turned, Phaira caught a glimpse of Theron's surprised eyes before she grabbed the lapels of his grey wool overcoat, yanked him down to her level, and kissed him.

At first, his lips were stiff with shock. Then they softened, and he softened. His arms slid around her back and, suddenly, her feet lifted off the ground. Phaira heard an involuntary squeak come from her throat. Then the sensory rush overwhelmed her: his enveloping warmth; how good he smelled; how forcefully he kissed her back.

She made a choice. Five long, woozy seconds of indulgence.

Now focus. Focus! This isn't about you.

Phaira broke away with effort, ducking her head. She waited, eyes closed, until she felt her boots touch the grass again. Under her scarf, the base of her throat was on fire. She resisted the urge to touch it.

"Is that what you've wanted?" Phaira began, her voice low and honeyed. "Is that why you gave me sanctuary, and transporation..."

Then she opened her eyes. "...and invented that HALO with my brother?"

She heard him catch his breath. When his arms loosened, Phaira stepped back, her tone sharpening. "What are you doing with me and my family? What's your endgame? A straight answer is all I want."

His silence made Phaira's chest grew tight. Theron didn't moved, his expression neutral save for the faint flush in his face. Finally, he slid his hands in his pockets of his overcoat, and shrugged.

"Fine," he said, his jawline a right angle of tension. "I told you I would bankroll your start-up costs. But I recognized that you come as a package deal. So I assessed my potential investment from all angles. And I assisted as necessary."

"Did you spend some time assessing Cohen, too?" Phaira shot back. Theron didn't say anything. A wave of disappointment crashed over her. "Where is he?" she demanded.

"I had nothing to do with that," Theron started, lifting his hands.

"You're telling me you don't know where he is?"

"That's not what I'm saying, I just - " He stuttered a little. "I mean, I didn't think they would just take him like that. He's so young - "

Phaira's heart leapt. "Did you set him up?"

"What? No!" Theron exclaimed. "I tried to warn him off, but I couldn't intervene. Not directly."

Warn him off. Couldn't intervene. So he was involved in all of this, whatever this was. Regardless, she had to ask. "I need your help."

"I've done enough, Phaira." His voice carried an undertone of fear. "I can't risk any more exposure."

"You coward."

The word visibly startled Theron.

"You know my brother is missing," Phaira went on. "You know where, you know why, and you won't help me get him back?"

"Like I said," Theron countered, his eyes blazing gold. "I can't get involved. Cohen should have never been recruited. But when I saw the danger, I did what I could to try and stop it."

She hardly heard his protests. *Oh, this is bad,* she lamented. *This is even worse than I thought. Cohen. He could be anywhere.* To her horror, tears pricked at her eyes. She turned away from Theron, willing them to reabsorb.

Long seconds passed. Darkness began to creep along the landscape, the pale pink of the blossoms turning a fiery orange.

"Phaira, I was four years old when the NINE attacked." His flat voice startled her. "I woke up in the hospital a month later. My mother, aunt and uncle were dead. My cousins and I were sent to live with our grandfather. I just wanted to be a normal kid, to forget that it ever happened. But my cousins could never let it go. And now they have the money and power to take revenge, to use whatever or whomever they want to make it happen."

Phaira turned her head, just to see his body language. His left hand clenched and unclenched, the veins pressing through the skin. It seemed like the truth. Question after question rippled through her mind. She might as well start with the most dangerous one.

"You're one of the Savas."

In her peripheral vision, she saw him nod.

Theron Sava. Phaira rolled the name around in her head, hardly able to believe it. "Your cousins are Savas too?"

"Keller. Xanto." Theron listed. Then after a short pause: "And Kadise. Or 'Saka,' as she went by online."

Her blood froze. Phaira looked over her shoulder, left and right, searching for any signs of surveillance. She had killed a Sava. This couldn't be happening...

"No one knows, Phaira," Theron was saying, in the midst of her panic. "You're not marked. She was a mess and it wasn't much of a loss, believe me."

How did even he know she was involved in Saka's death?

332 | LOREN WALKER

"My cousins are set on hunting down any of the NINE who might still be alive," Theron continued. "They've been building a team for months. Hired muscle. Hackers to shield their actions."

He paused. "And that woman Huma to protect them. I suspect that girl Sydel is still with her, too."

Horrified, Phaira backed away, but Theron caught her arm. "It's not what you think," he told her. "I didn't know she assaulted you, or took your friend away - "

Phaira's thoughts were spinning so violently, she couldn't even wrench her arm free. How had this happened? How had she gotten caught in this?

"I know. The whole situation is out of control," he confirmed under his breath. "But Keller is the oldest, the successor to my grandfather, so no one questions him. Xanto goes along to keep him under control. But Keller has the family's backing, the funds, and the connections. I can't stop them, even if I wanted to. But I think you can. And I've been trying to ensure that you have every resource to do so."

"Why haven't you joined them?" she choked out.

"I'm not like them," Theron emphasized each word. "I just want to be left alone. To make my own life."

"Well, I can't..."

Then the words died on her lips. Of course she was going to try to rescue them all. What else would she do? Even if she died in the process, it didn't matter.

Suddenly, his fingers slid off her arm. "I know where they are," Theron said quietly. "I can forward the coordinates. I don't know how much time there is. But I'm sorry. About your brother. And your friends."

He sounded genuine enough. But Phaira didn't want to look at him anymore.

So she unstrapped the longblade from her back and pushed it into his chest. When Theron's hand closed around the casing, she ran.

As Phaira wove through the overgrown trees, turning up her collar against the wind, she fought a sudden, desperate yearning to go back. Foolish, irrational, undeserving: but undeniably there. Even in the wake of everything revealed.

Phaira brushed a pink petal off her shoulder and shook her head to loosen any remaining ones. She had room in her brain for only one complex question: how to take on a crime syndicate, save her brother and friends, and keep everyone alive.

I V.

"There's nothing."

"Nothing?" Renzo repeated.

Anandi gestured at the topographic map, the small patch highlighted in blue. "It's the Kings Canyon in the West. Desert, mountains; preserved historical space, so little development. There's no access to satellites in that area, so I can't see if there's any activity within." She glanced over to Phaira. "You're certain that there's an underground base there? Doesn't seem likely."

Phaira didn't say anything. Could she really trust anything that Theron told her?

"So the only option is to go there, then," Renzo said grimly. "And see for ourselves."

"Is that wise?" Anandi protested.

"It's the only clue we have. We have to do something."

"And if you find the place? And the Savas?" Anandi pressed on. "What then?"

Renzo went to speak again, but Phaira interrupted. "I'm going to volunteer my services."

"What? No, you're not going to do that!" Renzo exclaimed, his hands gripping the head of the pilot's seat.

"Ren, how else will we get inside?" Phaira argued. "The Savas want warm bodies, willing to pull a trigger on command. I have the skill set, they'll see it right away. They'll take me in."

"You don't know that," Renzo pointed out. "You don't know what they'd do. They might kill you as soon as you're out of public view. Or ship you off for parts unknown. We don't even know who these Savas are looking to hunt down. There's nothing out there on that attack you mentioned, from twenty years ago or today."

Phaira glanced to her left. "Emir? Help me out here."

From the corner, Anandi's father pulled on his white beard. "It's risky," he conceded. "But I agree with Phaira; something must be done, and quickly."

He pushed himself up to standing. "Though she shouldn't be the one to do this. I will volunteer. Phaira can be my shadow."

"Are you crazy? Why would they trust you over her?" Renzo exclaimed. "Didn't one of them kidnap you?"

"There's history between the Savas and Ajyos," Emir said. Phaira caught his quick glance at Anandi: a warning for her to remain silent. "Enough to give them pause, if I remind them of it."

Anandi's forehead creased with worry. "Papa, no. What if they lock you away? Your heart - "

"Anandi," Emir interrupted gently. "As Phaira said: the Savas need hands, and not just to kill. They need to conceal what they're planning to do. Premeditated murder is still a crime. If I show up and I know about their scheme, if they believe their security is comprised, they'll think twice, won't they? Maybe even hire me to correct the issue. And then I can get Phaira inside. I sense she's capable of a resolution. And it's the least I can do to repay a debt."

"There's no debt," Phaira said uneasily. "It's not right to involve you, especially if you're ill."

"See, Papa," Anandi broke in. "It's not necessary."

The older man walked to Anandi and placed his hands on his daughter's shoulders. "I choose to get involved," he told her. "There's a larger threat here, even if you can't see it yet."

Her eyes full of tears, Anandi buried her face into Emir's arm. Then the two slipped out of the cockpit and into the *Arazura's* gleaming corridor. Even as their voices faded away, Renzo continued to look after them, his face unreadable.

Finally, Renzo wandered over to the pilot's seat, sitting down with a thump. Phaira placed her forearms on the chair headrest. For a long time, they were both silent.

"I'll go too," Renzo finally announced.

"Someone has to stay outside, Ren. If Emir can get me in, I'll do whatever I can to protect Co. And Sydel, if she's there too. Maybe there's a way to sneak them out of there and you can come for us."

"I can't let you do this. There's no way this will work. You'll be killed."

Probably, she thought. *But I'd rather it be me than Cohen.*

"Getting in doesn't worry me as much as getting out," Phaira said instead. "I can guess at the basic security measures in place: cameras, posted guards with orders to shoot to kill, but there's no way to know until I see it."

She paused, thinking. "But, Ren, if I can find them, if I can find a way out, you have to come as fast as you can. I don't know when that would be, it's so isolated out there; it could be just minutes of an opening."

"I'll be there when you need me," Renzo cut her off. "This ship is faster than anything in public operation."

He twisted to the right, so he could look Phaira in the eyes.

"No matter what," he repeated. "I'll be there."

* * *

Sydel listened to the whispers infused in the walls: the wonder, the paranoia, the anguish. This underground palace crackled with ghosts. And try as she might, she could not block out the old voices.

"Sydel." Huma's smooth voice floated through the space. "May I come in?"

The florescent light made her hair brilliant and white, but it also cast shadows across her face, deepening the lines around her eyes. When the door closed with a click, the woman's hand trailed down its frame.

"I feel it too, you know," Huma murmured. "All the energy of the NINE, still here, still vibrant. This place is incredible. If you only removed yourself from isolation, we could uncover so much."

Sydel shifted into the corner of the cell, and turned her back to the woman.

The hem of Huma's robe brushed across the floor, closer and closer. When finally settled next to Sydel, tiny pops echoed through the space: her creaking joints. The older woman sighed, long and low. At the edge of Sydel's peripheral vision, she could see Huma rubbing her bony hands together, again and again.

Why is she nervous? Sydel wondered bitterly.

"I think it's time you knew what's to come, Sydel," Huma finally said. She leaned into Sydel's line of vision; Huma's eyes were red at the edges, even as her emerald irises were bright. "Do you know when my abilities were activated?"

"I don't care." Sydel enunciated each word.

"I wasn't born with the gift," Huma said, ignoring Sydel's dismissal. "Not like you. I was a mother, a wife, a seamstress, just an ordinary citizen. Then, one night, I heard voices. I thought I was going mad. I could hear screams and shouts, but I was alone, no one near for miles. After an hour, it ended. I set it aside, and chalked it up to fatigue or dreams.

"But the next day, the world was inside my head: the thoughts and emotions of those around me, my husband, my family," Huma continued. "From that night on, I sought to develop my gifts to the peak of their abilities. I transformed that night, and I wanted more. And I went from fearing evolution to embracing it wholly."

Sydel lifted her head from her knees, wary but listening, as Huma went on. "For twenty-five years, I have been mastering my skills as an Eko, and then, remarkably, as a Nadi: reading, researching, traveling, experimenting, and at the same time, always wondering if there might be others like me."

"Some weeks ago, I received a meeting request from Keller Sava and his cousins: a command, more than anything else. He heard of my wandering efforts. I was terrified what they might want from me. But I was blessed, Sydel, for I learned of the existence of the circle of NINE, and their emergence exactly twenty-five years ago."

Huma's eyes grew wide. "Do you see? These people triggered my gift. They brought me to life. And they are the ones that I belong with, the only ones worthy to teach me."

"Are they?" Sydel said flatly. "You seem to get along with these syndicate men. How does one relate to the other?"

"Oh, foolish men and their lust for revenge," Huma scoffed under her breath. "They think they will right a great injustice? If the NINE are as powerful as rumored, it will be a mercifully short event."

"But the Savas are very powerful people, Sydel," she added, "with unlimited funds and access to the world. So by aligning with them, I gained their trust, their financial backing, and the means to finally conduct a proper search for others like us."

The volume of Huma's voice dropped even more. "Yes, it's true that my students have been diverting the family's attention with the notion of infusing Nadi into their weapons cache. But I'm sure you know as well as I do: the

further the Nadi is from its original source, the less po-
tent. Those weapons will be useless when they are taken
on the road."

Sydel didn't know that, and she cursed Yann for leaving her so ignorant. "So you are sending those men and
women upstairs to death."

"Their chosen path in life is killing, Sydel," Huma
corrected. "Their own deaths, while unfortunate, are
not unexpected. Why do you think the Savas recruited
them? They won't be missed if something goes wrong."

Suddenly Huma clasped Sydel's hand, her fingers hot
and strong. "There isn't much time," the woman whispered. "Very soon, one of the Savas will demand that
you send out a distress call to the NINE. They know you
can send telepathic messages far and wide, and they will
force you to claim that you are an ancestor... "

"Ancestor!" Sydel gasped.

But Huma kept whispering. "...and prod the NINE out
of hiding. If you concede to their threats, they will take
the first NINE to arrive and torture her, draw out the
location of the others before they slowly dissect her flesh
and desecrate it. Then the mercenaries will hunt down
the rest of the NINE. And Cohen will be forced into
service on pain of death. But you can stop this, Sydel.
Together, we can - "

Cohen, Sydel thought suddenly. *Cohen should be here, if
only to keep me from falling under her spell. I am already so tempted
to believe...*

Sydel yanked her hand away. "You lie. You twist words. I refuse to believe you."

"I understand," Huma said. She bowed her head, opening her palms to the ceiling. "Search my mind, Sydel. Verify that every word is true. I've already summoned Cohen Byrne as witness."

"I don't do that sort of thing," Sydel snapped.

"It's quite simple. Use the edge of your thumbnail to create an opening, and - "

"I know how to do it," Sydel interrupted. "But it's a crime against - "

The door to the cell burst open, making both women jump. It was Cohen, outfitted in black body armor, his hair freshly shorn, imposing as he loomed in the threshold.

"Cohen," Huma greeted him.

Cohen's face darkened in response. He leaned over to catch Sydel's eye. "Are you okay?"

"Huma has offered up her mind for me," Sydel said, still indignant. "To verify she tells the truth. She says she is on the side of good."

Cohen's features changed to a guarded, but sly expression. Sydel knew what he was thinking.

Now is our chance.

Maybe he was right. It would be easy. Cohen was stronger than the two women combined. He could restrain Huma, and Sydel could incapacitate her.

Or even more than that. She could paralyze the woman. Kill her. Control her. Sydel didn't know why she was so certain of her capacity to do such a thing. But she could do it.

It would be easy.

* * *

As they walked across the desolate land, the sun blazing above them, Emir began to sing. His voice was a rich baritone, and resonated off the dunes: an old song, some lovers' lament. Slowly, Phaira recalled the notes and lyrics, first in Emir's rendition, then in her memories.

The singing in the house stopped when her mother got a sore shoulder. Just a strain, she told them all. But when forced to go see a doctor, they discovered cancer in her bones, fast-moving and incurable. She deteriorated so quickly. Cohen was only four years old, so twelve-year-old Phaira and thirteen-year-old Renzo worked to shelter him from the worst. They put him to bed and dressed him in the morning; they took him for walks and adventures in the city. He was always with one of them; it was probably why he turned out so well-adjusted.

But late at night, when her little brother slept, Phaira remembered her stolen glimpses of their mother in the last days, how their father carried her from the bed to the bath, how the skin stretched thin over her bones.

Every hour, Emir needed to rest, sweat beading on his forehead, perspiration spreading under his arms. Staying at a distance, Phaira wondered if the old man could last in this heat. But eventually he would get up and start to walk again, slower each time, but moving forward.

Time passed. The landscape grew rockier, the dull sand turning to red earth. Emir had to watch his step now, dodging large rocks and crevices. He never looked back. If he had, he might have caught a slight shimmer. But to anyone watching, Emir was alone in the desert.

Five hours earlier, Renzo and Phaira were in the *Arazura's* common space, creating schematics, hypothesizing on what lay beneath the red sandstone range, the exact location of the coordinates that Theron provided. Mining her knowledge of government-run bases, Phaira laid out the probable design. An entrance somewhere at ground level, but also an emergency exit. Tunnels, ventilation shafts, perhaps some sort of aerial escape option....

"No," Renzo countered, staring at her notes. "I bet it's a designated no-fly zone. I bet the Savas have already thought of that. To keep the area clear. No witnesses."

"It is," Anandi chimed in from across the room. "Says it's government-ordered, but who knows. Recently renewed to protect natural resources from contamination, whatever that means."

"Okay, then," Phaira murmured, a little surprised. "You're good at this, Ren."

Renzo grinned at her. Phaira chose not to tease him in that moment.

Then her brother jumped to his feet, scattering papers in all directions.

"What's wrong?" Phaira cried.

Anandi and Emir turned in their chairs to watch Renzo rummage through a hidden floor compartment. When he rose, he held a crumpled ball of white material. With a few quick snaps, he shook it out: a wrinkled white bodysuit, complete with hood and mask.

Phaira made a face. "Are you that worried about contamination?"

"No." Renzo tossed it to Phaira, who caught it and held it between two fingers. "Put it on," he commanded.

"Why?"

"Do you have to argue with everything I say? Just do it."

Huffing, Phaira slid the white suit over her clothes and tucked her hair under the hood. She looked ridiculous, and her belief was confirmed when she turned around to the sight of Renzo smirking, Anandi hiding a smile behind her hand, and Emir with the faintest look of bemusement on his face.

"Aren't you adorable," Renzo snickered. "But look. Watch this."

He reached over and touched the narrow blue stripe on the inside of her wrist. Something shot through the bodysuit, stiffening the material. Then the fabric shifted from white to transparent, and Phaira with it.

"Whoa!" Anandi cried.

"Impressive," Emir said.

"Incredible, more like," Renzo nodded. "Just like she said."

"Where did you get this?" Anandi inquired, her eyes popping with excitement.

"It's a prototype, one of the scientists who helped with the *Arazura*? I guess she lost government funding for it halfway through the process. Anyways, I bought it from her and packed it away, I'd forgotten all about it."

Bought it? Phaira thought as she deactivated the suit. She glanced around the *Arazura*, taking in all of the shiny new construction. She assumed Anandi's friends had helped to fund its creation. But there wasn't time to think about it now.

It might have been a prototype, but the stealth suit was solid and still charged after hours of walking across the desert. Under the suit, her body was coated with sweat, and her calves ached. But she could see the crest of the massive Kings canyon, brilliant orange under the sun, just like the satellite images. And to her left, there was the outline of a stone foundation, half worn away by wind and sand; some metal bars and piping; and a cellar dug into the ground, a black hole against the red landscape.

Phaira felt for her HALO and the three additional ones stacked above it, all encircling the base of her head. It was still on. But it didn't lessen her nerves.

Twenty feet from her, Emir walked in circles. Suddenly he stomped on the ground, creating a cloud of red dust. Then he stepped a few feet to the left and stomped again. He began to sing again, each stomp and grunt in rhythm with his song, like a galumphing madman.

In that moment, Phaira was thankful for the stealth suit, so Emir couldn't see her laughing.

Then she heard the sound of a hinge creaking.

Emir darted over to the in-ground cellar. Phaira walked carefully in Emir's footsteps and peered over the edge.

Six feet deep and full of old glass jars and broken wood, the cellar's dirt floor shifted. Then something broke through: a trap door, debris pouring off as it lifted. The barrel of a pistol emerged, followed by a wary face.

Emir waved at the man with a big smile. "Hello!"

"Hey, stop that!" the man hissed up. "What are you doing here?"

"Good question," Emir called down. "A better one might be: how do I know your secret location?"

The man frowned. With that, Emir clumsily dragged his body over the cellar's edge. Clouds of dust billowed as his feet and hands made deep grooves in the red clay. His production made it easy for Phaira to also slide down and press her back to the earth, undetected.

The henchman held the trapdoor a foot above the ground, his Aegis firearm aimed at Emir. "I'll kill you, old man, without a second thought. You tell me what you know and why you're here."

"To assist. And be paid for my services, of course," Emir said. "I'd suggest letting me speak to the Sava in charge of security."

The man surveyed the cellar and the land above it. He was suspicious, naturally, but he was also young and uncertain.

Emir sighed. "They'll know who I am," he instructed. "I'm Emir Ajyo. Just ask one of them in there: Keller, or Xanto, I assume? I knew them as children. Plus, I fully support retribution for old crimes."

That last statement seemed to do it. The mercenary chewed his lip for a few moments.

"No guarantees, old man," he finally said. "Xanto is in charge of the hackers." He gestured for Emir to come in, lifting the trapdoor a little higher.

Emir frowned. "I can't shimmy under that door, son. Can't you see the white in this beard? You'll have to open it wider."

Phaira pressed her mouth together to hold in her laughter.

The henchman huffed and stepped up to the surface, turning to lift the trapdoor to a right angle. "Quickly," he said to Emir.

Crouching down, Phaira ran her fingers over the dirt until she found a stone.

Emir made his way to the opening; Phaira walked in his footsteps. As Emir stepped down, Phaira flicked the stone over the henchman's head. It hit the earth wall on the other side, and a wave of dirt and dust billowed down. The man jumped, dropping the door. Emir caught it, stumbling to his knees, but holding the door over his head. "What are you doing?" he bellowed. "Are you trying to kill me here?"

In the commotion, Phaira leapt past Emir through the entryway, landing hard on her hip and skidding down one step before she caught her grip.

On the surface, she heard the mercenary hiss at Emir to be quiet. As Phaira crouched against the dirt wall, she heard the smack of a fist on flesh.

Soon, Emir walked down the stairs. His eye was swelling, but his face remained impassive.

The henchman followed, securing the trapdoor and bolting it shut. The narrow staircase plunged into darkness, until the mercenary flicked on a portable light.

"Let's go," he said curtly to Emir.

* * *

When Phaira and Emir's solar trackers disappeared from radar, Renzo took in a deep breath. "They're in," he told Anandi, who sat nearby, waiting for the news.

And on their own, he thought. *Nothing to do now but wait.*

The *Arazura* was stationed on the West-Midland border. Trackers were given to both Emir and Phaira when they set out to walk the wasteland; they wouldn't work underground, of course, but at least Renzo could ensure that they were alive for the first part of this insane mission....

"Well, we've got time." Anandi sat astride one of the seats, playing with the orange scarf around her head. "So tell me about your sister."

"What about her?"

"I don't know. What's her story? What's her type?"

"Her type?" Flustered, Renzo shook his head. "I'm not talking about that kind of thing with you."

"We have to do something instead of worry," Anandi pointed out. "I'm just curious, don't get all bothered."

Renzo shook his head again, his eyes fixed to the console screens. A burst of annoyed breath came from behind, and then the sound of her boots hitting the floor. But when she stomped out of the cockpit, he didn't look after her. He couldn't. When Phaira and Emir got out, he had to fly faster than ever before. He didn't dare to let his mind be distracted by anything.

He had to be ready.

* * *

The most accessible memory was the night Huma first heard the voices: a young woman with sore shoulders, standing in a kitchen, looking through potted herbs to peer out the window. The first whisper made her still. The second made her body swell with fear.

Every room was searched. Then the great, winding streets outside, Huma's heart pounding as she searched for the source for the voices in her head. The cacophony grew into a blistering roar, the view tinted white with terror.

Then the noise began to fade. Within minutes, the world went silent again. Huma panted on her front porch, staring at the purple, florescent-lit sky, her tears frozen on her cheeks. Wonder seeped in, the memory taking on a faint orange glow.

Artificial. Outside influence. Too many times relived, Sydel noted. And there was something else mixed into the moment: a rumbling hunger for more, a hunger that bordered on panic...

Sydel put the recollection aside. Then she carefully lifted other strands of memory, flimsy as gossamer, searching for truth.

Huma, meeting with the Sava cousins, just as she had said. Huma hitchhiking, buried in libraries, holed up in hostels, developing her Eko and Nadi skills. Huma, sitting outside of Sydel's cell, rehearsing what to say.

At the edge of the cluster, something caught her eye: something deflated, faint and flickering. Sydel removed the strand and coaxed it into clarity. A grey, crumbling memory: a baby boy sleeping in the crook of Huma's arm. The memory was cradled with nervous, thrumming love, infused with the same kind of wonder as the woman's psychic awakening.

It gave Sydel pause. Did she want to know more about this woman's other life, before her decades-long search for power? On the surface, there was no other memory of a son. Huma made no mention of it when she talked about her Eko development. Had she abandoned her family in the name of knowledge?

Still another part of Sydel twitched to move to that section of Huma's brain that connected to the spine and to shut it off entirely. She could do it with a flick of her finger.

Sydel opened her eyes. Before her, Huma was pale and sweating. Cohen stood between the two women. His eyes turned to Sydel, questioning. *What do you want to me to do?*

Sydel shook her head. As she took Cohen's hand, Huma wiped her brow with her sleeve, worship in her voice. "Your abilities are extraordinary, Sydel, just extraordinary. So delicate. I barely felt any pain. To think, I might hold that kind of mastery very soon..."

Finally upright, Sydel gripped Cohen's elbow. His arm was warm and solid, as always. She used his strength to gather her courage.

"You have no further to evolve, Huma."

Huma's eyes went wide. Then they slowly narrowed. "What?"

"You are at the peak of your gifts. You have been for some time now. It doesn't matter who you meet, or how much you study."

"That's not true," Huma stuttered, drawing to her feet. "I have been evolving for over twenty years, every year growing stronger -"

"In your perception, perhaps," Sydel corrected.

Huma's nostrils flared. Subtly, Cohen angled his frame so he stood just in front of Sydel's.

"I don't believe you," Huma said finally. She sniffed, smoothing her silver hair back with both hands. "How could you possibly know such a thing? You are remarkable, Sydel, but you cannot speak to everyone's ability to evolve. When we finally make contact with the NINE - "

"All that talk, and you're still so eager for war and death?" Cohen interrupted.

"I have never wanted their deaths, you idiot," Huma snapped.

"No?" Cohen countered. "So infusing weapons with that energy, getting Sydel involved in all of this, it's for what? For fun?"

In his anger, Cohen took a step towards Huma. She raised one hand. "Step away from me, Cohen Byrne."

"And what about when this is done?" Cohen growled, the veins in his neck bulging. "What's your plan after that? Going to kill me when I've served my purpose?"

Sydel could see the tentacles of Huma's mind, rising, readying to strike. "Enough!" she commanded.

Cohen and Huma continued to glare at each other. Then they turned to look at her.

"You say you want to save them," Sydel continued. "So prove whatever authority you hold and send me now, Huma. Now, or nothing. Send me to the surface to end all of this."

V.

No visible cameras. Hallways in disrepair. Oxygen vents choked with red dust. Phaira gawked at the base's condition as she followed Emir and the henchman down the stairs. This was the gathering place for a powerful mafia family?

Then the halls began to brighten. Ahead, lights were strung around a metal door labeled 1. When the mercenary entered the keycode and held the door, Emir shuffled over the threshold, taking his time so Phaira could slip under his arm.

Inside, four men and woman were hunched over makeshift Lissome stations, their faces awash with blue light. One of the men had greasy black hair and a long nose, and looked utterly miserable.

Lander, Phaira recognized him. Was he the consolation prize for losing Anandi? Did they kidnap him and force him into service, like Cohen?

"Wait here," the mercenary said, jerking his head to the other hackers. "Don't move or touch anything. Say anything to them and you'll get a hole in your head."

Emir nodded, putting his hands behind his back. Phaira slid along the wall as the mercenary keyed in a code to the door on the opposite side of the room.

"Excuse me, sir?" Emir's voice rang out.

356 | LOREN WALKER

Phaira twisted out of the henchman's eye line as he leaned back into the room. Holding her breath, she glanced at the others in the room. Her flurry of movement had been noticed; their eyes were moving between the mercenary and where she stood. But no one spoke.

"Could you ask Mr. Xanto if I might have a chair?" Emir continued. "I can't sit on the ground like these young folks."

The guard huffed with impatience and turned away again. But now Phaira was close enough to slip through before the door slammed shut.

On the other side of the threshold, two flights of stairs coiled down, surrounded by rock walls. Red dust floated everywhere. Phaira stepped into the henchman's footprints as he clomped down to the middle floor, to the door labeled 2. But when he passed through the door, Phaira stayed on the platform. Finally alone, Phaira took in a few long, deep breaths. Stretching the overworked muscles in her legs and back, she wondered how much longer the charge in the stealth suit would last.

Before her, the door to Level 2 opened again. The same mercenary headed back up to the first floor, with a second man following: dressed in tailored black, a head of white hair on a relatively young face.

Keller Sava? Or Xanto?

Mid-step, the white-haired man paused, as if sensing her presence.

Then he continued his ascent. Sheets of dust fell through the stairwell. Phaira pressed her body into the wall, waving off any wisps of red.

When they were gone, Phaira peered into the second floor through the door's tiny window. As dusty-looking as the one above it, this space was larger, but far more crowded with men and women: guns slung across their backs, cleaning their weapons, arguing with each other.

A bunch of bored mercenaries crowded into an underground space? she thought. *I'm surprised they haven't started their own bloodsport.*

Phaira moved away and leaned over the platform's railing, peering down to the bottom of the rocky tomb. The top floor held the hackers; second floor, the muscle. Bottom floor: Huma, maybe?

She heard the door click open behind her, and froze against the rail. At the edge of her vision, she saw the silhouette of yet another man, heading for the stairwell. She turned her head just a little to see.

The physical similarity to Theron was striking: that same square jaw and jet-black hair, but his eyes were pale blue instead of amber, and there was a snake-like quality to this one, a twisted meanness in his face as he bounded up the stairs.

Keller Sava, she knew it.

And in his rush, she realized, the door hadn't closed behind him.

Sliding across the platform, Phaira used two fingers to ease the door open, as if a breeze pushed it. Then she slipped inside.

For several moments, she remained flat against the wall, observing each mercenary who walked by: their build, their weaponry, their awareness. Every variation of hair and skin color, build and muscle and scars, weapons over backs, weapons strapped to thighs. But the hired men and women had no cognizance of their environment, only themselves, it seemed.

And no sign of Cohen, she noted. Her chest panged.

But now I really need to get out of this suit. Too many people in this space. Someone is going to run into me.

The easiest option was to assume the appearance of the group. So Phaira focused on the female recruits. There weren't many, but a few wore the same bulky black body armor: likely provided by the Savas as partial payment for services. Some of the women wore scarves over their faces, or metal half-masks.

Then Phaira overheard one of them complaining. "It's too tight under my arms. If I move too much, it cuts off the circulation and my hand goes numb."

"So get another in a larger size," the other woman growled, gesturing to her own blood-red body armor. "Should have brought your own. Don't whine to me about it. Go get them to bring you another."

"I wasn't whining," the mercenary shot back. Her armor clicked as she walked through the partitions, and into a dim passage. Phaira stayed close to the wall, following.

Within the corridor, a blonde woman emerged from a door and almost ran into the masked soldier.

"Watch it," the mercenary snapped, shoving the blonde away. "Go and get me the next size up of this torso armor. Now."

The blonde in white nodded and scurried in the other direction. As the masked woman stalked back to her companions, a glint by her waist caught Phaira's eye. It was one of her 765-Calis pistols, neatly holstered in the women's belt: dirty, but the prototype design unmistakable. Phaira bristled at the disrespect. Huma must have brought them in and dumped it with the rest of the weaponry. But that meant that the other one had to be in somewhere.

Down the hall, the agent in white ducked into a storage locker. Silently approaching, Phaira lifted her hand to check for the HALOs at the nape of her neck: still stacked, still active.

Phaira peered around the doorframe. Inside, the agent pushed through racks of black-plated armor. Stacks of weapons were piled in the corners of the room, some older models of rifles and assault weapons, some that she'd never seen before. Somewhere in this pile was the other Calis, she could feel it.

The sound of heavy footsteps behind her. Phaira flattened her body against the wall, turning to check the source of the noise.

Nox.

Drenched in sweat, glowing with adrenaline. Slapping hands with another burly soldier before pushing through a door, twenty feet away.

When his companions passed her, Phaira moved.

The restroom held lavatory stalls and space to change, to shower, or just to sit. Nox had flopped onto one of the threadbare sofas, eyes closed, one arm slung over his stomach. The space was empty, otherwise.

Still in stealth mode, Phaira slid to the end of the sofa and rapped her knuckles twice on the wall by his ear.

His eyes popped open.

"Nox," she spoke.

Nox inhaled. He sprang to his feet, strode to the open restroom door, closed it and dragged a chair in front of it. Then, with a quick turn, Nox sat down, elbows over knees, looking down at the floor and muttering: "Here to save the day?"

Phaira's temper flared. "Really, Nox?" She yanked off the suit's hooded mask off and discontinued the current. Her white-clad body returned, a shock after so many hours as a living ghost. Nox didn't seem affected by the reveal, though. His face remained dark and sullen.

"I'm here for Sydel and Cohen," Phaira said shortly. "And you, although you're making me reconsider."

"Then you're being stupid," Nox retorted. "What's your plan, Phaira? You're surrounded by mercenaries. Pretty foolish to come in like this."

"Says the guy who works for a syndicate," Phaira shot back. "What are you thinking? Why would you get involved with these people? And then to put Co in their path - I can't believe you did that, Nox. I can't believe it."

"Hey, I didn't know they were going to recruit him," Nox objected, though with less venom than before.

"Recruit! Is that what this is called?"

"It was freelance work," Nox continued, ignoring Phaira's outburst. "Just a temporary job, like all the other times, some side money before going back to the offices. They've always treated me well. Keller showed up one night, so I introduced Cohen, just to brag a little. But I don't know, they decided that they wanted him to work. I tried to stop them, I really did. But you weren't there, you don't know."

Phaira said nothing.

"I had a plan, you know, to get him out," Nox said defiantly. "I've been working on it...."

"Sure you were," Phaira interrupted. "Sure looks like you're planning an escape, Nox, you and your friends out there. No, I think you like it here. And Cohen is just getting in the way of your fun."

With a growl, Nox slammed his fist into the restroom door. "You never hear me," he spat. "You always saw me as lesser, someone to just use as needed. Well, guess what, Phaira, the Savas think I'm a valuable asset. They think I'm worth having around. I'd rather be here than back at that office desk."

His voice dropped. "But I would never force Cohen into doing the same. I'd take a bullet for that kid and I will if I have to. This was all a mistake."

The freckles on his face grew darker. "And I don't need you to save me. It would be nice if you saw me for once, though."

A thousand words swam through her brain: declarations, accusations. There were years of memories between them, but she didn't recognize the man in front of her.

Then again, he probably doesn't recognize me either.

But there's no time to get into it.

Phaira unclipped one of the HALOS from the base of her head and flung it at Nox. At the last second, he snatched it out of the air. "What's this?" he demanded.

"You're so smart, you figure it out," Phaira said, pulling the hood back over her head. "I'm getting Cohen and Sydel. Do whatever you want, but stay out of my way."

Nox's glare wavered. Disgusted, Phaira restarted the suit's electrical current. Within seconds, she was already invisible and at the exit.

There was one last thing to do, though. Silently placing one foot on the chair, she shoved it with all her might. Nox tipped over with a shout. Phaira slipped through the space where his body once sat, her mind fixed on the contents of that storage locker.

* * *

In the darkness, Sydel could make out the silhouette of Cohen's broad back. She longed to rest her forehead on it.

Just a little longer, she told herself. *Hold together just a little longer.*

The sound of rusted metal-on-metal echoed throughout the tunnel. Up ahead, a door broke open, letting in a burst of sunlight. Sydel shielded her eyes with her hand and followed Cohen to the outside.

They had emerged onto a rocky platform, surrounded by orange-striped cliffs one hundred feet high. The wind moaned through the canyon. Sydel shivered.

Then Keller Sava blocked out the sun, looming over her. "This is what's going to happen, Sydel," came his whispery voice. "You're working for me now, without question, without argument."

Rattled, Sydel sought out Cohen, but Keller swayed to remain in her line of sight. He raised a thin finger to hover right before her nose. "You are going to send out an Eko distress call," he told her. "In all directions, in as many kilometers as possible. You beg your ancestors to come and rescue you. You say nothing about any of us here."

"I'm not - " Sydel started to protest, but at the sight of Keller's cold blue stare, she shrank back, swallowing her words.

"If you do so, without incident," Keller continued. "I'll let you leave."

No, you won't. She was quite certain of that.

When Keller backed off, Cohen took his place. His anxious face looked from Sydel to Keller, who was now climbing down to the canyon floor. Huma hesitated before following the Sava's path.

"We can run," Cohen mouthed to Sydel.

But his worried thoughts reverberated all around him: *Where would we go? How could we evade their hackers, their psychics, their mercenaries just begging for an excuse to attack something? What would Phaira do?*

"Just stay with me," she whispered, trying to keep her teeth from chattering. "Just stay next to me."

Cohen held her arm as she stumbled over the slippery rocks. Every step heightened her fear. She had no idea what might happen. She wasn't even sure what Huma and Keller were talking about: ancestors, the NINE. When she insisted on going to the surface, she thought to use her Eko to contact someone for help, NINE or not. Incapacitate Huma. Run for her life.

She wasn't expecting Keller to come along. But Keller was the leader of the entire operation, it seemed, and eager to begin his bloodquest. *He's here to ensure we don't try to escape,* Sydel soon realized. And he wanted the first glimpse of whoever might come. Maybe even the first kill. This man had no qualms about making a decision to end someone's life, Sydel could tell. Anything might set him off.

At ground level, they all took a moment to catch their breath. Dust kicked up and settled again. A bird's shrieking call bounced off the rocks. The heat intensified. Even as he swiped his forehead with his sleeve, Cohen kept his word and remained close to Sydel, blocking Keller from view. Huma panted for breath, red-faced and leaning against a boulder. For a very brief moment, Sydel felt a twinge of sympathy for the older woman; she was forty years their senior, after all.

Keller didn't seem to feel the heat at all. His eyes fastened on Sydel again. "How old are you, Sydel?" he asked, the word 'old' drawn out.

"I've told you, Keller; she's not one of the NINE," Huma chimed in, smoothing back her silver hair with both hands. "She wasn't even alive when it happened."

"She's familiar." The words were said with flat certainty. "Why is she familiar?"

"That's not possible, Keller, look at her, she's - "

"It is certainly not possible," Sydel said indignantly. "I've never left my commune before six weeks ago and I never attacked a person in my life."

Keller squinted at her. Involuntarily, her right hand twitched. Keller's gaze dropped to her fingers, and she heard his slight gasp.

He is afraid of me, she realized. *He really thinks I'm one of these NINE.*

A long pause. Then Keller ordered: "Over here. Out of the sun."

The group wandered into a shaded area that hadn't been smothered of life. Huma swept her hand in the direction of the base, hidden inside the cliff. "My students have activated the barriers," Huma announced. "Your men are at the ready within. Shall we begin?"

"Now," Keller told Sydel. "Do it."

Sydel's mind raced. She could pretend to call out to these people, just to appease this man. But when nothing happened, what then? Would Huma give her away? And what of these NINE? What would they do to her when they realized her deception?

The sound of a metal click echoed through the desert.

"Oh," Huma gasped, the color draining from her face.

The barrel of his silver firearm pressed into Cohen's left temple, Keller's face held no expression. "Now, please," he stated to Sydel.

Sydel's hands were on fire, but she forced herself to turn away from Cohen's bulging eyes. Slowly, she peeled open the barriers of her mind, like a flower forced to unfold.

Then she released one long, wailing cry for help in all directions. As it rippled over the landscape, she kept pushing, her call travelling beyond the canyon, through the trees and trenches. The pressure on her brain intensified. Her body twitched, but she held onto the wave as it spread outwards, further and further, biting her lip so hard that she tasted blood.

Then, there. Something. Someone.

The wave stopped. Sydel's consciousness gathered into a single focus, and swirled around the being that remained so still.

But there was nothing to latch onto, no emotion around this being: only frank observation of Sydel's presence. Sydel picked up a flash of green-streaked hair, of black eyes, a blue glow.

Then the being disappeared.

Confused, Sydel searched for some flicker of movement. She spread out her senses again, hunting.

Now and again she caught a glimpse of green. Closer, now. Much closer.

Someone grabbed her arm, jerking her back to her physical world. Keller glowered down at her. "Well?" He still held the firearm to Cohen's temple.

"Someone is coming," she stammered between gulps of breath. "Right now. Please, please put down the weapon. Please."

Keller looked to Huma. She was watching the exchange with a stricken expression. Did Huma pick up on the presence of this being? Perhaps not, the woman just nodded. Keller glanced back at Sydel, clearly suspicious. But he lowered the firearm.

Pushing Keller aside, Cohen leapt over to Sydel. "Are you okay?"

Even after that, he was still concerned for her wellbeing? Though Sydel wanted nothing more than to jump into Cohen's embrace, she gripped her upper arms instead, pushing her nails into her skin, willing her body to stop shaking.

Keller pushed all three of them in a circle, their backs facing each other. He gestured to his own eyes and then to the area all around. "Nothing funny," he ordered. Then he spoke into one of those Lissome squares, ordering Xanto to place all the recruits on alert, for the hackers to prepare for blackout conditions.

As he spoke, Sydel felt a knock against her mind: it was Huma trying to establish an Eko channel. But Sydel had already shuttered up her brain, terrified of the ominous shift in the air, the tension billowing, building.

A trace of sound rippled over the group, just a faint rustle, but enough for Keller to swivel to the east.

Then a silhouette emerged from behind the brush at the far end of the canyon. Sydel heard Huma's sharp inhale; the sound of Cohen's boot grinding the earth; the click of Keller's safety being shut off. Sydel's heart beat faster and faster, almost choking from the spasm.

The shadow stepped into the blazing sunlight, a mere thirty feet away from them. It was a woman: ghostly pale, with bluish hints to her lips and under her cheekbones. Deep brown hair streaked with green, parted down the middle and folded into multiple braids. The woman wore layers of shapeless cloth, hanging straight from shoulder to ankle, deep green and teal, with subtle leaf patterns and striped sleeves. Her feet were bare. Her black eyes found Sydel's. There wasn't much time.

Get away from here.

Huma looked between Sydel and the stranger. She sensed the exchange, but Sydel kept the channel narrow and impenetrable. *These people mean to kill you and your kind in vengeance,* she told the woman via Eko. *Run away.*

The stranger tilted her head. Her gaze shifted to the others. Huma clasped her hands to her chest with delight. Cohen didn't move or even breathe, so frozen in place.

Then Keller stepped in front of them all. His finger was tight around the trigger, but Sydel could see his arm trembling, his body pulsing red with energy.

Go! Sydel pleaded to the stranger. *They want to torture and use you to track down the others.*

The stranger didn't move. But her voice emerged in Sydel's head: soft consonants, her accent like water rolling in and out. *We know. These people have not been subtle. And we learned of your existence some time ago, Sydel.*

We? Sydel recoiled. Her eyes darted to the edges of the desert. *You know my name?*

I knew your parents. A long time ago.

Rough fingers dug into Sydel's upper arm. The Eko channel broke. Keller was in her face. "What are you doing?"

"Get off her!" Cohen bellowed.

Keller swung his firearm in a wide arc. Cohen had already drawn the pistol hidden in his waistband. Barrels aimed at each other's chests, neither man moved from his position.

Next to them, Huma took a small step in the direction of the stranger. Sydel sensed a ripple: efforts to make an Eko connection. But the green-haired woman ignored Huma. Her black eyes were fixed on Sydel, and once again, the connection clicked in. But before the woman could speak, Sydel sent a final plea down the channel: *Please, just go! She cannot be trusted. No one can, you must believe me.*

A shock of cold metal on her temple.

Cohen's cry. "Don't, Keller!"

Sydel didn't look at the evil man. She just looked to see if the stranger had left.

She was gone. Good.

"That was one of them," Keller sputtered, between hard bursts of breath. "She's ruined everything. She's one of them, I knew it from the start. Huma, you set us up!"

When Huma finally turned, there were tears in her eyes. "It's a mistake, Keller," she choked out. "Sydel was confused; the NINE must have done something to her -"

The gun barrel pressed into Sydel's temple. She closed her eyes, waiting for the blast.

Then Keller grabbed hold of Sydel by the hair. Yanked forward, limbs dragged across the ground, the sand and stone scraped her exposed leg before she caught her footing. Through Sydel's tearing vision, Keller's face was a swirl of red.

"We were like brothers," Keller was muttering. "I took you under my care, I even looked the other way when it came to this wretch."

Cohen lifted his hands. His firearm dangled from his thumb in submission. "Keller, please."

Behind Cohen, Huma kept looking back to where the stranger once stood. But there was nothing but sand and wind.

"Huma," Keller ordered. "Assemble your people. This isn't over." He twisted his hand in Sydel's hair; she cried out in pain as Keller propelled her up the stony ridge.

Fifty feet ahead, the entry into the secret tunnel swung open. At the sight of it, Sydel grabbed the hand that gripped her hair, clawed at the fingers, tried to twist away from the man.

A whistle of air. Sydel's cheekbone erupted in fire. Her hands flew to her face, just as the grip on her hair released. She dropped to her knees, spots dancing in front of her eyes.

Over the ringing in her ears, there were the sounds of struggling, grit and rock scraping underfoot, faint cries from the older woman, begging the men to stop.

But a calm version of Huma's voice was in Sydel's head. *Disarm Keller. Shut down his brain. It's the only way.*

Sydel's vision cleared, just in time to see Keller shove Cohen over the rocky incline. Cohen tumbled, head over feet; red scrapes bloomed on his arms and face before he finally skidded to a stop. Through the cloud of up-kicked dust, Sydel could see Huma in the background. Her hands were clasped to her chest, even as her eyes remained cold.

You can see that he'll never stop. He'll never let us free. You know you can do it. You must do it, Sydel.

Keller took aim at Cohen's heaving back.

"No!" Sydel cried out.

Keller stumbled. So did Cohen and Huma, as if hit by a gust of wind.

Then Keller was looming over Sydel again, snatching at her upper arm, hauling her to her feet. As he pushed her into the secret tunnel, Sydel caught sight of Cohen's scratched, horrified face.

Then the door slammed shut and everything went dark.

VI.

The soldier was right, Phaira mused as she emerged from the storage locker, moving her arms back and forth testing the black body armor. Tight under the arms. No air circulation. Not very well manufactured. She wondered if it would even stop bullets. Some digging had uncovered her missing Calis, miraculously still in one piece; it was holstered on her hip now. A curved knife was tucked in her boot. Her hair was now black, thanks to a CHROMA she found in a restroom, and she had splashed it with water so it hung stringy over her eyes. Mostly unrecognizable, she hoped. She'd kept the stealth suit on under the armor, and she already felt irritable and overheated. The bad temper could only help.

As she walked into the main space with all the partitions, working on her cover story, a high-pitched alarm went off. The men and women made loud whooping noises, and scrambled to assemble their weapons. Someone pulled on Phaira's armor, a man with a large scar across his cheek. "Come on! We're live!" he crowed. There was a mad, excited gleam in his eye. Blood thirst. Phaira remembered that feeling.

The man charged through the open door to the stairwell. The mercenaries filed in the same direction, heavy boots stomping, weapons clicking in holsters. Following the crowd, Phaira heard muffled orders echoing from below. She looked over the platform railing and took in the scene: the door marked 3 was still closed. Instead, the men and women poured into a concealed door on the bottom floor, built into the red rock wall, now swung open for entry. The white-haired man, Xanto, ushered the mercenaries into the tunnel within.

A secret way to the outside? Energized, Phaira slowed her descent down the stairs, letting others push past her in their eagerness. She caught a glimpse of red hair in her peripheral vision: there was Nox, along with all the others.

Shouts came from within the hidden passage. Xanto ducked inside, yelling something that Phaira couldn't make out. Ten paces ahead of her, halfway between the second and third floors, Nox was also craning his neck to see.

Then Huma emerged from the tunnel, pushed through the crowd and through the door marked '3.' Her heart in her throat, Phaira gripped the railing, ready to vault over and leap down to the bottom floor.

Then her little brother emerged from the same tunnel.

Cohen! she almost burst out. But the mercenaries were shoving him back into the darkness. He battled back, throwing his weight into people, grabbing at the wall for leverage.

Nox elbowed past the waiting mercenaries, yelling to Cohen: "What are you doing? What's wrong?"

"He's going to kill her!" Cohen shouted over the others. An elbow smashed into his nose, snapping his head back. As Cohen stumbled, one of the mercenaries shoved him across the platform, headlong into the door marked 3. At the same time, two men grabbed Nox on either side and propelled him into the tunnel. Phaira saw Xanto leaping on Nox's back, just before the door sealed, its seams now invisible to the eye.

The silence was deafening. Three mercenaries were left: two men, and that masked woman with Phaira's Calis. Their hands hovered over their weapons as they surrounded Cohen on all sides.

Phaira sprinted down the final stairs, streaked past them and leapt for her brother.

Cohen saw her coming and lunged. She ducked under his swinging arm. Then with a quick turn, she knocked out his knee and flipped him to the ground. He hit the metal platform with a loud bang. As the impact reverberated off the rocky interior, Phaira placed her boot to the small of his back, ordering: "Stay down!"

Cohen's body stiffened. Then he went limp.

In the time it took for the mercenaries' faces to move from surprise to suspicion, Phaira unsheathed her knife and flipped it to a horizontal grip, took a step over Cohen's body and waited. As it always did when she was about to battle, the world slowed down and everything sharpened into focus. She saw how the mercenaries' muscles flinched, the tension betrayed in the tightening of their jaw, noted their dominant hand, their stance, their likely plan of attack; it all assimilated in a matter of seconds, bundled into her mind, like a chemical reaction about to burst.

One of the mercenaries drew out his blade, holding it vertically, like a dinner utensil. The knife flashed in a wide arc, aiming for her face. Phaira deflected both blade and arm, and made a series of fast, precise slashes to the exposed underarm, the half-inch of exposed rib and belly, ending with a direct stab into the upper thigh.

As the man gasped, bleeding into his hands and dropping to the floor, the woman with the metal half-mask leapt onto Phaira's back. She was strong, her grip cutting off Phaira's airflow. With a quick burst, Phaira twisted and threw her to the floor. On the way down, she snatched the stolen Calis from the woman's holster, flipped it and smashed the butt of the gun into the mask, twice, then a third time. The woman howled, her hands to her broken, bleeding mouth.

The red walls turned blue. The shock-round blast missed Cohen's leg by only a few inches. Phaira swung her Calis around, the laser target landing in the center of Nox's forehead. Nox lifted both hands for a split second, before clasping them together and driving his fists into the back of the third mercenary's head. The shock-round clattered to the platform.

Phaira lowered the Calis. Nox lowered his arms too. They stared at each other. Familiar. So familiar.

Then Cohen jumped to his feet. *He's gotten more agile,* Phaira thought, before being crushed in a hug.

"I knew you'd figure out where we were," came Cohen's muffled voice.

He's stronger too.

"Okay, okay, Co, come on," she gasped.

As he released her, Cohen's face switched back to panic. "Keller has Sydel. He went crazy; he's in there with her, and now Huma too. I think they might kill her."

Phaira turned to the door marked 3. "Do either of you know the code?"

Cohen shook his head, crestfallen. "They change it every day. And this is the only way in."

"There's always another way," Nox corrected.

"He's right. Wait here," Phaira told Cohen. "Get those three out of the way," she added, nodding at the three writhing bodies on the platform before leaping up the stairs.

In the rush to get outside, the door marked 2 had been left ajar. Phaira peered into every partition, searching for stragglers. She only found clothes crumpled, food left half-eaten, satchels dumped on the floor. All abandoned to avenge some twenty-year-old wrong. Orchestrated by four children who never forgot what was lost.

Four. The number stuck in Phaira's head as she searched. Four children fused together by their violent loss. Four people forever connected. Trauma brought people closer together. Not apart. She knew that first-hand.

The corridor was equally deserted. But Phaira found her target in the storage locker with all the weaponry: the agent in white, cowering behind the door.

"What are you - " the woman began, then yelped as Phaira grabbed her by the neck.

Cohen and Nox stared as Phaira propelled the agent down the stairs. When they reached the bottom plat-form, the agent hit the door face-first. On the ricochet, Phaira was behind her, twisting her arm in a joint lock.

"The keycode." Phaira ordered, torqueing the shoulder.

"Don't hurt me!" the woman gasped. "Please, don't hurt me! I'll give you whatever you want, whatever I know. Just don't kill me!"

Phaira released her. The agent in white slid to the floor and covered her face with her hands.

"You were coerced?" Phaira asked, faintly sympathetic.

"Well, not exactly," the woman in white whispered through her fingers. "I have a lot of gambling debt - but please, let me go. I won't tell anyone, I swear. Here, here are today's codes to all the doors." She shoved a crum-pled piece of paper at Phaira. "Please. I just want to go home."

"Go," Nox said suddenly. "Get to the surface as quick-ly as possible. Then take cover."

The agent slid her back along the rock wall. When she hit the stairs, she took them two-by-two until she reached the top door and disappeared through it.

Phaira tossed a HALO at Cohen and showed him how to activate it. Then she offered the last HALO to Nox.

He shook his head. "I have one." As he pulled it from his pocket, his eyes flicked to hers as he looped it around the back of his head. Was there an apology in his expression? She couldn't tell.

Phaira punched in the keycode for the door. Cohen went for the handle, but Phaira stopped him, looking back at her old friend. "Come with us, Nox. Come on. Just like old times."

Nox held her gaze, and slowly shook his head.

"The hackers are still trapped," Phaira said, swallowing her disappointment. "And Emir Ajyo. White beard, older man. Anandi's father. Will you get them to the surface?"

Nox's profile was unreadable. "I'll see."

Then Nox leapt up the stairs, following the agent in white.

Impatient, Cohen yanked the door open and lifted his Vacarro firearm to his eyeliner. Ducking through the threshold, he swiveled back and forth, searching the floor, and then gestured for her to follow. Watching her brother, Phaira couldn't help but smile. He moved so differently, so full of confidence. Nox must have taught him well.

Then she dropped her smile, drew her Calis and followed him.

Together, they crept down a narrow hallway. The lights were even dimmer on this floor, casting hundreds of shadows. A series of doors stretched down either side of the corridor, a few ajar. Inside, Phaira could see small beds and dressers.

Pale light glowed at the end of the hall. In the open space, amidst low-burning candles, six bodies sat in a circle, slumped forward. What were they doing? Shielding the base? Shielding the soldiers? Both were likely. She wondered if they were using that Zephyr mixture.

There was a gentle knock against Phaira's brain. She jumped, pointing her Calis to the right, then to the left.

Movement in the circle of followers. Huma. The older woman's face was heavily lined, aged by twenty years, her face white with fear, her cape streaked with red dust. Her hand lifted in Phaira's direction. Her fingers shook.

"You," Huma gasped. "Why can't I - "

Phaira didn't hear the rest. Her vision sharpened, until there was no one but Huma in her view, fully illuminated. *I've waited a long time for this*, she thought, slowly and emphatically, for Huma to hear.

"Where's Sydel?" Cohen roared.

Huma faltered at Sydel's name. Her mouth opened and closed with no sound.

Then Phaira heard the unmistakable click of a safety being released. She snatched Cohen by the arm and yanked him into one of the tiny bedrooms, just as the floor exploded with gunfire.

* * *

Sydel's head struck the doorframe. She felt her brow split open as she crumbled to the floor.

Overhead, the bare bulb flickered on. They were in a cell on the third floor. And Keller was closing the door.

"You're one of them," he was saying. "You were there that day. Tell me who you really are."

Sydel pushed herself up onto her elbows, glaring at Keller from under her tangled hair. "I'm Sydel," she panted. "I am not - "

A burst of white pain, this time across her cheekbone. Warm blood trickled onto her cheek. Her eye socket began to swell.

Don't black out, Sydel begged her body. *Stay awake.*

"When I saw you," she heard Keller mutter over the rush in her ears. "I knew your face. I knew your eyes. You might have tricked that old woman, you might have bewitched that boy, but I remember you. I was the fool to let this go on so long. Everything is ruined. But you're going to tell me everything now."

His hand shot out, grabbing her by the collar, yanking Sydel to her feet. His opposite hand wrapped around her throat, gripping with enough force to lift her off the ground. Sydel writhed, frantic to wrestle away from his grip, but Keller slammed her back into the wall. She gasped at the shock of pain in her spine.

Then he let go. As she dropped, she barely had time to gulp for air before he grasped her chin in his hand.

"Tell me," he whispered, his face an inch from hers. "Just tell me the truth. You recognize me, don't you? I was only a little boy then, but I bet you do. I bet you were the one who left my father brain-dead and drove my mother to throw herself off these domes."

Keller's other hand slid up her throat. His thumb caressed her larynx, gentle as a lover.

"Oh, Sydel," he breathed. "I like to see that you bleed. I wondered for years if there was blood in a NINE's veins."

Then Keller lined up his thumbs on either side of her airway and squeezed.

Sydel clawed at his wrists. Black spots danced in her vision. She was going to pass out. Maybe die of asphyxiation. If he let her die. Flickering images, memories, bits of melody ran through her brain: the same pattern, faster and faster. A fire was building in her core.

No. No, stop.

But it was already consuming her: her eyes burned, her mouth burned, every organ engulfed with fire, burning from the inside out.

Over the din of the flames, Sydel could hear Keller's confused noises.

Then one of his index fingers lifted from her throat. Keller stared, spellbound as the finger slowly arched back.

Then the bone snapped. A scream of pain.

His hands dropped from her throat. But Sydel remained where she was, engulfed and out of control, barely cognizant of Keller's screams as each of his fingers snapped backwards, one after another, and more bones followed.

Too late. Too late. Too late.

VII.

From the sound of it, every one of Huma's minions was firing a gun. The hallway was riddled with dents, the floor covered with casings. Cohen crouched by the doorframe, gripping his Vacarro firearm, but Phaira could tell how terrified he was. Every few seconds, Phaira fired her Calis around the edge, just to keep them from advancing. In-between shots, she debated whether to surge forward and shoot Huma through the head. Phaira savored the image of a shocked Huma with a perfectly round bullet hole smoking in the center of her forehead, grey wisps, just floating away...

Despite the fantasy, there was an easier way. As evolved as they might be, Huma and those hounds didn't know what they were doing. And they certainly weren't paying attention to how many rounds were left in the chamber.

Sure enough, the cacophony of gunfire began to lessen, replaced by the sounds of panic.

Then Phaira's ears pricked at the sound of rumbling. She placed her hand on the doorframe. It was vibrating. Cohen felt it too, judging by his puzzled expression.

Huma's gasp filled the space.

Then the floor plunged into white.

Phaira's body lifted, soared and slammed into the opposite wall. Bright light swept through the floor, again and again. Over the roaring sonic waves, there was the sound of screaming. Despite her pain and blindness, Phaira managed to scoot her body into one of the cells and into a corner, covering her head with one hand, searching for Cohen with the other.

There he was, to her left; she yanked on his sleeve until he slid next to her. They huddled together, shielding themselves from the light. Phaira could barely suck in breath; her temporary flight had bruised her right ribs, by the feel of it. She fumbled with the strap of her torso armor to try and support the bones. The white flares seemed to go on forever. Her ears felt like they were bleeding from the strain.

Then, as quickly as it began, the light was gone. Phaira couldn't see. Was that some kind of advanced flash grenade? She fumbled for her dropped Calis, blinking to force her eyes to adjust. Cohen was a blur next to her, slowly coming into focus. He was on his knees, holding his head and crawling into the hallway.

Then Phaira heard her little brother gasp.

"What is it?" Phaira whispered, terrified.

Cohen stumbled to his feet and ran past her. Phaira forced her body upright, ignoring the blast of pain from her ribs, and hobbled into the corridor.

In the open space, it was a massacre. The six followers were scattered across the white floor. Some had hit walls and slid down to the floor, their limbs twisted behind them. Some had blood coming out of their ears or mouths, their eyes staring at the ceiling. In the center was Huma: her white hair streaked with pink, her body in a crumpled heap. Unmoving.

As Cohen stepped through the wreckage, his active HALO blinked at Phaira from across the room. In a burst of gratitude, Phaira silently thanked Theron for those strange devices; she didn't know what just happened, but she felt certain they would have been dead without them.

"Phair!" Cohen called.

Holding her ribs with one arm, Phaira stepped over Huma's body and another man's twisted corpse. Cohen examined a door, the same door as the others in this underground base, but this one had beads of cooling metal running down its edges. Heat radiated from the doorframe.

The blast had come from in there. Anything could be behind that door. It could be radioactive.

But before she could warn him, Cohen yanked on the door handle. It opened with a long, loud groan.

A burst of scalding air hit Phaira's face, followed by the rush of cool desert wind.

Inside was a square cell, with a cot overturned in the corner. Blue sky and red rock glistened through a small hole blasted in the far wall. Someone was huddled next to the opening, shaking, her long brown hair covering her face. And there was a man sprawled on the floor, face down in a pool of blood. Black hair. Scars on the back of his hands, the fingers snapped and deformed.

Phaira recognized the corpse in an instant. Keller Sava.

Cohen didn't seem to care about the body, hopping over the splatter. "Syd!"

Sydel didn't respond. Under the matted nest of her hair, Phaira could see the girl's fingernails digging into the scalp.

"Sydel?" Cohen tried again. He put a hand on her shoulder. Sydel jerked away. The cell filled with the sound of hissing. It was Sydel, Phaira realized; the girl whispered something in a steady stream of breath. A curse? A spell?

"Phair?" Cohen pleaded.

Phaira glanced at Keller's mangled body. Her impulse was to grab Cohen and run as far away as possible.

Instead, Phaira made her way across the room. Sydel didn't look up at her approach. Did the girl even know where she was? Or who they were? Maybe the HALOs were interfering. Reaching back, Phaira unclipped her HALO and set it on the floor. No change in the girl.

Holding her ribs, Phaira knelt down on the floor. Then she shifted to sit next to Sydel. The girl's scorching body heat hit Phaira. Smelling of blood and sweat, Sydel shuddered hard with every breath.

Phaira leaned over so her shoulder brushed the girl's. Then she spoke very quietly: "Sydel."

Sydel's grip on her head loosened, just a little.

Phaira craned her neck to peer under the bedraggled mess of hair.

"Sydel," she said, more firmly this time.

Sydel's hands dropped to the floor. Her head rose and turned, and her face was exposed. Eyes ringed with red. Angry purple bruises on her throat and jaw. Smears of blood on her face from a cut lip, eyebrow and cheekbone. Phaira grimaced. *What a mess.*

"You're here," Sydel croaked. Her brown eyes filled with tears. "You're really here. You found me. I knew you would."

"Do you know where you are?" Phaira asked. "Do you know what just happened?"

Sydel's eyes flicked to the left, just the tiniest movement, but Phaira caught it. *She knows.*

The room shuddered. Phaira's free arm shot out to brace Sydel against the wall, even as pain screamed through her body. A crunching noise echoed across the ceiling. Then the whole floor dropped down a foot. Sydel yelped, and Cohen let out a shout. They all looked up to where the wall met the ceiling. The metal buckled in the corners. Dust funneled through the blown tunnel. Phaira swiveled to peer through the open door. The bodies hadn't moved, but a thin layer of dust now covered them.

Something warm spread under Phaira's arm. Was she bleeding? Confused, Phaira lifted her right arm to check, but nothing was there.

Then she froze. She could lift her arm. No more pain.

Next to her, Sydel lowered her hand. Her voice drifted into Phaira's head. *Huma is still alive. You need to confront her.*

Phaira's hand shot to the nape of her neck. She didn't have the HALO on.

You don't need it. Sydel's voice was eerily clear. *You know what to do.*

"Hey, are we getting out of here or what?" Cohen asked, bracing his hands on both walls, as if to hold them up.

Phaira slowly got to her feet, part of her desperate for the pain of her ribs to come back. But there was no trace of it.

"Stay with her," Phaira told Cohen, working to keep her voice even. "Don't come after me."

In the open space, the lights flickered like a warning. No sign of life among the sea of bodies and shell casings.

But Huma was gone. Phaira stepped through the wreckage, searching the shadows.

And then she felt it. The prickle of cold, starting in her left side of her brain.

She quickened her step, heading for the corridor with the tiny bedrooms. Every room she looked in was empty. More shadows crept in.

Then Phaira's heart stopped for one long moment, followed by another.

Those icy fingers were snaking into a new section, she realized.

The hall began to turn sideways. She put her hand on a doorframe to steady herself. She had to resist: shut down her brain, deaden her senses, push down the panic.

No, she remembered, as her body started to shake. *Feel the fear. Let it go.*

Swarms of imagery coursed through her head: death and desertion and mind-rape, ice and burning blood. The sudden flood of adrenaline blinded Phaira, but the cold in her brain was receding, her legs were pumping fast, flinging her body through the fire, into the final room. And through the haze, Huma came into view, her mouth open with shock.

Phaira shoved Huma against the wall, one hand entangled in that silver hair, the other twisting the older woman's right arm behind her back. The impulse to slam Huma's forehead into the wall, again and again, was ravenous. The adrenaline was clouding her judgment, logically, she knew that, but the memory of the look on Huma's face: that sneering, superior look as Phaira screamed in pain, it was overpowering....

A thread of sound made its way into her roaring ears: Huma whimpering into the wall. Phaira's senses began to return. She felt her fingers digging into the woman's fleshy wrist, smelled the sweat in the woman's scalp. Then the adrenaline cooled, and her mind began to clear. She let go of Huma. The woman sank to her knees, her hands in her lap upturned, helpless.

"They weren't strong enough," Huma sobbed into the wall. "They couldn't shield themselves. I didn't teach them how. I didn't know she could do such things."

Disturbed, Phaira stepped back. So that blast, whatever it was, Sydel generated it?

"Phaira, please." Huma stared up at her, her face pink, and wet with tears. "You have to help me, protect me from Sydel. If you take me with you - "

The floor shook again. Screeching metal mixed with the crash of falling rock. Phaira jumped as the door marked 3 buckled. The stairwell was collapsing. Whatever Sydel did, there could be enough structural damage to make the whole place come down.

"Phaira, please." The older woman's fingers brushed her wrist.

Phaira jerked away. "Don't ask me for anything," she snapped. "Save yourself."

Her journey back down the corridor, punctuated by Huma's fading cries for mercy, was longer than any in Phaira's recent memory.

"Close the entryway," she told Cohen when she caught sight of him. "The stairs are gone."

Cohen threw his weight into the half-melted door. It groaned and buckled back into the frame. Collapsing against the wall, Phaira pressed the heel of her hands into her eyes, working to slow her ragged breath. Cohen's heavy footsteps passed. Phaira peered through her fingers. Sydel stood by the blown-open hole, peering through the rocky tunnel. Cohen was next to her, his hand on her lower back, speaking to her in a low, worried voice.

A living bomb. Sydel was a living bomb. Did she mean to kill everyone on the floor? Should she incapacitate Sydel? Could she, even?

"Phair."

Trying not to shudder, Phaira came at Cohen's beckoning, and squeezed past the two to look into the blast opening. It was clean through, the hole narrowing in diameter with only a foot of light at its end. They'd have to widen it to get out. But she could at least get her hand outside.

Phaira crawled into the space, coughing from the rising dust. It took some time, but with some shifting and wiggling, her head cocked in a painful angle, Phaira was finally able to get her arm through.

Her hand went cold in the wind. Her fingers scratched along the edges of the hole, feeling for a ledge. There: a tiny crevice in the cliff-face, wide enough to jam one end of her solar tracker in, the rest exposed to the sun.

* * *

Renzo awoke with a jerk. A pinprick of light flashed on the radar. Active! One of them was outside! Renzo smacked himself in the face to wake up. Just one tracker, though. It had only been, what, two hours since they went offline? Was it Phaira, or Emir? What about Cohen? Was Sydel in there? What if only one of them had survived? Should he wait for more signals?

The rumble of the *Arazura's* engines startled Anandi awake. Her legs draped over the armrest in sleep, she would have crashed onto the floor had she not grabbed her seat mid-fall.

"What's going on?" she cried, yanking herself back up.

"Someone is outside," Renzo announced as he rerouted fuel to the engines for added speed. At the edge of his vision, he saw Anandi cross her legs on the seat, activate the Lissome on her knee, expand screens and begin to furiously type. She was preparing for any attempts to jam their system, Renzo guessed, as he checked for wind speed, mapped out their course, anything to keep his mind occupied. Even still, his throat was parched from anxiety.

Come on, he chastised the ship. *Come on. Warm up, fire up.* Every second that passed heightened his panic.

Trust in your design, Renzo told himself. He ran his hand over the *Arazura's* mainframe. You know her inside and out. *You know what she can do.*

Excitement surged through him, a feeling he'd never experienced in all his mathematical discoveries. Gripping the throttle with both hands, he already craved the weightlessness of flight. He was ready.

* * *

Using a plasma grenade dialed down to its lowest setting, and Phaira kicking at the rubble with the steel heel of her boot, she was able to extend the rocky opening by another two feet. Phaira would climb out first to assess the situation, while Cohen created a makeshift sling so Sydel could hold onto his back. Of course, Phaira would be vulnerable, so exposed on the cliff-face. But with the stairwell gone, every drop and shudder of the ceiling demanded that they get outside as soon as possible.

So Phaira removed the black body armor and borrowed clothes, exposing the white stealth suit beneath. Phaira pushed her Calises into the girl's arms. "Don't lose those," she instructed. "I mean it."

Then she pulled the hooded mask over her face. The suit stiffened with electrical charge, and her body disappeared. Sydel and Cohen simultaneously gasped. Phaira ignored them as she crawled into the tunnel.

On the other side, it was a dead drop one hundred feet down. The rush of fresh oxygen made her dizzy, even a little delirious. Or maybe it was the aftermath of Sydel's blast.

Even farther away were the mercenaries, clustered around the bend of the canyon, two hundred feet away. Some loaded their weapons; some drew a strategy of attack in the sand. No one looked back in the direction of the base.

There were visible footholds on the cliff-face, so Phaira held onto the whole's edge and slid her legs out, searching for a shelf that could support her weight. Again and again, her foot slipped, dust crumbling down. Finally, she found a ledge, tested it, and shifted her body to stand on it, clinging onto rocky crevices. Had the men on the ground noticed? She could smell their pent-up energy, their hands ready to tear something, anything apart. But in their restlessness, it didn't seem that they realized the base was on the brink of collapse.

The solar tracker was by her right hand, still jammed into a crack, still blinking. Renzo should be here. Shouldn't he be here by now?

"Phaira?" she heard Cohen whisper through the tunnel.

What if something happened to Renzo while we were inside?

Phaira looked up to the sky, listening for any sign of an approach. But there was nothing: no sound of engines, no sonic boom. Another one hundred feet to the top of the canyon. She might be able to climb it, but she doubted that Sydel could.

A scenario popped into her mind: Cohen losing his grip while trying to carry Sydel, falling back as his mouth made the same O shape as Nican Macatia and Saka...

And what about Nox and Emir? Were they trapped inside? Was Nox able to get everyone out?

Phaira shook her head to clear it of the awful imagery. "Send her out," she called into the tunnel. "There's a decent ledge to the right. Sydel can step onto that one."

Sydel's profile came through the opening. The dried blood and purple bruises on the girl's face was highlighted by the sun. Then her pupils dilated as she searched for Phaira. Phaira knocked twice on the cliff-face. "Over here," she whispered. "I'm going to help you over to the ledge, okay?"

Sydel nodded nervously. As she wiggled her body halfway out, Phaira noted that she'd strapped the bundle with the Calises to her back. Satisfied, Phaira grasped the girl's wrist. Then Sydel let one leg drop down, feeling for the narrow ledge, grasping a bunch of roots to her chest for balance. Tufts of sand floated down. Phaira held her breath, but the mercenaries gave no sign of noticing. "Okay, Sydel?"

Sydel nodded, her body pressed against the cliff-face. *She's thin enough to flatten herself to nothing,* Phaira thought. *But Co won't be so easy.*

Cohen's head emerged next. Just as she feared, he grunted and struggled to push his wide shoulders through the opening. Phaira bit her lip as Cohen swore under his breath. *Come on,* she prodded in her mind, her eyes flicking over to the crowd below, again and again.

A loud screech sailed through the tunnel, followed by a muffled explosion from within. The cliff shook, and stones tumbled to the canyon floor.

Then the tension in the stealth suit's fabric softened. *The charge is gone,* Phaira realized with horror, just as her body reappeared, brilliant white and obvious against the red rock wall. In her panic, Phaira lost her grip. Swearing, she scrambled to find another foothold and grip something with her desperate fingers.

"Phair!" Cohen cried. He angled his body to get one burly arm out of the hole and snatch her forearm. Something pushed against the sole of her foot; it was Sydel, holding onto Phaira's heel and guiding it to a new crevice. Phaira jammed her toes into the space. Then she yanked the hood off of her head, gulping for air.

Ren, she yelled inwardly, *where are you?*

"Hey!" A voice echoed. Clicking sounds echoed through the canyon: weapons being primed. There was laughter too.

They don't care that we are escaping, she realized, her stomach sinking. *They just want target practice.*

"Give me the guns!" she commanded Sydel, straining to reach the girl. As her fingers brushed the top of the bundle, a gunshot rang out.

Phaira whipped her head around to find the source, but the closest mercenary recoiled, his blaster flying from his grip, his trigger hand awash with blood.

Another shot. Another mercenary fell back into the sand, a bullet torn through his throat. The rest of the group shouted and scrambled to take cover.

Speechless, Phaira followed the sound of a chamber being reloaded. To her left, the barrel of the Vacarro sniper rifle was visible through the hole in the cliff, Cohen's thick finger around the trigger.

Then the sun was gone. Clouds of sand and debris billowed up the cliff face.

As Phaira looked up, her hair whipping around her face, the *Arazura* loomed above the canyon. Through the dusty fog, Phaira saw the mercenaries assemble into rows and take aim.

The *Arazura* cleared the cliff edge, and began to rotate and descend, its nose facing the three on the rock wall. The engines angled to the men and women below. The backdraft blew them off their feet.

Grasping the cliff-face, Phaira looked over her shoulder to see Renzo and Anandi's faces through the ship's windshield. Renzo caught her eye and mouthed angrily: "What are you doing on the cliff?"

Phaira scowled and waved her hand, first at Renzo, then signaling to Cohen, who was now halfway out of the opening, the sniper rifle abandoned. "You'll have to jump," she shouted. "Then get cables and secure yourself. Fast as you can! You can do it!"

Cohen nodded. With some twisting and wriggling, he repositioned his body to sit on the hole's edge. Phaira watched as her little brother visibly gulped, bracing his feet against the rock. Then he pushed off and soared.

Phaira's breath caught as Cohen hit the nose with a slam, causing the ship to bow slightly. But Cohen found his grip and heaved himself onto the surface. Anandi was already leaning out, cables in hand, her black hair crusted with red dust.

Over the din of the wind, Phaira heard the sound of metal on metal; sparks bounced off the bottom of the *Arazura*, pounded by gunfire from below. Renzo was able to hold the *Arazura* steady as Cohen buckled himself to the ship. Then he reached out for Sydel.

"I can't," Phaira read Sydel's lips. "I can't."

Phaira's palms were growing damper every second. "Do it!" she yelled, kicking at the wall near Sydel's hand. "Stop complaining and do it already!"

Shaking, Sydel turned to face outwards, her feet sliding on the tiny ledge. Cohen's arms were out, beckoning. Frozen, the girl stared ahead for several seconds.

Then, suddenly, she jumped.

But it wasn't far enough. Her outstretched hands barely grazed Cohen's fingers before her body dropped.

In a flash, as if he had done it a thousand times, Cohen slid down the nose of the ship, swung across, grabbed Sydel's wrists in mid-fall and hauled her to the safety of the cable line.

Gunfire ricocheted off the rock wall. Renzo brought the *Arazura* closer to Phaira, trying to shield her from the bullets, but the winds blinded her. She could smell smoke and fire, pouring through the hole just above her, but her eyes were scratched with sand. Through the blur, she saw Cohen leaning off of the *Arazura's* nose, his hand outstretched. No time left.

In one swift motion, Phaira twisted away from the cliff and leapt.

"Go!" she yelled as soon as her body hit the *Arazura's* nose. "Ren, go!"

Renzo wrenched the throttle. Gusts of scalding wind blew into the canyon; Phaira could hear the mercenaries screaming. The *Arazura* lifted away from the smoking hole in the cliff. Cohen gripped Phaira's forearms in his huge hands, but her legs still dangled over the edge.

A burst of white-hot pain exploded in her side.

Phaira gasped, her body coiling into itself.

The *Arazura* rose and cleared the canyon. Phaira could see Cohen yelling at her, but she couldn't hear him. But she could see the great desert horizon and the spread of the massive canyon. It looked beautiful.

Suddenly, the cliff buckled and folded into itself, black and red clouds billowing into the sky. And just before she blacked out, Phaira saw the mercenaries turn on each other: flashes of metal, bursts of light, red splashes of blood hitting the sand.

VIII.

First, there was slow, spreading heat. Then a prickling kind of pain. Finally a cool wave washed over, turning the red into purple, and then white again. The blaze behind her eyes turned to azure blue: a clear sky without a cloud to be seen. The smell of saltwater, the briny mix of fish and seaweed. Whitewashed walls, a thatched roof.

Where was she?

Phaira slid her hand under her body. She wore a soft white cotton dress, open at the back. Her fingers brushed the spot that itched, just above her kidney. The skin was rough and scabbed over.

Her mind clicked with the memory. She'd been shot.

"Yes," came Sydel's voice. "But I healed you."

Standing in the doorway, Sydel wore a long white sundress. Her facial wounds were healed, her hair wound into braids again. But the girl didn't look young and scared anymore. Just still, and watchful.

Phaira coughed. "How long have I been out? And stop reading my mind," she added fretfully.

"I'm sorry," Sydel said, flushing a little. "Only a few hours."

Phaira sat up. Her body was stiff, but there were no jolts of pain. She ran her fingers over the small of her back again, feeling that scaly, tender skin. When Sydel first healed her in the Communia, it quickly scarred, but it still took several days for the wound to stop aching. Inside that base, Sydel had eased the pain of bruised ribs with a touch. Now this girl could heal over a gunshot wound?

"Where are my brothers?" Phaira asked faintly. "Where am I?"

"They went back for Anandi's father and the others," Sydel continued in that calm voice.

"So the hackers got out of there before the collapse? Nox got them out?"

"He did," Sydel said, a little too carefully.

Phaira's senses prickled.

Then Sydel's expression shifted from serene to sympathetic. "I'm sorry, Phaira. But I was told that your friend was inside, and they didn't find any survivors."

Phaira dropped her eyes to the floor. The wind picked up granules of sand and swirled them around the intricate tile. She focused on their patterns, trying to breathe. Nox. Aeden. Her chest grew tight. She was suffocating.

"You need time alone," she heard Sydel say quietly. "I'm very sorry about your friend. But thank you for coming after me, Phaira. And bringing me back into the world."

When Sydel left, Phaira slumped over. She ran her hands through her hair, again and again, trying to take in a full breath. All those people, dead. Nox crushed under rock. And what about Sydel? There were no witnesses to that brutal blast inside the base, save for her and Cohen. Who was to say that Sydel wouldn't explode

again and kill them all? As much as it pained Phaira realize, there was a valid reason for the girl's banishment
from Jala Communia.

But Sydel had healed her injuries three times now.
She'd done the same for Cohen, too, when he was caught
in the Vendor Mill explosion. And Yann's confession lin-
gered in Phaira's mind: how Sydel had been mind-wiped
several times, how the girl was not really a girl, but several years older. Did Sydel know any of that?

"Phair."

She lifted her head. One of Renzo's lenses had cracked.
Cohen bore a gash on his arm and sand burns across his
face. They were dirty and exhausted, but they were alive.

"You good?" Cohen asked, leaning over to peer at
Phaira's back.

Phaira swatted him away. "Fine."

"Don't be obnoxious. You need to be more careful,"
Cohen grumbled. "You're getting shot all the time."

Renzo glanced at Phaira, his blond eyebrows showing
over his glasses.

Despite her grief, Phaira allowed a tiny smile on her
lips. "You know, that is true, Co," she managed. "Far too
many bullets." She looked past her brothers. "Where's
Anandi and Emir?

Silence. Cohen rubbed the back of his neck, while
Renzo rolled his eyes.

"They need some space," Renzo said finally. "Going
back into hiding, I guess."

"I thought you'd be going with them," Phaira remarked.

Renzo shook his head. "Nope." The way his jaw set made it clear that he had nothing further to say on the matter.

Nox's face swam in front of her vision again. Maybe Sydel was wrong. "What about Nox?"

Renzo and Cohen glanced at each other. Phaira's chest constricted again. "Did Emir see what happened?"

"Nox burst into the first floor," Renzo said. "Told Emir, Lander and the other hackers to get ready to move. One of the Savas followed him, Xanto, I think, the one with the white hair. They fought, and Nox choked him into unconsciousness. Then Nox led the hackers outside, through that cellar with the trapdoor. Then he went back inside."

"He went back in?" Phaira gasped. "He was out and he went back? Why?"

But they all knew the answer. He'd gone back for her and Cohen. He was in that rubble. Buried in the collapsed base. Maybe even in the stairwell. She had to go back. He could still be alive, somewhere in the debris.

"Phair," Renzo interrupted her desperate thoughts. "We can't."

She shouldn't have been so cross with Nox. She should have listened to him. He was her friend, one of the few she ever had, and she'd trampled all over him...

"Word's already gotten out," Cohen told Phaira. "We caught patrol coming in on radar. We kept out of sight until they passed. They're there now. Cleaning up."

All three of them were silent. Renzo was the first to turn away, heading back the way he came. Cohen followed. Phaira searched the open bedroom for any trace left of their presence. Then she joined the line headed for the *Arazura*.

Ahead of her, Sydel appeared next to Cohen, taking his arm and stretching up to whisper something into his ear.

Phaira stared at the back of the girl's head, debating with every step.

* * *

The *Arazura* was the most beautiful manmade thing that Sydel had ever seen. Sleek and shimmering, made of pale gray and soft blue metals, the main level contained three compact, but cozy cabins, a clean kitchenette and lavatory, and a lovely common space with a round table, four chairs and two consoles built into the back wall. There was a lower level, too, that seemed to serve several purposes: storage, some kind of training equipment, all sparkling and new. Sydel ran her hands over the cool panels as she walked, marveling at it all.

A new start for the family. A new home.

Where her own home was to be, she didn't know, but Sydel tried not to dwell on it. Instead she complimented Renzo on his achievements.

When they climbed the ladder to the main level, Renzo showed her to a final door, tucked into a hidden alcove at the back of the *Arazura*. Sydel smiled. "What is this?"

Renzo jerked a thumb towards the door. "Behind the far wall, I put something - well, I did some research, and you probably need time to decompress or whatever. So if it's not right, I'll fix it."

Confused, Sydel went to ask for clarification, but Renzo was already striding away.

No more limping, she realized. *I wonder how.*

Then Sydel placed her palm on the door, enjoying the sensation of metal on skin, and pushed.

It was a fourth cabin. One side of the room was sparsely outfitted with a bed and a few pieces of scratched furniture. Her satchel lay in the corner, her few belongings from the commune already hung up. The other half was a medical bay: gurney and small bed tucked against the wall; intravenous bags and stands, shelves of glass bottles and boxes, everything white and clean and brand new.

Stunned, Sydel opened every drawer; inside, there were machines to conduct ultrasounds and x-rays, tools to monitor heart rates and blood pressures, and a number of other shiny items that she didn't recognize.

This was all hers?

Did she want to stay with these people?

Yes. I am safe here until I determine what to do next.

But what was Renzo talking about 'in the far wall?' Yes, there was the trace of a door's outline. It responded to her light touch, clicking outwards and sliding to the left.

In a space no bigger than eight feet squared, and void of any light, there was a metal cylinder with a ladder. When she stepped onto it and looked inside, deep, clear water met her eyes.

A sensory deprivation tank, Sydel realized, shocked. Her senses screamed for its relief. And yet she hesitated, studying the light that bounced off the water's surface.

In her mind, she travelled back to the desert. The heat of Keller's hands around her throat. How her body ignited from within. The man's lifeless, mangled body on the floor, drowning in a pool of his own blood. The moans from Huma in the other room as she lamented her dead subjects. Left behind, crushed by falling rock.

She was grateful. But after everything that happened, her gratitude felt trivial.

And wicked.

* * *

Renzo dismissed the first request as some kind of joke. But a new appeal arrived within the hour, and then three more. All posted out to the network, and all addressed to the same person.

Settled in the cockpit of the *Arazura*, Renzo expanded his Lissome and began a general search, pulling up records, recollections, personal entries and some encrypted files. There were stories everywhere, the same rumor, but the details slightly altered in every version. Someone launched a guerilla operation to destroy a secret criminal base in the Kings Canyon and rescue a number of captives. This person was from a covert ops background, an expert in the LRP field: Locate, Retrieve, Protect. Deemed highly dangerous, with several warnings not to engage in person. The same name attached, again and again. Phaira Lore. Phaira Lore.

Who did this? Renzo had no idea. There were no identities or cc to trace. He didn't dare to seek Anandi out for help, either. Not yet.

It didn't seem to matter that the stories were planted a few hours ago. There were at least twenty requests that sought to hire Phaira Lore's services for security, assassination, and mysterious item retrieval. From every corner of Osha, payment offered with so many decimal places that Renzo had to look twice.

Immediately, Renzo deleted the assassination requests. Then he studied the details of the other messages. His mind turned, considering.

Locate, retrieve, protect. It wasn't the worst job description.

Curious, Renzo brought up another search for any news on the Macatia family or their manufacturing plants. Nothing unusual; they were still the richest family in Daro, building a memorial statue dedicated in Nican's memory, even creating a new, improved version of their water purification tablets called "Nicans." Renzo made a face at that. But they hadn't reinstated the bounty on Phaira's head. They weren't behind this information spread.

But perhaps the leak was a good thing. The Macatias' blood money was almost gone. They needed income if they were going to stay mobile. And reputation was everything, as Renzo knew well. Whomever the source, a little assistance could only benefit them all.

* * *

Phaira sat on the top of the *Arazura*, looking up at the stars. The wind was warm and sweet, but it wasn't pleasant in any way. Too many questions. Too many changes clouding up her mind. Her time in Kings seemed like a dream, surreal and preposterous.

She hadn't contacted Nox's mother and father yet, though she knew she had to say something. But her throat closed up at the thought of his name.

The twisted grey cigarette smoldered between her second and third finger. Lifting it to her lips, Phaira inhaled deeply. Then she exhaled, surveying the horizon. From this vantage point, she could see the edges of two cityscapes, one to the east, one to the south, twinkling with lights. Some miles away, a train rumbled by, spewing smoke into the night air.

In her lap sat the Lissome that Theron had given her. Putting the mekaline down, Phaira popped open the black square and disassembled the circuitry, searching for a tracer. There was none. But she left it open and dead anyways.

The Ikani Mala identification packet lay next to her. She couldn't use it, of course. But it was too valuable to toss away; she could sell it for extra rana, if she needed to. For now, she would keep it to herself.

Phaira took another inhale of mekaline; she could feel the effects now, that familiar, blissful rush. Good, because her mind was turning again, this time to those unanswered questions about Theron's intentions. And her secret, aching shame at being played for a fool.

Theron had a hand in this bloodgame. Of course he did. Theron and his cousins were fused in their common tragedy; why wouldn't he be involved in avenging their lost family? Of course he never thought of Phaira as someone who could 'make a difference in the world,' as he'd said. Those were just empty words to try and recruit her to the cause. Another mindless mercenary to join the ranks.

Or, very possibly, a mindless mercenary to clear the path to power. Because on reflection, with Keller, Xanto and Kadise confirmed dead, Theron Sava was the lone successor to a powerful crime syndicate. It couldn't be a coincidence.

Phaira slipped the Ikani Mala passport into her back pocket, and kicked the dead Lissome over the edge of the *Arazura*. It made a tiny pinging noise as it crashed into the concrete platform. Then Phaira ground out the mekaline and blew it off the paneling.

More than any time before, Phaira and her family needed some kind of protection.

And loyalty, secured in whatever way would stick.

* * *

The air on the sixth floor of the abandoned factory was stifling. It grew warmer as the sea of people collectively gasped.

A girl grabbed at the arm of the man next to her. His conversation interrupted, Lander scowled and looked to where his friend pointed. Then his face went even paler.

"Phair - Ms. Lore," Lander stammered. His friends backed away, a circle of empty space around him. Lander's eyes darted to the exit. Cohen stood in the doorframe. Backlit, he was a wall of stone.

"Recovered, Lander?" Phaira cooed. Twenty feet away, she leaned against the opposite wall, pleased at how her white street clothes made her stand out in the black sea of fabric.

Lander wet his lips. Fear flooded through the room. The Hitodama members hid their faces behind their hands, whispering and staring.

"Can I - " Lander started, and then stopped. "What are you doing here?"

"You owe me," Phaira said. She lifted one hand and counted on each finger. "Didn't pay for the recovery job.

414 | LOREN WALKER

Tried to kill my family. Put a contract out on me. And then not even a thank-you for a genuine rescue. Not one shred of gratitude!"

"Not very nice," Cohen's voice boomed across the room.

"Thank you?" Lander squeaked.

"Little late for that," Phaira said as she pushed off the wall.

The room shrank back. Lander's eyes bulged and his hand fumbled under his cloak.

Really? Phaira thought wearily.

As Lander unsheathed a Compact firearm, Phaira was already next to him, disarming and sweeping his legs out from under him. The crowd cried out as he crashed to the floor. Then Phaira neatly cartwheeled over Lander's body and wrapped her legs around his arm, wrenching it into an armbar. As he howled in pain, Phaira kept her eye on Lander's elbow joint, noting the hyperextension. Then she tilted her head back, addressing the row of witnesses: "I'd stay out of this."

The upside-down eyes stared back at her. No one moved.

"As for you, Lander," she continued in a softer tone. "Try that again and I'll break your elbow and sever all the nerves in your hand."

Lander nodded, sweat dripping down his temple.

"You work for me now," Phaira told him. "You help Anandi keep our channels secure and knock out any tracers. You also remove any identifying information on us, on any of us, that gets out into the network. Do that and I'll leave you alone. Deal?"

Lander nodded again, looking like he was about to faint. "Deal."

Phaira released him. As she swung her legs around and rolled to her feet, the crowd of Hitodama stepped back. Phaira raised a hand to wave. "Go back to your party. Sorry to interrupt."

From his position in the doorway, she saw Cohen smirking. Phaira winked at him as she strode out of the room. As they headed for the exit, the floor remained silent for several seconds. Then the same words floated down the hallway, like a plume of smoke.

Phaira Lore. Phaira Lore.

* * *

When they returned to the *Arazura*, Renzo was waiting for them by the door, a stack of papers in hand. "We need to talk," he told his sister.

As Phaira and Renzo headed for the common area, Cohen smoothed his palm over his hair and worked up his nerve. As an afterthought, he tossed his heavy boots and jacket into his quarters. Then he padded down the hall to the little alcove.

At his knocking, the door creaked open. Her hair fell from their braided topknots. Her robe was loose, with one bronze shoulder exposed. Cohen tried very hard not to look at it.

Sydel smiled up at him. "Co."

"Hey," Cohen said. "How are you?"

Sydel lifted the bare shoulder. But her brown eyes were warm, even crinkling at the edges. "You're back. Would you like to come in? Tell me what happened?"

When Cohen grinned at her, Sydel shyly dropped her gaze to examine her bare toes.

Then her skin prickled. Someone was watching them.

Phaira, at the other end of the corridor. Her jagged blue hair framed her face. Her arms were tight over her chest, the biceps prominent.

Sydel tilted her head, inquiring.

But Phaira's expression didn't change. Her gray-green eyes were fixed on Sydel, unblinking.

"Syd?" Cohen's voice made her jump. "What is this thing?" Having slipped inside her room, he was now peering into the deprivation chamber.

"I - " Sydel started, and then turned back.

Phaira was gone.

That was a warning, she realized. *She's watching me.*

Sydel looked at her hands. They were clean and healed. But something pulsed in the center of her palms, like a heartbeat. Something rippled through the bones of every finger. And her core, though no longer aflame, smoldered like the coals of a fire. Waiting.

about the author

Loren Walker was born in Burlington, Ontario, Canada, and today lives and works in Rhode Island as a freelance writer and illustrator. EKO is Loren's debut novel.

The sequel to EKO is NADI.

Get publishing updates, character biographies and custom illustrations at her official site: www.lorenwalker.net

thank you:

to my family and friends, my eternal cheerleaders.

to my beta readers Ty Black and Jill Corley.

to my editor Wil Scott, Deranged Doctor Design, and the Book Designer for making EKO look good.

and to you, for giving this story a chance.

Made in the USA
Middletown, DE
27 December 2016